Too Asian,
Not Asian Enough

First published in UK 2011
by Tindal Street Press Ltd
217 The Custard Factory, Gibb Street,
Birmingham, B9 4AA
www.tindalstreet.co.uk

A CIP catalogue reference for this book is available
from the British Library

ISBN: 978 1 906994 24 2

Typeset by Tetragon

Printed and bound in India by Replika Press Pvt. Ltd.

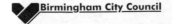
Birmingham City Council

Too Asian, not Asian enough

Edited by
Kavita Bhanot

Tindal
Street
Press

CONTENTS

Kavita Bhanot

Introduction

British Asian identity, as we know it today, emerged in the nineties with the success of books, plays, albums, films and TV shows by and about British Asians. Hanif Kureishi's 1990 novel *The Buddha of Suburbia* spoke to so many of us. We devoured this and then *Bhaji on the Beach*, *Goodness Gracious Me*, *Anita and Me*, *East Is East*, *White Teeth*, *Brick Lane* and *Bend it Like Beckham* – to name a few examples. For the first time, we South Asian immigrants or descendants of immigrants saw ourselves represented in the mainstream, and we were seduced by these images. They reflected and informed our identities. For aspiring writers and artists, they inspired confidence and allowed us to think that there could be a similar interest in our own creative work.

Today, twenty-one years after *The Buddha of Suburbia*, each time another British Asian novel, film or memoir appears we can't help feeling a sense of déjà vu. We see the same few narratives again and again, stories about generational and cultural conflict which, greatly simplified, go something like this: born or brought up in Britain, we suffer at the hands of oppressive parents. These comical or villainous figures (usually both) continue to hold onto the culture and customs of the place they're from, a country that should be irrelevant to them since they live in England now. They hold us back from the pleasures and normality of western life: they don't let us drink alcohol or eat meat; they don't let us go to pubs and clubs; they force us to wear

Indian suits or keep topknots; they're overly religious; they make us study hard and push us into careers that we don't want to follow; they don't allow us to have relationships of our choice and want us to have arranged marriages. When we resist, they resort to emotional blackmail or physical force.

We've seen many versions of this story: the sporty one, the northern one, the gay one, the domestic-abuse one, the academic one, the mental illness one. There is also a Muslim version, which seems to tell a different story, but at heart it is about a culture clash. This story sets out to reveal the truth behind the beard and headscarf: how a generation of young liberal Muslims overnight became religious fundamentalists.

These narratives have become synonymous with the British Asian brand. But for many British Asian writers the pressure to continue to write these stories – since they've become bankable, marketable formulas – means that the British Asian label has now become stifling. Some of us feel that these stories have nothing to do with our lives. Some of us identify with the themes but want to find other ways to write about them. Some of us don't want to write about our lives at all. It's these attitudes that you see in this anthology, in stories which might not usually be published, perhaps because their content or approach doesn't fit the expectations of the label: these stories might be considered too Asian or not Asian enough.

Some authors don't want to write about their lives, and this might be, if they manage to create such a space, the simplest, cleanest way to sidestep the suffocation of the British Asian label. We see such stories in this anthology: stories that are set in other countries and other times, and about characters who are not of South Asian origin. Bobby Nayyar's 'Phun' is set in an American university campus. Niven Govinden tells the tale of a woman who arrives in a European village to buy hair. Suhayl Saadi transports us to ancient Rome, through the eyes of a soldier's wife.

Writers should be able to write these stories about other people, other places, other times. To do so is an assertion of freedom and confidence. But it isn't always easy to find publishers for such stories;

and when we do, it might only be because our surnames or religion are a handy USP for publishers to use in their marketing pitches. For many British Asian writers, the only alternative to writing the British Asian story has been to write about an exotic India or political Pakistan, regardless of their knowledge and experience of those places.

Some of us do want to write about our lives or about Asian-origin characters in Britain but feel that these narratives – so ubiquitous as to define the 'British Asian' label – are nothing to do with us or they simply don't interest us.

Implicit in the expectation that we all have the same story to tell, there is an assumption that we're all the same, ignoring cultural, regional and class differences between us. British Asian is assumed to be a catch-all label for everyone of South Asian origin living in Britain, but the category doesn't speak to us all. It carries certain regional and class associations; most 'British Asians' originate from Punjab, Gujarat, Mirpur and Sylhet, and have been part of the working classes here. Those who belong to other classes, who have come to Britain from other places or are more recent immigrants, who have one Asian parent or whose individual experiences simply don't conform to the dominant narratives, can feel disconnected from this idea of British Asianness. Many writers I have spoken to have been adamant that they are expatriate Indians, Pakistanis or citizens of the world, rather than British Asians, despite spending all, most or a large part of their lives here. Others define themselves as black British.

Those writers who don't conform to the accepted idea of British Asianness, whose stories don't engage with certain themes in a certain way, can be perceived by publishers not to be gritty and authentic enough: not Asian enough. We see such stories in this anthology: for example, Rohan Kar's 'Sepulchre', about the journey that Mikey, son of a Muslim father and a Catholic mother, makes to Jerusalem to scatter his mother's ashes on the Tomb of Christ, or NSR Khan's 'Familiar Skin', which centres on Sonia, a privileged, bipolar, Muslim girl in a hospital psychiatric unit.

*

And then there are those writers whose experiences do overlap with the dominant narratives, and who do want to write about these experiences. I would include myself in this category. For us, the struggle is not only against the limited vision of the publishing and media industries, but also within ourselves. Aloo gobi, gurus, Bollywood, bhangra, saris, arranged marriages and the hijab might be aspects of our lives, so it feels strange to avoid writing about them. But to write about them seems to perpetuate clichés. We might want to explore our lives in true and fresh ways, but the representations in cinema, television and literature hang over us, making us self-conscious. The existing narratives are so pervasive that they form a barrier between us and the world; they bleed into our imaginations and influence how we write about our lives.

For some years I have been trying to write about a guru and the community around him, about a fictional spiritual group based in Britain. But the guru figure is a cliché. The precedents that hang over me – the film *The Guru, The Guide* by R. K. Narayan, *The Mystic Masseur* by V. S. Naipaul, *Hullabaloo in the Guava Orchard* by Kiran Desai, *The Buddha of Suburbia* by Hanif Kureishi – all share something in common. They all create an abstract, mystical, comical, ahistorical, sceptical picture of the guru figure – he's always an accidental guru, a fake. These versions of the guru have interfered with my sense of the guru and followers that I have known. Such representations coloured my early writing, in which I inhabited a sympathetic second-generation character who was sceptical of any form of faith, who looked at the community with the eyes of an outsider. This character was distant from my more traditional characters, who became caricatures because they had faith.

But then I spent five years in India, far away from British Asianness. I didn't go there to find myself, to go back to my roots. In fact I was very aware, as I worked in the English-language literary world of South Delhi, an elite cosmopolitan world of privilege, of being far away from my family roots in villages and towns in Punjab. Over time this awareness became discomfort. My appearance and my English education brought easy acceptance into this society, but I carried the knowledge of my working-class family background in Britain and my lower-middle-class family in Punjab, who didn't speak English, who would most likely be invisible to and even ridiculed by the same people who accepted me in Delhi.

I later moved to a village in Himachal Pradesh where I stayed for two years. During this time I also saw my family in Punjab frequently and both experiences began to give me a better understanding of the history and specificity of my characters: immigrants from the villages and towns of Punjab. Reading about that history and more specifically about spiritual groups or 'deras' like the one I was writing about helped me to place the fictional world that I was creating in a wider social, political framework, to develop a sense of its trajectory as well as the roots of its particularities. I learned, in particular, how deras, which often reject casteism or dowries and question individualism and materialism, can provide internal reform within North Indian communities: Critique and reform don't have to come from the West as they tend to in so many British Asian narratives.

It became apparent to me, as I looked over what I had written up until then, that while I had been writing about a community that I knew well, that I had grown up in, I had written about it, not from the inside with compassion, particularity and knowledge but from a distant and superior perspective. On the creative writing MA I took, the students, teachers, publishers and agents who came to advise us were predominantly white and middle-class. And those who weren't, shared – along with the bourgeois South Asian or the British Asian writers of the literature I turned to – a similar world view to those teachers and publishers. It seemed that in my writing I had unconsciously adopted that gaze, white middle-class or bourgeois Indian, upon a world that I knew intimately, that I had been a part of. It was a gaze that was not only unsympathetic, but that also allowed me to be lazy. Knowledge, depth, understanding, wisdom were not required; I only needed to present a slice of the 'reality' I had access to.

As the anthology shows, I'm not alone in objecting to the clichés of the British Asian narrative. It is an embodiment of a world view, which is not simply white or British, but more specifically secular, liberal and middle-class. By focusing on a simple culture clash, it creates unthinking dichotomies of East and West, Islam and the West, Asian and British, with a narrow version of 'British' assumed as the norm. It promotes an ideal of multiculturalism as assimilation, personified through characters, often second generation, who aspire to fit into British society – to be 'normal'.

When we write about our lives from this British perspective, 'Asian' or 'Islam' are simplified. We end up stripping specific traditions, rituals, religions and other forms of lived faith, 'arranged marriages' and parents' anxieties of their context and detail, of their history, politics and class, simply to make them more consumable. All these appear, as we look down at them, exotic, inexplicable, funny, but at the same time, as we stick to those expected tropes, strangely familiar.

Writing our stories from the inside can be one way to avoid clichés. In the stories by Harpreet Singh Soorae, Dimmi Khan and Azmeena Ladha, which all centre on Asian-origin families and communities, the lives of their characters have not been reduced or simplified for the consumption of non-Asians. In each story there is particularity and detail; the writer is a part of the world he or she is writing about, as if the imagined reader is not so different from the characters in the stories. This approach is one way we can write about our lives in fresh ways.

There are many writers who don't want to continue recreating palatable versions of the British Asian formula. We want to carve another space for ourselves, one where we can simply be writers or, if we don't buy into that idea of universality, where we can simultaneously be other things: women writers, gay writers, black writers, Punjabi writers, readers of French literature, dog lovers; or whatever we want to be, but without a label imposed from outside. And then when we come together, as we do in this anthology, under this umbrella for our particularities, we will challenge the label; broaden it, change it, make it new.

Too Asian,
Not Asian Enough

NSR KHAN

Familiar Skin

STEVIE

I'd seen a lot of girls brought in here like that. Not aggressive exactly. But troubled; in your face. Random, pacing. She did a lot of that pacing, up and down, up and down the women's section. Hours; up and down. Listening to her iPod. Dancing to her iPod. She was gorgeous, actually, doing her own silent disco. Then suddenly she'd start howling. Like a wounded fox, or something. I saw her clinging to the knees of a nurse. It was disturbing.

She's wasn't exactly beautiful, not a size six or anything, but glamorous. Fit. A lot of cleavage. Nice cleavage, though; sort of classy, not slaggish. She looked Italian; Brazilian maybe (in my dreams). Yeah, she was interested in me. But she was interested in everybody. All the girls, all the boys. She's wasn't the kind of girl I go with, really. Except that there was something familiar about her. It worked my nerve. Wondering where we'd met before.

She got given a room on her own; not one of the shared rooms on the ward. I thought maybe it was 'cause the Psychs thought she couldn't cope. She seemed so posh. Fragile. But she didn't seem scared. In fact, it was almost like the other girls couldn't handle her. She was a bit unsettling. Elisha was playing with her breasts in the smoking room (which was unsettling enough as it was), and we were all trying to ignore it and this one just went up to her and said, 'Don't do that. Your baby boy will smell you and will weep for his mother.'

Elisha is like, 'Do you know me? You don't know anything about me!'

'I can see through your skin, to your mind. If I believed in Allah I would say that he told me these things.'

Weird really. 'Cause Elisha did. Have a baby boy, that is.

Did I wanna shag her? I shagged Elisha when she came in raving. She wasn't keen to have me near her after that. I'd shagged a lot of them when they were flying. More when I was flying. But it's cold, man. Dark. It's not even passionate, anonymous sex. They actually don't care who you are. You're just part of their story. And I didn't want to make their story worse. But sometimes it's just impossible to refuse, ain't it?

JED

We had spent six hours in A&E waiting to get her admitted. She'd thrown herself variously at the security guard, the mental health social worker, the duty psychiatrist and a female nurse. Before I brought her in I had found her draped round some low life in Soho. I was exhausted by her: the oscillations between warm adoration, violent rage and ugly-face weeping. She complained constantly that her head was noisy from listening to everyone's thoughts. It was a shame that she couldn't hear mine. In those six hours I wondered why I'd stayed with her. Long before the manic depression, we faced decay. At first I didn't care; I never got to meet her family, I wasn't allowed to answer the phone in case her father called, had to ship out every time he came round. I wasn't even allowed to go to his funeral. But after a while it was undermining. The feeling that her culture was afforded more respect than I was. And I couldn't understand the loyalty. Her father was an inconsistent, firebrand, disciplinarian of a man.

For me, she was never really Pakistani. There were too many things about her that didn't fit with the image, not least the smoking. Her family were educated, westernized. They holidayed in Paris not the Punjab, for God's sake. It felt as if all the 'Asianness' was just for show, something to make her white friends uncomfortable.

In A&E she wasn't Asian. She was just bipolar. And I was keeling over from the strain.

SONIA

I couldn't form thoughts I was proud of. I couldn't sustain one mood, one course of action, one strategy for longer than a minute. For a second I would have hope, and then? Loss of all perspective; 'waiting to die'. I hated my volatility and rage at Jed. The anti-psychotic medication was neither pleasant nor effective. It's taken with a pill for Parkinson's disease for the tremors. And as it slows the metabolism, it brings with it gargantuan appetite. I knew that in days I would not only be suicidal but, worse, many dress sizes bigger.

I could still hear people's thoughts; see what the nurse was thinking: that she wanted to leave her husband; what she'd fed her family that evening before she came. And the other patients? One of them was stashing his diazepam to sell on the other ward, another wanted to sleep with me. But with the meds, I knew that although I could still hear the noise, it was not real. At least that is what I am told. But sometimes the things I see, the thoughts I hear, are the truth.

After days I finally came down enough to wash. I found six shalwar-kameez neatly folded on the bed. I must have asked for them; Jed had left them. I didn't remember. I couldn't imagine why. I never wore them outside. Jed didn't like them. He said they alienated him. I'd wear them at home for comfort. Comfort as in food. Comfort food. Like hot roti. When I was little I told Papa that my favourite food was freshly cooked chapatti with butter. He'd replied, 'Yes, but someone had to stay in the hot kitchen to make it for you.' So when Jed was out, at his Lib-Dem meetings, I would stay in the kitchen and make the roti for myself.

It was too late to ask for different clothes and I couldn't wear what I was admitted in. Far too provocative. Most of the clichés about bipolar disorder are true. A manic episode *does* start well. You feel liberated; can do anything, be anything and, as it appeared in my case, wear anything.

STEVIE

That morning in the smoking room I didn't even recognize her. I went for my early morning fag, before the cleaner got in, and there she was. Legs up on the chair, smoking a roll-up in a Pa . . . Asian pyjama sari-type thing. Beautiful swathes of pale embroidered fabric wrapped around her. But odd. She wasn't fucking Brazilian or Italian. How had I fucking not noticed that? I mean odd, that she was smoking and a roll-up of all things. But she was undeniably Asian. But still, somehow, familiar to me. I wondered if she reminded me of a Bengali girl at my secondary school. But she wasn't really like that.

I think a lot of the others didn't notice or care about the change – you've got to be aware of reality to notice a thing like that. But Tony noticed. Nasty, AIDS-ridden, body-arted poof. He wasn't ill! There was nothing wrong with him save that he was pure evil! He started needling her that morning. I mean, you have to be evil to start on at someone at six-thirty a.m., don't you?

Subtle at first. 'Hey, Stevie, have you got a spare fag. I didn't get a chance to go to the Paki's.' A sly look in her direction.

'You can't call them Pakis any more.'

'Stevie, I'm not referring to a person, just the name for a shop.'

'Fuck off, Tony.'

And she didn't say a word. She just stared, frowning at Tony. She didn't avoid him. But she didn't take him on. She just kept looking at his face and then his hands.

Thankfully, some of the girls came in. Elisha cooed over her: 'Oh, I love what you're wearing. God, Sonia, you look great. I've got a scarf that I don't wear that would really suit you.'

The whole day Tony took pop shots at her. The funny thing? It weren't about racism, I don't think. She just got more attention than he did, and he didn't like that. He *saw* her. Do you know what I mean? She wasn't just Asian to him. And he wasn't picking on her because she was Asian. She was a person to him. He just didn't like that person.

I should know. My dad's a racist. I don't blame him. When I left for the army at sixteen, my sister and her baby were living with us in a two-bed council flat. When I got out at twenty-three she was still there. And the empty flat next to us went to a Bengali family. Twenty years on, Somers Town is Bangla Town. It's not the same place he grew up in. I don't blame him, but it don't make it right.

But still, racist or no racist, Tony was having a go and she seemed powerless against it. I felt protective. Not 'cause she was Asian. 'Cause she was pretty, of course.

SONIA

I was relieved to see that Tony was not in the smoking room. His relentless jabs had been ruining my recovery. There was only Stevie. I liked him, at first. He was nice-looking: French crop, intense blue eyes, gaunt, tiny scars dancing on his face. Gentle manner about him. But something about him made me feel uncomfortable. I've done some terrible things because of mania. Many, thankfully, I can't remember. Some I can. Recurrent pictures in my mind cause waves of guilt and distaste to pass through my whole body. I've slept with a lot of men I didn't know. But this feeling about Stevie, it felt as if something more than sex had happened. I couldn't pin it down.

He didn't smile. He always smiled at me. He just stood against the wall looking edgy, paranoid. I wasn't sure why he was in hospital. He seemed normal. But Elisha said he was in a state, at first. I wondered if he was getting ill. He wouldn't move from the wall. He let the ash from his cigarette fall onto the floor. I wondered if he was okay. I placed an ashtray in his hand. He shrank away from me as if I repelled him. I was afraid for a moment that he might become violent. And then I realized what he was doing.

He had been trying to hide the graffiti on the wall. PAKIS OUT OF THE SMOKING ROOM. For one second I thought it was Stevie. But of course not. Tony. I should have done something about him the day before. I've never been good with words. In an article, a symposium, a lecture room, yes. Not the playground, the street, the student summer pub job. Not the smoking room. Some people create a force field by their demeanour, their presence, their language. Not me. Presented with a threat, I'm silenced. My only response?

Inappropriate, disproportionate, violent rage. I could blame the illness, but it's not that. I've felt that way since I was very small. I had no words for Tony. I just wanted to punch him so hard that all his piercings fell through his lower intestine and descended out his colon.

STEVIE

What happened next was crazy, even for the ward. Sonia, despite my best efforts, eventually saw Tony's handywork. Unlucky for him, at that moment, Tony sidled up to the smoking room. She didn't say a word. Just lunged for him. Grabbed him by the neck. A couple of the others came in and saw the graffiti and starting shouting at Tony, saying it wasn't on. Nobody seemed that bothered that she'd pushed him up against the wall and was squeezing his neck with one hand. Suddenly it seemed like half the ward were there screaming at Tony, and then the morning shift nurses flew in like the military police, hauling patients away, ordering them to be quiet.

And suddenly, I don't know how, Tony was on the floor. And she was kicking him and kicking him. His back, his head, maybe his face. And odd, all the time, she was crying. When I finally got a handle on what was going on, I pulled her off and dragged her to the visitors' room.

JED

She'd asked me to bring in more items from home. Her prayer carpet and her father's Koran of all things, this time. I'd bought her some toiletries from Bond Street, like her father would have done. I was looking forward to seeing her. I'd got the sense she was improving, less hyper at least. As I walked in to the visitors' room I saw a bloke I'd seen sniffing around her before. He had his back to me. Looked like a squaddie from the posture and his cropped hair. I'd been worried about her in there. She was so vulnerable when she was manic, throwing herself at everyone. The ward manager had assured me that the female and male beds were separate, but I wasn't consoled. The rest of the ward was mixed. I hadn't liked the look of that bloke.

Within a split second I realized that she was with him. He was holding her. Kissing tears from her eyes. This was different. I had seen her with men before. I've saved her from men before! But she was down now. Her mood should have been more stable. What I saw was intimate.

They didn't see me. I walked out, left her stuff at the nurses' station and went home to look for flats to rent. I never saw her again. I used friends as intermediaries to arrange the collection of my stuff.

SONIA

I felt like I did when I was little. It had nothing to do with mania or labile mood. It was rage, pure rage. The kind of rage I'd felt before, but not acted on. Not like this. Not since I was tiny, ten, maybe. Papa had picked me up from my girls' private school to buy sweetmeats for Eid from Ambala on Drummond Street. We'd gone to Selfridges first to buy me new clothes. But we spent more time in the men's section looking for yet another suit for him. 'Something light for the summer,' he'd said. He was always so smart. That day in sharp, pressed slacks and a cashmere blazer, ostentatiously walking with an ivory-headed cane. I had hated his canes. Hidden his canes. When my parents moved house they a found a collection of wooden spoons, Papa's belts and some of his best canes in the attic.

We got lost somewhere on the wrong side of Euston. It was getting late, but Papa was adamant he knew where he was going. He oscillated between irritation with my anxiety and interest in my school stories.

I saw them first. From a distance. I can't work out how I knew that they meant us harm. I had no reason to fear white people. But I did fear those boys. Three of them. They were young, not men yet. But they seemed big to me. Big enough. I tightened my grip on Papa's hand and he in reply loosened his. He continued to talk about nothing in particular. But he seemed distracted. And older. And frailer.

They were on us so quickly. I can't remember all they said. It was foul. Papa hated bad language. They knocked my school panama off.

'Aren't you gonna pick it up then?'

'Look at her. I've never seen one dressed like that.'

I bent down to get it, but Papa fiercely jerked my arm. He seemed more angry with me than them. He was smiling, but I remember feeling that he was afraid. That I wanted to protect him in some way. That I didn't know how. I hated them for making him seem weak. Or maybe that's what I think now.

He was staring at their hands, their pockets. He told me later that he was checking for knives, knuckledusters. Anything that would have made this a real attack. They had not come prepared. Or at least not prepared for him.

'Now, I am going to give you all a chance.'

He raised his walking stick up to shoulder height and held it across his body like a defensive sword.

'If you leave us alone. You will remain unhurt. If you pursue this cowardly behaviour. Then' – nodding his head – 'I will be forced to take direct action.'

They jeered. One seemed to step back pulling the other with him. The one in the middle seemed more dogged. He squared up to Papa. Only for a second. Papa's stick swiped out knocking the boy in his chest. He was winded, retching slightly, falling forward.

The other two fled. Papa started to move away. He looked exhausted, broken.

And then . . . I was on the boy. I kicked the back of his knees. He went down easily. His chin hit the pavement, splitting. Blood started to spread from the split. And I was there, kicking his face, his eyes, his nose. How dare he? How dare he make Papa weak? How dare he frighten him?

Papa grabbed the back of my blazer and in seconds we were in a taxi on the Euston Road back to Highgate. He was quiet for the whole journey. Except for, 'Well, it is their country.' Nothing more.

At the weekend he took me out to celebrate my 'victory'. Papa loved telling stories, but he never told that one again.

STEVIE

I don't know what happened, really. I've seen blokes get into fights like that before. Hell, I used to get into fights myself like that. My mum got sick of it. That's why she sent me to the army. Maybe I should blame my mum for where I am now. But this was different. This was a bird, a woman. This was Sonia. I felt sorry for her. What's the word? Compassion. I felt compassion. I wanted to protect her, not from Tony, but from herself.

And the rest? Yeah, I fancied her. I might have tried to think differently at first, but I did. But it was more than that. I wasn't expecting that kind of sex when you, literally, really wanna eat them. From that first kiss in the visitors' room all I wanted to do was touch her. Be with her. Talk to her. Kiss her to the bone.

I couldn't work out what it was we had in common, but there was a connection. Was it mental illness? I don't think so. Mine was 'cause of the draw. Years of trying to puff away memories of the army. Mates of mine from the Gulf got jobs, settled down. But I never got off the starting blocks. Drug-induced psychosis, they call it. But her? Manic depression? I mean, when you've been on the ward a while, you realize that they are not so different, all these mental illnesses. But Sonia and I didn't talk much about it.

I've always thought upper-class people – you know, proper posh – and working-class people get on better. Middle-class? Well, they're too frightened, up their own arses; trying to pretend to be something they're not, apologizing for what they are. Upper-class people aren't ashamed of what they are. They're themselves. Maybe it was that. Because Sonia was posh. She might have been Asian, but she had some money and clout behind her.

I loved her in her Asian clothes. She looked beautiful, she did. She took my breath away sometimes. And I loved all her stories about Pakistan. She looked so happy when she was telling me about their houses in Lahore and Karachi and her aunties. She told me a little about her dad, her 'Papa'. Being upper-class don't protect you from everything, I suppose. But she did love him.

I would tell her about growing up in Somers Town and the Bengalis there. She was nothing like them. I told her about my dad and the way he was, is, with foreigners. I told her bits about the army, the Gulf War. Not much, but more than I've ever told anyone. We tried to tell each other everything. We did try.

It felt like she was getting better. There were bad days, returns to the silent disco. But more where I could see what was really Sonia and not the illness. And the more I got to know her, the more it felt as if I had always known her. Sonia said the reason we felt so familiar was because we'd met before. She said that in Islam men and women are made from the one soul. And when you meet your beloved, you know them, 'cause they are the other half of your broken soul.

She said a lot of things. The way I felt, feel about her now, is that nothing will ever be so exciting as when we first met. We healed each other. We did. We healed our broken souls. And I have never felt so whole.

SONIA

I know people asked what the hell we had in common. I may have been ill, but I wasn't demented. Friends, who visited me, warned me that I was losing Jed. I didn't care. I know he took care of me. But he denied me so much. When my cousin, my first cousin, died in Pakistan a few years ago Jed asked me why I was sad. He told me that Tariq wasn't part of my life, because I hadn't seen him for a while. That Pakistan wasn't part of my life because I grew up here. That I shouldn't be overdramatic. But Stevie. I could have told Stevie anything. And we imagined a life after hospital together. I could imagine it.

And I know that Jed looked after me, but I also know that I repelled him. He couldn't bear my anger. When I cried he would just walk out. Stevie knew me. To be loved is to be known and Stevie did, he knew me.

I felt myself getting better. And I felt myself getting fatter. And I wondered how Stevie could still desire me. And, of course, it made sense, as it always does, even now, to ditch the meds. The anti-psychotics, the mood stabilizers, the tranquilizing benzodiazepines, even maybe the sleeping tablets. Not hard really. It's easy to emulate a swallow. Swallow; stick out your tongue, the meds tucked in the side of your cheek.

STEVIE

She told me she'd stopped taking her meds. I didn't see a problem with it, at the time. I didn't realize that bipolar disorder is with you for life. I know that now. She seemed okay. In fact, she seemed better.

She had more energy, enthusiasm. And she was so hopeful for our future together. I got swept up in all her joy and plans. The holidays we'd go on, the people she'd introduce me to. She really made me believe that it would work. I want to believe her, even now.

Yeah, there were a few hiccups. She was a little more impatient than before. She'd get irritated when people were just mucking about. She started to complain about too much going on, people being loud, about a noise in her head. Little signs. Little things that reminded me how she was when she first came in. But nothing to worry about. She seemed to have it under control. If anything she was even more loving with me. We'd sit for hours just talking and kissing.

We were sitting in the dinner room. It had amazing light in that room. When the sun was out, it just poured in. She said that I looked like an angel with the light on my face. She was stroking my face and touching each one of my faded scars. She asked me where each one was from. Above my eye, a fight with my cousin and I fell on the stairs. On my cheek, my only bona fide knife fight, and you could barely see it. And my chin. I started to tell her the story and then I felt uncomfortable. I'd never told anyone the truth about that scar. But you feel like you need to be pure. Clean. With someone you love. With 'the one'. Start fresh. I lied to my mum. I didn't wanna lie to Sonia.

And I suppose that injury changed my whole life. I came home with my face in a right mess. My chin felt like it was open to the bone. The rest of me wasn't much better. My mum had never seen me in such a state and she went mad. I suppose she panicked. I think she thought I would end up dead if I stayed in Somers Town. She had me down that army recruitment office quicker than . . . Well, you know, quicker than most things.

Sonia is holding my face and looking at me. 'I can see through your skin. I can hear your thoughts.' And I thought, Oh God. Not a-fuckin'-gain! She's getting ill. We can't go through this again. Not that mind-reading thing.

'I know you,' she said. But she was right. She did know me. She could see my memories.

SONIA

Most people assume we split up because I got ill again. People who know me assume it's because I couldn't forgive Stevie. It wasn't that at all.

Stevie tried. We both tried. I didn't hate him. Yes, in one split second I had remembered his face. But the Stevie now, the Stevie I met in hospital, the Stevie who had suffered so much, that was not the Stevie of twenty years ago.

It was Stevie who could not forgive me. The little girl and her Paki dad who mashed up his face. The little girl who humiliated him in front of his mates. The little girl who ruined his life.

STEVIE

That little girl, she was mad. I didn't defend myself. I could have. But it was pointless. I knew, by instinct, that there was something wrong with that little girl. If I'd fought back she would have done something worse. I don't think even her father, her Papa, could have controlled her at that moment. I think there will always be something wrong with that girl.

Gautam Malkani

Asian of the Month

T hey could hear the electrical surge as they stepped out onto the stage. Had the act of stepping out activated the lighting; or had the lights been on before? No audience, of course; this was still part of the audition. More an audition for the audition – that's what both of their agents had told them.

At stage left, the first one starts shielding his eyes. Wondering if he might get a suntan from the sycophantic spotlights. Wondering if he *should* get a suntan. And if the women among them will sunbathe with no clothes on.

At stage right, the second one starts setting up his stuff. His traffic-light lighting, his speakers, his tape deck. His twin steel-tabla-like turntables. Then, without being instructed – for there is still no one around to instruct them – he stops and stands upright. 'So,' he says to the contestant at stage left, 'who the hell are you?'

The contestant at stage left smiles as he answers. 'I'm the Asian of August. Don't you remember? We already met each other – during the last round.'

'Well, you all look the same to me. Anyhow, nice to meet you and all that bull and baloney – my name's the Asian of April.'

'I know,' says the Asian of August. 'We already met each other. During the last round.'

Due to self-inflicted injury, tonight the role of Asian of August will be played by his able understudy. Please queue at the box office for a full ticket refund.

For the moment, it is just the two of them. Like they've both turned up at the wrong auditorium. More lecture theatre than auditorium. More disused TV studio than lecture theatre. The Asian of April tries to imagine the spectacle of a live studio audience. Then he turns once again to talk to the Asian of August. 'Where do you reckon the others are then?'

'The judges?'

'No, the *others*. The other *months*. Why the hell ain't anyone else here yet?'

'No idea.'

'Well, was anyone hanging about backstage?'

'Like I said, bruv, I've got no idea.'

'Don't be calling me bruv, okay. I ain't your bloody brother. I ain't even your bloody blood brother. We might've got the same skin colour as each other, but we sure as fuck ain't got the same blood.'

The Asian of April then pulls out a razor and slices his left little finger to prove it. But he knows he should really be slitting his throat. Just slit through his throat and be done with it. The tedium of his life is killing him. Slowly but surely, the small talk is shutting him down. He supposes that it's killing all of them, though. They should have all become bankers or accountants or consultants – then they'd be dead and wealthy and happy by now. They'd be staring at brochures and menus and televisions – not four hundred full-frontal backrests. Four hundred futile erections from four hundred flip-down plastic chairs.

Tonight's interval drinks are even better than the real thing – with new, improved recipes formulated for a sweeter aftertaste.

The Asian of August walks towards an onstage vending machine – backlit and sweating from its own fluorescent tube-lighting. Or just sweating from the heat of its refrigeration system. He opens an out-of-date can of Pepsi. He doesn't think to wonder why a vending machine is standing between them on the stage. 'I'd offer you some of this refreshment,' he says to the Asian of April. 'But I suspect you'd be better off smoking a joint.'

Both contestants try to remember how they felt back in the beginning. They'd been warned there'd be a degree of psychological stress involved. That entertainment would be a function of their failure.

'Or maybe you should just try meditating,' continues the Asian of August. 'Or even masturbating. Although the others might be here any minute. They'll probably all arrive at the same time. All ten of them. And the judges, too.'

The Asian of April wonders whether he can wander backstage to smoke, meditate or masturbate. After all, the real-time, round-the-clock surveillance format was so last season. But any scope for stress release is removed by the sound of footsteps. The mental disturbance of stage props. 'Who's there?' he shouts.

'I'm sorry I'm late,' replies a lone latecomer as she steps out into the light. In her right hand, a machete; in her left hand, a rubber chicken.

'I don't believe we've met,' says the Asian of August.

'I don't believe it either,' says the latecomer.

The Asian of August dons his best indifference. The latecomer scrolls through her smartphone. 'You ain't late,' says the Asian of April. 'Only the last one will be late. Anyhow, what's your name?'

The not-late latecomer smiles and strokes her machete. 'I'm the Asian of October and November,' she says. 'Otherwise known as the competition's first and only Consecutive Asian. But for short you can just call me the Asian of Autumn.'

The Asian of August asks whether that means there'll only be eleven contestants in total. The Asian of Autumn shakes both her own and her rubber chicken's head. She says there'll still be twelve of them. She explains that July was a tie so the judges put both July's finalists through to this round. The Asian of April tuts before declaring that the judges were a bunch of dickless eunuchs: 'They should've just chosen one of them. After all, it ain't like the loser could accuse them of racism.'

Mirror, mirror on the dressing-room wall, who is the most authentic of us all? Mirror, mirror on the bedroom ceiling, are those tattoos across her ass-cheeks genuine?

Today's round will be round three – though some of them still refer to it as round C. It had taken a year to whittle down thousands of contestants to twelve Asians of the Month, and it would now take eleven weeks to eliminate each Asian of the Month until there remained only one. The trouble was, the first two rounds had outfoxed everyone – but instead of eliminating all the contestants, they'd eliminated none.

Back in the penthouse, the candidates broke rule number nine and convened for a post-round post-mortem. The problem for all of them had been the judges. In the absence of their mothers, the question of who judged them was as much metaphysical as procedural. They'd all been expecting to face a three-strong panel of white, middle-class marketing professionals. They'd all dressed down to demonstrate their street cred and their general state of material and existential deprivation. They'd all thought to themselves with their own respective glints in their eyes: *I* know how to work this system we've been placed in. Ain't nobody gonna accuse *me* of being too privileged to be ethnic, too educated to be authentic. But, as round one began, the judges turned out to be a panel of Asian media pundits.

First up, the pundits scolded the Asian of January because of the bruises on his manga-style mangoes. Next, the Asian of February was dismissed for having sweated her way into Oxbridge. The Asian of March was berated for failing to lie prostrate for her aunties and uncles and parents. The Asian of April was attacked for being offensive to his fellow Asians. And so on and so forth until the Asian of December was disqualified for having too many holes in her fishnet stockings. Because, as every authentic Asian media pundit knows, the bona fide deprived dress *up*, not down.

'There's a reason for all this stringency,' one of the Asian judges told them. 'We aim to facilitate an environment so authentically pure that both positive discrimination and negative discrimination result in identical outcomes.'

So, for round two, the contestants all wore brand-new suits, designer jewellery, religious headdresses and sacred threads – only to find that, this time round, the judges comprised the previously predicted panel of white, middle-class marketing professionals.

Audiences are reminded to leave the auditorium in an orderly manner. Because acts of ethnic violence can seriously harm you and others around you.

Four more months trickle in over the next thirty minutes – each with their own equipment. Another rubber chicken and another machete. A modified set of manga-style mangoes. A free-standing pole-dancing pole with detachable Indian-tinted dildo. A portable, electric funeral pyre with self-cleaning function and saffron-scented smoke.

The Asian of May strolls up to and spits at the Asian of August. 'Listen, August, while we wait for the others, let me tell you what a disgrace you were in front of the white judges.'

The Asian of August smiles as he wipes May's spit from his eyes. 'Well, I thought I did pretty well. Those people think I don't use toilet paper and yet I still had them eating out of my hands.'

'But have you forgotten that you represent?'

The Asian of August examines the texture of May's phlegm.

'Did you hear me, August? I said, you represent. Whether you want to or not, you can't escape the fact that you represent your race.'

The Asian of August shakes his head. 'I'm sorry, May, but how does that even begin to make sense? How can I be representing all Asians when my act only features flying Asian paedophiles?'

'Is *that* how you want to portray your people? The descendants of all those who died for your freedom.'

The Asian of August maintains his composure. He knows contestants on these sorts of shows are supposed to scrap and squabble. You can't have drama without conflict and you can't have conflict without giving the audience a sense of the dramatic. They call the genre 'reality' so that the squabbles and the fights don't need a narrative plot device.

'Well, perhaps my next act should feature an Asian axe murderer?' he offers. 'After all, surely nobody's going to think *all* Asians are axe murderers? What do you reckon, May? Would you prefer it if I opted for an axe murderer?'

'Fine – but only if they don't actually kill people. And don't say I didn't warn you, August. If you don't represent well, then Asians won't like it and if Asians don't like it then white people will think it's inauthentic.'

Customers claiming a refund for tonight's tickets should send in their original booking documentation – not photocopies, scans or faxes. Brokers' or intermediaries' notices are also unacceptable.

For round three, they'd each been sent a set of written instructions. Engraved in aluminium and wrapped in velvet. More of a statement than a set of instructions. More of a sentence than a statement:

CANDIDATES ARE REMINDED IT IS NO LONGER SUFFICIENT SIMPLY TO PROVE THEMSELVES AUTHENTICALLY ASIAN – CONTESTANTS MUST ALSO DEMONSTRATE THEIR LONGEVITY AS OUR SEARCH FOR A SUSTAINABLE ASIAN CONTINUES.

In response to this sentence, each of the contestants hit upon the exact same sartorial strategy: ethnic dress, but clean-shaven and secular above the neck. They also adopted the same ideology: the shortage of Asians isn't because of discrimination; it's because of a lack of applications. The same micro-economic theory: it isn't because of the size of the Asian market; it's because of bootleg discs, illegal downloads, a lone legal copy loaned around like herpes. Even the same aesthetic sensibility: the beat isn't too rhythmic; it just needs the theme tune from *Knight Rider* to be thrown into the mix. The book isn't too vernacular; it just needs subtitles. The screenplay doesn't labour tired questions of divided identities; it simply shows the torments of being torn between two cultures.

By way of preparation for today's round, the contestants back at the penthouse applied these same strategies, ideologies, theories and sensibilities to their individual modes of talking, walking, dancing, singing, chanting, eating, drinking, coughing, fucking, sucking and vomiting. Every move carefully followed by a countermove for maximum creative paralysis.

The revolution will not be streamed over the internet, but if you sign up for a year's free subscription you can view it tomorrow night at the following address.

Fed up with foreplay, the Asian of May tries speaking into an onstage microphone. 'Hello?' she says. 'Anyone there? Can someone at least please tell us where we're meant to be waiting?'

'Here,' says a voice from the speakers above them – as if the spotlights are the eyes and the speaker-grilles the mouth.

'Here?'

'Yes.'

The Asian of August snatches the microphone. 'And what exactly are we waiting for?'

'Authentication.'

'Authentic Asian?'

'Yes.'

The Asian of May takes back the microphone: 'Well, I refuse for my act to be defined by my own Asian-ness.'

The Asian of June duly agrees: 'And *I* refuse for my act to be defined by the Asian-ness of the actual act.'

Next up, the Asian of Autumn: 'By your removal of the restrictions of my ethnic identity, I've become even more ethnic than I otherwise would be – because that's how authentically Asian I am.'

The Asian of March: 'Your format forces us to compete to be D-list villains instead of D-list celebrities. In accordance with western Marxist critical theory, it means not only are the masses in the audience deceived, so are the contestants on the stage or the screen.'

In the same fashion, each Asian of the Month slowly morphs from a state of resignation to a state of sociological revolt. Mangoes and rubber chickens are flung with violence into the non-existent audience. Smoke from the electric funeral pyre starts to reclothe the strippers, silencing the spotlights and choking the speakers. Its patent still pending, the cremation machine looks more like a bed-sized toasted sandwich maker. Wheels for ease of portability and a flame-grill function for extra flavour. When the device was unveiled to the panel of Asian judges, it was labelled, The Family Barbeque. When rolled out in front of the white, middle-class marketing professionals, it was rebranded, The Pyre This Time.

'I am not an Asian,' declares the Asian of June as he douses the electric funeral pyre with a bottle of eau minérale. 'I am a free man. A metrosexual, metropolitan man.' He continues speaking through the spits and the sparks: 'My metropolitan identity consigns to history all your dead-beat debates about whether I am torn between being British and being Asian. In my metropolitan identity, I am not even a minority. I do not suffer from racial discrimination or economic deprivation. I do not get lost in dreams of the motherland or work with my mother in a corner shop or her family's flock-papered Indian restaurant. I do not support India at cricket *or* England – I support whichever team has the best-looking female fans. I do not hear sitars in my head and dream of my mother in her favourite sari. I do not have any angst about an arranged or a semi-arranged marriage. I do not do terrorism, fundamentalism or Bollywood films. Because, frankly, I'm too busy building my own brand of Britishness; trying to get into the record business; spending my parents' hard-earned income on designer trainers, designer clothes and designer smartphones; driving around in an unstolen Audi and spending my evenings trying to get laid by fit-looking women . . .'

The smoke-choked speakers interrupt him before he can finish: 'The candidate is advised to save his protestations for the judges.'

'You mean you ain't the judge?' joins in the Asian of April. 'Then where the hell are the judges then?'

'The candidate is advised to save his protestations for the judges.'

'Yeah, but who the hell *are* the judges this time? Are they white or are they Asian?'

'Don't be so colour-centric,' retorts the Asian of Autumn. 'All that matters is whether they're educated or ignorant. And whether they can be overruled by the audience or by the advertisers.'

The spotlights sear down with enough force to flout factor-fifty sunscreen: 'The candidate is advised that the judges will be identified by the judges.'

'Oh just shut the fuck up,' shouts the Asian of April as he smears toasted-brown funeral flesh across his own face. 'Or I'll climb up there and smack up your grilles with my Garba sticks.'

'Can you just calm down?' the Asian of August urges the Asian of April. 'If you start smashing stuff up then you'll definitely lose.'

'Why?'

'Because that's not what Asians do.'

Divya Ghelani

Your Incredible Excuse

He couldn't ride a bicycle and he couldn't fall in love. Not since Beetle had left him. But he would reveal only the former to the broadsheet newspaper that had contacted him out of the blue to ask, 'What is the one thing you are most ashamed of not being able to do?' Antje Awan, the author and broadcaster with whom he went to university, had recommended him to the journalist. The email, opened in his inbox at exactly 2.47 a.m. on Wednesday 14 December 2010, had made him cry.

Dear Abhi

Anjte put me in contact with you.

I am composing a double spread in the arts review section of our newspaper on the subject of highly successful celebrities and the one thing they wished they could do. The article, entitled 'Your Incredible Excuse', will give the British public an insight into the more human aspects of the public figures they know and love. It will be a playful tongue-in-cheek piece composed entirely of personal testimony and we would love for you to be involved. Please respond by tomorrow (Wednesday 14 December) with a short answer to the below question.

'What is the one thing you are most ashamed of not being able to do and what's your incredible excuse?'

All best wishes,

Maya Hendricks

It was actually two questions parcelled up as one, just as the sender's 'all best wishes' had been bundled together, *all* of them, in a way that felt both annoying and insincere. The writer of the email had simply *presumed* he would be able to respond at short notice because they had a mutual contact, which irritated him. Maybe it was because he wasn't that big a celebrity? Maybe Begum Shafak or Terence Wainwright, who read the ten o'clock news, had been given two weeks to respond, and Abhi was a mere afterthought in a desperate journalist's frantic mind; a young man making his way, a friend of a friend and only half a year into his TV career. Of course *he'd* respond.

Abhi, who had resorted to Facebook stalking after trying, unsuccessfully, to sleep for four hours now, and was finding the sender of the email to be most disagreeable. Curious, he Googled her name and found a long list of 'lifestyle' articles written by a pretty, a *very* pretty, young Iranian-looking woman. Abhi looked at her photo again. He sent a brief, animated response.

> Dear Maya
> Will do! How nice of Antje to put us in touch!
> All best wishes,
> > Abhi Archarya
> > BBC Breakfast News Presenter

His mind projected an image of Maya Hendricks standing semi-naked in his newly fitted kitchenette, making herself a cup of Iranian coffee. Fragile as a Chinese vase, Abhi held the daydream and slowly, slowly left his desk to slip under the warm covers of his futon bed. Gently, he pushed his right hand into his jogging bottoms and closed his eyes in anticipation of the sweet release that might help him relax enough to sleep. But just as he began to wade into his new fantasy, just as he began to conjure that image of Maya Hendricks doing exactly what he wanted, the sound of Beetle's laughter interrupted him. Abhi stared up at the whitewashed ceiling and sighed with disappointment. He hated it that he missed her. *That damn Beetle!*

Again, Abhi sighed. He reasoned it would be better to distract himself from the subject of women altogether. Ensconced in his new

John Lewis Brisbane Quilt duvet, Abhi Archarya, aged thirty-four, began compiling a mental list of things he could not do: he couldn't ride a bicycle; he couldn't do quick tidy-ups of his flat (only big ones, and then only to music); he couldn't tell long jokes like other men; he couldn't unlock doors under pressure (his landlord had told him to go Zen and *then* turn the key); he couldn't parallel park or touch-type and he couldn't . . . *Beetle*, he still couldn't get Beetle out his head, no matter how he tried. Abhi was restless, more awake than ever before.

In all fairness to her, it wasn't just the trapped Beetle of Abhi's mind that was causing this particular bout of insomnia. He had slept well in the immediate aftermath of their break-up, defiant in his belief that life without her was going to be just fine. No, it wasn't just her. It was his job that had been keeping him up of late. Ever since he'd begun the early morning shifts at work six months ago, Abhi had acquired a nervy new internal alarm clock. His actual alarm, set for five each morning, left him too wired to sleep and too useless for anything else. And no, the fully expensed taxi ride to work didn't help. What if, one day, the taxi didn't pull up outside his bedroom window and Abhi overslept? What if the taxi did arrive, but he didn't hear the doorbell? What if he got into the taxi, left for work, went into makeup, got his notes and presented the news only to find that the whole sequence was just one long freakoid dream designed by his subconscious to mess up his life?

'Hot milk, okay hot milk,' he muttered up at the ceiling, throwing back his duvet and surrendering himself once again to premature day.

3.02 a.m. Standing in his kitchenette, with the warm glow of the streetlight outside, Abhi's fingers riffled beyond the numerous boxes of tea in the dark of his cupboard. There was tea for all occasions; Sleepy Time, De-Stress, Detox, Inner Goddess, Mildly Spiced Indian Chai tea, Green tea, an untouched Puerh brought over from Hong Kong by the BBC Financial Correspondent, Samantha Bodden, whose ex-girlfriend ran a New Age shop out there. Unsatisfied, Abhi's hands continued their search until they found what they were looking for. It was the watermarked Robertson's strawberry jam jar his mother had given him on her last visit to London. It contained shaved pistachio nuts, cardamom, cashews, almonds and sugar, all interlaced with delicate saffron hairs that looked weirdly ethereal to Abhi, like beautiful alien antennas. A few days ago, the same concoction had helped him sleep when nothing else would. He opened the old jar and inhaled its warm cardamom scent.

Abhi realized he was crying. A prickly hotness burned his cheeks. He raised his fingers to his face, as if exploring it for the first time. Yes, there were tears. Why was he crying? Abhi felt anxious and disorientated, like a man who had lost his keys. He backtracked, retraced his steps: He had read the email, responded, raised himself from his desk and returned to bed. Then, exasperated, he had wandered into the kitchen to make himself a cup of hot milk. It was then that something inside him had begun to thaw, causing tears to roll freely. But why? Abhi's eyes searched the flat for an answer and found it, finally, in the open laptop on his desk. 'Of course,' he whispered to himself. Shaken by the discovery, Abhi stood stock-still, staring into his memory.

14 December. Today was 14 December: the date of Beetle's mother's death. For four years, Abhi had marked it with her, an occasion that had made him feel both privileged and loved. Still, there was no need to cry. No reason at all to cry like he was crying now, stood in the cold new kitchenette, waiting for the milk to boil. It had been ten months, after all, since Beetle had left him, carrying her bright red suitcase out of their smart Kensington flat. It had been eight months since he had moved to Ealing Broadway in an effort to erase all traces of her. And, by and large, he had managed it, except for moments like these, when she came blundering into his consciousness unannounced. 14 December. She'd done it to him again. That damn Beetle!

Beetle (aka Bernadette McKenzie) was a journalist. She was the politics editor of a respected left-wing, liberal magazine: a lower paid but intellectually superior job to Abhi's BBC TV news anchor role. She was a short, smart woman with an American accent and designer bangs that cut across her forehead like a three-fifteen deadline. She had the intellectual edge in their relationship, was always snorting and guffawing at the dubiously sourced news reportage she saw Abhi and his cohort turn into stories and recount on TV each day. She would have laughed at Maya Hendricks' email request, referring to her as a 'lifestyle journalist' or a 'list-monger', categories Beetle reserved for anyone working in the 'inane, nepotistic, Oxbridge, balls-fondling' arts sections of the British print media. Beetle was a direct sort of a woman who lived and breathed politics, and it wasn't just Abhi she served it to straight.

When Abhi had expressed concern at their meeting his parents together (after all, Beetle was white, upper-middle class, half Scottish-American and half Jewish), she had insisted on a gathering the following week.

'Don't be so stiff, Bug!' she had said.

When Abhi's parents arrived at his London apartment with their usual plastic bags and Tupperware boxes filled with cooked food, Beetle had greeted them wearing a black Stella McCartney dress and pillar-box red stilettos. She had drunk dark rum in the kitchen with his mum, had argued about the Maharishi with his dad and had told him, in her post-rum pensiveness, that Islam was by far her favoured religion. Later on that evening, Abhi had caught Beetle in their kitchen, plaiting and un-plaiting his mother's long, oiled hair, twisting it into new shapes as they talked, an intimacy unfolding before him.

The odd thing was, they had all gotten along so well. It was Abhi who had spent the evening sullen and nervous, hovering on the periphery of rooms, waiting for his loose cannon of a girlfriend to hit someone in the face. But Beetle was Beetle was Beetle and Abhi's parents had sensed this. Abhi's father had even emailed him one of his weird messages to say just that:

Abhi
  Bernadette is a nice girl! Mum wants to teach her cooking. Carrots growing in the garden, but they are too small. Maybe I did something wrong? Ask in your BBC. Hi to Terence Wainwright.
  Love,
      Papa

It was always tense for Abhi, introducing his old life to his new one. Though Abhi loved his parents, loved them so much, he'd never told them he felt like a freak. Even among the two people most proud of him and his achievements, Abhi felt shame, a surfeit of it. The truth was he couldn't remember a time when he did not feel it. It was monstrous, the things he'd achieved!

He still remembered those three long winters during which his parents had refused to pay for heating, so Abhi could continue at the private school he had grown to hate. As they worked, he was chased and beaten by the local white boys, was rejected by the richer ones at school. Abhi had grown up associating success with the cold that had settled in his bones. Success was lonely, cold and strange. There was always that fear of being found out. So when Beetle McKenzie came along, with her loud American intellect and her soft, kind heart, Abhi still couldn't open up. Everything was buried so damn deep. He was willing to give everything of himself to her, but for that deep, dark kernel of shame. And who was she but another one of them, that conveyor belt of Alfies, Francescas, Sandeeps and Lisas, the bastards he'd honoured and hated so ferociously to get where he was. And for what? For Beetle McKenzie to keep trying to prise him open like a live oyster on her dinner plate? For Beetle, everything had been debatable, solvable, manageable . . . but he wasn't like that. So what if she was a 'serve it to you straight' sort of woman? If Abhi 'served it to you straight' he felt like the sky would shatter and fall down over everything. It was like the whole game was bloody rigged! Stupid, clever, straight-talking Beetle. God, he had loved her.

It was 14 December. Each year on this day, Beetle and Abhi sealed off the world in memory of Mrs Beetle. Abhi had never told Beetle, but in the four years they had been together, he had grown to look forward to her mother's death day more than his own birthday. 14 December had opened Beetle up even more, brought out someone softer, more fragile, a Beetle who needed Abhi more than he needed her. He found it odd and wonderful that she could spend it with him.

For Beetle, the day had its ground rules and Abhi was more than willing to obey. There would be no laptops or mobile phones, each would take the day off work and in this stolen pocket of time they would remember Mrs Beetle. The first anniversary was five months into their relationship. Abhi had never met the dead woman, but there he lay with his gorgeous new Beetle on her couch, smoking the last of the weed she'd bought for her mother, an attempt to alleviate the pain of the cancer that had taken her in the end. By the second year, Beetle and Abhi had moved in together. They made cranberry and banana oat bread in the swish breadmaker Mrs Beetle had gifted her daughter before she died. Then Abhi had sat with her under the duvet, watching Grace Kelly movies, listening to Beetle as she laughed and cried intermittently. The following year – the year of the abortion – Beetle had ignored Abhi's phone calls and spent days at a girlfriend's house listening to Nina Simone on her iPod, her mother's favourite singer. Abhi sat alone in their flat, longing to stroke Beetle's hair, make her feel all right. But by 14 December last year, things were much better between them. In high spirits, Beetle had rented a cottage in the Lake District. The plan was to watch *Forest Gump* in the morning (Mrs Beetle had liked Tom Hanks), and then hire bikes in Windermere to cycle through the National Park, an activity that would be followed by an indoor picnic. Ashamed, Abhi had waited until after the film to reveal that he could not, in fact, ride a bike. Beetle had been furious.

'Why do I make you so nervous? Why can't you just tell me the truth?' she had asked, her green eyes glinting with incredulity.

He had stared at the TV screen, unable to respond. Beetle left him in the cottage, hired a bicycle alone and didn't come back until evening; her face flushed and blotched with cold. Abhi had laid out the picnic items perfectly for her, spelling 'I'M SORRY' with cheese sticks. He'd even lit a fire with real logs, the first in his life. After they had made love in that very English rented cottage, Beetle had fixed him with her gaze, serious and kind.

'Life should be so cool,' she had said. 'You just need to loosen up from time to time. You're so stiff sometimes, Bug.'

The alarm read 4.15 a.m. Still, Abhi could not sleep. He warmed his hands with the mug of hot milk, inhaling its sweetness, and looked out onto the street below. He made out the shadowy figure of the big-bellied Turkish newsagent. He was pulling up the metal shutters of his shop window in anticipation of the oncoming day. Previously a Polish family had owned and lived in the flat above the shops, but Abhi preferred this new Turkish family, with their bored teenage girl cashier, their odd business plan that involved converting the traditional newsagent's into a jumble sale: plastic buckets, steel colanders, pitta breads and succulent vegetables as well as cigarettes and lottery tickets. In the first few weeks of his own early morning shift, Abhi had been warmed by the man's insistence on starting early, his morning ritual of opening up shop, followed by a coffee and newspaper at his counter. Abhi felt an affinity with him, an unspoken closeness. He felt they were brothers, morning crusaders, and considered it auspicious if he spotted him. But today it wasn't just the old Turkish man Abhi saw. He had seen something else, another shadowy object. He took a long slug of his mother's hot saffron milk and pulled the blind back a little further.

It was a bicycle. A slim burgundy frame, a hybrid; somewhere between a racer and a mountain bike. There it stood under the warm glow of a streetlamp, unlocked and beautiful, glinting its metallic burgundy splendour, broadcasting its presence to no one. Intrigued, Abhi forgot his tears, forgot Beetle McKenzie. He opened the window, wide enough to poke his head out. Things were changing. The Turkish man had entered his shop. He was making coffee and reading his newspaper. Again, Abhi eyed the bike. It was still there, a hot girl waiting for a date. Abhi checked his alarm clock: still forty minutes before the taxi arrived, taking him, his brogues and his newly pressed suit to present the news at BBC Television Centre in White City. Forty minutes and no bike owner in sight.

Abhi unlocked the door of his Ealing flat and made his way onto the street outside. Eager not to be seen by the shop owner, he kept his head down, and made his way stealthily towards the bike. In no time at all, he was stood in front of the old newsagent's, sporting the jogging bottoms and the hoody he'd worn in bed. He took the bike by its handlebars and led it toward the empty road. 'Okay,' he said. 'I'm going to do this.' As he climbed onto the seat, he felt the same relief he had felt as a boy, happiness that his feet touched the floor.

Right. Right. Here goes, he thought. Abhi pushed off with his right foot, teetered cautiously, lost his balance, fell first to the left and then to the right. At his most audacious, he managed two whole seconds of blissful balance before swerving to a halt. Then he went ahead once more, managing to lift his feet off the ground, coasting along the road for three whole seconds. Bolder, he added pedalling. First two rotations of the pedals, then four! After several runs, he was rolling along the road on his bike. It was only on his last run, going faster than he could believe, faster than he had ever gone before, feeling at once exhilarated, free and fearful, that the latter emotion took over and Abhi braked hard. The bike stopped abruptly and he went shooting over the handlebars.

A stinging sensation on his palms and knees. And he'd bloodied up his face! He remembered his five o'clock TV news slot and moaned. This realization was followed by a short bout of swearing. It took him a moment to become aware that the bicycle was hurting his left leg, and he shifted position slightly. It was then that he heard the sound of slow feet on gravel.

'Are you all right, love? Let me get you up. Eric? Eric? Come here. Will you come here? This young man's had a fall.'

It was a heavy-breasted old woman with thick arms and a wrinkled, concerned expression.

'Oh, love. You should come in to ours to clean yourself up. It's not pretty, your face.'

As Abhi looked at the old woman, fear set it. Maybe she'd seen the theft; maybe she'd seen it all.

'I was going to take it back,' said Abhi, stumbling over the bike as he tried to raise himself.

But she seemed concerned only with his bruises.

'Come on, love, up with you now. Eric? Eric, wake up will you? You coming out or what? We've got ourselves an injured man.'

With the old woman's help, he heaved the bike to one side and made his way up to what could be called a standing position.

'There you go. Up you come, my lovely,' she said, shaking the dirt from his sweatshirt. 'Dear me, that's a sore-looking face you've got there.'

Abhi grimaced. David Rogers would have to take the morning slot.

'Name's Gladys,' said the old woman, holding out her hand and gesturing towards the front door of her flat, only metres away from them.

'Now. Tell me one thing. You're not a drunk, a rapist or a murderer, are you?' she asked briskly, as if getting an unwanted task out of the way. Abhi shook his head vehemently, gladdened by the fact that she hadn't mentioned theft.

'Well, that settles it then. You had better come in and get yourself cleaned up.'

It was unorthodox behaviour for a Londoner, inviting a stranger into their home so early in the morning. Abhi wanted to tell her that he himself lived close by, but she was making her way back to her flat, expecting him to follow. He didn't want to go back just yet. He was feeling too shaken, too full of a cold ache in his bones.

'Can't sleep these nights. That's how I heard you. Eric! Get up! We've got ourselves a guest,' she said, holding the door open and guiding Abhi to the living room.

'That's it, sit down love. I'll get you some Dettol for your bruises.'

Gladys reminded him of the dinner ladies he had known at school; there was an ease about her, an indestructibility. When her husband finally arrived, he nodded silently at Abhi and seated himself on the chair in the corner of their small living room. But, just as Abhi got comfortable, that unspoken fear encroached upon him, the fear that their poverty might contaminate him. Eric turned on the TV to display rolling news. Abhi's initial anxiety was quickly replaced by the more rational concern that the couple might recognize him from TV. It would be too awkward: a BBC news anchor in a stranger's home having fallen off a stolen bike. He braced himself, but neither the silent old man nor his wife behaved as if he were a criminal or a TV celebrity. Gladys handed him a cup of coffee. Softly, she applied antiseptic to his face. 'Don't you worry. You're sorted now.'

Abhi smiled.

'Please,' he said. 'Can I use your phone?'

She took him to the corridor, where an old-style blue rotary phone was sat on a high table near the door. Abhi dialled.

'Hello, Fran? It's Abhi,' he said. 'I've got a 5.00 a.m. shift today, but I've had an accident.'

Abhi could feel Fran's disdain from the other side.

'Who's going to replace you?'

'It was an accident with a bike. I don't know . . .'

'Are you all right?' asked his producer as an afterthought. Her concern felt laboured.

'Yes, yes I am. But it's my face,' he replied. 'Bloodied up completely. No, I'm afraid makeup won't do it. Not today.'

Abhi heard Fran shout David Rogers' name across the newsroom. She told him to keep her updated throughout the week, made her excuses and said a rapid, slightly annoyed goodbye.

Back in the living room, Eric was still staring at the TV. In his blue-striped pyjamas he watched the news like he watched Abhi, semi-present, as if the world was one long, strange movie.

'He doesn't talk much,' said Gladys, pointing over at her husband. 'But he says what he thinks when he's got something to say.'

Silence. Abhi felt a stinging sensation on his face. There was blood on his cheek.

'You look like one of them Turkeys over the road,' she said suddenly, reaching again for the bottle of antiseptic. Abhi sat politely as she dabbed it on too roughly. He frowned, remembering the bike. He hoped someone else hadn't stolen it from the lawn outside Gladys's flat. He wondered if it had been wise to leave it out at all. A framed photograph on the mantelpiece caught Abhi's attention.

'Is that your granddaughter?'

'That's our Amy when she was little. We like to keep it there. There are others around the house. Makes her feel a bit closer to home,' said Gladys.

'She lives abroad?'

'You could say that. This is her place, really. We travelled down from Hull to look after her for a couple of weeks when she first fell sick, but we ended up staying with her for the whole year.' Gladys shook her head. 'About your age, she was.'

Besides her, Eric sat in silence and watched the screen. Abhi began to wonder if he spoke at all.

'She was trouble. You do wrong to the dead by dressing them up prettier than they were in the first place. But she made her peace in the end. I just wished she'd done it a bit sooner. I'd have liked for her to find a nice boy, get married or whatever you call it these days.' Gladys laughed gently to herself.

'Please,' said Abhi. 'You've been so kind. Thank you. I should leave you both to get some sleep.'

Gladys nodded and, as she raised herself up with much effort, she motioned to Eric in the chair beside her.

'Come on then, up with you, let's see our guest to the door.'

Abhi left the flat, escorted by Gladys and her husband. He picked the damaged bike up from the cold morning grass, feeling a deep pain in hands, knees and chest. His face felt sore and bloody. Still, he took the bike by its handlebars, and started pushing it back up the hill towards the newsagent's. At his back, he heard the old man shout. 'Here lad! Aren't you gonna get back on?'

As the sun rose, Abhi remembered Beetle after the abortion. How tired she had looked in the hospital, how shut out he had felt when she had pushed him away. The abortion had been their mutual decision, just as ending their relationship had been, but Beetle had refused to speak to him for days. When she finally began accepting his calls, it was to say that she loved him, that she didn't want to change anything, just to learn how to live with what had already been changed. Abhi had felt relieved. It was *his* Beetle talking again, that rational, strong, 'serve it to you straight' woman he so adored. Soon after they moved back in together, Beetle had called his mother for consolation. So easily, she had done the one thing Abhi never could. He wouldn't have believed it, a woman of that generation supporting the unmarried white girlfriend of her son through an abortion. But they had talked for what seemed like hours, the two women, after which Abhi's father had arrived by train from Leicester, bringing with him home-made kaju katli in a pink-lidded Tupperware box, just in case Beetle needed strength. His eyes sunken with sorrow, Abhi's father had told them to pray for themselves, for each other. 'When there's nothing more to do, you pray,' he said. 'A true heart's prayer, it comes from a broken place.' To his surprise, Beetle had nodded. She promised his father they would.

When evening came, Abhi saw his father to the door. As he hugged him goodbye, he wondered whether he and Beetle would pray together that night, but she did not mention it again. The following day, normal life had resumed. He reasoned that his Beetle was back together with him, so what was the use of looking back?

Now, in his morning kitchenette, Abhi smiled. He raised a mug of still-warm saffron milk to Beetle McKenzie, to Mrs Beetle, all the lost souls of 14 December. And in that moment of calm contemplation, he opened his laptop and began to write.

14 December, 2010
Subject: Your Incredible Excuse

My parents were newlyweds when they fled Uganda in 1972. In that absurd twist of fate experienced by countless other middle-class Ugandan South Asians, they found themselves on a derelict council estate on the outskirts of Leicestershire. I was born in England five years later and I suppose I took it upon myself to rectify this gross misunderstanding. Both my parents worked in the local biscuit factory until retirement. As they worked, I accepted a partial scholarship to the local private school, top marks in high school exams, a First Class in English and History from the University of London, a postgraduate certificate in Journalism at City University. I worked for several years as a researcher for Newsnight, followed by a fast-track TV news presenter traineeship with BBC Worldwide. My parents are proud of me. But there are many things I still wish I could do and my excuses aren't all that incredible. I wish I could be more myself, say it when I need to without my tongue faltering in my mouth. I wish I could feel better, have more pride, less shame, be more open with people, be less scared.

I can't ride a bicycle. I was too scared to learn how to on the street where we lived. For me, the experience of watching children riding bicycles has always been anxious and beautiful. I don't know how they do it! They are so young and so able to balance, so free in spirit and so fearless of falling. They might teach a man like me a thing or two. Perhaps now that my father has retired (and while his body is still robust), he might still be able to teach me to ride and fall. Because I suppose you can't learn how to balance without a few falls here and there. It's late in the day, I know, but we all have to start from somewhere.

Abhi Archarya
BBC Breakfast News Presenter

NIVEN GOVINDEN

La Coiffeuse

S he drove with a head rush. On every trip to the mountains Paulihna felt the same mixture of trepidation and euphoria: a series of tight knots bunched in her chest, and a sudden hollowness to her breathing. Both she and the company knew the loopholes; villages that were remote, away from whistleblowers and municipal eyes. Mostly they were only accessible by ancient bridges: monuments of worm-eaten wood or crumbling masonry. That was the thrill. What brought the oxygen back, and her concentration with it, was a decrease in acceleration and a recognition that in every instance there was a long day ahead. A job to do.

If the village had a square she would find people. Otherwise, she went into the local bar or shop.

'I'm buying hair today. Let your women know.'

In the hour or so it took them to organize, to offer – or to hide – those with the longest hair, she made herself comfortable. She enjoyed the local specialities, possibly a bottle of wine or a glass of spirits, depending on their generosity. And they were often generous, filling her up in the hope that she would treat them well. Be gentle. Her stomach was proof. She'd been on the job eighteen months and put on thirty pounds. For all these kindnesses, softly attempting to please with the offer of blankets if it was turning cold, or prehistoric stereos for her car, she found that her reputation preceded her. In this village, for example, the owner of the café where she announced her business was loading her table with salami, olives and soft, bland sheep's milk cheeses. The food was good, which was in his favour. In other places, she'd ignited rows for far less. The café owner's wife and young daughter, no more than ten years old, peeping curiously from behind the kitchen door, both had geometric bobs; thin and choppy, the mark of a city hairdresser's handiwork. They would be spared.

'I'll be setting up here. The company will reimburse you for any loss in trade.'

During training, her employers had drilled her in not offering choices. She followed this instruction to the letter: choosing her location to set up shop, holding firm on price, staying blind to tears. She did not console, but offered a routine stream of words if the customer's hysteria threatened to jeopardize the entire job. Shaven-headed brides were not an uncommon sight in this part of the world, she often said. In the Middle Ages it was virtually a trend. What would you prefer: to have the hair on your head and walk down the aisle in rags, or to be able to afford the cloth and seamstress for the dress of your dreams? That the money she offered barely covered the cost of flannel, let alone silk, meant little to her. It was only on her drive back to the city that she gave any thought to what she was leaving behind.

A queue had started to form outside the café, but she kept them waiting until she finished the roundel of cheese and the small pitcher of aniseed digestif. From what she could see, half of them would be of no use. Though they had the length, the condition was lank and weak; a combination of caustic shampoos and poor nutrition. There was no point in taking anyone's head that was a B or C grade because her clients expected the best, as did their clients. No one would ask where their hair extensions came from, but there were certain illusions to be fulfilled: healthy, organic, virginal, consenting. The women for whom this shorn hair was destined hoped to assimilate the nutrients and karma of these innocent donors through their weaves. That by melding this foreign hair into their own they would become good, wholesome people, whose uncomplicated beauty had returned.

When the time came to inspect them, she fought through the sloth induced by gorging on rich, salty food. Her fingers pored over scalps for signs of lice, hair dyes and dry skin conditions. She looked for split ends and breakage. Three teenage girls with early signs of alopecia were sent away only to rejoin the queue on their mother's orders in the hope that they wouldn't be recognized. The line trailed the perimeter of the square and down into the valley: sacrificial women, desperate and hopeful. Twice she spotted the teenage trio, clumped together like bread rolls placed too close together in the oven, and twice she swatted them away. On their third attempt she called for the café owner, peeling off a handful of notes for him to police the line. In all, there were over two hundred to be inspected, and they were a nervy lot.

'Please,' implored the mother of the alopecia daughters, breaking through the group to speak with her. 'I must have brushed their ponytails too hard.'

The grip on her arm was warm and damp with sweat. It didn't sit well with the aftertaste of the soft sheep's cheese. Nor did it say much for the villagers' manners. Paulihna preferred civility to be upheld in spite of the circumstances. Rudeness wasn't the way to do business. She did not approve of begging and other lapses in personal standards.

'Madame! Please, madame. Look at the shine on it.'

'They're diseased. No one will want it. Don't let me see them in the line again.'

'But it's still good what they have,' the mother insisted urgently, shaking one of the ponytails loose and tugging on it. When she let go, a good proportion of hair remained in her hand.

It was a shame. They were the only redheads in the group, and the length, what there was of it, would have been perfect. As she looked at them for a final time, she noticed the mother's high hairline peeping from her scarf, suggesting something thinner and patchier than her daughters. They didn't stand a chance. The café owner prodded them until they started to move, with a familiarity she found distasteful. The mother's continued pitch carrying up the hill.

'Take it! It's still good for your money. You can stuff it in chairs or mattresses!'

When the café owner returned, red-faced and breathless, his neck wet with exertion, she sent him back to retrieve them. The line was likely to turn on her if she did not show some compromise.

'You can stop thanking me and get her in the chair,' she said, addressing the mother, aware that she would only pay a tenth of what was originally offered.

'Hold her hand. The girl's hair is very dry. It's going to hurt.'

There was no ceremony because none was needed. They came willingly. Also, she knew them better; she knew she could get away with treating them like this. In larger communities she would have shown more organization: setting up the clothes rail from the trunk of her car, hanging a line of clear plastic bags to house each particular hair colour and type, and sometimes, when a show was really needed, even displaying the small cardboard placard that announced her company's credentials, which featured a phone number they would never call, a website they would never visit. Faced with a hostile audience who needed converting she was capable of giving the full song and dance, playing the demonstration DVD from her laptop and selling herself as a charitable benefactor fighting the ugliness of competitive gangs who roamed the mountain villages. She warned against teams of brutal men, who would probably rape the girls as well as shaving their heads. She was putting herself in danger by doing what she was doing, she'd tell them, but it was only because she wanted to avoid here what she'd seen elsewhere: women of all ages defiled and pruned like commodities. Combined with the money offered it was a solid gold pitch, one which she saw as a fulfilment of her training, nothing more. Other colleagues may have crowed over their results in the privacy of their cars afterwards, but this didn't come naturally to her. She was physically exhausted by the end of it. A victory celebration would take up too much energy.

She was alone as she swept up. It was evening. Families of shorn girls, keen to hurry their flesh and blood examples of need and shame ran indoors, feeling suddenly conspicuous in spite of the fact that most of them had stood in line. In company terms, it was a sheep-dip day. Almost the entire flock had been treated.

The café owner poured her another small carafe of spirits.

'Well, you weren't as rough as the others might have been.'

'It's the way I have to be. I don't want to lose any hair.'

'Like I said, not as rough.'

'Do you speak to all your customers like that?'

'Sorry, madame. It was observation, nothing more. There was no intention to offend.'

Their eyes held for a moment and she thought of possibilities. That if she had stayed in her village this would have been the most that she could aspire to: washing dinner plates in a cracked kitchen sink while her husband sexually appraised the out-of-town clientele. He too was brooding, she thought, his eyes roaming for signifiers underneath her clothes: the location of her wallet and style of her underwear.

'Was it done to you?' he asked.

'What?'

'Your hair. It's so short. I was wondering whether it was done to you. Why you'd do this.'

'No. It's just the style I prefer. I've always had short hair.'

'I'm sure your mother wouldn't have allowed it. Nor your priest. How would you have set foot inside your church with hair like a boy's?'

'You know nothing about my church. Or me, for that matter.'

'Again, I apologize if I have caused offence.'

She felt tightness in her face, a marked pithiness to her breath.

'The cheese,' he said. 'You asked specifically for that cheese when you came in. Only someone from the mountains would've used that particular name for it.'

'What of it? We all have to come from somewhere.'

She'd been bred in rural communities like this one. Barren hamlets where ambition was blotted by the landscape; where all were tethered to agricultural rituals of child-bearing, preparing food, the worship of their god. She'd despised everything about it, plotted her escape from childhood. But even with her city clothes, the elocution lessons that had neutralized her accent, her two-week crash course in European languages, and carefree bouts of spending that contravened all she'd been taught, she still felt prickles cluster across her shoulder blades when a community's eyes rested upon her, conscious that her background should not give her away. She was nothing like these people. She was better than these people. She was here because she had something to prove: to them as well as herself.

His manner was making her nervous. They were both aware of it, squaring up with each other from either side of the bar. He no longer pretended to dust glasses and liquor bottles that had long been undusted. He put down his grimy cloth and stared at her inquisitively, like an older relative who asks questions they already know the answer to, just so you will give a voice to your foolishness.

He gestured at the hair, all five bulging sacks of it, resting on the table top. It turned out that no intricate sub-categories were needed to label it, bar the alopecia sisters. They were all so in-bred here. Each bag carried the same scrawl across the front: *Black*.

'What are you going to do with it?'

'Would it make any difference if I told you? It's not like the girls can have it back.'

'I suppose not. Here, have another drink.'

A second carafe was pushed in her direction. They always tried to get her drunk. Thought they could get things: money from the float she carried, the bagged hair, her lower half. In one of the villages, where the company's visits were both needed and despised, they clumsily attempted to hijack her car as she left, and hold her to ransom at the roadside.

'Take your hostages,' she'd said, kicking the sacks contemptuously at them. 'It's no skin off my nose. Except you won't have a clue what to do with it. Your women have been paid fairly for what they've given. What you're doing doesn't serve anyone, least of all your families.'

But she understood. She was well aware of the broken skin and bleeding scalps she'd left behind. The fear of those who'd sat in the chair unwillingly. Child prodigies and other lynchpins of the family reduced to a market price to pay for necessities: giving their hair for bread, medical bills, tractor repairs.

The group who forced her off the road had threatened many things, including sex. But they were out of their league, incapable of carrying anything out. Experience had taught her that if men were going to do things they didn't tediously list them out beforehand. Their voices were loud, their anger real enough, but their chins dropped and their eyes became bloodshot jellies as she stood her ground.

The café owner did not have the anger of those men. His actions came from a more spirited place, or perhaps they were those of a gambler, hungry to play her at her own game.

'Drink,' he said. 'It's fine. You've had a long day. You should relax.'

But she declined and started to pack her things, aware now of the aloneness between them; knowing that nothing good resulted when married men encouraged single women to relax over a glass of alcohol. In the city his exhortations might have produced a different outcome, she thought, admitting to herself that his face and physical build were favourable. But she felt stifled by the shabby bar, which recalled the same trapped feelings of her childhood. The city was solid, set in steel and concrete. She didn't like the softness of the earth here. Her heels sank into the grass as she methodically loaded her car. Each step felt like walking into quicksand.

'That was my sister, by the way,' he said, following her out.

She was drunker than she realized; she needed help with the sacks that wouldn't stay in the boot despite her repeated attempts.

'Who?'

'The one with the daughters. You paid me to keep them away.'

'Have you got a problem with that? You never said at the time.'

'They need the money.'

'Looking out for your family. That's nice . . .' she began, before an elongated belch forced its way out; a corrugated rattle echoing around the square. The close air between them stank of aniseed and undigested salami.

The café owner laughed, the sharpness of his features melting until he looked like a child.

'Spoken like a true mountain girl!'

'I get it now. You're a baldie too. Runs in the family.'

Under these trees, in these surroundings, drunkenness made a lout of her. She thought of her mother goading her father late at night in the bedroom, of insecure husbands abusing wives and neighbours for ill-judged slights. She walked to the other side of the car and, with some difficulty, opened the glove-box.

'Take this, if we're sticking to the old customs,' she said, handing him a bottle, 'because you look like the old-fashioned type. I've had my free lunch and got plastered on the house, so now I give you something in return.'

She held a clear bottle filled with a viscous green liquid that glowed phosphorescent as the clouds overhead broke. Shampoo.

She laughed hard at her joke, bringing forth more corrugated belching. They were all dumb here and worthy of being laughed at. Every hungry belly and shorn head that stayed here because they were too traditional or too frightened to move. Who became sitting ducks for chancers like her. Passive, dumb, trusting bastards who deserved everything they got: poor crops, violent marriages, starving babies.

'You're drunk.'

'I just drank what was put in front of me. We're taught not to offend.'

'You looked like a women who could handle her drink. Obviously I was wrong.'

'I'm following the company rules. Stylists must not vacate the location until every stone has been turned. A lost sale is a wanting customer.'

His eyes tightened to pin-points. 'What do they call you?'

'A stylist. Je suis une coiffeuse.' She giggled, flirtatiously.

The name, the false prettiness of it, like the synthetic cakes she saw in the windows of city stores, left a sharp taste in her mouth. A poisoned well. Gun metal. But this was something she would not share. She was earning good money now, which would not be maintained by agreeing with whatever accusations were thrown.

She was struck now by a sudden freshness of air hitting her face and neck, and realized that she was being carried with some speed into the car. He frisked her for keys before tumbling her into the passenger seat, slamming the door behind her. His fingers were as hard and deft as a masseur's, one of the many luxuries she now enjoyed in her new life. There was, however, a contrasting sensation, one which transported her back to the church porch where a priest had frisked children for cigarettes and other contraband before Sunday school. It was a memory that quickly sobered her up.

'You won't make it out in this state. I'll drive you across the bridge and then you're on your own.'

She argued the toss for a couple of minutes, allowing him to think that he was doing her a favour. Mostly, it was because she missed conflict. Few people challenged her. She realized how boring that power had become.

He turned the car roughly and accelerated hard down the hill. The bumps and turns she felt in her belly distracted her from his scrutiny. She imagined herself to be on a rollercoaster, but then she realized she was the only passenger whose hair blew in the breeze and that it wasn't a pleasant dream at all. Though the engine thundered between them, she could still hear his breathing, hard and sharp, indicating a singular focus.

'We took your prices,' he said, 'but it's never enough, is it?'

'What was that?'

'I said, you should get home. You're tired.'

They all thought of it as some master plan, disregarding her explanations that this was an arbitrary exercise. If they'd all refused and shown no hospitality she'd have packed up and gone elsewhere. They needed the concept of fate to decipher a square filled with shaven heads, not the reality, which was that she chose random villages from the company's emailed list. All the stylists employed had their own particular methods. Her eyes always gravitated to the names closest to her background: *ish, nish, kesh*. Slowly working up to the day when she'd return to her village and show them who was boss.

The bridge was faithful to its construction. Its tarmac wobbled, arches squeaked under the car's weight.

'Why have we stopped?'

His silence made her fearful, as did the instability of their position: floating among treetops with an eye-line level with the stars. Her head drummed with rough alcohol and an enhanced state of her own gravity; how little there was around and below her. Even in this metal box she felt flimsy and transparent; light as a feather blown on the breeze. She didn't even want to open her mouth, scared of how her echo might sound across the ravine, another indicator of how much space there was around her, and how it would never close in.

She'd reached a compromise with the men who'd cornered her in the other town. She stripped off her top half and shaved her armpits. Her choice. Hair for hair. They had a good stare while she did it. One of them did something to himself behind a tree. It was all part of the job, so long as she came back with the hair.

The café owner's silence told her that he, too, was searching for compromises.

'The car's rattling. Can't you hear it?' he said, pulled off his seatbelt and got out of the car.

Whether this was a trick or not was unknown to her. All she could hear was the drum rattle in her chest; the pounding in her ears. She was aware of a heaviness in her gut, as if her body was fighting weightlessness.

She wanted to look and see what he was doing, but that would force her gaze outwards, to the broken wall of the bridge and what lay beyond it: water, so deep it was hidden from the moonlight.

'Hurry up,' she shouted. 'I'm running a business here!'

She searched hard to dredge her earlier sarcasm, hoping her voice wouldn't reveal how little she cared. But he didn't hear, or chose not to, and headed to the back of the car where he pulled hard against the tailgate and bumper.

She felt the chill against her ears as the boot opened. His head was bowed and out of sight, but the rustling from the bags was real. A grunt of exertion as his fingers broke through plastic and pulled hard.

She tugged her seatbelt to get out, but the bottom was caught in the door and wouldn't release. The door itself clicked uselessly, safety locked from the outside.

'What are you doing?' she shouted, knowing that the words were trapped in her throat, and realizing she had to show some fight to the last. It would be expected in her report. But his earlier words were right. She was tired. She would not mention that she was dizzy with drink, too comfortable to get out of the car, her shoulders relaxing as they melded into the upholstery. Aware of what was happening, but not caring.

They could never know this. Not while she still had a voice.

'Have you found the rattling? Have you? I've had trouble with the boot lock for weeks.'

All around her, hair tumbled over the side of the bridge; balls of black and red cascading with the wind, like candyfloss on invisible wings.

KAVITA JINDAL

Special Delivery

DAY 7

of my new existence. I have a plan to make it bearable, and this evening my little project has worked perfectly again. If I can go on a detour three or four times a week without my hosts suspecting anything then there will be delight in the world, harmony in the star charts, new hives for bees and funding for the Arts. Et cetera.

I am already in the bedroom, changing out of my work shirt and into a T-shirt, when I hear them come in. My office shoes are in the hall, but a female voice floats upstairs anyway: 'Mee-heer, are you home?'

'I'm home,' I call back. Not that this is my home; it's hers and she's letting me stay as a house guest until I find a flat to rent. I've been here a week. It feels like seven years.

'I'll get some dinner going,' she calls. I hear her say something to Atul that I can't catch.

I must go down to pretend to help. But I'm bushed. I'll lie down for just two minutes. Just. Two. Minutes. The bulb shines its yellow light into my eyes. The bulb is shaded by one of those round paper contraptions that were sold everywhere – Ikea, Habitat, John Lewis – in the last decade. Cara, whom I am learning to refer to as 'my estranged wife', with the emphasis on *strange*, would never countenance such a lampshade. This particular once-white paper orb is covered in a thin film of dust. Cara would rip the thing down.

49

Has she arrived home yet? Has she found the open pizza box on the tiled path to our front door? Currently *her* front door. I have been manipulated into exile or 'am trying a new way of habiting', depending on whose viewpoint you want. It's a pepperoni pizza. The red of the pepperoni amid the yellow splodge of cheese picking up on the dark red tiles of the path. There's artistic vision in my plan.

Outside the window, the cloudy sky has darkened further into the smudged blue-black of Pantone 433C. If Cara isn't home yet, then she's likely to surprise a fox eating the pizza when she does get back. I hope you make a real mess, fox; smear the pizza on the path, you diseased little fox. Cara might come home tired, but she'll bring out the mop to wipe off the goo. She might even have to slosh a bucket of hot water to get rid of the smell and get the tiles looking clean.

'Mee-heer.' What is it with the woman below? Why can't she pronounce my name properly? Mihir. Soft *i*, soft *i*. Mihir. Not Mee-heer. A bit much when I can pronounce her name correctly. First vowel, barely enunciated; second vowel, long *e*, as in eek.

'Yes, Denise?'

'Dinner's ready.'

We sit at Denise's kitchen table, Atul, Denise and I. Looking at my hostess, who has kind eyes but frumpy shoulder-length hair, I'm reminded of what Cara once said about her: 'You can tell she's not a creative person.'

'How?'

'There's no spark of it, no flash in the clothes she wears or the furnishings in her house. So, well, if she is imaginative, it's well-hidden.'

'She could *do* inspired things rather than just look artistic.'

'But we know her. She doesn't *do* creative.' Cara had shrugged. 'It doesn't mean anything. Denise is one of the most likeable and dependable people I know. That's what's great about her.'

I pile a mound of dependable Denise's penne with sundried tomatoes and tinned tuna on to my plate.

'I steamed some broccoli for you, Attle,' she says, too sweetly, pushing a plate of the greens towards him.

Okay, she can't pronounce her own husband's name. Why haven't I noticed this before? But then we've never spent a week living under the same roof. For me, it is already too long. And who knows? Possibly for them, too. It's not like Cara and I are known for our easy-going qualities. But Atul was so welcoming when I arrived, and he and Denise are making a real effort to coddle me. Atul is my best mate, after all. Even so, he'd looked shocked to see me wiping down the skirting boards on the staircase on my second day as house guest; a Sunday, incidentally.

'What are you doing?' he'd gasped. I'd tried to explain. Cara couldn't bear dust gathering in crevices. Because of Cara, because of having lived with her for far too long, although less than seven real years, I was programmed to clean when I saw grimy skirting boards. It was Cara's fault.

'But I'll stop now,' I'd said. Then I waited for them to take themselves off to their bedroom for weekend conjugal relations before I surreptitiously crept out to finish the job. I'd already cleaned the skirting boards in my room and the tiny guest shower room. For the grooves I'd used a toothbrush, the one Denise had given me on the first night, when I'd arrived after phoning Atul to ask if I could stay a few days. As if I'd storm out of my house without my own toothbrush.

I'd hit on the pizza plan on Tuesday. All day at work, instead of coming up with a new design for the lettering on Stavio's fat new highlighter pens, I wondered how to get at Cara. Driving back to Atul's place in Balham instead of my own quiet road in Putney I'd been overtaken by a pizza delivery idiot skittering his purple moped along the road. He almost crashed into a traffic island before wobbling right in front of my car, forcing me to choose between braking hard (not good for the car), or killing him. I raised two fingers at him. He raised four back. But the moron had given me an idea. I U-turned then and there, paid out five pounds for a foul takeaway pizza, drove home, to *my* home, and threw the open box on the path, letting the pizza slither out. Greetings, Cara.

DAY 13

I think the plan is working well. I have mashed pizza on the path a total of six times. I have thought about hanging around to see her reaction, but it would be too risky. I would love to see her scrubbing

51

those tiles. It is exactly the sort of minor annoyance that will drive her *up the wall*. I know the mess is being cleaned up, but I want to know for sure that *she* is getting as worked up as I expect her to. But then I wonder, what if I spy on her and see that she's ignoring that evening's pizza slop; that she's sitting on the sofa instead, feet encased in her knitted bootees, legs up on the stool, watching *Miss Marple* with a glass of chilled white wine in her hand. (I can't stand white wine.) But, of course, I wouldn't be able to look in anyway, because Cara always closes the curtains before she sits down to watch TV. And what excuse would I give Atul and Denise? Going out is fine, they are gagging for me to go out, but presumably I should have a plausible story. If I was sighted hanging about my own home by a passing busybody, they might mention it to Cara, who would then put two and two together. As it is, I stop by in haste now, parking a few doors down and donning a cycle helmet and bulky yellow jacket, so that even if neighbours happen to be looking out, they won't really be able to tell who it is in the early evening darkness.

Happily, at dinner tonight (farfalle with asparagus and olives), I get confirmation that all is not well in Cara-land. Denise starts to speak in a confidential, soothing voice. 'I spoke to Cara today.' She waits for a reaction. I give her none. Atul glances at me and I look blankly back to show it's cool with me.

'What does Cara have to say?' Atul asks his wife in a non-committal tone. Translation, which we can all hear loud and clear: Hey, babe, go easy; don't upset my friend or by extension, me.

'Cara's a bit distressed, but I mean, not about this' – Denise waves her hand apologetically around the table – 'but something else entirely.' She widens her hazel eyes. 'She's being picked on by some local teenage gang.'

I feel a twinge of worry for Cara, but it subsides. Denise looks at me as if I should be rushing to Cara's aid. But I am living here now, Denise, see? I'm not Cara's minder.

'What gang?' Atul asks. 'Why?'

Denise carries on with her story in a calming, I-was-made-for-counselling voice. 'Apparently, a couple of weeks ago, she reprimanded these three youths who were standing on the pavement just outside her house throwing beer bottles at passing cars. She told them to stop. "Yeah, what's it to you?" one of them sneered. "It's not right," she told them. "Don't do it." And then she backed down a bit and said, "Don't do it standing here, anyway. Go elsewhere for your fun game." They left, but they made a throat-cutting gesture at her as they did so.'

I'd heard this story from Cara on the day it happened. I'd told her to call the police if she wanted; she'd grunted as if that was a useless suggestion. That was the week every conversation was actually a quarrel. No matter what I said, I got a snort in reply. It went on all week, until late on Friday night I packed my bag. 'I'm taking the car,' is all I said by way of goodbye. She'd grunted.

Denise continues with her account. 'She thinks they're targeting her now. She said that for the past three days *in a row* they've left a stinking half-eaten pizza on her front path.'

Atul frowns in extreme puzzlement, so I copy his expression. 'Is she sure it's the kids?' he asks, finally. 'A gang is wasting eight quid a night on terrorizing her with *pizza*?'

Not eight, five pounds, I want to say. Not fancy pizza, Atul. These low-grade ones cost under a fiver. I keep my lips sealed, even press them inwards in sympathy at this outrage to my ex-front-path.

'Well, she's not completely sure, but she guesses it's those local youths she had an altercation with. Attle, that's why I've offered your services.'

'What?' Attle is definitely startled.

'Well, you know, since we're friends with both of them' – she nods towards me – 'we must treat them fairly. With equal support. I'm sure Mee-heer will agree.'

Mee-heer won't, but no one is asking Mee-heer really.

Denise is using the counselling tone again. '*He* is staying here, so I thought we should offer Cara our support, too. It's a difficult time for everybody.'

Not least for you, I think. I have been your uppity guest for almost a fortnight.

'What kind of help have you offered Cara?' Atul asks, sounding a bit desperate.

'Well, I said that you could stake out their home, just for a couple of evenings. If you parked there, say from four onwards until Cara got back, you would see who's leaving the pizza. You'll have a description. You might even be able to get a photo.'

'Jesus, Denise, I'm busy. I don't have time to sit around in cars, waiting for loons to show up.'

'Just a couple of days. Not tomorrow, obviously, it's too short notice. But you could arrange it. At least once next week. On Monday or Tuesday?'

'Jesus, Izzy. Hire a PI.'

When she doesn't respond, he says, '*You* do it.'

He gets a look. You know, the wifey look. The one that brooks no argument.

He glares at me. What did I do? Then Denise turns to me, too. 'Unless you want to help, Mee-heer. Although' – she delicately wrinkles just the top of her nose – 'Cara did say she wanted to have nothing to do with . . .'

'Ya, ya, I'll go one afternoon next week,' Atul interjects quickly.

I take the dishes to the dishwasher and stack them on the counter. Denise stands there like she's waiting for me to do something. She's looking at me with a schoolteacher's stare when you haven't quite finished a task. She *is* a schoolteacher, so this must be the look her pupils receive – strict but kindly, hint of twinkle, hint of steel. I get it. I'm meant to put the dishes in the dishwasher. Cara could never tolerate a stranger – well, a newbie – in the house filling the dishwasher. There are only certain ways the bowls are allowed to go in. And the large plates are always on the left; the small ones on the right. Two spoons of the same size do not sit together. They never get properly clean if you do that. Wooden-handled knives *never* go in. But the inside of Denise's dishwasher is haphazard. As I rearrange the breakfast dishes so that I can stack the dinner plates the right way, I think about Atul staking out my home, or Cara's home as it is now, next week. That's Plan One brought to an effing halt.

I slide in the dishwasher racks and close the door. What I can do is finish Plan One on a high. A proper blast. Five pizzas, why not?

Three squished into the path for smelly gloop on Cara's heels; two
upturned to show their colours when she switches the porch light on.

DAY 24

as house guest. Dinner is a stilted affair. Atul and Denise are fidgety,
their eyes skating over me, but also not quite meeting each other's. I
wonder if they know about the five pizzas. Do they want to accuse
me, but can't bring themselves to, despite instinctively grasping the
truth?

Denise fairly chucks dishes onto the table. I wheeze in surprise. It's
not pasta! We've got brown rice and chicken breasts and spinach.
Denise nudges the plate of spinach over to Atul's elbow. He's been
ignoring it studiously, but nudge by nudge it has come closer and is
almost being pushed onto his place mat. He gives in; he helps himself
to some and then pushes the dish away with a quick roll of his oval
eyes. I've already served myself a healthy helping and as I look down
at the wilted spinach on my plate I feel a cramp of sorrow in my
stomach. Atul, a samosa-and-parantha man, who believes 'if it ain't
fried, it ain't got no taste', is being looked after. These veggies that
Denise thrusts on him are a form of love. I swallow and stab my
fork into my spinach.

It is up to me to provide some sparkling conversation to lift the
mood, but I find I can't. I have spent the last few days gnawing weakly
at life, with life gnawing back. I've stayed late in the office, texting
Atul to say I'll be home after 10 p.m. I've eaten crisps at my desk. I
don't want pubs or people. So the three of us sit quietly; lost in our
own worlds, our mouths chewing in unison. After we've cleared up
and I've scrubbed the pans to make them look dazzling and new,
Atul invites me to sit back down at the table to finish the bottle of
wine, it being manic Monday and all. Denise says she'll leave us to
it. I sense that they've planned this. She offers me an explanation,
saying she wants an early night because she's fasting the next day.

Atul swings round in unfeigned surprise. 'Fasting? For what?'
'Your mother rang to remind me. It's Karva Chauth tomorrow.'
'Already? Again? So soon?'
'Yes.'

'You don't have to fast, Izzy, you can just ignore Mum. I'll tell her you didn't eat until you spotted the risen moon. You stood outside, wearing your wedding bangles, peeping through the strainer, waiting. Ha. As if you'll be able to see the moon through the clouds.'

'Oh no, don't lie to her,' Denise says. 'I don't mind, really.' For the first time this evening she actually looks into his face. 'I quite like the idea: fasting for the wellbeing of my husband.' She is all liquid eyes and tender mouth. Atul puffs out visibly, his chest growing an inch and his neck straightening up.

'Goodnight, Denise,' I say as she wafts upstairs in a warm glow.

Atul pours out wine, insisting on fresh glasses. Is he becoming like me? The dishwasher makes its swilling sounds in the background along with an erratic rumble or two. The tension in the room has melted and we sit companionably.

'Mihir, yaar,' Atul asks me softly, 'how's work going?'

'Great. Although I'm not concentrating as much as I should. I'm redesigning the labels for XT shampoo; guess what, instead of cylindrical clutchable bottles we're moving to elongated trapezoid containers. Big deal, huh? Didn't get any sample labels done today, but I'll knock out a couple of ideas tomorrow.'

'Good, good.' He lets me slurp down some more wine. 'And how's the flat-hunting going?'

Atul is such a sweet guy that I know this is the closest he will come to telling me my time is up. I must leave him and Denise in the peace they deserve. I feel sorry for him. But before I speak, he hurries on. 'You know if you want to talk about . . . Cara – or what happened, or your . . . feelings – you can, I mean, I know how to listen . . .'

'Thanks, yaar,' I say and feel red wine dripping out of the side of my mouth.

In their guest room I lie back on the small bed and stare up into the deep yellow light of the bulb, which gently illuminates all the dust on the paper shade that surrounds it.

It was kind of Atul to ask. But what can I tell him? Cara, obsessive-compulsive Cara, is bored of marriage. Been there, done that. She wants to live on her own, despite the mad bad youths and the burglars.

I can't tell Atul that this came about after our last trip to India for my sister's wedding. Cara was surrounded by these jumped-up, pumped-up Bombay boys. Maybe she's dallying with one of them. Maybe all that interest turned her head.

What I do know is that everyone can see I've been wronged, yet it's Cara who steals their sympathy. I will move out from here soon; heck, I'll have chosen a flat by next week. My temporary needs are simple. A one-bedroom place, freshly painted. A window that overlooks a green space: a communal garden or a park or someone else's well-tended garden.

The problem with living alone after so many years of co-habiting is going to be this: who do you blame for what your life has slid into? Who do you blame for the lethargy, for the visits not made, for the sarod that sits reverentially in its own corner not being played? Marriage is an institution that turns you into a round shape sinking into a round hole.

Now that I have to acquire edges, who do I blame if I remain a round peg submerged in a round hole? The world will close up above me, forgetting I am there. I won't remember anyone's birthday and no one will remember mine. The old Mihir I knew has already been rubbed out.

Everything is Cara's fault. I try an experiment to prove my hypothesis. I pull myself up to sitting and I throw my socks, one by one, across the room. I lie back down. I last three seconds before I am compelled to sit up and fetch them. I was always tidy. People occasionally said that I was obsessively tidy, but those people had never met Cara. Once you'd seen Cara's standards, you would know that I was only in the middling league of such behaviour. Of course, despite her hygiene-and-order fixation, or because of it, Cara gets sick all the time. I place my socks on the carpet again, but this time in the spot I have assigned for them, by the roller suitcase I brought with me, and I sink back on the bed, feeling better.

Everything in its place. First, I find the right flat. Second, I think of another way to madden my estranged wife. There is, after all, a purpose to my life.

Rajorshi Chakraborti

All You Can Dream

L ondon: November '99.
   One evening, my flatmate Gombrowicz proposed that we should visit an exclusive men's club, with chandeliers, candelabra and, most of all, costumes – costumes for every whim and depravity one could imagine.

   'Everyone in the City with any class is raving about it, not that you would know, Dasgupta, in your Formica office where your colleagues bring their own rice to work and return meekly every evening to their wives. Man, once you were in London why you didn't quit beats me. What is the point of being the head of a losing outfit? Weren't you admitting to me you barely managed to attract five million pounds in new investments last year? In Bishopsgate, you would raise more money if you closed the office and simply rented the space.'

   Our other friend Mehta and I had grown to accept such gratuitous abuse as a form of affection, as an integral part of the Gombrowicz torrent. Besides, the three of us were so starved of any form of interaction, aside from seeing one another most nights, that in the matter of a special evening out we didn't require much persuading.

Inside the club, it was as though many De Mille movies were being filmed at once. Costumes had been mentioned, and we immediately noticed the chandeliers, candles, champagne and long tables that Gombrowicz had promised, but we hadn't been prepared for the sets. The first thing to gape at when we arrived and lifted our eyes from the grandeur at ground level was a giant fifteen-foot balloon that floated from the foyer ceiling. It was shaped like a diva with huge breasts and curves in a shiny gold dress, and a jewel-encrusted peacock's tail crowning her head. She had a smile painted on her face but no eyes, and carried a fan in one hand. Part balloon and part plaster, she was lit from within and hung above us swaying slightly: if you stood directly under her on the rim of the central fountain, and stared up or down into the water, you could admire her carefully crafted legs as they disappeared into her dress, right up to her anatomically precise, illuminated pelvis. At intervals throughout the night, the house lights would dip and she'd slowly revolve, casting kaleidoscopic flecks of colour over the entire hall.

Butlers in formal dress were working in front of us, alongside other male attendants who sported no more than bow ties and thongs, and gathered the clothes heaped up outside a giant bathtub in one corner. We later discovered that this could accommodate twenty bathers and had a winding stair on the side, but you couldn't peek inside unless you climbed the steps yourself.

All of this was housed in a building in Bayswater that resembled a wedding cake even on the outside: seven floors high, ornate at every opportunity with patterns, parapets, balconies and figurines, but blind in each of its eyes because all the windows had been blackened. Inside, the central hall must have been nearly a hundred yards long, and it rose as high as the main roof with the other floors arranged along walkways round the sides. A chamber orchestra was playing classical music to our left, hundreds of people were strewn around the vast space, and three lifts with golden doors manned by bellhops in full uniform – gold braids, shiny buttons, chin-strapped hats and all – ceaselessly transported guests to and from the main floor.

As our eyes grew accustomed to the variety of sights we realized there were couples here as well as the many groups of men, and also a few elderly gentlemen, some of whom were already undressed and being assisted into the bathtub by thonged attendants. A small number of people sat around the centrally-placed grand dining tables, but most had chosen the large sofas scattered everywhere; you could also stretch out on a chaise longue by yourself.

And it was soon obvious that the women, without whom all the splendour would have been superfluous, were justly celebrated for their costumes. Some passed by in transparent, clinging gowns with nothing underneath; others wore long, tight-fitting skirts with nothing above. There were the usual dominatrix types in shiny black outfits brandishing whips, but then there were nurses, circus girls, tigresses, newscasters in trouser-suits and glasses, squaws with feathers and painted faces, geishas in kimonos, secretaries with their breasts exposed, mini-skirted schoolgirls, even a housemaid so authentic that Mehta missed a beat wondering if she might be his Lisa. Gombrowicz bowed and the girl raised her skirt as she hurried past, and the similarity extended right to the absence of any underwear.

It was just as well we'd had an induction meeting when we entered, so bewildering was the array of delights on offer. Besides, we would never have appreciated the intricate organization behind these extraordinary appearances had we not been adequately briefed. Not just appreciated: left to ourselves without any knowledge of the system, we would never have been able to participate in the pleasures around us that were only apparently so open and accessible.

At the introductory meeting, we were informed that All You Can Dream (we learnt the name of the establishment for the first time from the leaflet handed us: there had been no signs at the front or anywhere else) operated more or less like a theme park. One paid upfront at the desk, £150 per head, which covered each of us for all the services we'd enjoy that evening. We were then handed a card with a number and ushered into an auditorium, where we first watched a computer graphic film, rather like the safety instructions on a flight, pointing out the building's floors and various sectors, its exclusive and open sections, and finally its fire exits and emergency arrangements.

Next, we were told that we could freely wander into anything that was unlocked throughout the club. This included passing through or peeping into rooms that were curtained, as long as we never interfered in whatever was going on. The customers in such cases were aware of, approved and probably wished to be spied upon in their pleasures. For example, in the first chamber we entered there was a huge apparatus to vertically string up a man, legs and arms apart, by fastening his limbs to its four corners with elastic mechanisms. A naked man with a large erection wriggled happily before us, and we watched as a woman in a g-string and high heels first sucked him for a while, then licked his balls, before resuming her painting of his body. She was sketching dirty drawings all over him with a brush and black ink and describing to him what she drew, what activities her figures were performing. Now and then he asked her to draw in a particular area as you might request someone to scratch you. This could be around his penis, on his inner thighs, his earlobes for which she required a stepladder, or as we saw, with the tip of the brush beneath his buttocks.

To come back to the meeting, chaired by Troy, our maître d' for the evening, we learned that AYCD, like anywhere else, worked on the basis of queues, except it was so arranged that we would never actually encounter two people in line behind one another. Again, it was like awaiting your turn in an amusement park, or for your gate to be announced at an airport. Several discreetly placed screens would flash whichever number was ready to be served. Until such time as it was your turn, you enjoyed full access to the open facilities, which included unlimited drink, lounging and frolicking in the bath, and wandering anywhere you wished within the building. When your number appeared, you were free to proposition any woman you fancied, as long as she was not on her way to another client.

Once in the bedroom, the rules were just as flexible. Of course, no one was watching the clock or stipulating how long you should take, but the house rule was, to phrase it simply and memorably, that you only *came* once – though you could stretch that to include anything you liked. Here Troy smiled at his own joke and we all laughed with him, relaxing as we slowly realized that the rules weren't invisible alarms after all, and were only meant to facilitate our pleasure. And there was a bonus – even though you could only come once, it wasn't as though you were then dumped into a cab and sent home. You could remain for *seconds*; it was included in the price of your ticket. You would have to acquire another number at reception and await a full turn of the wheel. But the house closed at seven in the morning, so there was no reason – unless it was an exceptionally busy night – why most people wouldn't earn a 'second ride' if they waited.

Troy then offered some instructions about suggestions and complaints, followed by an introduction to the range of accessories we could request. He assured us that their wardrobe was vast, as well-equipped in contemporary costumes as it was across historical eras and cultures. And every girl could recite for us a list of the house toys at our disposal; we only had to allow her twenty minutes to prepare herself and return.

Noticing Mehta and me in his audience, Troy specifically mentioned that he hoped it wouldn't offend some of us if, in the course of the evening, we saw the odd woman passing through the hall in a burka. If a certain customer ordered it, that was what they provided him. Embarrassed at being singled out, Mehta reassured him we weren't Muslim and it wouldn't bother us for a moment. I could hear in his voice how eager to please he was, out of sheer awe of the sights and the system; I felt the same way myself.

Similarly, continued Troy, there were customers who wished to sample the experience of partnering Africans in their traditional tribal costumes, even if the girls were sometimes white because none of their black employees were immediately available. This clarification was presumably for the benefit of a black man seated one row behind us, but he just nodded and appeared very grave. I thought he should lighten up and enter into the spirit of things; he hadn't after all been dragged here unwillingly. How could political correctness cohabit with no-holds-barred pleasure?

Troy's penultimate point was about dos and don'ts with the girls and the strict rules regarding their safety and protection. Each girl would individually spell them out as soon as we entered a bedroom, but the crucial thing to remember was – never to hurt her, ever. The penalty was instant eviction. Of course, one might request to be hurt if that formed part of one's tastes. Also, we were never to employ a particular appliance or a toy on a girl if she refused, although again we could demand for anything to be used on us in any way we wanted, and she would comply to the best of her abilities. The girls at All You Can Dream were highly trained, well-compensated and motivated professionals, just as we were in our own working lives, and each of us should remember and respect that.

Finally we were told about the monthly newsletters we could pick up at the door to browse through while waiting, which included a section full of suggestions for deepening and prolonging our pleasure, and some great offers on accessories and toys. Troy's last word to the hungry, caged bunch before him, as he unleashed us on the house, was 'Enjoy', but with that only us single men were released; the couples stayed behind for some special details and protocol to do with threesomes.

'I had never imagined it could be this way,' were my first words as we re-emerged into the main hall. 'So clean, so safe, and, above all, not in the least bit sleazy. So well-managed, regulated, organized. And you can take as long as you like, ask for whatever you want, *and* if you wait, you can buy one and get one free!'

Gombrowicz was the only one not convinced. 'This wasn't what I expected at all. If I try to remember everything he said, I'll forget to look at my woman, and my dick might forget to stand.'

Mehta couldn't miss such an opportunity. 'Yaar, Gamru' – I'd noticed he'd shortened his name in the last few weeks, but Gombrowicz didn't seem to mind – 'make sure you don't let it all out at the start, hanh. The Pole must stand tall. Pace yourself, okay, breathe deeply; otherwise you won't earn full value for your money. Do a little this, then change and do a little that, you know what I mean.'

'And you ensure your heart doesn't stop beating and we don't have to telephone a real nurse. After all, as you keep reminding us, you are nearly the same age as Dasgupta's father. Are you sure it still stands up every time, especially on such a grand occasion as today? You were practically calling Troy "sir" back there; sure you won't be too intimidated during your performance?'

'Huh,' huffed Mehta. 'Go ask Lisa and countless others if you want a customer satisfaction report. I'm telling you, if they had one of these places for women, I could be working there. Because, you know, I've lived a long time *and* I run a hotel, so I've grown to like them in all shapes and sizes. And allow me to offer a timely piece of advice that might benefit you both tonight – the old "good from far, but far from good" rule often applies. In many cases, the ones with the more obvious qualities to appreciate aren't up to scratch when you probe deeper. Age has made me realize that; so my suggestion to both of you is, before you choose your woman, look for that gleam in the eyes to see if she can give you something really special.'

Such was our mood as our first few drinks were poured: light, curious, full of reassurance and anticipation, choosing from the varied liqueurs and canapés that circulated around the tables, laughing and comparing the properties of the different bundles inside the attendants' thongs, or the many delectable girls that promenaded by as free gifts for the eyes.

But our first impressions hadn't been wrong, and this was indeed a busy evening. Besides, we hadn't arrived all that early, because Mehta insisted only children went out to play at nine so that they could safely return to bed by midnight. One o'clock turned to two, then three, and we were still fifteen numbers away. Gombrowicz was now plainly napping after consuming gratis spirits and liqueurs for three hours non-stop, and I kept embarking on the long march to the nearest bathroom every twenty minutes. There were guests on other couches who had also dropped off, though the bathtub was as popular as ever. But I admitted, and Mehta agreed, that we needed at least a few visits to this place to feel at ease naked in front of everyone. I was happy at being light-headed already – I believed it would erode my inhibitions at the moment of reckoning.

The sullen young black man from the induction meeting had been sitting across from us all night, and our eyes had met several times. He had been abandoned by the group with whom he had been drinking, office mates presumably away enjoying their turns, and he suddenly walked over to join us.

'So, how far away are you then?' I asked him once he was seated.

He was number 204, three places after us, and he was seething. 'Don't you find this disgusting? Look at what they offer you. You sit around for hours waiting for them to keep their promise, and they tease you so that you won't leave, but that's the way it will be all night, because they are so greedy they invite in many more people than they can service. Do you know how many girls work here? Fifty! And I am number 204. How will they ever reach our turns?'

Mehta was surprised by the extent of his aggravation. 'Calm down, yaar, your turn will come just like everyone else's. Is your need getting pressing? Maybe then you should quickly visit the loo,' he joked with the appropriate hand motions, and we both burst into giggles.

But this annoyed the man even more. 'Take a look around you. Have you seen another black face tonight? No, it's just me and the two of you. Don't you find that strange? Why did you come here?'

'Yaar, for the same reason as you. Have a drink, na? You've worked hard, now play hard. We've made up most of our money in liqueurs already. They're not swindling you; otherwise everything wouldn't be free and unlimited.'

'No, I didn't come here for the same reason as you. I only came because my boss and everyone in my department was coming. It was a big night out. They made me sign up and I couldn't refuse.'

'Man, you must work in a merry office. Where is it that you take such merry outings together?'

He named a major Swiss investment bank. Without our asking, he proceeded to inform us that he was from Nigeria and, moreover, the only black person in his office. His colleagues always joked about it. As it was, he claimed, his position was precarious, and his performance and competence were judged extra closely. If he hadn't come along, it would have been a mark against his name.

'But if you feel like that you should move elsewhere.'

'Move where? They are all the same. My bank isn't the problem; the system is the problem. And because it keeps us so well fed, we feed it with everything we have. If we opt out or fail its standards for even a day, there are thousands willing to take over because they have heard the rumours of our salaries and our bonuses.

'I was at a meeting last Thursday. Our clients were from a large South African diamond corporation, who were being pressured by their government to do more about the incredible death rates among their miners, something like thirty per cent, because most of them are migrants and many take home HIV to their families. That is why we were meeting in London. We are their financial advisers. Should they release more money for hospitals and health education, was the question they would shortly place before their shareholders. Our recommendation was an absolute no, supported by many legal arguments and counter-proposals. And this is the firm I work for. And you, you said you are from Pakistan, right? You should see what kind of things they force through in your country.'

'India,' corrected Mehta. 'We are both originally from India.'

'That's even worse. The point is that we attend these meetings silently while they make decisions that affect millions of our countrymen. And we are rewarded with a fat pay-cheque for keeping quiet, or worse, for preparing the report that leads to the decision. There's the tragedy, that people like you and me have the education and the training to know better.'

'Man, if they don't announce my number within the next ten minutes, I'm going to ask to be paired up with her,' said Mehta, pointing at the revolving diva in an effort to lighten the mood. But the African only shot him a glare of uncomprehending disgust and remained resolutely focused on his subject. Mehta went back to staring despairingly at his own lap.

'You know, one thing I learned in the City is that the rich will only grow richer while the poor will never even understand in how many ways they are being swindled. Underneath the appearance of rivalry and competition, people like my colleagues and seniors are the most cohesive group of all, the most class-aware, because they've been prepared for their roles from earliest childhood. They were groomed in the right schools, where they were introduced to the friends with whom they would grow up to run the world. And this training is formalized in the world's best law and business schools, where they teach you the one universal secret about power – cooperate in controlling single-mindedly the structures and institutions of society, and shaping its systems and laws, and you'll collectively reap the rewards. That's it. You don't need to be a dictator. It's much more discreet than that, there are much cleverer ways to do it, more streamlined, less heavy-handed, absolutely open yet barely visible.'

Although I was still trying to look awake and attentive out of politeness to the Nigerian, Mehta had given up the effort and closed his eyes. Gombrowicz suddenly awoke with a start, and I realized that Mehta's head had drooped onto his shoulder. They had the right idea, I reflected bitterly, nothing short of outright rudeness would drive this menace away. Did these endless sermons also come free here, like the booze? Ice-cold water couldn't have worked better as a sure-fire turn-off. They should hire this guy to go door-to-door helping out premature ejaculators.

'Is it my turn yet, Dasgupta?' Gombrowicz asked drowsily after shoving Mehta's head to the side.

'No, but I'd welcome some company while I keep an eye on the screen,' I pleaded as subtly as possible, looking away from the African. But it was no use, and I could only watch as Gombs finished his drink in one swig, raised his legs, curled himself into a foetal position so that Mehta couldn't lean on him, and went back to sleep. Mehta piled up the cushions at his end to give himself something to rest against, and I wondered if I should head to the toilet and only return here to wake up the others when we were one or two numbers away.

But even my slight delay while I was making up my mind, allowed the Nigerian to resume his tiresome, one-track, completely out-of-place harangue.

'You observe the way it works here: this place is a perfect example. They don't interfere with anyone's personal freedom. It's a very important illusion, and a most effective distraction – the sensation of feeling free. Let people feel at liberty to paint their hair yellow or screw each other up the ass, or visit brothels such as this. Ultimately they all have to shop at Tesco, and work to keep up with the mortgage, and go deep into debt to pay for the pleasures you constantly seduce them with, and that is how you own them. Meanwhile, in the sweatshops and mines and factories and fields and the torture cells and hospitals over there, where we come from, lives are destroyed every minute. You don't even need to be a mafia boss any more. Why run the stupid risks and spend your life in constant fear? No, live legally, live openly, a white-collared life, honoured by your community . . .'

I had gone back to feeling strangely paralysed, hating myself for enduring this unrelenting verbal violation, yet unable to close my eyes and fake sleep, and unable also to walk away. But at this point, when even the cocktail waiters appeared to have been frightened away from our table, I finally managed to clear my head and formulate an objection, although it fell far short of the simple 'fuck off' my tormentor deserved.

'Look, I don't know your name, but I have to ask you to stop saying "you" when you're talking about these imaginary world-dominators of yours. I'm just an ordinary punter here, who can't even keep his friends awake. I don't own anybody that I know of, so please stop saying "you" all the time.'

But perhaps my words were slurred, or he didn't understand my accent, because although he shut up momentarily, the Nigerian didn't look as if he'd comprehended my objection. Instead, he shook his head and took up another train of thought.

'Do you know, my government spent fifteen thousand pounds to send me to the LSE to understand precisely how this whole game works, so that we can finally stop being its pawns? And I accepted this bloody job only after promising myself it was just for a year, for the experience, to observe the other side and learn their dirty deceptions. But now I'm trapped; I have a big mortgage to pay each month, and so I actively help in robbing my people, while spending my nights sitting in a place like this with you. And for what – so that tomorrow my colleagues will treat me as one of the boys? Hah, as if you and I will ever be one of the boys.'

'Look,' I said, once again briefly finding my tongue, 'maybe you have a point, but I must clarify what I really do, because you seem to have formed a strong misconception about me. First of all, I work for an *Indian* company, not a Swiss bank or anything western. It's an Indian investment fund that invests people's savings and pensions back home. My job here is to attract more foreign money to India, rather than exploit poor people, which is what you are describing.'

Aside from this meek rebuttal, it was too late in the evening for me to respond articulately to this incongruous explosion of paranoia, conspiracy theory and conscience, but I thought that in the throes of his personal crisis he was missing the point and entirely misplacing his blame. He was a homesick social misfit, who, moreover, was desperately aroused by the visual stimuli around us, and annoyed by how long it was taking to get to the action. Fair enough – but none of that justified marching up to complete strangers and accusing them of stealing from Africa. In my silent indignation, I finally found the resolve to walk over to Mehta, wake him up and suggest a trip to the loo, before we went and checked the number on the screen.

It was 4.30 a.m. by now, and we were still ten numbers off. Gombs was asleep where we'd left him, but there was no way I was returning to our African radical, who amazingly hadn't budged from his spot. So we decided to ride one of the lifts and discover more about the floors upstairs. I was too tired, and grateful for the sudden, delicious silence, to even give Mehta an earful for leaving me alone to face such an insane onslaught.

On stepping out, we were surprised to find that these upper levels were far less opulent than the central hall. On the third floor, most of the rooms were shut. Here the ceiling was only ornately painted, as in a film set, instead of the decorations being actually carved. It was the same story with the walls: the patterns were just paintings. The landing went right around the hall until you returned to the lift, but when I tried a door at the far curve I realized it too was a painting. For some reason, this really startled me and I called Mehta's attention to the discovery.

The corridor was darker as we walked round, but the next twenty doors – I tried every one of them – were likewise . . . *paintings*. It seemed a momentous finding, and in a flash I understood why they'd done it – to make the place appear grander than it was, believing no one would ever check amid the free-flowing alcohol and sexual euphoria. I was overcome by a greater rage than I can now explain, and suddenly I grasped the point of the Nigerian's diatribe. How were we all going to be allocated girls if most of this place was an illusion?

There were no girls and no rooms for us. I had to return immediately and confront Troy about this. But before that I wanted to forge a rock-solid case, so that I would have all the evidence I required. And on my way to Troy, I must remember to offer my apologies to the Nigerian, perhaps even transform him with his bubbling outrage and formidable verbal gifts into a fellow plaintiff. So, shouting to Mehta that I would see him downstairs, I strode over to the lift and continued to the fourth floor to ensure they'd played the same trick here. Of course they had, and on the fifth as well. I would just check the sixth before I marched straight down to Troy to complain.

That was where they awoke me at seven, when they were clearing up before closing – in the dark turn of the sixth floor far away from the lift.

'But I didn't get my number,' I protested. 'Shouldn't Troy know about this? Shouldn't there be a refund?'

One of them was kind enough to inquire what my number was. When I told him, he conjectured that I must have slept through my turn, because that night they'd reached number 204. I declared I didn't believe him; that I clearly recalled they hadn't even got to 200. To which he replied rather clinchingly that the turnover was much faster as morning approached because people wanted to leave and be home while it was still dark. We both knew he'd closed me out with that objection, and there could be no more question of any refund.

In the light outside, I located Mehta and Gombs. They had obtained the same answers to the same objections. A few other stragglers were led out as well, but the African wasn't among us.

'Nigerian ko dekha?' I asked Mehta as we crossed Bayswater Road to hail a taxi.

'No, the bastard must have fucked and left,' he replied sullenly without looking at me. I could see he was shivering in the morning cold.

'What a hypocrite, huh?' I marvelled. 'Chutiya talked like he was a priest-in-training, until the time came to screw.'

'I've seen plenty like that,' said the sage Mehta, as usual flaunting his life-experience before us. 'Some fuckers need the whole guilt-trip thing to get themselves hard and horny. He was using you for foreplay, I'm telling you.'

For some reason this ludicrous suggestion tickled Gombrowicz's funny bone, and the two idiots began cackling in unison right there on the pavement in the mist. I refrained from replying, and instead hailed a cab travelling in the opposite direction that neither of them had even noticed. A few minutes later, as we sat bundled in the back speeding homewards, I briefly wondered if the driver had guessed where his early-morning passengers getting on at that junction were coming from. I felt slightly ashamed at the thought, but decided that whatever he assumed about us was better than the truth, which was that he was taking home three morons who couldn't get laid in a brothel.

RAJEEV BALASUBRAMANYAM

The Tablet of Bliss

Our hero has fifteen tattoos.

On his back: his sons' names, a winged cross, and the words 'Guardian Angel'.

On his left arm: a picture of his wife, her name in Hindi, the words 'Forever by Your Side' and 'Ut Amen Et Foveam' – *So That I Love and Cherish.*

On his right arm: the Roman numeral 'VII', two angels, a classical design, the motto 'In the Face of Adversity', and 'Perfectio In Spiritu' – *Spiritual Perfection.*

Running from his nipple to his groin, a Chinese proverb: 'Death and life have determined appointments. Riches and honour depend on heaven.'

His body was his work, his body was a work of art, and we have ruined it, Malini and I.

But no, my wife is not to blame.

I am a proud, proud man. I have a scar running from my eye to my chin. I made the mark myself after I painted my last wedding portrait: Mr and Mrs Sanjeev Shah from North Harrow, who requested that their Audi Q7 – 'Keeps you and your family safe' – gleam grey in the silence between them.

But this was how I paid my bills.

My name is K– and I am a political miniaturist. My works are vast, spacious, sweeping, panoramic – oh yes! – but with detail so

73

tiny I can fit all humanity on a shrinking white canvas. The closer you look, the finer a story you hear.

Hiroshima: 6 August 1945: twenty seconds before impact

Banks, restaurants, offices, cafés, brothels, railways, dentists, hospitals, schools. Children, parents, invalids, lawyers, thieves and priests. Above them all, three aircraft, cross-sectioned: the *Enola Gay*, the *Necessary Evil*, and the *Great Artiste*. Colonel Paul Tibbets, smiling, crying, erect. It has been my habit to strip away surfaces as I please. X-ray upon X-ray. Skin sheared. Walls removed. Life in all its allness. You can even see his semen.

New York: 9/11

Similar to *Hiroshima*, but we cannot see inside the plane.

London: 7/7

Sex, everywhere sex. London's whores in basements and castles. Royals piercing bleeding mouths. Parliament and palace laid bare. In a Liverpool Street hotel, Netanyahu is on the phone. In Downing Street, Blair is too. In Russell Square, a bus spews arms and legs.

They didn't like this one, and I was punished. 'A propagandist.' 'An inciter.' 'Crudity of style.' 'A heavy hand.' And then. Nothing. They simply left me alone.

We lived off one salary after that. I became aloof. In anger I cut tiny drawings all over my body, the pain loudspeaking to my brain in protest. I cut a whip into the sole of my left foot, a flame into my right; I was going to remove my toe when Malini intervened.

'I've been to the doctor –'

And soon we had no income at all. Like these folk . . .

Manchester is not a city I would visit by choice. Like wool against my skin, the air is damp and smells of beer. 'Whalley Range', a name like a public school joke, stinks of human filth: I have read the history. Controlled by Quakers, no pubs allowed, which means the sinners abused in their homes and look . . . weak, proletarian genes soaking in their sweat-drenched piss. Yes, I am a bitter man.

College Road. Second gear.

The moral is not this, but this is, nonetheless, a fact: mere foolish, inelegant pride is irrelevant beside that which threatens to zip night's curtains over our world for ever with the kind of zeal found only in the serially psychotic and which goes by name of cancer. To put it less adamantly, I needed the money.

But pride is a curious thing.

Speed bumps the size of camels; I splutter onward and to my right it looms like a metaphor. A building like this does not belong here. From behind iron gates higher than two men a spire lances this festering black sky. This building belongs in Oxford, not here.

I have read about it. They used to train priests here, who then died of dysentery in Africa and Asia. The university bought it from the church, then the GMB bought it from the university and union activists learned to yell at their overlords, persuasively. And then it was sold, again.

They say he never goes out, that he drinks, smokes, snorts, spends days on the internet ogling the blue-eyed blonde he used to love, as did we all.

When he first entered our lives, my words to Malini were affected and false: 'He's a charlatan.'

Whatever did I ever mean by this?

Only dissimulation, fear of within. I was in love with him, you see, but only after I destroyed him did my heart speak to my brain with such clarity.

But we were all in love with him back then; this is not a cult, this is not about red-tops or the ignorance of the masses; this is essential to the *soul*. This is why once we had gods, and why we now mourn them, from time to time . . .

That first night I may even have paid him a tribute, hot against my oversheet, my cancerous wife asleep in pain. I saw his face and gasped in devotion . . .

. . . Then in the morning I went with the others and, like an artist, feigned cynicism and anger.

The brief was as follows. In honour of the forthcoming Olympics, twelve artists would paint portraits of the same subject. They would hang for twelve months under twenty-four-hour lighting in Trafalgar Square. We would receive £120,000 if *in twelve hours or less, we succeeded in capturing the spirit of the man who so aptly captures the spirit of the Olympics.*

The time limit, of course, was necessary because they couldn't afford him for longer. There would be three sittings, each of four hours, and all twelve artists would work concurrently with no extra sittings, no cameras. The work could be continued in private, however, so long as the final deadline was met.

We convened in a usually derelict warehouse in Leytonstone. There was plenty of champagne, which no one touched, and twelve easels fanned around an empty space. He was exactly twelve minutes late. Most of us believed we were too good for this nonsense, and lost no time in announcing this, though others attempted to justify themselves (postmodernity, and so forth), but once he arrived, all that was forgotten.

The room went silent at once.

Darkness settles nervously, as if it could recede at any time. I doubt even the locals know he's here. These houses, on either side, seem ordinary enough, a mixture of middle-class and aspirational. I think there was a consensus to exclude him from the media, the modern equivalent of public stoning.

But here he is. I can hardly believe I'm looking at it . . .

A brass plaque with a single word, archaic as a pagan carving.

BECKHAM

And now the gates are opening, very slowly. First gear.

I clutch at my awful heart, but my alarm was false. *I*, at least, still have my health.

Down the gravelled entryway, alert to signs of life, but I can't see any. No lights in this house: a cross between a cathedral and a castle, which feels like a tomb. It would be impossible to make a joke within these grounds; the darkness would snuff it out at once.

But there, a lamp breathes colour into the air. I see roses, blue-grey in the thickening dusk, and to my left a fountain. Beside the lamp is a wooden door with an iron handle. I park and lock the car. Attached to the door is a note, which I open.

K– Make yourself at home. I won't be long. David.

When I first met him, David Robert Joseph Beckham (born in 1975 in Leytonstone) was unassuming, charming, modest, and – yes, I dare, I dare! – beautiful beyond belief. His hair had gentle highlights, less obvious than in his youth, and his eyes were little tablets of bliss, begging to be swallowed. He was dressed simply in a black V-neck sweater, Versace jeans, and loafers. None of his tattoos were on display. He seemed shy, nervous, excited.

The lighting in that room was all natural – most of the ceiling was glass – but, in here, I can't even find a light switch. There's an oil lamp on the kitchen table, which throws a golden disc sufficient to illuminate a bottle of wine, a pair of mugs and two wooden stools. I sit and wait.

My portrait was all about the eyes. They were slightly too large, and the rest of him was out of focus, the colours dulled. But I worked a long time on that blue. I was up all –

'Mr Beckham.'

I have bowed: it was not my intent.

He is wearing a grey woollen overcoat, black builder's hat and grey jogging pants. His feet are bare. And sunglasses, thick and black. Only the voice is the same.

'You must be K–.'

'Mr Beckham, it's very kind of you to see me. I know my letter was a little strange.'

'Not really.' He laughs, less high-pitched than I remember. 'There isn't much I find strange any more.'

'Mr Beckham, would it be all right if I asked *you* some questions first?'

'Anything you like.' His face in the lamplight is smooth as slate. 'I don't even have electricity in here. I don't know or care what they're saying.'

They're not saying anything!

'It's just, could you, would you describe what happened to you after the portraits were hung? When did you start to feel . . . different?'

Malini is starting to feel different pretty quickly.

It started with a pain in her abdomen that had her screaming for most of the night. An ultrasound revealed a ten-centimetre cyst on her right ovary, which was removed in emergency surgery. Two months later, the pain was back, and the doctors removed an even larger cyst, but this time they took the ovary too. A month later they told her she had ovarian cancer.

In my paintings, I began to draw people without their skin or flesh. A critic called me 'sick'.

We were told the cancer was in its early stages and hadn't obviously spread, but it was aggressive, so she would need a cycle of six Carboplatin chemotherapy treatments after a course of IVF treatment in case the chemo made her infertile.

All in all, Malini spent twelve hours under anaesthetic, thirty hours in chemotherapy, and missed almost one year of work.

'It was the speech, you know, at the party. Everyone was staring at me, but I couldn't stop talking. They thought it was a wind-up, even the papers.'

I smile.

All that happened was that at the press conference when the portraits were unveiled, David Beckham stood up and, with cameras flashing like mini-Hiroshima blasts, he started talking about Iraq.

'When we voted for Blair we thought the swords would turn into ploughshares, but he set fire to Baghdad and it just wasn't right. I don't understand how he could kill so many people. I just can't understand it –'

When he started crying, his minders intervened and led him away.

It made the papers, but mainly as a joke. 'Beckham's trying to be political. Isn't it sweet?' Or, 'Beckham's trying to be political. What a dick!' Or, 'Wearing a sarong wasn't enough?' A couple of left-wing journalists applauded him ('he's growing up'), but most people dismissed his words as attention-seeking, including me. I assumed his publicist had written the speech, directions included (*sobs profoundly*).

But then he turned up at a Galaxy game with a full beard. And after the game, in which he scored for the third time from inside his own half, he told the world he was refusing to shave out of 'solidarity with my Muslim brothers'.

There was talk of Islamo-chic and 'the compassionate footballer.'

'I got some hate mail, but I've always had hate mail. I don't usually read what they write about me, but I *felt* stuff, K–, stuff I'd never felt before. And, yeah, you can say compassion, but there was also anger. I've never been, like, angry . . .'

To put it mildly, David Beckham went wild. He grew his hair long, very long, and his beard seemed to go on for miles. Galaxy let him go, but not before he'd told them, and the country he lived in, to go to hell.

So he came back to Britain, told the press he wanted to be ambassador to Iran, and then he met the prime minister. But he was too far gone by then. The establishment couldn't see any advantage in him. They were just embarrassed.

To her credit, Mrs Beckham defended him at every opportunity. 'David's just standing up for what he believes in, can't you see that? *Cunts.*' She would spit that word, with malicious love. I know this love: I've seen it in myself, every time I took Malini for chemo.

But then he went further. He declared that Britain was a 'fascist state', that reparations had to be paid to every country ever colonized, and to every one of its ethnic minority citizens, starting with the Muslims who'd been raided or searched. And then he went on a tour of 'the free world': Cuba, Libya, North Vietnam, any country that would have him, exhorting the people to stand up and throw the whipmasters aside.

*

'I just knew what to say, K–. I would open my mouth and everything felt . . . right.'

By then the nation hated him, more than any other public figure since Hitler, probably. His picture was on the front pages every day, but never with out-and-out vitriol; it was always ridicule, painting him as insane, a laughing stock. Comedians devoted entire sets to him; every broadsheet turned into *Private Eye*; he was a satirist's, and a psychiatrist's, dream.

'Well, it *did* hurt, K–. If you thought someone was mentally ill, would you laugh at them? *Would* you? But that was all *anyone* did, and it was all so cruel, like the way kids are cruel. I can still hear that laughter sometimes. That's why I'm glad it's silent in here. The walls are thick.

'And then Victoria left. That was the hardest.'

I pour us both a little wine.

Again, to her credit, she insisted, near screamed from the rooftops, that she would always love him. She constantly referred to him as 'her David', but she said it was breaking her heart to see him like this. That was all.

In any case, I don't think he had any need of her.

He was going to another level.

The day before the Olympics began, David Beckham announced that if all Anglo-American forces and capital did not withdraw from Iraq in the next twenty-fours hours, then he would kill himself in public. No one knew where he was any more. All we knew was that in twenty-four hours' time, David Robert Joseph Beckham's life would end.

So we waited.

I thought he'd do it at the opening ceremony, but Malini said he wouldn't go near it. Once *he* appeared, the world would simply turns its cameras off and – in any case – he didn't *need* television. He could do it anywhere, and show it live on the internet. In any case, she said, it was obvious where he was hiding.

She tossed me the car keys.

We drove there together, that warehouse in Leytonstone with the glass ceiling. And Malini was correct. Dressed in a black judo suit, David Beckham was sitting on the floor staring into a laptop. Even from across the room we could smell him. There was no water up there.

As we walked towards him, he told us it was too late. He had already swallowed the poison. An estimated 1.5 billion people were going to watch him froth and choke his way to death. The camera – he gestured at the wall – was already on.

But Malini started running at him.

In response, Beckham did a delicate little chassé, like sidestepping a tackle, but my wife – so thin after her treatment, but still so alive – stopped, pivoted like a gymnast and, after reaching into her jacket, stabbed David Beckham in his eye.

He pulls off his sunglasses. The right socket is bare; it looks smooth, like snakeskin.

'I suppose that's when it all ended,' he says. 'But I remember everything, though not in the warehouse, not so well. When I think of it, it feels like a movie I wasn't really concentrating on. It's funny.'

'But. Look. You have to know . . . you have to know why I'm here.'

He doesn't reply. Just refills his mug and looks at the floor.

Those famous feet may soon be dribbling my head around the room. But this is what I came for.

When I'd finished my portrait, I added something extra, in miniature, something so tiny you could only have seen it with a magnifying glass, unless your eyesight was exceptional, but even then you'd have to know what to look for.

It was all painted inside a highlight in the iris of his right eye, smaller than a grain of rice.

The miniature depicted a David Beckham in a small house in Iraq with his family – Victoria, Brooklyn, Romeo – as a mortar explodes between them, fired from a British tank. We can see the screams on their faces, a noose of fire tightening around them.

I have a friend who is a vet. He removed a malignant tumour from a dog. When I told him I wanted it, he knew me well enough not to ask why: there is no why, in art.

I crushed the tumour with a pestle and mixed it with paint.

It's made of cancer, that little drama.

The thing is: when I saw him at that first reception, when he cried and had to be taken away, I could see it *in his actual eye.* I don't know how it happened. Like a sixteenth tattoo, my miniature had stamped itself on that little tablet of bliss.

It was Malini who insisted we find him. Even I didn't know she planned to do *that.* Cancer-free, Malini is in prison now. One and a half billion people watched her stab the world's most famous footballer in the eye. But the world doesn't hate her; she's no Myra Hindley. They've only forgotten, as they've forgotten the man in front of me.

Beckham isn't speaking; he's still looking at his shoes. I count to a hundred, then stand and walk to the door.

As I'm opening it, David Beckham speaks:

'*Thank you.*'

'*What?*' I say.

'Thank you, K–. Thank you both.'

'For what?'

From outside I can hear, for a moment, a child laughing, but then there is silence once more. He lifts his head, surveys the room.

'For this.'

Only when I'm in my car do I begin to understand. The wrought-iron gates have closed behind me and through them I can see a stonewashed black sky and the lonely silhouette of the spire. Perhaps a hundred people will walk past here tomorrow and think . . . nothing.

I drive away, down this dark, deserted street.

MADHVI RAMANI

Windows

When Mrs Sharma found herself locked out of forty-two Foley Feild – yes, that is Feild, not Field – her first instinct was to cry, which was ridiculous because Mrs Sharma never cried.

Last time she had cried was right after her hysterectomy, but that was on purpose. Her son, Raj, and his dumpy wife had come to visit. She knew that she looked a bit grey and frail from the operation, and so had decided it would be a good time to ask for the house. The house that she had always wanted. A house to die in, she said. Add to that a few tears, and bingo – the house was hers. He had made the down payment, and she paid the mortgage with her pension and the rent from the townhouse. Well, it wasn't a big deal – she had given birth to him, after all, and they spent more money on that damned dog of theirs than they did on her. If she hadn't made plans for herself, they would have eventually chucked her into a nursing home, like her sister, Ganga.

Ganga had lost it in there, repeating the same phrases about how she didn't want to collect the milk, make the dough, dust the cobwebs and so on and so on. Echoes from their house in Rupali Society. It was the nursing home that killed her. Mrs Sharma had told Ganga's son as much at the funeral, and threw in a curse that he be reborn as a rat for good measure. He looked like a rat, too, which was a sure sign that it was going to happen. Needless to say, she no longer spoke to him, or any of Ganga's other imbecile brats.

If Ganga was still around, she would have a spare key. She was the only one of Mrs Sharma's five siblings who Mrs Sharma had kept in touch with. Raj would be at work, and he only visited at the weekends. Sometimes, when he was busy, he would skip a weekend. Today was Monday.

As Mrs Sharma stood in her garden, tears filled her eyes, turning the solid house watery. It was no good thinking like this. She blinked the tears away, and focused once more on the house. It was the best house she had ever had. A three-bedroom semi-detached in the suburbs. Mostly white people here, away from all those spitting, gossipy Indians. Although she had been disappointed to learn that her next-door neighbours were black. Not even pretty black, that nice freshly fried puri colour, but proper black. She had feared loud music all night, but so far they had been surprisingly well-behaved. When she had lived in Kisumu with Harish, they had been surrounded by blacks. Well, anything was better than that crowded house in Rupali Society where six of them lived with no privacy at all under the watchful eye of their mother, a woman who had something against people sitting down. That journey, by ship from Porbandar to Mombasa then by coach to Kisumu, was exhilarating. She thought she was getting out, escaping to a life of luxury. Whenever the coach slowed down, she heard the Africans shouting 'Jambo! Jambo!' and thought that they were selling gulab jamens, her favourite sweets. It was only afterwards that she learned that 'jambo' means hello in Swahili, and that life in Kisumu was no luxury. Then there was the flat in the middle of that dirty Irish neighbourhood and, when the kids got older, the townhouse. That had been okay until Harish died, and a new influx of Indians came in. Besides, all that up and down over two flights of stairs had started killing her knees. Now, however, she finally had it: a proper house of her own. Except that she was locked out of it.

She had gone to put the bins out for collection. Normally, she went out the back door and dragged the bins from the back garden, through the side alley and out to the front. This morning, however, she had gone out of the front door, walked round to the back and, by the time she had dragged the bins to the front, the wind had blown the front door shut. She couldn't remember why she had done it that way round, but that's what tended to happen nowadays. A slight change of routine, of the normal way of doing things, and she found herself confounded.

The wind picked up, lifting her thin sari and making the leaves rustle. The sky was gathering heavy clouds. Her tulips, red and yellow, had already closed their petals. They were lucky; they could shut themselves up in their protective little houses whenever they wanted. Soon, it would rain.

Mrs Sharma tried the back door again. Undeniably locked. The sliding patio doors were sealed shut. They were double-glazed, as were all the windows, which also remained obstinately shut. She made her way round to the front of the house via the alleyway, running her fingers along the rough, hard bricks as she went, admiring the impenetrable, foolproof nature of the building, but at the same time feeling trapped by it. Brick after brick packed tightly together, not a gap between them. Halfway down the alley, she remembered the window. She looked up. A little sash window with red and green stained-glass patterns, older than the other windows, was positioned about halfway up the stairs, about a metre above Mrs Sharma's head. If there was one window she might be able to get through, it was this one.

She went to the front of the house and wheeled the green recycling bin back down the alleyway, parking it directly below the window. She tried climbing on top of it, but the bin was very high and Mrs Sharma was not in the practice of hauling herself up onto mountainous objects. She tried again, placing both hands on the flat surface and using all her strength to pull herself up. Years of lifting babies, rolling chapattis and scrubbing surfaces finally paid off; her arms held out while her flip-flops scrabbled against the side of the bin, and she managed to plonk herself on top. She stood up and realized that the pleats of her sari had come undone. She quickly re-pleated them and tucked them in. Her head was level with the window and she could see inside. She tried to push the bottom of the window upwards. It rattled in its frame, but was locked. If she could just put some more strength into it . . . but it was no good. She sighed. The first drops of rain started to fall. She looked around; propped against the wall at the garden end of the alleyway was her trowel.

She climbed slowly down from the bin, trying to ignore the pain in her knees, fetched the trowel and went through the whole palaver of getting back on the bin again. This time, she pushed the tip of the trowel in the little gap under the window, using it like a lever. It took a bit of effort, but the locks snapped and she was able to lift the window up. She stuck her head through and breathed in the familiar smell of cloves and incense. Then she placed her hands on either side of the ledge, pushed off the bin with her toes and started to wriggle through.

About halfway through, she found herself in a regrettable position. The front of her body was suspended mid-air above the stairs, while her lower half stuck out of the wall at the side of the house. She was balancing precariously on her hips, flailing around to keep that balance. It was like swimming in space. She hoped nobody was looking. After a few seconds of this, she decided that the best course of action would be to reach for the banister. She stretched her hands out and almost fell down head-first in the effort. She needed to get a bit closer. She continued to edge herself nearer with her swimming action, then made a desperate grab for the banister once more. She made it.

She pulled the rest of her body into the house and found herself stuck again. Her toes were on the windowsill and her hands on the banister. She had to get down, but how? Her arms ached and her legs trembled. The bottom half of her sari was clinging to her calves, wet with rainwater. Well, she couldn't stay here for ever; she was just going to have to jump. She counted to three, but found that she was still hanging on after 'three'. So she said three Hare Krishnas, knowing that if she didn't do it this time it would be a bad reflection of her faith. She pushed off the windowsill and her body went flying forwards. Her feet stumbled on the stairs, but her hands steadfastly gripped the banister and she managed to steady herself. She released the banister, warm blood rushing to her arms, and sat down. Mrs Sharma began to laugh. She had done it!

Once she returned to her senses, she went up to her bedroom and took up her usual place on the rocking chair by the window. The patchy grey sky was spitting rain onto the empty street below. She wanted to tell someone about her little adventure, but could think of no one to call.

Mrs Sharma put her glasses on and started to read her weekly copy of *Garavi Gujarat*. A car swished by, but didn't stop. At around two o'clock, a group of girls, who should have been in school, walked past, shouting and shrieking. She watched them disappear at the end of the road, taking their laughter and exaggerated gestures with them. At 3.30 p.m., she went downstairs and made herself a cup of chai, with a plate of cornflakes sprinkled with lemon juice, salt and chilli powder, and settled down for the most interesting part of the day.

It had stopped raining and Mrs Sharma moved the net curtain back and opened the window slightly, letting in the cool, pond-smelling air. Shortly after, the red car belonging to the black woman pulled into the drive of the neighbouring house. She got out with her son, who was about eight years old. His uniform, which was neat enough in the morning – although Mrs Sharma had noticed that he'd neglected to tuck in a piece of his light blue shirt round the back – was now completely dishevelled. The bottom of his left trouser leg was caught in his sock, and the right one had a scuff on the knee; chalky grey scratches surrounding a patch of slime green. If Raj had come home like that, he would have got a slap. The mother, followed by the boy, went inside the house.

It was Monday evening, which meant karate. At 5.30 p.m. they would leave the house again. This time he would be dressed in a white costume, which looked like something they might make you wear in a mental institution were it not for the yellow belt around his waist. When Mrs Sharma first moved in, he used to wear a white belt, which completed the asylum look perfectly.

In about fifteen minutes, the black girl would walk home with her friend – another black, but an extremely pretty one with long limbs and a graceful manner.

Presently, they rounded the corner. As they got closer, Mrs Sharma listened carefully to their conversation, but, as usual, she couldn't comprehend what they were saying. She understood the words of course – Mrs Sharma had always prided herself on her excellent

English – but these girls used them in ways that made no sense: 'Mr Fenton is safe', 'that film is sick', 'Darren poked me on facebook'. Mrs Sharma didn't know what face book was, but everyone seemed to be reading it nowadays – she had even overheard Raj mention it once.

The girls reached the house and, as usual, the pretty one waited while her friend walked up the drive and unlocked the door. Then she raised her arm and waved elegantly, like the gesture of a Kathak dancer. Mrs Sharma waved back silently from behind her curtain.

A car growled closer. Probably the newlyweds at number seven coming back from work together. They did everything together. They even wore matching colours; this morning she was wearing a purple dress while he sported a purple tie. Mrs Sharma didn't know if they really were newlyweds, but they acted as if they were. She was waiting for the day that their nonsense would come to an end and they would finally start behaving like normal people. However, the vehicle that came round the corner was not the newlyweds' silver Golf, but the little white van belonging to the builder who lived opposite Mrs Sharma.

Mrs Sharma had a magnificent view of his house from her window, but this was wasted on such a boring person. The builder lived alone, hardly had any visitors, and drew his curtains as soon as it got dark. Sometimes she caught the flicker of the TV in the front room, but the lights were always out by ten. Mrs Sharma knew that he was a builder because of the things he loaded into his van and the way he looked. He had a beer belly, thinning grey hair and wore dirty T-shirts coupled with cement-flecked jeans that exposed his backside when he bent down. The only element of surprise was that he came and went at irregular times.

The black father came home shortly after his wife and son had left, ranting and raving like an idiot. When she'd first moved in, Mrs Sharma thought that he had serious problems until she realized that he was actually talking on the phone.

The nurses, who lived next door on the other side, would follow at around seven, because they had left at eleven that morning. Although their shifts changed regularly, they were usually on the same shift and came and went to work together. They probably organized it that way so that they would be safe coming home when they did nights. Sensible girls. Today, however, by the time the nurses came walking down Foley Feild arm in arm, Mrs Sharma was fast asleep.

She awoke to the familiar whirr of machinery, punctuated with the occasional thud, clap and tinkle of breaking glass. At some point she had moved from her chair over to the bed. She lay there for a few minutes, before realizing that she had forgotten the recycling bin in the alleyway. The lazy dustbin men would never collect it from there. She got up and hurried to the door re-pleating her sari as she went. She went out the back door, and dragged the recycling bin to the front, but it was too late; the truck had already passed.

Irritated, she dragged both bins into the back garden once more. As she was doing so, she glimpsed, on the other side of the fence that separated her house from the black house, a little window, positioned, like hers, in the middle of their wall. An idea flickered in her mind. She dismissed it, but as she ate breakfast, settled down in her rocking chair, watched the newlyweds leave wearing navy blue, the family with the blond boy in the wheelchair get into their Jeep, the blacks get into their two cars and drive off, it kept coming back to her with renewed force. When the street was quiet once more, Mrs Sharma went downstairs.

She tied her house keys to a handkerchief and in turn tied the handkerchief to the end of her sari, which she tucked into her waist, so that her keys dangled from her hip. She went outside, fetched her trowel and walked with it by her side towards the black house. The exterior was more or less like her house, although the rose bushes were not as well-tended. The windows glassily reflected back images of the street, giving no indication of what lay within. Birds chirped and, in the distance, cars breezed past on the dual carriageway. Mrs Sharma turned sharply off the street, and walked down the alleyway. Their sash window was exactly like hers. She walked round to the back garden to find something to climb on; she couldn't very well drag their bins in from the front drive.

Wet tennis balls, once yellow but now mouldy green, an upturned bucket, badminton rackets and a home-made barometer lay around the garden. Mrs Sharma contemplated the plastic garden furniture; the chairs would be too low and the table, although a good height, was too wide for the alley.

She took the chairs to the alleyway one by one and stacked them on top of one another just below the window. Then she put the upturned bucket on the chairs and stepped on top, feeling the plastic bend beneath her weight. She quickly wedged the trowel into the gap between the sill and the bottom of the window and forced it open. Then, she started to wriggle though. A strong smell of coconut . . . a tinge of something burnt . . . a whiff of aftershave. She moved quicker this time, scared that someone would see her, muttering 'Hare Krishna' as she inched her way further and further into the house. The carpet was beige, the banister was a dark polished wood and, beyond, was the open door of the living room. Before she knew it, she found herself gripping the banister with her feet safely on the stairs. She paused to catch her breath, wondering what to do next.

She made her way cautiously down the steps, the carpet compressing beneath each footfall. In the hall, a few pairs of shoes surrounded a shoe cabinet. Mrs Sharma shook her head. All they had to do was perform one simple task to help keep the place tidy. Near the front door, an electricity bill lay on top of a pile of post. Two hundred and eleven pounds. They spent a lot. She took a few steps into the living room; school books, newspapers and a laptop lay around in much the same fashion as the garden. It reminded her of those days in the townhouse, when she was continuously trying to return things to their rightful places. Kids. She was glad that she had gotten rid of hers, but, despite herself, felt a pang of nostalgia.

She stepped out of the living room and continued down the hall. The dining-room door was closed. Maybe someone was in there, she thought as she crept past, a sleeping grandfather perhaps, whom she had never laid eyes on. Or worse, a mad member of the family, or a criminal under house arrest. Her fears faded as she passed the door and entered the kitchen, where the smell of coconut and charring were stronger.

Black specks surrounded the sink area, where someone had scraped off the surface of burnt toast. Mrs Sharma had to resist the urge to start tidying up. She felt sorry for the mother. She could not fathom how she had coped with working and running the house when her own children were young. Just looking around, it seemed exhausting.

She opened a cupboard at random: pepper, thyme, salt and a bottle of some dark brown powder labelled 'jerk'. She opened the bottle and sniffed it. She could tell it was spicy, like garam masala, but different.

She untied the handkerchief from the end of her sari, making sure that the keys did not clink, and laid it out on the kitchen counter. Then, she tapped a bit of the jerk stuff onto the handkerchief and wrapped it up before replacing the bottle. What would Raj think, if he saw her now? He'd put her into an asylum for sure. A thought struck her, How on earth was she going to get out? She couldn't go back through the sash window; she'd need to put something on the stairs to climb on just to reach it, which would be far too dangerous. She tried the back door that led out from the kitchen – it was locked. She tried the front door. Locked. Where did these people keep their keys?

Then, as obvious as daylight, she saw the windows. She went back to the kitchen and opened the one by the sink. She picked up her handkerchief and keys, climbed onto the counter and out the window, pushing it shut behind her. She returned the bucket and chairs to their previous positions as accurately as possible, and left.

At home, she walked through the rooms of her house. It seemed as if she had not been here for years. It was like wandering through an Ikea store: unslept-in beds, empty wardrobes, perfectly positioned ornaments. When she had moved out of the townhouse, she had told the kids that they needed to pick up their stuff, or else she was throwing it away; she was not a storage centre.

Exhausted, Mrs Sharma lay down. A couple of hours later, she awoke with a growling tummy. That evening, instead of watching the street from her rocking chair, she made herself a chickpea curry with some chapattis, using the spices in her handkerchief instead of her usual mix of Indian spices. The curry tasted hot and peppery with a hint of cinnamon. Satiated, Mrs Sharma went to bed with the knowledge that she had discovered a taste for something new.

The next day, as she watched the residents of Foley Feild leave, she calculated which house to enter next. Her gaze rested on the newlyweds, both wearing black cardigans. Delightful thoughts of disturbing their wardrobes so that they could never match again danced in Mrs Sharma's mind.

She waited until the nurses, who lived next door to her on the other side to the blacks, and directly opposite the newlyweds, left. Then she waited another ten minutes before prowling towards her targeted house with her trowel. Just as she was about to duck into the alley, she noticed a white fixture above the top right-hand window, flashing a red warning light. A burglar alarm. Mrs Sharma continued to walk past the house, down the street. Quite a few of the houses had alarms. At the end of the road she crossed and started walking back. These houses were on the periphery of the view from her window, so she didn't know much about their inhabitants.

She passed an old English woman clipping the rosebushes in her front garden. Mrs Sharma knew that she lived there with her husband, and that they didn't go out much. The woman smiled at Mrs Sharma, and Mrs Sharma smiled politely back. She imagined making friends with the woman, going over for a cup of tea poured out of a floral teapot into a dainty porcelain teacup. Isn't that what happened in English neighbourhoods such as this? But Mrs Sharma had already passed the old woman and was approaching her house. She panicked. What was she going to do now? Go back home? And then what?

As she approached the nurses' house, she noticed that they did not have an alarm. Not her ideal choice of house. Nurses reminded her of her time in hospital. They were all sensible and overly cheerful, which irritated Mrs Sharma. She always tried to give them a hard time when they fussed over her – not that it had any effect. She turned into the alley.

The bins were round the back and Mrs Sharma, now quite the expert, scrambled through the window, feeling that familiar rush of excitement as she landed on the stairs. She went upstairs and through the open door of the master bedroom, expecting a tightly made bed and hospital-like cleanliness. The bed was crumpled, clothes and odd pairs of high heels were strewn on the floor, and a spilt ashtray was on the crowded dressing table. Mrs Sharma wondered if she was the only one in the street who knew anything about housekeeping.

She trod carefully round the room, picking up dresses and un-comfortable-looking knickers, inspecting them as she went before dropping them onto the floor again. The nurse wouldn't be able to tell if anything had shifted. At the dressing table, a half-smoked cigarette that looked like a bidi lay beside the ashtray. She sniffed it: marijuana. When they were young, just before Mrs Sharma got married, she and Ganga went on a trip to Punjab, where they had some bhang. She remembered feeling elated and relaxed at the same time after drinking that sweet, milky drink. She would have liked to try marijuana again, but she didn't smoke. At least the nurses were having some fun.

She picked up a small pot labelled anti-wrinkle cream. She looked in the mirror and inspected the lines on her face. The deepest were two vertical furrows on her forehead, just above her nose. She opened the pot, put her finger into the cool cream and rubbed it into her forehead. She looked at herself again. It made no difference to her wrinkles, but her forehead felt silky. Mrs Sharma had always used Ponds. The sound of an approaching car disturbed her thoughts. She put the cream down and went to the window. It was the white van. The builder got out and stood at his door for a moment. He searched his pockets, then fiddled around with the potted plant by the doorstep. He went inside.

Mrs Sharma went downstairs and left via the back door, the key for which was, thankfully, inserted in the keyhole.

The following day, Mrs Sharma tried to gain access to the house where the blond boy in the wheelchair lived, but was confronted with a monotonous brick wall. She ventured down a few other alleys belonging to houses across the road and discovered that they were all the same. None of the houses on that side of the street had a sash window. She wandered up and down Foley Feild and came to the horrible realization that all the other houses she was familiar with on her side of the road had burglar alarms. She went home and sat by her window, gazing listlessly at the street, locked out.

On Friday afternoon, Raj called.

'Mum, I called a couple of times this week, but there was no answer. Is everything okay?'

'I was out.'

'Oh, good. Keeping busy then.'

'Are you coming round this weekend?' she asked.

Raj hesitated. 'Shalini and I were planning to go to Ila's this weekend.'

'Ila?' repeated Mrs Sharma. The leaves on the trees seemed to be beckoning her. The builder came out of his house and got into his van.

'Mum, are you all right? I know it's not my place to say, but you two ought . . .'

Mrs Sharma's gaze fell upon the plant by his doorstep. She stood up. 'Yes, yes, say hello to her from me,' she snapped.

'Really? That's great –' But before Raj could finish his sentence, Mrs Sharma had slammed the phone down and was hurrying outside.

She crossed the road and looked at the plant. The ends of its leaves were yellowing. It needed watering more frequently. She looked under the pot, then ran her fingers through the crumbly soil. They touched something smooth and cold. A key! She quickly took it out of the pot, inserted it into the door and turned.

The house seemed strangely feminine. Photos of the builder with a wife and two children crowded the living room, and floral plates and porcelain ornaments lined the surfaces. It was cluttered. Mrs Sharma couldn't stand clutter.

Upstairs, the box room was covered with old football posters, their ends peeling off the walls. The bookshelves were empty, apart from a couple of dusty tennis trophies. On the door of the other bedroom, a handmade sign informed visitors to 'Keep Out'. Mrs Sharma peeked in: crusty glittery nail polish, a dried-out feather pen, a tall CD rack holding just one abandoned CD. Mrs Sharma closed the door and continued to the master bedroom. Before she had the chance to look around, she heard a vehicle.

She muttered 'Hare Krishna' as she crossed the room and went to the window. It was the white van! She hurried out of the room and started down the stairs, but could already hear the rumble of the van in the driveway. Silence. She turned back. Maybe she could climb out of a window on the second floor. She panicked as she heard the sound of the key being inserted into the lock. The front door opened, letting in the gentle rustle of the outside world before it was shut again. Mrs Sharma looked out the window of the master bedroom. There was no way she could escape from there. She frantically looked around for a place to hide, trying to ignore the movements below her. Opening the wardrobe would make too much noise. Heavy footsteps ascended the stairs. Mrs Sharma got down on the floor and slid under the bed. Sinister clouds of dust surrounded her in the dim space. Two big boots entered the room and stopped in front of the bed. The bed creaked and lowered as the builder sat down. For a moment Mrs Sharma thought that she was going to be crushed to death. Surely he could hear her breathing, as she could hear his. He took off his shoes and socks, the sweet smell of sweat attacking Mrs Sharma's nostrils.

He stood up. A zip was undone. The jeans came down, with a pair of boxers inside them, and the builder stepped out of them, one foot at a time. A T-shirt landed on top of the jeans. The wardrobe door slid open. Some things were put on the bed. The builder lifted one foot, then another onto the bed. He was, unmistakably, putting stockings on. Then some more movement and Mrs Sharma saw him step into a pair of high heels.

The high heels walked to and fro, then left the room. He was clearly a nutcase. She had to escape. She scrambled out from under the bed and ran to the stairs. Sounds could be heard from behind the half-closed bathroom door. Then the bathroom door opened and a big woman with red hair and a floral dress came out. Mrs Sharma and the woman stared at each other for a second before they both screamed. Mrs Sharma bolted down the stairs, with the woman stomping after her. A high-heeled shoe went flying past Mrs

Sharma, but she kept going. She opened the front door and ran across the road to her house, frantically trying to fit her key into the hole, sensing him behind her. But as Mrs Sharma stepped inside and closed her door, all she saw was an empty street and the closed door of the builder's house.

She went upstairs to her chair and sat down. Her whole body was trembling. She watched his house, but there was no movement. It remained solid, still. After about an hour, when her heart-rate had slowed down, she noticed a movement behind his net curtain at the window opposite hers. His dark shadow remained at the window and he appeared to be staring directly at her. Could he see her? She thought about calling Raj, the police even. But what would she say, how would she explain?

When the black woman and her son came home, their staring competition ended. He disappeared from his window. Maybe she had imagined it? But a minute later, he came out of his house and crossed the road. The unfamiliar sound of the doorbell – an obscenely cheerful *ding-dong* – sang his arrival at the front door. Mrs Sharma sat perfectly still. The doorbell rang again; twice. He knew that she was in.

He couldn't murder her in broad daylight, could he? She could scream as loud as a suburban fox. She got up and trod cautiously to the door. She opened it.

The builder towered above her, his face red.

'What you saw you had no business . . .' he growled, waving his big hands in her face. Those hands could easily strangle her; she wouldn't even have chance to scream. Who would discover her body? She would rot, alone in her house for days, before anyone came. A sense of despair and loneliness came over her. The builder paused in his tirade. Mrs Sharma looked into his eyes and realized that he, too, was like her, all alone in a house that had once held his family.

'If you're, you know . . . maybe you'd like to come over for a cuppa sometime,' he said abruptly, before turning and walking back to his house.

A cuppa? thought Mrs Sharma. She'd never heard anything so ridiculous in her life. A woman like her going over to a strange man's house for a cup of tea.

That weekend, however, as she whiled away her time, she contemplated his offer. No, it would not be right for a woman like her to go over to a man's house to have tea. But maybe he wasn't a real man. Maybe he was like a hijra. After all, hijras were very powerful. Shiva himself was half-female, half-male. Maybe he was a woman trapped inside a man's body. Sometimes, we all get trapped in lives that we don't really choose, thought Mrs Sharma.

At four o'clock that Sunday afternoon, Mrs Sharma walked across the road and knocked on the builder's door.

BOBBY NAYYAR

Phun

Carly lived in the same apartment block as me. East 53rd and Dorchester, six blocks from campus, just round the corner from a Starbucks and a Hollywood Video. She was Illinois all the way, born and bred in Peoria, schooled at U of C, living in a studio apartment on her student loans and part-time earnings, in a block that faced a blacked-out cinema. She lived on the fifth, while I was whittling away my stipend on the third. In those days she was doing her MA in Art History, while I had just started writing my doctorate thesis on 'The Crystallization of Memory in the Works of Italo Svevo'. Okay, so we hadn't set out to change the universe, but we both believed in what we were doing.

I first met her when she was moving into the block. She was sitting pretty in the lobby on an old leather trunk, surrounded by cardboard boxes and stuffed polythene bags, wearing a tweed blazer (typical grad student), jeans and a crisp white blouse, her hair brown with blond highlights, a fat-free face with high cheekbones, makeup, sharp eyes not addled by any weight. Youth. I bet she slept no more than seven hours a day and went jogging by the lake three times a week. Conservative like her parents, but sexually vigorous. A drinker, to excess when she was a freshman, but now, nevermore. She still didn't know how to dance. Perhaps she was in love with one of her supervisors, though not enough to do anything stupid, but she had thought about it. I looked at her; she looked at me and offered a wavering smile. In that second or two of eyeballing I thought I knew her and that she knew me.

I told her my name, she told me hers. I outstretched my hand; she took it, but remained seated. I offered no resistance; she shook once for me and laughed at my feigned passivity. I liked looking for signs. I believed you could learn a lot by touching a woman's hand, like her past, present and future were contained in the brevity of that moment. I was encouraged by her reaction. I asked her if she needed some help moving.

'No, that's okay,' she said, her eyes a powder blue. 'I have a guy helping me. He's just moving the car.'

I turned and looked out the front-door window. There didn't seem to be anyone else around. I told Carly that I'd be seeing her and headed for the stairs. I didn't want an awkward wait for the elevator. As I opened the fire door I saw him come in. An East Asian man, no more than five six, smallest glasses I had ever seen. I rushed up the stairs before he could see me. For the rest of the afternoon I wondered why someone, anyone, would choose to view the world through such small windows.

The new term started. Under advisement (coercion) I took on an Italian 101 class. In preparation I bought a blazer from Sears to cover the thinning elbows of my shirts, and I wore contact lenses instead of spectacles. But I couldn't look my students in the eyes. I was a teacher, instantly I had some caché; walking around campus young women would say 'Hi' to me, each one testing to see how I would say 'Hi' back. Eighteen-year-old women. For a few weeks each year they would flock to beaches like sea turtles and bare their breasts to the rising sun. They would flutter their eyelids when I looked at them, like I was whispering Petrarchan sonnets in their ears. It wasn't me they wanted. It was something else.

I spent less time in my tiny office in the Regenstein, more in my studio apartment. My desk jammed against the window, to the right of a fan I had installed when the heat and humidity had become unbearable. I saw Carly now and then, usually around East 53rd or in the new cafeteria on campus. We talked a few times, ate lunch together once. She wasn't the type of woman to be seen alone, she was either with a few girlfriends or the East Asian guy. I couldn't figure it out. Most couples mirror each other in a manifest display of narcissism, yet they couldn't be more different. They hardly spoke; I had never seen them hold hands. My default explanation for these types of relationship was a disproportionate member or a trust fund that had come to fruition. I opted to keep my distance, as I did with all of the women I found attractive.

In mid-November she knocked on my door. I was making coffee. I asked if she'd like to come inside; she said okay, though I could tell that she didn't want to stay for long. She looked at my unmade bed and the piles of books on the floor. I glanced at her as she crouched to pick up a book. In spite of the cold weather she was wearing a dress.

'You speak French?' she asked.

I pretended to be busy with the cafetière, turning to look at her from the kitchenette. She held up a copy of La Rochefoucauld's *Maximes*. I nodded.

'I love this book. Do you have a favourite?'

I looked into the deep black of the coffee and saw myself reflected. The question was a test of sorts. Luckily in this instance, unlike many others, I was prepared.

'Il n'appartient qu'aux grands hommes d'avoir de grands défauts,' I said dryly.

Carly laughed. She was looking for a place to sit, I thought I might be on to something if she chose my bed. Instead she sat at my desk. She glanced out the window then started to flick through the book. I put her coffee on the desk, and sat on the short edge of my bed. We were only a few feet apart.

'You've underlined number two hundred and thirty-one,' she said, turning to look at me.

'Which one's that?'

'C'est une grande folie de vouloir être sage tout seul.'

I didn't know what to say. The line means that it is the greatest folly to want to be wise all by yourself. I remembered underlining it at one of my low points, when academic life felt like an endless trawl through a library, not quite able to find the book you need.

Carly took a breath as if to speak. I looked up. Her eyes had softened, like clouds that have brought rain and thunder. She put the book down.

'A few of us upstairs are having a pot-luck dinner this Saturday. I was wondering if you'd like to join us,' she said, trying to smile.

'I can't cook.'

'Neither can I. Just come.' She sipped some of the coffee to show her willingness.

I told her I couldn't go, made up an elaborate story of what I'd be doing. I had no idea where it came from. Like my hero, Zeno Cosini, I told lies with no compunction. The truth only came when time or my intellect failed me. Carly took another sip and got up. Her face flushed pink as she walked to the door; she wasn't used to people turning her down. I needed to say something, anything. I put my cup on the floor.

'Is your boyfriend going to be there?'

'Who?'

'The East Asian guy.'

She leaned against my front door and crossed her arms.

'You mean Phun? He's not my boyfriend.'

The pink turned to red. She opened the door and left.

There are worse things than being alone, the poet Bukowski said. Solitude is as much a personal choice as happiness or wrath. I decided to make amends. A few days later I wrote Carly a note, put it in the internal mail rather than slipping it under her door. Not quite a billet-doux, though life has taught me that the three greatest words after 'I love you' are indeed 'I am sorry'. I didn't hear back from her. The pot-luck dinner came and went. The weeks drifted by like the flakes of snow falling across Illinois, the cold only biting when the wind blew.

For Christmas my parents decided to spend part of their savings on a month-long cruise. There was no point in going back home. I didn't know what I would do. My thesis was at an impasse, I couldn't bear to spend any more time in the Regenstein. I trudged through the snow, rented movies and avoided morning dishes by eating out at night. There was a gulley of restaurants near East 53rd. The waitresses all knew me by name. After eating I was faced with either calling in on a few friends, who had sacrificed their holiday time to study or write, or to go to bed early. One night I drifted down to the Ida Noyes hoping to find a diversion.

The bar was below ground. During term time it was full, now there was more furniture than people. Half the lights were off, the kitchen was closed. As a counterpoint the jukebox was still on, but at this time of the year, when the clientele consisted of the depressed and terminally lonely grad students, no one was prepared to pick any tunes. There were much bigger decisions to be made. To be or not to be. All that jazz. I sat at the bar and asked for a Red Rock. I scanned the room. There were a few single men sitting at tables that were meant for two. If the night dragged on long enough we'd probably end up drinking together. There were a few couples and, on the far side of the room, a couple of booths with small groups of women. They made the noise for us, we tried to listen. The point was to break the deadlock, to approach. I was too sober. I concentrated on drinking. I looked again after my second drink. I was fairly certain that Carly was there. I waited for her to come to the bar.

She saw me as she approached. I gave her the option to ignore me; I didn't try to make eye contact. She leaned against the bar as she asked for another pitcher of beer. I asked her if she'd join me for a drink. She gave the faintest of nods, steadied herself to take the beer to her friends then came back. I asked the barman for two more bottles of Red Rock. She sat on my right side. I always took that as a positive sign.

She asked me why I was still around. I told her. She told me that her parents were divorced and had families of their own. She couldn't bear to choose, or make the commute between them.

She raised her bottle. 'To parents.'

The clattering of glass was the closest thing to music in the room. We drank, we looked at each other, Carly smiled.

'What star sign are you?' she asked, no trace of mirth in her face. She was drunk and deadly serious.

I told her.

'I'm a Capricorn,' she said, pleased with my answer. 'Capricorns are headstrong, maybe stubborn, but we know what we want. We'd be a good match.'

I took a swig. 'I'm glad the stars think so.'

She looked down the neck of her bottle. 'You must be lonely.'

'How could you tell?'

Carly shrugged her shoulders. 'Look at us.'

I liked her much more when she was drunk. I wanted to think that the note had swayed me in her favour.

'Where's your boyfriend?' I asked, testing the water. She drank some beer, clearly she had to think about it.

'You mean Phun. I told you, he's not my boyfriend. He's my guy. He's special.'

'What does that mean?'

'We go out sometimes. He's always there for me. But he's not like your average guy – he doesn't crave definitions. We don't measure what we have by any parameter. It's so refreshing.'

I arched my eyebrows. There was only one of two questions that could follow: one philosophic and sentimental, the other crude and unoriginal. I went for the latter. Carly looked at me, not surprised, not even shocked. I knew she wouldn't answer. If she was a man, she might have at least winked. I moved on.

'How did you meet him anyway?'

'At one of his concerts. He's a composer – veeery talented.'

I looked at my hands. A composer. Where did composers come from these days? I had to ask.

'Ohio. But if you must really know, he was born in Cambodia.' She touched my arm. 'Do you want to meet him?' She looked at her watch. 'He should be here by now.'

We finished our drinks, Carly said goodbye to her friends and we went outside. The cloud-covered sky looked bruised, a deep shade of purple. The sidewalk had been salted, the camber of the road was covered in slush, while the wide bank of grass that divided East 57th from East 58th was covered in a fresh layer of snow. Carly tiptoed across to the divide. I followed her. She checked her cell.

'We could walk,' I offered. She looked at me. There was no point in trying to sound chivalrous. I wanted her on my own, we both knew it.

'He'll be here,' she said, her words white puffs of smoke. 'He's busy working on a new piece. It's going to be performed by the SPCO next year. You should come.'

'I'll think about it.'

'Don't be like that.'

'Like what?'

'You know.' Carly picked up some snow and started to compact it into a ball. 'Don't shut people out. You'll regret it someday.'

I turned and muttered something, blew steam out of my nose. In my mind the night was far from over. But Phun still puzzled me. I couldn't comprehend why a man would chauffeur a woman, be there whenever she asked and yet be content to be called a friend. Maybe he just didn't know what he meant to her. I figured that the rest of the night depended on what Carly did with her snowball. If she threw it at me, then we were on to something, if not, then she'd probably call it a night when we got to East 53rd. She concentrated on pressing the snow into a fist-sized ball. I looked around, we were alone, we were forgotten. Carly took a few steps back.

'Watch this,' she said, grinning.

She leaned back and threw the snowball at the battered sky. It rose, arched and fell like a comet, dust and flakes trailing, all lost against the clouds, disappearing before it could hit the ground. Phun pulled up in a silver PT Cruiser and beeped his horn.

'Come on.' Carly beckoned. 'You sit up front.'

We got in the car. Carly introduced me. I shook Phun's hand; he made no reaction, either to me or to her for that matter. The roads were covered in patches of black ice and he drove slowly. I looked back at Carly, where she was sprawled across the back seat.

'I think she's passed out,' I said to Phun.

He looked in his rear-view mirror. 'Sleepy,' he said.

Phun stopped at a traffic light. I saw it as my opportunity to ask him about Carly. I asked. He looked at me. His face was small, cheeks sunken, hair cropped close to his skin. He pushed his small glasses up.

'It's better to love than to be loved. Don't you think?' he said, as the lights changed.

I thought about it until we turned off Blackstone onto East 53rd.

'I guess so,' I said. 'But where does that love get you? Does it get you to the end of the street, to the front door –'

'It gets me wherever I want to go.'

For a guy who talked about love he sure sounded sinister.

He parked outside the apartment block. Carly got up; she didn't need any help getting out of the car. We all went inside. I pressed the button for the elevator. I thought something might happen. Carly looked at me, she wanted to speak, but she was past the point where the alcohol gave her energy. It was some time after 2 a.m. We got inside the elevator. Carly pressed the third-floor button for me, which came as a crushing blow. I looked for signs and yet ignored them at every corner, for what was desire without ignorance? My floor came. I murmured a goodbye. Carly wrapped her arms around me and kissed my lips. I wasn't sure if she would remember it in the morning.

A few weeks ago I saw Carly for the first time in years. I was at Wrigley Field with my wife. Carly was there with her boyfriend. By chance we were seated in the same row, though she didn't notice me. The Cubs were playing the San Diego Padres, Carlos Zambrano was in sight of throwing a no-hitter, Derrek Lee was ejected for fighting. I alternated between watching the game and glancing at her. During the break in the fifth inning I pointed her out to my wife, who said it was okay if I went and talked to her. I waited until her boyfriend had vacated his seat then squeezed my way to her. It took her a few seconds to recognize me, but when she did, she stood up and we hugged.

We traded stories. She didn't get a dream job at the Art Institute, or any other museum. Instead she was teaching art history at a community college in Evanston. I had made it as a low-level academic at Loyola University, teaching Italian literature, including a special course on Svevo. I was paid to teach bored students what a crystallized memory actually is. Carly hadn't married, but had been with her partner for nearly three years. He was an English teacher. I had married an Italian woman. Smiling, I recounted how we had first met in the Regenstein and the months of courting that ensued. Carly looked across at her and was impressed. I didn't tell her that my wife's name was Carla. When our conversation dried up, I remembered that night at Ida Noyes bar.

'Whatever happened to Phun?' I asked.

Carly looked at me puzzled, then figured out what I had said.

'Oh, we broke up a long time ago.' She looked at me wistfully. 'But it turned out all right. Last I heard he was in New York writing scores for movie soundtracks.'

I nodded. We both looked to the outfield. Carly asked me if I was happy. I said I was. She nodded. Her boyfriend came back. I got up and shook his hand. There was nothing more to say. I sat back down next to my wife and kissed her cheek. The Cubs lost to a homer in the ninth.

NIKESH SHUKLA

Iron Nose

He's opted for Snoop Dogg's worst album, the third one, *Paid Tha Cost To Be Da Bo$$*, the one that everyone hated, the one that sounded like it was farted out in a half-stoned slumber. He's opted for us all to sit around his glass coffee table, instead of in the leather sofas by the huge television. He's opted for Charlie to be his provided refreshment of choice, but gives me the number of a 24-hour alcohol courier company, so I can get myself some beer and cigarettes like a square. The rest of them have their heads down over the glass table and silky food parasites are travelling up their nasal cavities; a communal sniff and snort sounding like a Metropolitan line train hitting the tunnel between Finchley Road and Baker Street.

My cousin's massaging Felicity's blackened feet, his palms grey with the grime of the sodden dance floor she barefoot strutted around on an hour ago. No one is talking to me. I've ousted myself from the group by opting for beer and cigarettes. I quickly scan my memory banks for exactly how I ended up here.

Twelve hours ago, I was having lunch/dinner (linner) with Isla, a girl I'd met during the week, completely infatuated with her, playing back that moment on loop where she told me I had beautiful eyelashes and my stomach did that little lurchy thing, that burn and fizzle, and I knew I'd know this girl for a while. Ten hours ago, I arrived at 13a on Gerrard Street in Chinatown, a decadent and grimy bar, my new hangout in central (on the off-chance of being there rather than East), now that the Dive Bar's been closed down, gentrified and turned into a consumer wine bar. I saw my cousin and said something cheesy like 'stick a fork in me, I'm done'.

Eight hours ago, we were in South Kensington while my cousin looked for this townhouse-converted-into-a-toff-club called Light House. Seven hours ago, it's my round and I find two bottles of beer cost me over a tenner. I look at the label; they're ordinary Budweisers, costing £1.90 each across the road. Five hours ago, we're dancing, meaning that my cousin's friends are guffawing to each other and I'm no longer being ignored. I'm locked in an ingenious jukebox in my head where all the songs are set to the same tempo as the cheese erupting from the disgusting speakers. Two hours ago, we left so they could buy more coke and opted to go back to Tom's house so they could snort without scrutiny.

I'm stuck next to this guy no one has thought to introduce me to. I'm safety in numbers. He's vibrating. He's flaring his nostrils and licking his lips as the white worms are given tails on the see-through eighties coffee table. He eyeballs the scaly powder with his left retina and with his right, fixes himself on my cousin's fingers as they knead Felicity's feet. Her small fat toes are lacquered with silver. She's throwing her head back and guffawing at one of my cousin's puns. They only work when you're in this state. I scan the proprietor's CD collection while I sip my beer and light up a cigarette. The guy next to me waves the smoke away, prodding it like it's full of leper-bacteria.

'Hey,' he bellows at my cousin, his volume control malfunctioning. 'You know what they used to call me?' Everyone but my cousin and I gives a knowing titter and they lower their heads to the table. The guy next to me crouches forward.

'Iron Nose,' he says, without any acknowledgement that my cousin is listening. He's too busy caressing Felicity's feet as they bump off his fingers. The two of them roll their heads back and his massage becomes more fervent, her groans more suggestive.

'They said I could hoover anything up here.' Iron Nose taps a nostril as he emerges for air.

No one is talking; they're tuning into the music and thinking of something witty to say.

'Who used to call you Iron Nose? You said "they" but didn't say who "they" are,' I say. I'm pissed. My internal-censor control malfunctioning.

'What? No, my name's Suleman. They call me Iron Nose.' He looks like at me like I smell of pure arse dags, little dried crusts of shit dangling out of his iron bum.

'I like you,' he erupts in my cousin's direction. 'You and me, we're alike. You see, not much Asians would do what we're doing. We're breaking down barriers, you know. I mean, we've got it all. We have amazing jobs; earn a fuckload of dollar; fuck whoever we want; and we like the snort of the finer things in life. Who wouldn't want to be us? I mean, listen, my dad grew up in some village in Pakistan, like a Paki, like a Paki with no money. He would hate this. That's why I like you.' He gestures to my near-mute cousin, lost in waves of neverwhere. 'You get it. You like it. You see it. You take it. And you know what? You're not like the rest of them. You know what it's like. You can feel it. I like you. We're the only two Asians I know who would do this.'

He manages a lingering look at me that, between his twitchiness and my pissed delayed reactions, feels like it should be more subtle, like he meant it to be quickfire, but it feels like a mongoloid stare attack.

'Look, this stuff here is perfection. Do you believe in reincarnation? Because I don't, but if I do I want to come back as the Sheikh of Burma. Imagine all the yayo and poontang I could snuffle up with that kinda cash.'

My cousin nods him away. Felicity has her eyes closed and is mmming herself and he is following her lips with his eyes, trying to work out the best moment to lean in for a kiss.

Iron Nose feels ignored. He looks at me and resigns himself to the inevitable conversation. He's not willing to initiate it. I scan my drunken lists of conversational gambits for something inoffensive to bring up.

Yayo
Poontang

Bad rap
Being Asian
Reincarnation possibilities

We've exhausted these already. Anything else?

Politics
Religion
Careers
Nasal hygiene

'So . . . what do you do for a living?'

'Listen, I work hard, okay? Don't get me wrong, I work seventy hours a week. I like to unwind on Friday nights, you know? I work hard. I work really hard. This is just how I relax.'

'What do you do?'

'I work in an office. I . . . listen, why are you so interested? Who are you?'

'I'm his cousin.' I point to my cousin who has succeeded in touching his lips to Felicity's, her face looks so numb that it might fall off with the force of his chin pressing against her.

'And who invited you here to this sacred place? You know this is a sacred place. This place is our nirvana. You're Hindu, you understand that, right? Nirvana, perfection, Krishna.'

'Yeah. I understand.'

'Listen, I am a new breed of Paki, you know? I snort cocaine. Don't be too shocked by that. Don't be too shocked by the things that go up my nose. Just because your mother comes from a village and your father is your mother's brother and you were born on a banana boat – but you don't get it, do you? With your beer and your cigarettes; you know the Koran expressly forbids intoxication, and cigarettes just smell. I mean, have some self-respect. You need to stop intoxicating yourself and get yourself on the path to righteousness. Don't judge me. I work hard. This is how I unwind.'

'You're Muslim?'

'Yeah, I am. Why are you so interested in me?'

'Well, snorting "yayo" counts as intoxication.'

'Ladies and gentlemen,' Iron Nose announces to the group, who all stop and look over at him. 'I have an announcement to make. Our beautiful Asian friend has brought his family with him. Do not talk to him; he will ruin your high with his questions.'

No one is quite sure how to respond.

'Hey, guys,' Felicity suddenly brays. 'I had no idea we knew so many coloureds.' She fires a look at me. 'Don't be offended by the word, darling. If I use it, it's because it's ironic. Okay? And you need to understand that your cousin is my friend and if I've got coloured friends, I can call them coloured all I want. That's part of the privileges.'

Luckily, my need to get out of this room coincides with the desire to go for a shit. I get up and ask where the toilet is.

Unhelpfully, our patron looks up from snorting a line off his girl-friend's big toe and tells me to 'follow the smell'. In my head, I grimace; outwardly, I'm neutral. Ice-cold. The flat is small with weird velour carpets. It feels like a box room adjoining a bedsit. However, its location, in the heart of Kensington, darling, makes it more expensive than any property I'll ever own, ten times over.

I push into a door that turns out to be the bedroom. Some anal sex is being perpetrated on a large TV screen on one wall, but otherwise the room appears to be empty. I open another door, but it's a cupboard crammed with spear-fishing equipment. Behind door number three, I find a cubbyhole with a sink, bathtub and toilet.

Close the door.

Pull down jeans over hips.

Pause.

No matter how drunk I am, that pause is important. It's the pause when you've finally sat down for a poo, you're desperate, can feel it pregnantly poking through, labouring towards the water and you just pause. Regulate. Let it out at your own speed. And once it comes out, it eases downwards, everything empties at a cathartic pace and you find yourself having that all-important poo-gasm.

Pause.

Unload.

Pause.
Unload.
Splish splash splish splish splash.
I search for my beer and with the hand I won't be using to wipe myself down, take a long victorious sip. I've conquered the poo gods. They've allowed drunken me to unload without too much consternation and constipation.

Iron Nose is standing in front of me. His arm is around my cousin. He's pointing to a wrap in his hands, containing, he stresses to my cousin, the special stuff, the stuff that's too good for the white man . . .

'They've taken all the other best stuff already. Time we kept some things for just us. Justice. Just us. Get it.'

My cousin is feigning passivity. He's internally licking his lips at the special powder a few inches beneath him. They acknowledge me then ignore me as they crouch over the sink. The bathroom's so small, I'm now barricaded in. With no other option, I start wiping myself down with my non-beer-drinking hand.

They close in and close around the sink, bending their faces towards the nirvana powder. I look up at Iron Nose.

'There was this girl, she loved Asian cock right, she just wanted to feel brown cock slide inside her. She had had an Indian butler once and he once showed her his cock when she was eight, and she'd fantasized about his cock ever since. And when she hit sixteen, this was like last year or something, she was in the club telling me this story while we were bumping the yayo and I'm thinking, she doesn't even realize I'm Asian, right? So I say to her, like, love spread your legs, cos I'm Asian and I'll happily ram your sweet candyfloss pussy into spiritual enlightenment. And you know what she says? No brown man does coke, there's no way you're brown. And I laugh, like, listen, babydoll, I'm a pioneer, I'm breaking down barriers, darling. I'll snort it off your pussy while reciting the Koran if you want me to, baby, and you know what she says? You're not a real Asian, you're a coconut. I had to laugh. Isn't that funny?'

My cousin is passive. He has built himself into an ivory powder tower.

FLUSH
FLUSH
FLUSH
FLUSHhhhHHH

I stand up and start pulling up my jeans.

Iron Nose whips round and presses his forearm against my neck and pins me back over the cistern.

'What the fuck, get off me, you prick.'

'Where did you come from? Have you been watching us? Are you trying to tell my daddy on me? Is that it? Did my dad send you? Tell him I saw his spy as soon as he entered. His spy doesn't have nothing on his son. You tell him to leave me be.'

'Get off me, you prick.'

'Seriously, who are you? Where did you come from? Who invited you? Are you a policeman? Are you a reporter? Are you from *Eastern Eye*?'

'What's *Eastern Eye*?'

'That Asian newspaper . . .'

'Just get the fuck off me.'

SWISH
SPLASH
DRIZZLE
SWISSSHHHhhhHH

My cousin is rescuing me in the only way possible. He is silently holding the showerhead over Iron Nose's hair, and the streaming cold is making him squeal and bellow and he releases me and I push him aside down into the bathtub, where he falls with a thud. My cousin drops the showerhead in his lap and follows me out.

'Hey, guys, help me up. Asians stick together. Brothers, eh? Fuck those white guys?'

We return to the lounge. I'm nonchalantly swigging my beer like I own the joint. Cocky. I tell my cousin I'm going to leave.

No one looks up. As I'm walking out, Snoop's crooning on yet another lazy tune from a lacklustre album. I hit the stop button, murmuring that the album's shit, grabbing my bag and putting the beer bottle down on the glass coke table. People are starting to stare. Iron Nose has emerged from the bathroom, his top off, wiping himself down. I finish hitching up my trousers, tighten my belt and head towards the door. I've had enough of Asians tonight.

ISHANI KAR-PURKAYASTHA

The Sky Is Always Yours

Isn't life funny? So many years I have spent yearning to go back. Now that finally the time has come, I no longer want to.

You see, I hadn't realized how beautiful it is here. I have spent the last fifteen years looking down at the pavement, or forward into Amal and Anu's futures, or backwards over my shoulder to make sure no one was following me. I had, though, never looked up. Until this last year just gone by. Don't ask me why. It is just a sense I had, in the pit of my belly, that something was set to change.

Today, I have decided to spend the whole day looking up. It's spring. The sky is bright blue, and trees that were barren just a day or two ago have erupted in pink blossom. The locals are in T-shirts, but I still have my jacket on. Despite the passing years, I still have not adjusted to the climate. Although I do sometimes wonder if India will be too hot for me now.

Lately both my children, but Amal in particular, have been complaining bitterly of the Delhi heat. Amal is the older of the two (and Anu the more mature). I shouldn't be surprised: people keep saying how much more sensible girls are than boys. I have to take their word for it. I haven't been able to witness this firsthand in my children. I surmise what I can from our telephone conversations and emails.

They are both doing well. Anu has completed class twelve and started college. She is doing her degree in biology. And, as for Amal . . . he is shining. Bhaiya is always so proud of Amal's achievements.

'Didi,' he said to me yesterday on the phone, 'all your sacrifice has been worth it. He is a brilliant scholar, my Amal.' Recently, Bhaiya sent us the 'family' photo from Amal's graduation day; the three of them are arm-in-arm smiling seriously at the official camera. How grown up my babies look.

Bhaiya, my older brother, is their local guardian. Never married. Never interested in having his own children, but circumstance has moulded him into a surrogate parent. Now, it is always 'my Amal'. I have never corrected him, feeling mean even for thinking of it: he is Amal's uncle, blood relative. It goes without saying that I am immensely grateful for the way he has looked after my children, for the affection he has developed for my son, but I cannot help this petty jealousy. Of course, I have never said a word. Not even to Amal's father. Instead I have capitulated to Amal's needs. When, in the summer, Delhi got too hot for him to study, I persuaded Amal's father to buy him an air-cooler. When, in the winter, Delhi got too cold, we bought him a heater. When he needed money for a college excursion, we found it.

On the plus side, I have never been short of shifts. My regulars are Mrs Barua in Northolt and my two days a week looking after Priya Singh, but other than that I am inundated with requests to help with the cleaning, or the ironing, or at the shop round the corner from where we live. You see, I work hard because that is why we came. Job after job. Dawn to dusk. I polish, and wash, and scrub, and when the skin on my fingers wears thin from detergent, I lift, and sort, and pack stock. I am not the only one. Amal's father also grafts for the children. For him it is harder because back home he was a maths teacher, but you cannot be a maths teacher here without all the paperwork to say that you are qualified, and you cannot get the papers if you dwell in the shadows of society. So, Amal's father works in the restaurant. He is fifty. He wears a uniform of cheap black polyester trousers and a white cotton shirt and he runs from table to table, kitchen to table, between clicking fingers and impatient managers, who are neither as clever nor as qualified as he is.

But, no, I should not be too negative. In many ways, we have been fortunate. London has been kind to us. Or, perhaps I should say, this little corner of London has been kind to us. It is a mini-India. Though infinitely more organized and cleaner, still there is a hubbub that survives even the sharpest days of winter: shop fronts remain flung open; piles of karela, aubergines and chillies tumble across aisles full of determined, sari-clad shoppers who wear sneakers instead of sandals; men with grey stubble and round bellies stand on street corners touting for business, earnestly rubbing their hands together. Pictures of our many-armed deities gaze at us from windows and, though we are in London, though the sign on the street corner reads London Borough of –, though the traffic lights go from green to amber to red and cars pause politely at pelican crossings, there is still some semblance of chaos here that makes me feel at home.

So, I wonder . . . why did I not spend more time gazing up? These last few days I have been struck by the swarms of people who look like me – dress the same, move the same – forever looking down or forward or backwards. It is a shame. If there is one thing that I wish I could tell my comrades now, it is this – always look up because wherever you are, the sky is always yours.

For Amal, these little pearls that I have gathered will be irrelevant. He is arriving today. Can you believe it? My son. My son is arriving today. This evening, from Delhi via Dubai to London to take up his post in the UK head office of one of India's biggest software exporters. He was not supposed to come for another month, but there was some last-minute emergency, so they are flying him in – in *business class*.

Mr Amal Trivedi will sit in an office made of steel and glass. In a shiny suit and polished boots, he will stride confidently upon this land where we have existed for so long like ghosts. He will take it all for granted – the land, the sky, the sun. So, it has been worth it.

I glance at my Casio watch. It's nine in the morning. I better return home soon and start preparing some food for his dinner. It is the first time that Amal will be eating his mother's cooking in fifteen years. He used to be such a fussy eater. No matter what else was on the table, he would always ask, 'Mamma, you made "peshal" omelette today?' The only thing special about it was that there was no spice in it – just egg, milk and salt. Part of me wonders whether I should make it tonight. But he is an adult now, a valued company man, who is bound to have developed more intricate tastes. Yesterday, Amal's father lost his patience with me. He said that I had lost my head, that I was acting like some big shot or other VIP was coming to visit.

Amal's father is a good man; he does not like to see me fret this way, but I cannot help myself. I dither over a sophisticated menu, but part of me hopes my son will remember the significance of 'peshal' omelette. I finally decide that I will have some ready, a sort of standby option, in case he asks for it. I make a mental note to let Amal's father know. You see, I won't be here when Amal gets home. I am going to receive him at the airport, hold him in my arms, but then I will have to go.

As I finalize the ingredients for tonight's meal, I veer towards the greengrocer. But then I stop. This is silly. He is my *son*. My flesh and blood. I carried him for nine months. Amal's father is right. I need to calm down. So, I do a U-turn and head back towards the underground station. I am going to Waterloo.

I have made this journey countless times to see Lucy, my solicitor. But, today, it is different. It is a Saturday. The seats are not crammed full of people with their noses in their newspapers. I don't read the papers any more. I stopped when I realized that more lies can be told in black and white than in any other colour. To tell the truth, I hadn't noticed until I came to London, because back in India the lies had never been about me.

It's not every day, not even most days, but often enough, maybe two or three times a week, sometimes a headline, often a handful of paragraphs tucked inconspicuously amid reams of unrelated lines. And then my skin prickles when you, the men and women of this country, *look* at me. I prefer to be disregarded, but there are days when I am the headline . . . my face burns and I imagine that everybody can tell that it is me. I am the immigrant who is squatting uninvited in your country.

And then I think, Is that not what you did? Were you not squatting in my country not so many years ago? We are not so different after all.

Yes. I am taking. But you, too, have taken. At least I have worked from day one, for everything that I have. I have never begged. I have never stolen. And I have never killed anyone.

I take a deep breath. Today is different. There are no newspapers in sight. The girl sitting opposite me has long brown hair and blue eyes. She smiles at me. She reminds me of Lucy – there is no tension in her eyes.

I first met Lucy almost a year and a half ago. I didn't choose her. We were assigned to each other. I was lucky. You see, Lucy cared. If you had told me that people like her exist, I wouldn't have believed you, but Lucy cares for my cause. Lucy also cares for me. In the beginning, the distinction was irrelevant: I did not have the luxury of dissecting the motives of the men and women who volunteered themselves to help me. Now, that distinction is all that matters.

Lucy and I were first introduced in January. I remember there was a slight delay for Christmas. Our neighbour's house had been burgled while they were away with some family friends. Two days later, the police were knocking on our door appealing for witnesses. They didn't find witnesses, but they found me.

Shortly afterwards, I was referred to Lucy and the process began.

I knew I had no leg to stand on. I knew it, but you never really silence the irrational voice of hope in your head, do you? At any rate, I couldn't.

On 10 March 2005, I had my first hearing. They said no. Afterwards, Lucy took me out for a meal, nothing fancy, just a burger. She insisted that we appeal. As many times as we have to, she said, and clasped my hands in hers with such force she made me forget who I was.

'You think there is chance for me?' I asked.

'More than a chance.'

She said I had been here for a long time, that this was my home. She told me we would win.

That night, I rowed with Amal's father. I asked him, did he ever feel ashamed when he looked in the mirror, or was he proud of the life he had given me. That night, for the first time in fifteen years, we raised our voices, and all the other families in our shared house must have heard us, heard everything we said, our filth and our indignities.

For so long, we had been so cautious, careful not to make noise. It makes me bitter even to remember. Fifteen years, we have spent in one room – a spacious double (what should have been the lounge) in a house converted into two flats with three couples per flat. We shared a kitchen and a bathroom between six. Fourteen times we had made love in that bed; once a year to commemorate our wedding night. We would lie awake for hours, deep into the early morning so as not disturb anyone, and then we would do our business in hushed, illicit thrusts.

It was always our overarching concern to remain quiet. So, our arguments were disagreements; our moments of happiness were agreements that we would acknowledge but never celebrate. So, maybe my behaviour that evening was not so shocking after all. My head had been pounding from the lightness of it all; from how easily the verdict had tripped from the judge's tongue. I was the last case of the day. I imagined him pondering what he would have for his dinner as he wrapped up my destiny in a few mechanical sentences.

Of course, I burst. It is extraordinary that it hadn't happened sooner.

Lost in thought, I am surprised when Waterloo sneaks up on me. For Lucy's office, you come out and turn right, but today I'm not headed that way. I am going, instead, to look at London, at this beautiful city that has been my home all this time without me noticing.

The sun is out. It is the first sunny day of the year and the south bank of the Thames is basking in warmth. The promenade is busy with loosely dressed amblers who have nowhere to go. Men and women sit on benches; in front of them, the river is a shimmering feast of blue and gold, a bevy of ferries glide to and fro prettily along its lengths. I want to sit down, too. I hesitate. From the other side of the river, the Houses of Parliament are watching me. Am I entitled, I want to ask. I want to scream at imaginary men on velvet-lined pews. *Am I entitled at least to sit?* But, then, I sit down anyway. What is the worst that can happen?

A few feet away, a couple of uniformed parking attendants head towards the railing – one is African, the other Indian. They look like recent arrivals. How, I wonder, did they make it? In their uniforms, entitled to stroll and sit on benches, on a par with the natives. Why can I not have what they have?

To my left, wide-eyed tourists take flight over London in a giant Ferris wheel. I am overcome by a sudden whim to take a ride on the Eye but it is *thirteen* pounds. I hesitate. I want to be up high. I feel like an addict in need of sky, but thirteen pounds is half a day of scrubbing floors and I need to save. Amal might be coming over, but there is still Anu to think about. She is getting to a marriageable age. Back in Delhi, they will be expecting big things from us and we cannot be mean with our children's futures.

Think of the bigger picture. I am used to chivvying myself along, but it doesn't work today. I don't go on the London Eye and it makes me intensely sad that, even today, after so many years, I cannot bring myself to be frivolous.

By the time I get back, it is five o'clock, too late to cook. Amal's father starts on me immediately. 'Where have you been?' he asks. 'Why aren't you picking up your phone?'

'It didn't ring.' I tell the truth.

'You checked?'

I admit that I have not. I sneak a look at it now. Eight missed calls. I swear I did not hear it.

'We have to be at the airport in one hour,' he says. 'Lucy's been ringing non-stop. And Amal's flight . . .'

Mid-sentence, he stops. His eyes grow soft and he shuffles towards me. The worn, brown fabric of his tericot trousers has bunched up around his belt and his shirt sleeves seem empty. His arms are made of skin. When we first married, he was the strongest man in the village. 'It is a big day for us,' he says.

I nod. I can understand perfectly. He is excited. We will see our twenty-one-year-old son for the first time in fifteen years. He is proud of Amal, who is coming here to shine, but he is also anxious that the room is spick and span. While I have been out, Amal's father has been busy tidying our lives away. Suddenly, I feel him around me. I am being pulled into an embrace. It is awkward; his smell fills my nostrils, my arms are trapped under his, so I cannot reciprocate.

His urgency throws my balance. I feel detached, but I don't have the heart to stop him because he is subsumed in the moment. Finally, he pulls away and I notice that his eyes are moist. 'I'll miss you, Meenakshi,' he says.

That makes me sad. Of all the silver screen actresses, Meenakshi was his favourite; when we started courting he said that he had found his very own Meenakshi. And he was my Dharmendra. That was before London, before he became Amal's father. Today, as I am about to leave for Heathrow, for the first time in the fifteen years we have been here, he has called me Meenakshi, but we are old now.

'I should get ready,' I say and disentangle myself from him.

I head towards the cupboard. I feel his eyes on me as I take off my blue and black striped T-shirt and elastic-waisted jeans. Underneath his gaze, my body feels heavy. The last time he saw me naked I was a lithe twenty-something. I was never a head-turning sort of girl, but I used to be pretty and coquettish in the way of youth.

From the top shelf, I pull out a pale pink chiffon sari. I fasten the petticoat and blouse then wrap the sari expertly around me. He is still watching. I tie my hair into a bun and apply some deep red lipstick. I want to look good today. In fact, it has never been so important as it is today.

'You are beautiful,' he says.

I look at him. I don't know why he is saying these things to me. I wish he would not.

Lucy is already at the airport when we arrive. She trusts me, but understandably she is anxious. Her reputation depends on people like me turning up. She comes at us like a hurricane, as always, relentless in her optimism. I am tired of her today. 'Where have you been?' she asks.

I don't bother to explain; we are late, but still in time. I turn to study the arrivals screen. Flight EK 001 from Dubai is delayed. Flight AI 102 to Delhi is on time. This cannot be happening. Amal's father is still fixed on the screen. I look again, I cannot see words any more – just a mass of flashing lines. Beside me, I see Amal's father's expression evolve from disbelief, to shock, to horror. He turns away from me, not towards me. He cannot face me. He cannot bring himself to console me. How can he? What can he do? I shouldn't blame him; it just so happened that the day the police came knocking he was out working and I warned him not to come back.

He was lucky. But still, I blame him. He was the one who persuaded me to come here. He was the one who convinced me to overstay – *for the sake of our children*. And, with each passing year, as the 'A' grades stacked up, the prizes, the possibilities, I reconciled what I had done with what I had to do. Dreams don't stop at borders. They don't respect passport controls, international agreements or the bureaucratic et cetera by which entitlement to dream is apportioned. Yes, I am guilty of succumbing to our dreams but that is all you can hold me to account for.

Lucy is looking at me now. 'I'm so sorry. We have to go now.'

'Just . . .' I am as bad as Amal's father. I give in to a sob. I am exhausted.

Lucy puts her arm around me. AI 102 is flashing *Final Call*. EK 001 has an estimated time of arrival only twenty minutes away. I cannot miss my flight. Lucy won't let me.

At the check-in desk, a uniformed officer is waiting for me. 'Mrs Trivedi?' He is an Indian. British-born Indian. 'Would you like to come with me?'

'Yes.' Lucy answers for me. I am surprised at just how keen she is to see me off.

The British-born Indian officer has a weary face. He signals for me to follow him. I cast a glance at the screen – it is unchanged. EK 001 is still twenty minutes away. I say goodbye to Lucy. I do not thank her. I already have. Then I turn towards Amal's father. He cannot bring himself to look at me. I do not know when I will see him again. So, I touch him on his arm. He slowly moves his hand and covers mine. We do not say anything for a moment.

'Give my love to Amal,' I say. He nods.

'And Anu . . . my . . .' He struggles with his sentence.

Strangely, the situation is giving me strength. I peel myself away from my husband, from Lucy and from this great country that has been my home, and follow the officer through immigration. As I am escorted, my transit through the airport is seamless. The officer doesn't say much and keeps a safe distance. I wonder if he is embarrassed of me. Maybe it doesn't occur to him that we are from the same place, or that it is just a generation or two that is the difference between his situation and mine.

I arrive at the gate with a few minutes to spare. Despite the apparent rush, the gate is closed and passengers are waiting obediently to board.

Now that the officer has left, I am no different to the others. No one but me knows that I have overstayed, that I will never come back. Through big glass windows I catch sight of the elegant manoeuvrings of large aircraft. AI 102 is pulling up. The screen tells me that EK 001 has landed. Amal is somewhere in this airport. We are standing on the same soil.

You may think it strange that after so many years without seeing my son, I am now distraught about a handful of minutes. I cannot explain it, except to say that I long to hold my son in my arms. I deserve these few minutes.

Ladies and gentlemen. We are now ready to board flight AI 102.

First it is the wealthy travellers, then people who need help, then families, then finally just seat numbers. Mine is right at the front, so I wait. And it is just as well.

There is a glass panel that separates those who are leaving from those who are arriving. It is a handful of centimetres thick, if that. When I see Indians pouring out from the belly of another aircraft I realize that EK 001 has pulled up alongside us.

Would all passengers from rows K to rows W, please come forward for boarding.

I no longer know or care what row I am in. I am standing at the panel. My heart is thumping. All I want is a glimpse. Just one glimpse. Is that okay? Am I entitled to a glimpse of my son?

Would all passengers from rows . . .

And then I see him. He is taller than he was in the graduation photo. He has wavy hair like his father and a confident stride. I want to run towards him and say 'I am your mother', but this glass panel is between us. I am staring at him. He has seen me. I gesticulate. I point to my chest, then to him. I think he understands. I think he is walking towards me. I cannot breathe because he is so bright. But now . . . before he has made it to the glass he is moving away. There is confusion on his face. He doesn't understand. I am inventing this connection. There is no connection – why would there be? The last time we were together was in 1990, Delhi Airport, when Meenakshi and Dharmendra were leaving for London. I am a heavy-set old woman now. I am behind a glass screen. This is not how a son expects to see his mother. It is not his fault that he does not know me.

'Madam . . . you have to board the plane now.'

It is one of the airport staff. They have come to take me away. Amal is receding into the throng of new arrivals. I am going.

'Yes, take me,' I say. 'I am tired.'

HARPREET SINGH SOORAE

Bubbly Kaur

Bubbly Kaur panicked a lot and this time it was deep. I usually cringed when I saw people's names in my inbox, but I always smiled when Bubbly bubbled up.

What would have happened if I had been born an elephant?

This was the kind of thing that preoccupied Bubbly.

She was worried.

It was our fate to have been born geniuses in an age of mediocrity, in a provincial town of indolence and contempt.

Birmingham; city of a thousand artisans, cradle of the industrial revolution, second city of Albion, birthplace and strangler of Bubbly Kaur and me.

I met her outside the coffee shop on Grove Lane.

– You're wondering why I'm wearing a pink T-shirt? she said. I'm wearing a pink T-shirt to make people think I am in a light, pinky mood. But ever since this thought assaulted me I have had no peace. Me as an elephant. What would have happened?

Our connection was the join of kindred, frustrated spirits. We had resolved that our magnitude would defeat this city and the petty ruses it employed to grind us into two point four children and pavements lined with saloon cars. For us there would be no Indian petit bourgeoisie; no Edgbaston or Handsworth Wood; no philistine Sutton Coldfield; no abandonment of striving for higher meaning and life.

– Bubbly, I told her. You usually worry about unimportant things. But this one is important. If you were born an elephant I would keep you in my back garden and stand naked before you every morning.

– Oooh. That's nice.

People walked past in blue and blurry clothes. The man from the Vietnamese grocery waved at me. I continued.

– Yes. Then I would fill up a paddling pool with warm water so you could sup it up and spray me with your trunk and I would take a shower underneath. Every morning. You could shampoo my hair as well, before showering me.

A vision before her eyes.

– I could reach up and tap on your bedroom window with my trunk whenever I needed something, too.

– That could be done.

But she still seemed in a crisis.

– What about my mum and dad and brothers and cousins? Would I ever have known them? I can't imagine life without them.

– Maybe they would be elephants, too.

But this did not placate her.

We decided to seek inspiration at Dudley Zoo. Soon we would be leaving each other to attend university: Bubbly at Oxford, me at Wolverhampton. My genius failed me at the last minute, during exams, when I had a nervous episode. Nevertheless, true genius adapts to circumstances, and Einstein did not even finish his degree. From Wolverhampton I planned to launch a thousand enlightenments and revolutions of the mind.

Into the Black Country on the bus we strove, like Marlow chugging up the Congo, into the starkness of Sandwell, to the lard of Dudley. Bubbly had recently attended an exhibition of contemporary Hungarian art at the Walsall Gallery. I sneaked in after her and was ejected for fighting with an obnoxious lunatic who had accosted some innocent pensioners in front of me. It turned out that the man was Laszlo Strobl von Liptoujuar, the world renowned Magyar abstract performance artist, and I had ruined his interpretation of Samuel Beckett's *Catastrophe et autres dramaticules*.

I later complained to the *Birmingham Evening Mail* that I was making a creative statement about the spiritual crisis of Walsall, its regeneration from an industrial hub into an outlying province of the service revolution, a protest against the neglect of Birmingham's younger brothers. But to no avail. Only Bubbly loved me for my act of genius and protest. Only she could see past the black eye the mad Magyar had inflicted.

Soon we arrived at the zoo. We found the elephant enclosure and stood watching them being scrubbed and attended to. They seemed to be smiling.

– It would have been a strange thing if I had been an elephant, Bubbly said. But maybe I would have done panic and thought to myself in elephant paaaarp: 'But what if I had been born a human?' And that would seem so incomprehensible.

– Bubbly, you're right. Good point. Those elephants are happy, and so are we. They cannot imagine the absence of their universe and its constellations any more than we can. One day we will be nothing, though, everything shall be absent, all those we love, but until then, you are Bubbly wearing a pink T-shirt.

She pondered my words and mumbled 'the absence of my universe'. I thought about her naked nipples.

The zoo keeper shovelled elephant shit. A trunk curled and seemed to wave to us. Bubbly rested her head on my shoulder.

– But what if I was born a monkey, instead? she said.

I sighed and talked philosophically about how everybody on Earth at some point in their life fantasises about having a pet monkey who would do everything for them: change the TV channel, wash dishes, iron clothes, cook dinner, scratch their back, clean the windows, eat surplus bananas.

– We would always be slaves. Monkey or man, we are destined to work.

We adjourned in a mood of futile melancholy to the cafeteria. I had begun sneezing at the smell of shit and straw. Terrifying brats scampered around the tables clutching plastic animal souvenirs. Bubbly placed her books on the table. Tomes on quantum theory and the works of Seneca. I tried to hide my copy of *Bhangra Superstars* magazine from her. But to no avail!

She considered me and sighed in disappointment. I was ashamed, but claimed research, and the need for Punjabi geniuses to keep in touch with the common culture of those we arose from. Bubbly spoke again. I wanted to caress her naked body. She slapped my face. I had carelessly spoken my thoughts. I told her this was an attempt to stay in touch with my base instincts. She conceded the validity of this, in theory.

– As those elephants conceptualize the latest existential crisis I have experienced, they also represent a scheme for the ascent of you and me, she said. Just as the ancestor of the modern-day elephant which resides at Dudley Zoo evolved from the mammoth and mastodon, so do we, the offspring of the children of migrants, also evolve from the primordial swamp of Indian life in the second city. Our grandparents worked with their hands in factories and sweatshops sewing clothes. Our parents worked in less demanding roles, achieving a degree of education and working in offices, carrying out chores involving basic mathematical and literary skills. Already we have evolved from hands to head in the space of one generation. But for you and me, for us, it is our destiny to blow open our skull caps and litter the world with our genius and ideas. Otherwise the whole endeavour shall have been meaningless, our existences would have been banal, our lives as Punjabis in England forgotten. We are peripheral, ignored, marginal, invisible. We must act to raise our voice or we shall be annihilated and forgotten. We must venture out into that unknown world to make ourselves. Do you not agree?

I nodded my head slowly and looked sage. Bubbly turned to the side and said:

– I need a chocolate éclair. Buy it for me, please.

We consumed chocolate éclairs. Soon she would be in Oxford mixing with Rhodes scholars. Soon I would be in Wolverhampton University law school mixing Skol with beans on toast. Could our destinies be so different? What was the meaning of this cleavage between us? What was the meaning of cleavage in and of itself? That luscious valley of promise and bounce. I was overridden with the erotic urge.

So I turned to Bubbly and held her in my arms. I told her that it would be our destiny to escape from the clutches of our small parochial families and flee into a world of art, literature, love, science, passion, debate, away from the tired salons of Punjabi life in Birmingham. She became as excited as I was, and spoke of the eager, eternal aspiring spires of Oxford, and I dreamed of nothing, but I told her that Wolverhampton would be the midwife to my revelations to humanity.

We caught the bus back home, riding beside the plebeians, and I held Bubbly's hand. She allowed me to do this occasionally as an experiment. When our palms mated I dashed the evolution of our genius to hell. The evolutionary stage of handicraft was a step that was grasping life with physicality, it was a stage when work was created by the body and was tactile, gruff, solid and real, rather than the abstract theorizing that we sought. Such electrical liveliness sparked inside my soul, merely by having a part of my body contained by her. I imagined her containing other parts of me. She slapped me again because I had spoken out loud my thoughts once more. Some plebeians ahead of us laughed at me. I expect with my Magyar-inflicted bruising I looked either comical or tough to them.

How we were hated by all others for our pomposity and genius! But to an ant a butterfly looks pompous for her colours and ambition.

We walked along Soho Road, and cunningly avoided being beaten up by working-class Indian youths envious of our genius.

– Watch out for those proletarian Sikhs, Bubbly said. They are enraged because we are bourgeois Sikhs.

– They just can't handle the fact that we are bourgeois Sikhs and they are still proletarian Sikhs, I assured her. Don't worry, if we are accosted, I have a few cutting epithets about their peasant manner and lack of aspiration prepared.

But I had no call to use them. Soon we reached the streets which would presently be lit with lamps as the summer day faded into a blue night. I kissed her and said:

– What will become of us, Bubbly?

She pushed back her shoulders.

– Well, I imagine we shall grow old and die. Along the way I will become known as the Sikh Spinoza. Perhaps we will experience joy; most probably we will shrivel and cringe as all living things do. But our fate is to sprinkle secretions of genius around those we meet.

– Indeed. I grunted.

– Yes, she assented.

– Yes indeed, I reflected.

– In deed and in action we shall sail forth beyond the known horizons, she exhorted.

– We shall paddle there if we have to, I added.

– Yes, she asserted. We shall theorize new dimensions, elaborate new art, calculate new mathematics.

I wondered, Could that really be? Could we will ourselves out of the universe we were contained in, change the lines on our palms, alter the time allotted to us and the course God's proxies had given us? I thought of something profound to ask her.

– Bubbly, if you could go back in time in a time machine where would you go back to and what would you change?

She hitched her thumbs in her belt and stuck out one hip. How I wanted to caress and squeeze and ferment her. She pushed her glasses up her nose and said:

– I would change the composition of the jury that sat in judgement on Socrates in 339 BC, to ensure his acquittal and further enquiry. What would you change?

I wanted to tell her that I loved her and before killing Hitler at birth I would have changed my exam papers so I could have passed and gained a place at Oxford where we could explode our skulls and be geniuses together, but I shivered and all I could say was:

– I think I would go back to last week and change my socks. I've been wearing the same ones for a week.

But she was not even listening. At the corner of the street, Tramp Master was watching us. We walked towards him. Above us the sky was transmuting into a blanket for the world. We looked at the phone box that he had called home for so long. It had been severely vandalized and had a notice of removal on its side. Bubbly cleared her throat and spoke.

– Sir, what is the meaning of this?

Tramp Master smiled and said:

– Smashed up public telephone boxes are a sign of mental disturbance.

Sad pianos seemed to play in the silent swirl between us. Tramp Master shook his head philosophically. I asked where he would sleep now that his booth was being dismantled.

– Only one evening remains, he said. This is technological Darwinism. The mobile telephone means the extinction of the public payphone species. Soon all that will remain is the cracks in the pavement where they used to stand.

– So where will you go? I replied.

– Oh, don't worry about me. I, too, will be extinct soon. I feel my time is coming.

I was scared and almost offered him my sofa for a few nights. But I would get battered by my parents for bringing the Tramp Master home. I knew we would miss his wisdom. There was never that faint urinary tang or red-faced confusion around him that most tramps held. He laughed at me.

– I would not sleep in your house. You think you're happy because you have a home? Let me tell you something. It took the Buddha years to get to the point of enlightenment underneath the banyan tree. I have become enlightened in this phone booth. It sheltered me and taught me the truth. When you look at nature you think it is beautiful and consider flowers to be things of sublime beauty. But, in truth, they are pustulant, erupting sores. Nature is a flux of life and death, creation and destruction; there is such ugliness and turmoil in what you think is beauty.

Once again he left me astonished and my tongue paralysed. Bubbly was speechless, too, but tried to hide it by looking at him with suspicion. He picked his nose.

– So the destruction of this phone booth and the extinction of public payphones is a technological equivalent of this flux of life and death, of uprising and destruction? I asked.

He pondered, collected his can of Special Brew and rubbed his beard.

– Yes. In a way, this is the truth. When we accept this we can accept the violence as part of a cycle we are all subjects of.

– Then smashed up phone boxes may not be a sign of mental disturbance, Bubbly said, rather a manifestation of the universe's logic?

He looked at her and smiled.

– We have spoken enough for today. We shall meet at some point
in the future. I must find a new shelter from tomorrow. Allow me to
sleep for the final time here.

We took our leave of him and I kissed Bubbly on the cheek. She
kissed me, too, and said that it had been a most enjoyable day of
leisure anointed with some agreeable philosophical speculation.

As I lay in bed I imagined Bubbly naked in front of me lecturing about
semiotics or Sanskrit. I chastised myself for sullying my conception
of her in such base terms, and then went back to thinking of her
naked and writing equations on a blackboard.

I really was a genius. Outside, Wolverhampton awaited me. If
only I had not passed out in my exams I might have got the grades
I needed. But such is life, and not a year can ever be wasted, lest the
worms and maggots find warmth in your soul.

The world was more mysterious than God had intended to make
it. Of that I felt sure. We are the core of our own universe, all else
revolves round our souls. But in reality we are all provinces of some
capital city, in which life ascends, and which we are unaware of.
To escape to life and find the centre, that was our task. Bubbly
was holding the reins of the carriage that would take us forth into
understanding and escape.

I could not stop thinking of the time last week when she had listened
to my pleading and pulled down her blue jeans from the back just a
little so I could see the top of her panties. This was the mystery and
forest, deep in that ruffle and lovely skin, musk and silk. I telephoned
Bubbly and we discussed how we would be joint winners of the Nobel
Prize for literature. I allowed her to win the prize for physics. We
wished there was a Nobel Prize for lying in bed and day-dreaming. I
knew we would be all right eventually. But after she fell asleep I could
not rest and I dialled the number for Tramp Master's phone booth.
There was no reply. I imagined bloody flowers erupting in silence.

*

So I think of her cleavage and feel at peace. Her twirling spirit will always be my refuge. We will wake tomorrow and eat cornflakes for our souls, and ponder again how our paths of confusion might become paths of glory.

RESHMA RUIA

Another Life

Twenty-eight years ago, I stopped in Manchester en route to America. It was to see Gupta, an old school friend of mine. He was in the second year of his accountancy degree.

'Manchester's small and cosy. It'll be easy for smart guys like you to make money here. Why don't you stay on for a bit?' Gupta said, squeezing my hand. We sat in the bus shelter eating our fish and chips, waiting for the number 215 to Levenshulme, where Gupta rented a one-bed flat. I checked Gupta's face to see if he meant what he said. His eyes looked lonely. I stared at the sky grey with rain. I stared at the dull huddle of buildings. I said to myself, He's right. It'll be easy to shine in a place as gloomy as this.

'I think I'll stay on for a bit!' I slapped his back and said I'd get a job, make some quick money and then carry on to America. I'd feel happier with some English pounds in my pocket.

We were like brothers, Gupta and I those days, sharing rooms, whining about the cold and the thin English girls with their bony thighs, who giggled at our accents but let us squeeze their breasts in the cinema halls.

I turned fifty-five last year.

'So, when's the celebration, PK?' Gupta asked when I met him for a drink after work. 'Fifty-five's a big number. You're getting on, old man,' he said as he drank his orange juice.

'It's only a number,' I replied, staring at his grey lips sucking in the juice through the straw. 'There are things I'd still like to do.'

'Like what? Don't tell me you're still banging on about America. You've been dreaming about it long enough,' he said, sneering. I pushed the bowl of peanuts towards him, shrugged and looked around.

It was late afternoon and the Victoria wasn't busy. A young man in a black biker jacket stood fiddling with the shiny knobs of the fruit machine by the door, while the woman behind the bar chewed gum and polished beer glasses. Her eyes were far away. There was music playing, but it was new stuff that I didn't recognize.

'Cheers.' I finished my beer and got up to buy another. When I came back, Gupta was still waiting for an answer. He was an accountant; he liked to get to the bottom of things.

'Maybe Geeta's throwing a surprise party for you or what?' he said, his face suddenly eager. I got the feeling he'd not been out much lately. He was careful with his pennies.

'Fat chance,' I said, lighting a cigarette. 'I'll be lucky if she remembers. Anyway, what's the big deal? It's only a number, and you could always throw a dinner, I'm your oldest friend, after all.'

Gupta waved away my suggestion, saying he had enough bills of his own to start adding more.

'I think you should hire an American car, an Impala or a soft top, maybe a Chevrolet and visit Scotland. Get away from the business; get away from your family and Geeta's long face.' Gupta chuckled. He was in a good mood because I'd bought him two rounds of drinks and it was a Thursday, which meant he'd be soon going home to have sex with his wife.

Why did Gupta bring up America? I thought as I drove back home. The rain was falling steadily and thick clouds had eaten up the last of the afternoon sun. A hearse passed me on the left-hand side. I looked at the blurred faces inside the cars that followed; the rain on the windows smudged their faces, streaked down their cheeks like tears. Gupta was right. Manchester was an accident. It was America I'd wanted all along.

'Why do you want to mess with America? It's a godless place. Stay here. Bombay's booming.' Those were Father's words, thirty years back. But my mind had been made up.

'I want to try my luck in America,' I'd said, thinking of the film studios in Hollywood and their hunger for a fresh face and then thinking of my job as shipping clerk with Wadia & Sons. I told Father I was sick of taking three buses each day to work only to push files around. I wanted something better.

'That's the problem with you. Always thinking you're cut out for better things.' He had spat out the words along with the betel nut he was chewing.

Father was nearly sixty by then, an old man, and I was his only child. I understood his bitterness, so I didn't answer back. I let him carry on. Mother would have backed me, told me I was right, but she was dead and gone.

'I'll be back,' I promised Father as we stood in the queue at the State Bank of India. I watched him draw out his savings. Eight thousand rupees for a one-way ticket to New York via Doha and London. It was a lot. Travel didn't come cheap those days.

'You'll get the money back in hundred dollar notes, not these worthless rupees,' I said, carefully slipping the money inside my wallet. He'd nodded then in a way that showed he didn't believe me and didn't expect to see me again.

He watched me fidget with my travel papers and passport. When it was time to leave, he broke a coconut for good luck and pressed a silver coin in my hand.

'At least pretend to be sad,' he said. 'And wipe that stupid grin off your face.'

But I made the mistake of breaking the journey in Manchester, where I met up with Gupta, got caught in the business of making money and Bombay and America turned into nothing more than just names on a map.

When people asked me 'Where are you from?' at trade fairs and meetings, I didn't think twice before answering, 'Manchester, of course.'

*

The following week, instead of going through the unpaid accounts at the warehouse, I celebrated turning fifty-five by buying a personal number plate for my car: PK 1. I attended an auction in Stockport, where I outbid a Mr Paul Kennedy by five thousand quid. A month later, I told Geeta about the number plate; didn't mention the cost, just said it was a bargain, a deal I'd picked up from a grateful customer in Ireland whose back I'd covered when the stocks were low.

'That's so sweet of him,' she said, but didn't want to know more. Her hands were dipped inside a big glass bowl full of flour.

'What are you doing?' I asked, hoping she'd want to go outside and look at the car with its new number plates.

'Baking bread.' She looked at me, waiting for a comment.

'What's wrong with Warburton's?' I didn't have much confidence in Geeta's cooking.

'Sammy wanted to try home-made bread. He said that his class teacher was going on about the wonderful smell of home-baked bread.' She scratched her nose and the flour settled like chalk dust on her nose and her chin, making her look like an Indian snow-woman.

'Good luck, just make sure you don't burn the kitchen down,' I replied before going out to stand on the drive admiring my shiny new number plate already screwed on to the Mercedes. I had half a mind to knock at Mr Peters from next door and bring him around, but then I remembered he was English. They didn't like being disturbed.

About ten years back, I took out a big mortgage and we shifted from Longsight with its noisy Caribbean neighbours to Timperley, where the streets were quieter and the houses had names like 'Fairholme' and 'Chatsworth'. We finally got English neighbours on both sides, proper ones with English as their mother tongue, and every Christmas I dropped them a bottle of Johnnie Walker. Our house had a small garden where I tried, without much luck, to grow a mango tree.

'Too, too lonely,' that's all Geeta had said, when the woman from Bridgfords first showed us the house.

'What do you mean?' I asked as the agent stood waiting on the front step, hands in her pockets, a tight, polite smile fixed on her lips. I pointed out the electric gates and the garage attached to the house. Geeta still shook her head.

'What more do you want?'

'It's big and I love the gates, but I'll miss . . .' Geeta hesitated before telling me that she'd miss her daily gossip sessions with Mrs Ahmed, our neighbour in Longsight. The two women did their weekly grocery shop together.

'Think of Sammy. There are better schools here. He'll get more attention,' I told her.

Once Sammy's future entered the picture, she said yes straight away.

'Lucky bastard.' Gupta's mouth had hung slack in envy the first time he came around for dinner. 'You've done all right; a house in Timperley and only ten minutes to the motorway. But, your council tax will be higher, band G or maybe even H.' He'd enjoyed telling me that.

In the early days, Mrs Ahmed, the old neighbour, would call by and Geeta, proudly flinging open the doors, would show her the en suite and the Italian leather sofa set from Arighi Bianchi, eyes brimming with pride. But then one day, her visits stopped.

'People are too busy these days,' Geeta said, her lips shrinking into a thin, trembling line.

The invite from Coopers arrived soon after I'd bought my number plate.

I read it out to Geeta: *'Ben Lawton requests the pleasure of your company at a golfing weekend at Mowbray Hall on . . .'*

Geeta was surprised. 'Why have they invited you? Don't they know you don't play golf?'

'Why shouldn't they invite me?' I was quick to hit back. 'They've done my accounts for almost five years now, high time I was shown some recognition, some respect.'

'But, it's all a bit last minute,' she said, looking at the stiff, cream-coloured invite. 'Next weekend, what do they think, you're just sitting around, doing nothing?'

It was a Friday and I was in no hurry to leave for work. We were finishing breakfast and Geeta, dressed in her usual uniform of blue velour tracksuit, was slicing an apple, head bent low and mouth open in concentration. Breadcrumbs clung to her top.

'Don't cut any for me,' I told her. The only fruit I like are mangoes.

'Mangoes are late this year because of the drought in Gujarat. Ravi's won't get them until next month,' Geeta said without looking up. Ravi Food Store in Rusholme was where Geeta did her weekly Indian shop on her way back from the temple.

'These are for Sammy,' she said, arranging the white skinless slices of apple neatly in a semicircle on the plate.

'How come he's not left for school?' I looked at the cuckoo clock above the sideboard. The hour and minute hands disappeared long ago, maybe in the house move, and now we relied on the bird coming out and chirping the time.

'He's in bed because he's not feeling well,' Geeta replied as she got up to fill the kettle. 'He says he's got a headache, so I told him to take the day off.'

'This is the second time this week he's done that. Skiving school, with his GCSE's just around the corner. Do you know how much fees I pay each term?' I said in a low voice, but loud enough so she could hear my disappointment above the hissing kettle.

I stuck the invite on the fridge door, behind the Eiffel Tower magnet, a freebie I'd got from a trade fair.

'So, will you go?' Geeta asked, ignoring my comment about Sammy. She buttered another piece of toast and pushed the plate towards me.

'I might as well. But I'll need a new suit,' I said, helping myself to the toast. 'The one from Debenhams is looking a bit shabby.'

'What's the point, wasting money on a new suit? Get your brown one dry-cleaned and we'll wait for the January sales to buy a new one,' Geeta said. She'd always valued practicality above beauty. It was not her fault. It was the world she came from, a world I recognized less and less each day.

As she bent down to open the sideboard in which she stored her Indian snacks, her hips flared out in her too-tight tracksuit bottoms. She pulled out a Tupperware, grabbed a fistful of salted cashew nuts and shoved them in her mouth. The salt left a faint white dusting on her lips.

My reflection stared back at me from the kitchen window on the opposite wall. Instinctively I sucked in my stomach and ran a quick hand through my hair. My jawline was still firm and I had a full head of hair. It was turning silver, but I was in good shape for a fifty-five-year-old. I still did my press-ups before going to bed each night. Unlike me, Geeta was giving up on herself, allowing the careless pounds to wrap around her five-foot frame, year after year.

The golf invitation remained stuck on the fridge. I felt its promise each time I entered the kitchen. Geeta casually referred to it in her conversations with her sisters in Bombay. She called them dutifully, every Sunday at 6 p.m. Indian standard time.

'Yes, the business is doing well. PK's so busy with all the orders . . . not so cold in Manchester now and he's been invited to an exclusive dinner at Mowbray Hall. Yes, just like Buckingham Hall with the Queen and all.' Her cheerful voice travelled down the telephone line into her sisters' waiting ears.

The way she said it, you'd think Mowbray was a household name in Bombay, like Michael Jackson or Muhammad Ali.

But I liked the little white lies Geeta fed her family about the business doing well. Only I knew better as I drove up to my warehouse in Grotton, week after week.

The day before the golf do, I nipped into Kendalls on Deansgate and bought myself a new Italian suit with a crimson silk lining. Back at work, I rang Ben, my contact at Coopers.

'Just received your golfing invite. It must have got delayed in the post.'

'Glad you can make it, PK,' he said, assuming I'd say yes anyway. 'I'll be there myself. You do play golf, don't you?'

'Haven't played for some time,' I said carefully, looking up to make sure Margaret hadn't heard me, but she was busy photocopying. I'd moved the stationery cupboard and the photocopier to my room on her advice. It was to stop the girls pilfering little things, staplers and printing papers. Costs that soon added up.

'You'll be fine, PK,' Ben assured me. 'I've got some useful people coming up for the weekend.'

'Useful?' Ben did my accounts. He knew the score.

He lowered his voice as he told me there were bankers coming. They'd be useful for tapping into loans for the Italian cutting machines I wanted for the hemming floor.

'You'll never guess who else is coming.'

'The Queen?' I joked, but I had a dull feeling in the pit of my stomach as I said this; bankers meant figures, which meant doing sums, showing how my annual profits were quietly tumbling down, year after year.

'Cedric Solomon may also come, schedule permitting.' Ben's voice was reverential.

'Really? How did you manage to rope him in?' I sat up straight and repeated the name so Margaret could hear me. She was standing by my chair, holding some invoices for me to sign.

'We were at school together. He's doing it as a favour really. You know how busy these guys get.' There was a pause. 'His wife's coming too. A real stunner, she is. You'll like her.' Again those hushed, cathedral tones. Ben could have been talking about God.

'Count me in, Ben,' I said and put the phone down. My mood had lifted.

'Margaret, Cedric's coming to the golf do.'

'That's good news, I suppose,' she said in a guarded voice that gave away nothing. 'We're trying to get into the catalogue market. You could have a word with him about investing in it,' she said, as she pulled out a hanky from her sweater sleeve and blew her nose. She was constantly either coming out of a cold or going down with it. She blamed the damp walls of the warehouse.

'You think so? A big man like him, would he be interested?' I lit my first cigarette of the day and considered the possibility. 'No harm in trying, I suppose.'

Hope was like a bird flapping happily inside me. Margaret was right. Solomon was a shrewd investor; he might want to take a chance on me.

I could have been another Cedric Solomon, I thought, as I watched the girls leave the office promptly at five. I'd worked in fashion long enough, not the glossy French sort one saw in magazines, but the cheap, cut-price variety, specializing in rip-offs of designer gear. I called it my homage line.

'It's your actor's eye,' Geeta would say. 'That's what makes you so good.' I'd alter a pocket here, a zip there and sell it wholesale to the discount chains. I'd become a hit right away, something to do with timing and women wanting to spend more on clothes. The orders had poured in from as far away as Portugal. I'd posted Father a newspaper cutting with a photograph from the *Grotton Evening News* that said I was 'the new face of immigration in England – an employer bringing jobs to deprived areas, not a scrounger on social benefits'.

'*Don't tempt fate,*' he wrote back in his doctor's illegible scrawl. '*Luck is like a fruit; leave it hanging on the tree too long, it will ripen and rot before your eyes.*'

He was right. At fifty-five, I owned a warehouse the size of two football pitches, but most of it was either shrouded in darkness or crowded with unsold stock. Unopened cartons of batik print dresses, stacked high, almost blocked my office door. I couldn't miss them as I went through the tenders for NHS nurses' uniforms. The August rains had chased away yet another summer and I was stuck with two container loads of unsold flimsy frocks with their sunshine prints. Looking at them made me want to pick up some scissors and slash through those dresses then run home to bed and pull the duvet tight, right over my head.

'*Don't fool yourself things will ever get better. They just tick-tock along, until one day you wake up and boom, the whole thing explodes in your face.*'

That was Father's last letter to me just before he died. I wanted to tear it up, but Geeta told me to keep it. 'The dead are always watching us,' she warned, her voice small and fearful.

Now I took it out from the drawer and read it again. I had written to Father the day we lost our biggest account. A ten-year partnership that came to an end in a short, sharp fax from the head buyer: 'We will not be renewing our contract. The management has decided to re-evaluate its cost structure.' I later found out they'd opened an office in Kowloon.

My world was changing fast. The profit margins on my dresses were shrinking and the big clothing chains were going direct to China and

Bangladesh. Cheetham Hill was crowded with others, smarter and younger, snapping at my heels.

'Monghia Textile's no longer the leader of the pack,' I'd told Margaret last year, and she'd shaken her head sympathetically.

'It's the way of the world,' she said. Margaret was from Scotland, where they were used to expecting the worst.

I was tempted to tell Geeta all this, but I'd stop myself when I saw her hoovering the stairs, or running after Sammy with a glass of milk. She had worries of her own. I could read them in the lines that cut her forehead like a knife. One day, Sammy would be grown up and gone. And then there would just be the two of us, and the silence hanging like a thick fog in between.

'Here, give us a hug,' I'd say to Geeta, after another lousy day at work. I'd slip an arm around her waist, my fingers searching for some softness, but no spark lit up between my wandering hand and her sleeping flesh.

Suhayl Saadi

Mosaic

The light that filtered through the painted window barely tempered the darkness. The carafe lay where it had fallen. A trail of dull, red liquid slowly separated into droplets, which resembled the small, Britannic grapes that decanted into a wine for slaves and idiots. The tiles felt like lizard scales through her undergarment and the wall at her back was ice. She tried to breathe. Every time he went to war, she would fulfil her role.

Laura pulled her subucula tight around her and began to sway. She gazed at her manicured toes and became aware of her hand as it fingered the dolphin-shaped brooch fastened over her left breast. Then she gripped her sides, the places where he had touched her. She traced her index finger along the elegant, immutable patterns of the floor mosaic.

The night before the day that now was dying, she had poured the saffron wine into two goblets and had readied the vial, had tilted it, had watched the strange blue substance glide along the glass.

She closed her eyes, pressed her palms to her face, watched the pattern break up.

Marcus. The back of his neck. Always warm when she caressed the skin, as though she held his being in her fingers. She felt him stiffen, then it was gone. He turned, smiled, opened his eyes. Dawn blue.

During the night, he had told her that with each dawn she replenished herself. She was not like the ones who emerged from the forests that shadowed the land beyond the furthest Wall . . .

He had gazed into the distance and whispered the words, '*Fib, Fortriu* . . .' Familiar, frightening words that made her feel naked in a Caledonian wind. But then the feel of his strong fingers moving over her scalp; the memory of a song.

It was morning. She rose from the cubile and walked quickly into the annexe. The mosaic was cooling. Reflected in the bronze mirror, her skin was vellum. Marcus overflowed with *virtus*, *pietas*, *fides*, while she had only her feelings, herself, the love of *luxus*. She would sacrifice; he would rape.

She splashed scented water over her breasts and between her thighs, dried herself and then returned to the cubiculum, where the morning light flattened everything into uniformity. Marcus was awake, stretched out in their marital bed.

She offered him a full washing jug, but he avoided her eyes.

A Primus Pilus, on campaign he existed wholly as flesh, blood and breath. Laura knew this, without need of logic, just as she knew that the water that flowed beneath the mosaic created invisible patterns, which occasionally would rise almost into the plane of her perception.

The smell of freshly baked bread and the cries of its sellers drifted in from the street. The sweepers had already passed by and soon it would be the turn of the soldiers . . .

Marcus stood at the head of the First Cohort, his body shining into the sky. The drums began to boom: one note, repeated over and over in a somnolent rhythm. She was entranced. When he lay with her at the moment of greatest rapture, he would whisper to her in cithara tones, in a voice so like her own imagined voice that she felt as though she were gazing into glass, or into his great bronze shield. She had gazed into the burning metal and had felt the loosening from this life and the undulating tide of war; and, at those moments, Laura wished that she had been born a man.

The breeze caught the edges of his scarlet cloak and the feather-tips on his helmet and it seemed as though the day was merely a reflection of his armour and that he, Marcus, was his words, purring in her ear, enticing, dishonest. 'Soon, I shall return and we shall lie here again,' he had said.

At last, she was compelled to close her eyes and let the tears flow. She felt unclothed as he inclined his helmet's plume towards her at the moment of silence. And the moment drew taut the vines and palms of the city, and she could have remained for ever in that place, huddled among thousands of other women, all of whom had pulled their cloaks up over their heads as they wept with pride.

They had been betrothed in Aquae Sulis, in Britannia Prima, when she was six and he, ten. They received gold rings, each fastened by a knot. The auguries had been favourable. Their fathers had mingled in the same circles and Marcus had drawn her attention often, with his near-black hair cropped in the style of the old Republicans. He had moved like the wild sea in spring.

The night before the wedding, Laura gave all her dolls to the guardian spirits of her father's house and clad herself in a white tunic, double-knotted at the waist, while her hair was coiled by the ornatrix in six locks upon her head. She bathed in amber light as the delicate fabric of the *flammeum* caressed her hair and face. The next morning (after a sleepless night), the contract was signed and the old woman took her right hand and linked her fingers with those of her husband-to-be. '*Ubi tu Marcus, ego Marcella.*' Laura did not eat much at the dinner, which her father had provided, and later, as she was being led in procession to the bridegroom's house, she felt as though, at any moment, she might dissolve into the night.

As was the custom, Laura pretended to hide in her mother's arms, only to be wrenched away and, as the torches flared violently, the smell of burning hawthorn mingled with the hulking presence of the black bull at her back. Voices encircled her – *Talassio! Talassio!* – and the flame itself seemed to dance music of flutes. The bull would be sacrificed, its blood would flow across the mosaics of the night and would soak the cloth of her virginal *tunica recta*; its blood would become her blood.

She felt the touch on her palm of her new home's door-posts and lintel as she smeared them with oil and flowers. Beneath the window-sill, a painted image of the erect *fascinus* held the evil eye at bay. She felt herself lifted like a small bird into the house of a man. The old woman who had first joined their hands together led her to the bridal bed.

The first night, he had been hungry to gaze through the eye which lay in her belly and she had feared, yet, at the same time, longed for, his hunger. And, though the years had moulded them, yet still, on his return from war, she would feel his rapacity as though it were the first time. Initially, she had been surprised; she had expected him to be sated, after all the killing and the whores, but he had become a skilled engineer of sensation so that at times – during the long, cool nights of *primo vere* – their love would become a shining blade and in those few, precious seconds, she felt that she might almost . . .

Soon afterwards, when his legion was posted to Apamea, she had swum naked with him in the Syrian springs as the day burned above them. She had stretched, letting her breasts grow taut, and he had grabbed her and they had joined like porpoises in the sapphire pool.

She carried the tableau of her wedding night in her head, not as a past event but as though it were recurring continually within her. The words they had spoken would be engraved on her tomb. *Where you are Marcus, I will be Marcella*. Every time he went back to war, it was as though he were withdrawing painfully from her body.

She had gone, one evening, to beyond the boundaries of the *colonia* of Eburacum, to a northern hag in a town of the dead, and there, in an airless grotto of yew trees, as night rotted into day, she had learned how to kill with stealth. At last, she would join with him in the unity which could exist only between killer and killed. She would cradle his dead god's head the moment before immersion in pools of magic wine, and his locks would sink between her thighs, where they would be held fast along the lines of her *subucula* and there, at last, she would know that he would never leave her again, would never be able to hold himself up for sacrifice, would not end both their lives in the blood and metal of myth, in the cold, blue forests of Fortriu among the painted mothers and the golden shrines.

She had run her finger around the rim of the glass, felt its cold smoothness, the unity of its structure. She had cut her finger on the glass and some of the poison had run onto her skin. She closed her eyes, forced her panic down, and thrust her hand into a bowl of water, watching as the blue and red had mingled and dissolved into tiny worms. As the surface of the fluid settled, a shape began to emerge. She had felt it rise alongside her, a long blue skin. Efficiently, she separated the wine and mixed the poison into a goblet.

On that last night, they had lain together after the struggle and smiled at each other as the silence filled with the ebb and flow of the black river, which ran beneath the marshes of the Isurium. She had seemed to hear him say:

'You will be left with the emptiness and I shall know this and, yet, we will persist in repeating the pattern, because I, Marcus Lucius Cato, do not wish the future to be borne on the backs of worms.'

And she had seemed to reply:

'But I, too, wish to be free from the shackles of love and death. As Paulina and Seneca were, I am not so different from you, Marcus Lucius. *Ubi tu Marcus, ego Laura.* Why cannot we rise as one above the flesh of our ancestors? Is this too wine-drenched a vision?'

And the Primus Pilus had frowned. Then, after all, he had gone to bathe and the sinews of his legs had been a *cithara* in her head and he had donned *tunica* and *toga* and, finally, sandals and he left her burning beneath the terrible gaze of his absence and, again, she shivered in the bed and clenched the sheets with her thigh muscles and wished she could be entombed, there, in the *cubile*.

All around the city, the courtesans would dance and Laura, too, would slide across the mosaic, and she knew that there would be no offspring for there had been none in ten years with Marcus and so the danger was measured, patrician, ironical and held no taint.

As always, Laura had presided over the preparation of the evening meal. Just the right amounts of pepper, cumin, garlic, thyme, silphium and liquid garum from Cades. They ate stewed crane and, this time, they ate alone.

As he took the goblet from her, their skin touched but she steadied her hand and donned a mask as she had done so often before. Yet her eyes slid to the left as he sniffed the liquor and she knew that she should have worn her sandals, yet still she held herself to the cold slabs of the mosaic and he looked at her again and then, in one smooth, quick movement, he tipped back his face and drank the wine.

Confident, facile, he smiled and removed her *subucula*, ran his long, killer's fingers along the luminescent skin of her breasts, her loins, her thighs. And, in the depths of that night, amid the hush of the city, as they joined together, Laura felt the stars burn into the moon-flower of her back. He sliced her flesh with the blade of his tongue and she bled freely, feeling, for once, untrammelled because at last it seemed that there was nothing between them.

The evening after the legion had departed, Laura lay in bed and watched the day creep away like an illicit lover across the mosaic and, at a certain point, she began to feel weightless. In this state, she sailed out over the rooftops and across the river and she came to the place that had not yet become a field of battle, but which already held the stench of death, and she followed the trail of a long funeral procession in which the people wore the masks of their ancestors and there she saw, lying on a bier, the body of Marcus. His torso was naked, mangled, and his face, alone, was unmasked. The eyes which had brought spring into hers were half-closed and were sunk deep into their cavities. She slipped through the globes and she was in the tissues, in among the clotted, unmoving cells. And, thus, she came to occupy every portion of his being: Marcus the Boy against whose *toga praetexta* her hand had inadvertently brushed; Marcus the Lover; Marcus the Soldier and now, at last, Marcus the Corpse, the entity which, even now, drew her on, out along the cold, Caledonian paths of the forests that lay beyond the Bodotria river and then further through the night, down a steep slope into the pooled blackness where the newly perished would find themselves. She shivered beside the white bodies and felt the pull of the river that flowed behind her and at which she dared not look.

The sound of oar-on-wood gathered form and grew louder until it filled the night. Then, silence. She felt the body that she was in turn on its axis and saw that, like an army of dolls, all the corpses were doing the same. She opened her eyes – until then, she had not realized they had been closed – and she knew the face into which she was staring . . .

She drifted, lazily, towards the light from a burning torch.

A movement, too fast for her to catch, along the windowsill.

The day had gone and she found that she was able to make the stars appear and vanish at will. The dream of the forest and the river was familiar, repetitive. Then she woke up a second time and, lying next to her, she felt the shape of emptiness. She would much rather have lain there, right through another night or, perhaps, for ever.

By now, he would be far away on some darkening northern road. The crowds long since fallen away, amid fields of kale his chariot would slow, his cloak pulled around his chest and the legion whore, some barely tamed, big-hipped Taexali Pict, would be waiting for him in a murky *popina* along the way.

But Laura did get up, as she always had, even though, in the act of waking, washing, rising, she knew that she was fastening her own life's myth.

In the distance – from which direction she was not sure – she heard the sound of a man scattering beans to the evil spirits. She was unable to recall whether this day was one of those when the gates of Hades opened and the Good People came rushing out to torment the living.

As she applied the white lead paste to her skin, Laura noticed the empty vial. Only it wasn't quite empty. She picked it up and rolled it between her thumb and her forefinger and she felt the glass burn against the place where she had cut herself, the day before. It seemed no different from the scores of other vials, which contained the various components of her makeup. Even as he marched, ever northwards, through the mountains and the ice, even as he mounted the stinking whore, even as he slit the throat of his enemy, he was diffusing through the blue of its substance. The concentration had been insufficient to kill, but had been enough to end the singularity upon which independent existence was contingent. Laura now knew that the only way she might become one with the essence of Marcus would be if she, too, allowed herself to flow, without structure, through the poison, through the unnamed tracts of land beyond the Wall. He would never escape her again.

She put on a clean *subucula* and poured herself a *modicum* and then, carefully, she let the potion drip into the wine. Her hands were shaking and she found it strange that she had been able to steady them, before. The blue poison had become concentrated at the bottom of the vial and she knew that this dose would be more powerful, perhaps infinitely so.

The stars were reaching their apogee, and she could see herself, half-reflected in the glass of the goblet. Her face seemed elongated, skeletal. Then she remembered. It was the face in the dream. She had entered his corpse and had spread herself through the tissues which had formed him and now, once again, she was about to dissolve into the blue of his eyes.

She shut out the image and drank, quickly. The wine tasted bitter; it took all her strength not to spit it out. She laid the goblet down, but at the last moment, her hand trembled, causing it to overbalance. Laura felt unable to stop both goblet and carafe from falling sideways off the table and smashing onto the floor. They made a hollow, distant sound. Shards of glass fragmented the picture of the mosaic, like light scattered across the face of the world.

Carefully, Laura stepped away from the window and sat on the floor. The cold began at the root of her buttocks and crept steadily upwards. The fire had gone out. She could feel the spaces between the tiles, and the lines formed by the spaces. In the sky beyond the window, groups of stars seemed to rise and spin, and then to shrink and become still, and then the cycle was repeated with another cluster and, in this way, Laura watched the *pantomimus* of the night and she felt herself grow light and tremble, and then dance in tandem with the stars. Tiny red trails emerged from the globules of wine and crept like fingers across the mosaic. She felt the fingers caress and move through her body, as she had moved through that of the dead Marcus and she knew that it would be his last campaign and that their world was soon to end, but that now she held him within herself, for ever, just as the stars were held, dancing, in the mantle of the sky.

DIMMI KHAN

My Faithless Lover

S ami had a date with a drag queen.
It was all he could find on the internet.

Heat clawed at his legs from his black leather pants (a mistake), the zip on his T-shirt was pulled down exposing his chest hair. He was wearing guy-liner and a smile, swaying to the music, B-grade Asian tunes for the early part of the night.

Club Noorjehan was in full flow on top of a working-class faggot pub: the trannies and the bis and the lesbians and the gays and the uncertains and the fag hags and the fag bangles and the drug pushers and the musicians. Everyone knew you got big in the Asian music world if the gays loved your toons first.

Sami nodded at the regulars. They never exchanged names in Club Noorjehan, just body fluids, tragic stories of the closeted Asian, fashion tips, movie updates, gossip. When you left this place you didn't remember who you'd seen. They never remembered you either.

Music morphed between Bollywood, Bhangra, R&B and Lollywood. *Turn me on, turn me on.* Rocky gyrated against strangers, letting straight girls touch his chest, keeping gay boys at a respectable distance.

He was here to dance, not chance.

Sweat sluiced down his neck, so he went to the gents to wash his face, the cold water refreshing, as groups of people stood around.

Checking others out, being checked out.

When the buffet arrived at midnight, a tranny put on a show for everyone. Dressed in a lengha, he/she performed 'Kithan Guzari Raat Ve' – asking 'Where did you spend last night?' – from the movie *Dulari*. The crowd went crazy, throwing monopoly money at the hijra.

'Milne ki arzu thi hamein, ab woh bhi poora ho gayi,' said the hijra. *I had a desire we should meet, and now that has been fulfilled.*

'Thanks, Chandramukhi,' said Sami.

'Chandramukhi loves without the hope of being loved in return. You know me now, so don't be a stranger . . .'

'Sweet. So what's your real name? Chandramukhi is from *Devdas*, right? The prostitute with a heart? And only one Paro?' Sami said.

'Chee. Uss kuttee ka naam mat lo.' *Yuck. Don't mention that ungrateful bitch.*

'Bit defeatist, though? Chandramukhi, self-sacrificing lover and all that?'

'Ask the flame why a million moths happily die for him; even he won't be able to say . . .'

'I don't know what those who decide about sin and virtue have destined for you, Chandramukhi, but if we should meet in the hereafter I know I won't be able to deny you,' Sami said, quoting Devdas's parting line to Chandramukhi.

Chandramukhi feigned coyness.

Sami became aware of the attention they were attracting. Him – with this she-man dressed in a green outfit straight from the movie, wearing a load of fake courtesan jewellery.

'So, go on. What is your real name? I'm not a stranger now, remember?'

'By heart my name is Chandramukhi . . . but by body I am Akshay Kapoor . . .'

They danced to a few songs, then Chandramukhi disappeared into the throng.

Sami continued pressing his body against unknown entities, a solitary glitterball casting a sinful glimmer over them all.

*

The guy winked and Rocky smiled.

'Nice dimples,' the man said. He didn't look gay. He didn't sound gay either. 'Has anyone ever told you that you look stunning? Like Shahid Kapoor.'

'The Bollywood actor? Oh yeah, I get that all the time,' drolled Sami.

'What's your name?'

'Sami. You?'

'Rocky.'

'Hey, Rocky, nice to meet you.'

The music kicked in again and they danced for a while. Rocky had moves, manly moves; he kept trying to subdue Sami, grabbing his arse and singing in his ear. By minute seven Sami gave up.

One of them had to bottom.

They went to smoke outside, Canal Street revellers shrieking around them. They found an empty table and sat down.

'What do you do?' Rocky asked.

'Web design,' said Sami. 'You?'

'Business.'

'Let me guess, you run your dad's newsagent's? Or grocer's? Or clothes shop?'

'Joker . . . nope, travel agent.'

'That was next on my list.'

'IT is hardly a non-Asian profession, is it?'

'You know there are billions of us in the world. Who's to say what constitutes an Asian profession any more? We do every profession from toilet-cleaner to astronaut.'

'I see you have a brain, as well as beauty. Nice.' Rocky blew smoke towards him.

'Thanks. You're not so bad yourself.'

This wasn't a lie. Rocky had fair skin, hazel eyes, thick, jet black hair flopping into his eyes, preppy style.

'You come here a lot? I haven't seen you before,' said Sami.

'I get around. I've seen *you* before.'

'Are you stalking me then?' Sami said.

'Joker . . . you wish.'

'Nice view,' Sami said, looking down the packed street.

'The best view is the one I have right now. Of you.'

Sami took him home to his Deansgate flat, a detached building that stood looking out at the locks.

'This is like Chandramukhi's brothel,' said Rocky. 'I saw you with Akshay at the club.'

'You know Chandramukhi?'

'Everyone knows Chandramukhi. He's been in love with me for months.'

Sami pouted.

'Don't be a fag, stalker-type, love; it's not reciprocated,' Rocky said, laughing.

In the morning Sami found a scribbled note and a gold chain on the empty pillow: 'Dil maang liya, magar jaan bhi aapki' it read. *You asked for my heart, but my life is also yours.*

Sami put on the chain, stayed in bed and smelled Rocky on his sheets all day.

Sami didn't mind his satellite status when he had a boyfriend to hide.

Maybe he was counting fifteen from two sevens, or making *One2Ka4*. One-night stands didn't transform into dreams-come-true, but Rocky had ticked every box on his internal perfect partner card.

Good-looking, own business, romantic. Great shag. A second date beckoned.

The bar was dark, with pink mood lighting, and empty because it was a Thursday. It reminded Sami of the bar from *Buffy the Vampire Slayer*.

Rocky was running late. They had arranged to meet by phone while Sami was wandering around Selfridges, imagining what it would be like to be the boyfriend of a rich businessman who lived in Hale Barns.

Chandramukhi, the drag queen, aka Akshay, had texted.

CHANDRAMUKHI TEXT: Rasiya Bada Beimaan.

'Rasiya bada beimaan?' Sami muttered.

It was a line from *Devdas*. *My lover is faithless.*

Lover? Sami thought that was pushing it. He barely knew Chandramukhi/Akshay. A hairy man in a sari was not lover material in Sami's eyes. Not like the gorgeous Rocky. Maybe the freak was jealous?

And faithless? Sami had hardly cheated on him.

SAMI TEXT: What can I say? Devdas is drunk on someone else now.

Sami felt a thrill at the notion that somewhere in the secretive world of gay Asians he was a topic of garam – that he was hot gossip; that people had already found out about them. *Them* being the word du jour. How fabulous. How camp.

Rocky turned up looking like a model. Casual glamour, jeans ripped at the knees, biker jacket. His hair flopped into his eyes and shone as if it had been polished. There was a diamond stud in his left ear.

'Like your bling,' Sami said.

'Joker . . . you look pretty smart yourself,' Rocky said.

'Well, I didn't know what we were doing so I dressed for everything. Trousers and a shirt. Black. Can't go wrong.'

'You ever wear any other colours?' Rocky asked.

'I'm wearing red kaccha *underpants*.'

'Nice. Maybe you can show me later.'

'We'll see. Get me a Coke.'

'A what? Cock?'

'Naughty boy,' said Sami.

'Am I allowed alcohol?' Rocky asked.

'I don't own you. Sure. Whatever you want.'

'Will you kiss me later if I drink alcohol?' Rocky asked, licking the corner of his mouth as he spoke.

'Who says I'll be kissing you at all?'

'Joker . . . I have a feeling.'

'Let's see,' said Sami.

'We will. I'll get a vodka and Coke. And for you, just cock. I mean Coke.'

'Shameless,' said Sami.

'Do you smoke?'

'No.'

163

'Do you mind if I do?'

'I don't own you . . .' Sami began.

Rocky paid for drinks, dinner and a night in the Lowry.

Sami felt like a queen.

The film had ended, the were lights off, Rocky was lying naked next to Sami.

Sami watched the platinum eternity ring Rocky had given him dance in the muted light.

'How many boyfriends have you had? Actual boyfriends. Not just shags.'

'Does it matter?'

'I'm curious,' said Sami.

'Seven. Maybe eight.'

'What? As in actual boyfriends? Men you lived with?'

'Lived with, no; that would be four. But seven long-term guys.'

'Wow.'

'How many have you had?' Rocky asked.

'None,' said Sami.

'One?'

'No, I said none,' Sami repeated.

'And I said one. As in me. Number one.'

'Don't presume,' Sami said.

'Joker . . . I've already cum up your arse, how much more presumptuous can I get?'

'Did you love any of them?'

'I could lie to you and say no. But the truth is that I did. I thought I did. In honesty, what I feel for you, even in this very short time, is so much more intense and meaningful. I know now that I have only ever loved one of them.'

'Who?'

'The one in my arms right now,' Rocky whispered.

Sami didn't like to admit it, but his earth moved. Well, the bed did anyway.

He felt like his life was complete, in this cold corner of this cold island, with a man who said he possessed him.

164

Sami wanted to be possessed. He ran his fingers through Rocky's hair, damp with sweat, their bodies sickly moist from the sex and the showers in between.

Now they lay sated and enthralled.

Sami did. Rocky seemed to have fallen asleep.

They went to Birmingham, a city where neither of them knew people.

Rocky paid for a five-star hotel, an apartment in the Rotunda, taxi rides, dinners in restaurants with waterfalls, even spent five hundred pound on a jacket for Sami.

They felt free, walking hand-in-hand through the gay bars and clubs.

'This is amazing,' Rocky said.

'What?'

'This. You, me, this feeling. I didn't think it could feel so real. I think I love you more than life itself. Promise you won't ever leave me.'

'Why would I leave you?' Sami said.

'Because you are so beautiful. Someone will snap you up, and you might get bored of me. I know this is the real deal; I have so many other guys to compare it to. But you? You might wonder if this is real, might want someone else to compare to me.'

'Rocky, you're a sentimental fool. I'm not a slag. Well, okay, technically I am, but not really. You're what I've been looking for. I'm not going anywhere.'

'Still. In the back of my mind I think you are. I wish I could bind you to me for ever.'

'I am bound to you. God forgive me my transgression, but I feel our souls are connected. I feel you are my all, I understand the poems of Ghalib with you.'

Sami was breathing hard, his words rushing out in an attempt to convince this delectable man that indeed he was Sami's raison d'être.

'Ghalib? You joker. Time will tell,' said Rocky.

'Aye dil e nadaan . . . ishq par zor nahin,' said Sami. *My naive heart . . . there is no mastery of love.*

Sami wondered how Rocky could not see himself. Every male (and a lot of fag hag) eye in the club was turned in his direction. Rocky exuded charm and sexuality just by *being*. He felt a pang of envy at this. Maybe he wanted to be the desirable one? That was crazy. Rocky was his.

Nobody would take him and one day he would prove it to be true.

Chandramukhi would have to play second fiddle in real life just like in life.

Sami took an early day from 'work', which meant shutting down his laptop in his flat and heading to Wilmslow Road to see Rocky.

The travel agency had pictures of beautiful destinations – Mauritius, Maldives, Pakistan, India, Sri Lanka – in the windows. But it was barely mid-afternoon and the closed sign was on the door.

Sami pushed against it and the door opened. Inside was empty, except for Rocky on his laptop, which he hastily shut.

Here we go, thought Sami, the cheating begins.

He asked Rocky to get him a drink. Sami opened the laptop, investigated and felt sick. It was worse than cheating. It was a site for slaves and masters. Sick S&M play.

He left before Rocky came back.

'I knew you would look at my laptop, that's why I left it there, no password,' Rocky said.

'I don't think we will work. What do you do? Meet these guys – and what? Be like a naked waiter or wear a dog collar and be their slave? Maybe you should go and debase yourself in Chandramukhi's kotha with all the other whores! You disgust me.'

'Don't fucking judge me, okay,' Rocky said. 'You don't know what it's like. Go and sit in your ivory touch-me-not tower. The rest of us have real issues.'

'Real issues? What's so real about some sick porn site?'

'It's not porn. Look . . . when you've had as much sex as I have, when you've lived with men and had access to sex every day, it gets boring. I need a little . . . extra to get excited.'

'Aren't I enough?' Sami said.

'You are amazing; you are the first guy I've been with where I didn't need any of this. That's how I know I love you. But if we are going to continue . . . I need sometimes to do this . . . and I want to do it with you.'

So Sami let Rocky tie him up with wires and belts and ties. He allowed Rocky to force him to lick his boots and trainers, they played watersports.

Sami let his disgust breed deep inside, his revulsion at how low he had fallen; his devastation at the destruction of a fantasy into a nightmare fester.

He gave up his decency for Rocky.

Just to keep him.

After that, Rocky called Sami his jaan.

His *life*.

'I need a favour, jaan,' Rocky said.

They were in Sami's flat, naked, postcoital, watching *Veer-Zaara*.

'Anything for you,' Sami said.

'You might regret saying that,' Rocky said, kissing the top of Sami's head.

'I doubt it. You are my world. My life. My all.'

'Joker . . . I hate to ask, but there's no one else I can ask. I mean, I could ask one of my exes, but they might, you know . . . there might be strings attached.'

Into Sami's mind flashed images of Rocky in the arms of beautifully chiselled white men. Jealousy at the notion that Rocky had enjoyed these men fizzed with the idea of Rocky being with anyone else.

'There's no need. What is it?'

'I know, but I don't feel good asking you. It's okay, forget it. Maybe I should ask Chandramukhi . . .'

'Chandramukhi? The stalker drag queen? How can you even speak to him?'

'I know, but he's sweet. I feel sorry for him. I'll ask someone else. I haven't known you very long. It's okay.'

'Tell me. If you really love me, ask me,' Sami said.

He had vile images in his head, Rocky and Akshay wrapped in a discarded sari.

'I just need some ready cash to pay the lease on the premises. I didn't expect the lease to be due and didn't save enough cash. I can't pay it using a credit card either. Some stupid rule they have. I don't want to ask my parents, they already think a travel agency is a waste of time. They want me to be an accountant. That was my degree.'

'After you've spent so much on me already . . . How much do you need?' Sami asked.

'How much have you got? Ready cash?'

'About five grand.'

'Oh . . .'

'I can get you more. A loan if you want. Ten grand. Will that be enough?'

'Yes. Thank you, jaan. I'll pay you back in four weeks. On my honour . . .'

'You lost that at thirteen,' Sami said.

'Joker,' Rocky said and kissed him. 'Okay then, I swear on my jaan . . . I love you. More than anyone ever.'

Sami was ready to sign his life over at that point. The next day he applied for the loan and transferred it along with his savings to Rocky.

Rocky insisted he sign a contract, for Sami's sake.

Secure and safe, and bonded for ever.

They went to London.

Rocky paid, got them a hotel in Holborn. It was pure luxury. The evening was set up as an extravaganza.

They went to a play, a dramatized version of *Devdas*.

Brit Asia's royalty were there. Soap stars, TV stars, radio DJs. As they hobnobbed around the Indian Embassy, Sami dared to ask a couple of them to take photos with him.

Rocky was deep in conversation with a film director. Even, it seemed, the leading lady of Brit Asian cinema wasn't immune to his charms.

'You got a light, mate?' Sami heard someone ask.

'No sorry, I don't smoke. I don't think you can in here anyway.'

'Fuck that. Is that your friend?'

Sami turned around and was faced with a girl with a bob cut. She was wearing a red cocktail dress with gold stars on it, and a matching dupatta thrown over her shoulders. She had gold and ruby earrings to match and plenty of bling on her wrists. She looked like an accident between a Christmas tree and a wedding.

'Friend? Yes, I suppose.'

'Hey, we're all on the down low,' she said, sipping her obviously alcoholic drink. 'Everyone in this room has something to hide.'

'I'm not hiding anything,' Sami said.

'Sure. Like, for example, I hate that fucking bitch over there. Thinks because she's sung backing vocals for Bally Sagoo she's all that.'

'Who?'

'That bitch over there. I went to uni with her. She may sing like an angel, but she's got the talons of a wanker bastard. But when we meet I act like we're sisters. The dagger is held hilt upwards, so she can't tell how sharp the point is.'

'Oh,' Sami said.

He had no idea to whom the woman was referring.

'She took an instant dislike to me. I think she was jealous, didn't know how to react to me. Fucking cunt. I loathe her. Do you swear?'

'Not always,' Sami said.

'Shame. I'm Moomy by the way.' She force shook Sami's hand.

'I'm Sami.'

'Sami? Is that your real name?'

'Yes. Moomy? Is that your real name?'

'Don't get smart with me. I eat boys like you for breakfast. Or rather they eat me.'

'Nice. But I'm not such a big fan of the bushy plate,' Sami said.

He looked over for Rocky, who was now engrossed in conversation with a theatre actor. A rather gorgeous theatre actor.

'Such a shame. He's got the moon waiting for him and he's fucking pissing up against a tree. You need to walk away from him.'

'What? Why? You don't even know him.'

'I know his type. Men. Fucking bastards the lot of them,' Moomy said. 'Not you, though. I can tell. Not you. You're a nice man. Such a shame you're . . . into *friends*.'

'I just like experimenting,' Sami said.

'Sure you do. Don't we all. But between me and you, fuck it, leave him. He's going to break your heart, and I can tell you won't get over it.'

'Thanks for the advice.'

Sami felt sad, knew he looked it. Moomy was right, in a way. He was terrified of Rocky ever walking out on him. Of late, things had started to mellow. Their sex life had gone from multiple times a day to furtive, infrequent blowjobs where Sami did all the sucking and swallowing.

Sami wondered if Rocky was getting it elsewhere. From men off his S&M sites.

They'd stopped seeing each other as often and now every time Sami turned up to surprise Rocky he was never at the travel agency, which always had the closed sign on the door. It was only ever open when Sami texted to say he was on his way.

London was an attempt to pacify his doubts, show him that he was still Rocky's jaan.

'I gave him a lot of money,' Sami said. This crazy drunken woman was nothing to him and he just blurted it out.

'Fuck. How much is a lot?'

'Ten grand.'

'Fuck me. Are you loaded or what?'

'Not really. I don't have ten grand to throw away. And now I'm not so happy. He's changed, and I don't think I want to be with him any more. But I can't walk away because I won't ever see my money again. I feel trapped.'

'Fuck it. Ask him for your money. If he's a good guy, he'll give it back to you. If he's a shit, he'll run off. Either way, ten grand is nothing to save your heart and yourself. Trust me.'

'Thanks. I don't know why I told you that.'

'Men do anything for me. Tell me everything. But you, I don't know. Maybe deep fucking down,' she said, jabbing at his chest, 'you want to be me?'

'I doubt it, love. I don't date trannies,' said Rocky, coming up to join them. 'Who's your friend, Sami?'

'Moomy. This is Rocky.'

'Rocky? Ha. Fuck. Well, I might be Sami's friend. But I don't fucking well want to be yours,' Moomy said.

'Charming,' said Rocky.

'She's drunk,' Sami said.

'She can fucking well speak for her fucking self,' said Moomy.

'Obviously didn't graduate from etiquette school, did you, darling,' said Rocky.

'Rocky, man, don't be rude, she's my friend.'

'Friend? Don't be an idiot, you just met her; I saw you.'

'Did you? I thought you were so far up that actor's . . . forget it . . .' Sami said.

'No come on, Sami, tell him. Don't fucking chicken out now, don't be such a wet pussy. You, dickweed, Sami has something to tell you.'

'What?' Rocky's face was hard; he was obviously pissed off now.

'Nothing. She's drunk,' Sami said.

'I gave you a fucking lifeline. You should have taken it.' This last comment was directed at Sami.

Sami wondered if it would be rude to dump Rocky after all this fuss. Maybe he'd give it a few more weeks, see if the romance and the passion and the grand filmic love came back.

He didn't get the chance. A week later Rocky disappeared. His phone was disconnected, his email account closed.

When Sami went to the travel agency he found the landlord there, wanting his money. Rocky hadn't paid any rent for six months and had sent all his bills to the landlord's house.

'Do you know him? The boy who took lease?'

'No . . . not really . . .'

'Akshay. His name Akshay Kapoor?'

The dagger was held hilt upwards, but the point was twisted in Sami's heart.

Chandramukhi/Akshay's number was also dead.

Sami felt as if someone had run over him, crushed all his bones, and then propped him up and tried to make him stand.

Not being out, where could he turn? Not to the police, nor to his family, nor his friends.

Rocky had taken his heart. And his cash.

Rasiya bada beimaan.

My lover is faithless. My lover is a fraud.

Azmeena Ladha

Two Pearls

I find her buried by a frangipani tree and I want to smile. These are the flowers she made into buttons as a girl and I think how lucky she is to be surrounded by these flowers, this scent. And then I decipher the K for Kulsum.

It was because of me that they never called her Moti. 'We can't have two daughters-in-law called Moti,' they announced when she first emerged from the hold of the dhow. She appeared not to hear them, or not to care. Her face displayed only relief: relief that she had finally arrived in Mombasa after a stormy voyage lasting six weeks instead of four; that I had sought her out from all the passengers, recognized her from her studio photograph despite her dishevelled appearance; relief, too, that the box of Kashmiri saffron from her parents had survived the voyage. She talked hurriedly of the passengers who had perished, of the sack loads of rice ruined by the seawater and thrown overboard. 'We are going to call you Kulsum,' they declared, silencing her with a garland. She bent to touch their feet, sought their blessings, acknowledged them as her new parents.

I never called her anything, not for months. We didn't like each other. I didn't like her because she was prone to prattling without any notion of her place at the bottom of our in-laws' hierarchy, because her dowry consisted of the gaudiest saris, and because she cried so frequently for the Ma she had left behind in Gujarat. She didn't like me because she never stopped answering to the name Moti.

She didn't know much for a thirteen-year-old. Some passing palmist in Gujarat had long ago foretold that her parents would one day beget a pearl and when no such pearl was forthcoming and when, after six boys, her mother delivered a girl they were convinced that she must surely be the pearl the palmist meant. That's why they named her Moti, waited upon her, let her talk as and when she pleased, spared her the daily drudgeries. And when the idea of a marriage in Mombasa was mooted, her parents believed they were truly blessed.

I had to teach her everything when she arrived: how to peel vegetables economically; how to fold bed sheets down to the same size and stack them neatly and quickly; and, most importantly, how to keep her head covered in the presence of our father-in-law. She never understood that when our father-in-law returned home in a midday temper, complaining about the settlers and the slum that lurked in the bazaar, the only thing to do was to feed him, fan him, and never stand in front of him. She would never have overtaken me in becoming his favourite daughter-in-law, even if she had lived. He tended to dismiss her within minutes of her entering a room.

Her husband dismissed her too, mostly. When he didn't, after a few forbidden swigs of imported whisky, he made his demands on her in the night. I heard her pleas through the partition and moved closer to my own husband so as not to listen. Mostly, though, her husband loaded his mud-covered chains and chicken wire into the box-body trailer and drove off into the interior for days at a time. My parents-in-law never mentioned his occupation in my presence. Never: despite my witnessing the stack of elephant tusks under their beds, and despite my delivering them a grandson and becoming keeper of the safe deposit keys. My husband, may Allah rest his soul – my loving, abstinent husband, simple and content to trade in glass beads with the Masai and to buy a jasmine garland for my hair each Friday – he never mentioned his brother in my presence either.

Her husband wasn't there on the day her fever started. It was not a convenient day for a fever. I had already quartered the last of the season's limes and laid them out to dry on the terrace; the pickle was to be mixed and bottled by the end of the day. Her fever would have to go away.

Our father-in-law returned home at midday and threw a bundle of crisp, creamy-pink bank notes onto the dining table. 'Florins!' he sighed. 'We have to have florins now. Rupees are no longer legal.' Our mother-in-law tried to make light of it, to comfort him. She asked him to read us the English words on the notes: The East African Currency Board. One florin. King George V. 'Tell us,' she pleaded with a smile, 'tell us again why the V means five.'

'The natives won't forget this,' he said. 'Their wages have just ceased to be legal tender.'

The fever did not go away. She lay in bed with a jug of water by her side and a cold compress on her forehead, but her fever remained long after the turmeric stains from the lime pickle had washed out of my fingernails, long after the natives were forced to take a cut in their wages. It must have been then that I tired of nursing the fever and managing the household without her help. With my chin out, shoulders pulled back, and remembering my place as the mother of the only grandson in the family, I ventured a family announcement: this girl needed to see a doctor for her fever, and I would accompany her.

The box-body that might have driven us to the dispensary was nowhere near Mombasa that week. We walked, setting off early in the morning, long before the sun had time to get angry. We walked slowly, and along as many of the cool narrow gullies as we could find through the Old Town. We rested under an occasional awning. The brand-new Japanese fan in the waiting room was broken when we got there. The doctor gave her some quinine tablets. He said it was malaria.

I had had malaria; my parents, my brothers and sisters, we had all had malaria. But this malaria was different. Some days our mother-in-law called it a dhow fever, other days it was an Indian fever, but always, she insisted, it was a fever that the young bride must have contracted before her marriage. Did they know the cause? And had the itch begun? Was that when I understood it was not malaria, when she began itching down there in her childbirth place? I know that I was afraid to know, afraid to allow such thoughts inside my mind, or inside the family.

The quinine tablets did nothing to relieve the fever. Nor did cold compresses or bags of ice. The itch grew worse. She was vomiting and, on our mother-in-law's orders, she was confined to her bedroom. It wasn't proper to wander around the house letting the servants see her scratching that place. I took muslin squares into her bedroom, thinking that perhaps a cold compress down there might soothe her. It only made her irate.

She became too weak to step out of bed. Did her husband come home during that stage? He must have, she lay in that state for several weeks, maybe months, and yet nothing about him comes to mind. We sent the houseboy to fetch the doctor. He asked to examine her. The sores began to ooze as I lifted her stained underskirt. A smell of pus rose from her bed and filled the room. That's when she raised a fleshless hand towards me, as her tears flowed past her plaits and into her pillow. That's when I first smiled at her. I touched her cheeks that day, dabbed them, and I called her Moti. The doctor made artificial coughing noises as he turned away from the bed. He said he didn't need to examine her after all and that perhaps our houseboy could collect some medicine from the dispensary.

I spooned holy water into her mouth that day, called her Moti again, and when she opened those piteous eyes and stared at the blank wall, I kept calling her Moti. That's when she uttered the word Ma again; it's who she thought I was.

I made frangipani buttons for her later that day. She had wanted to teach me to make them when she arrived a year ago. I had called her childish then, for playing with flowers and behaving like a thirteen-year-old instead of a daughter-in-law. She would pick a frangipani flower and press its milky stalk into the earth to dry, then hold the flower in one hand and with the other gently bend one of the petals back far enough to thread through the stalk. She would bend the next petal back and thread it, and the next, until all five petals were threaded and all that was left to view was a perfect button: a turmeric-yellow middle with pale white edges. Or pale pink, depending on the variety. It's the pale pink frangipani that showers her now.

It was the day our father-in-law brought home a handful of the silver shillings that were to replace the short-lived florins. Our mother-in-law did not suggest reading out any English words that day. We just held the coins, noted the king on one side, the lion on the other, and passed them round to each other. And when I took a shining shilling into her room to show her, she had stopped breathing even though her eyes were still open. They sent most of those shillings to the mosque that evening, as a donation, together with a tray-load of food offerings and a jar of lime pickle. And they sent a telegraph to her parents in Gujarat. When her parents replied, they regretted the loss of their pearl and hoped that Allah would grant each one of us much strength to bear our pain.

The K for Kulsum comes into focus again. She could write K and Kh, and G; just those first three letters of the alphabet. What she really wanted to learn in exchange for her button-making skills was to write the word Moti. 'Show me how you write *your* name,' she had begged when she was well.

'No,' I had scolded, reminding her that I was her elder by three years and would not be tricked. 'You have to learn the whole alphabet, all the consonants and all the vowels. Only then will I teach you to write Moti.'

A young attendant is walking towards me, limping or leaning, I cannot tell. He carries a watering can so full it spills along the path with every other step he takes. I clutch my bundle of notes, Kenyan shillings I have exchanged for the sterling of my adopted country, rehearse the lines I have so long planned to say on this occasion. I have come to order a new headstone, I will say. There is a name missing. We left out a name on this stone.

'Would you like to water this grave?' he asks, in Gujarati, as gently as though this were a recent bereavement. He puts the watering can down with the handle turned towards me.

The sun has not been up long, but already the notes feel damp in my hand. I swap the bundle from one hand to the other.

'Thank you.' I know that I shall not be able to lift the watering can.

'Your sister or something?'

I nod. Something.

'Died young, didn't she?' He can read Gujarati, not just speak it, like my children. And he has calculated her age. 'Would you like to recite some prayers? We have verses written out on a board. Shall I fetch them for you?'

'No, no, it's all right, thank you, this water is enough. I have come to –' They are here. Three figures have appeared at the gate in the distance, familiar figures. I see them beyond the attendant's shoulders. They have seen me. They are following the path he has just watered with his overfilled can. My grandchildren. The youngest, nine, waves as he quickens his step towards us. My time is up, I must make haste.

'I have come to order a – Is your superintendent in his office?' I point to the stone hut by the gate.

'My brother?'

'Is your brother the superintendent?'

He nods.

'Is he in the office?'

'Office is padlocked, auntie. My brother has gone to London, UK. Gone for his youngest daughter's marriage.'

I try not to appear agitated, try to smile at the attendant. I swap the bundle of notes from one hand to the other, again.

Seventeen, twelve, and nine years old, two girls and the youngest a boy, my three grandchildren walk towards us, keeping their English voices low, as though not to disturb anyone. They have been patient with this request of mine to visit the cemetery on the first morning of our arrival, while they explore the town for half an hour having promised under all circumstances to obey the seventeen-year-old.

The attendant hears the children, turns his head, realizes they are with me. 'Shall I fetch more water?' The kindness has not left his voice.

'Thank you, I am sure this will be enough for us all.' I want him to go away.

Perhaps he senses this. 'Don't worry about the watering can,' he says. 'You can leave it here when you have finished, it will be safe. I will collect it later.' He leaves us. He has a limp.

'We found the ice cream place you told us about. It's open, can we go there now?' The nine-year-old reaches for my hand.

'Ma, are you ready to go now?' asks the eldest. She is older than the girl buried under this frangipani tree. She glances at the tombstone. It is not a script she is familiar with. She learned her alphabet at a young age, as did her siblings. They go to school; they read and own books, write essays. They have not yet mastered the art of folding bed sheets down to the same size, peeling vegetables economically, making lime pickle. They may not need to.

'Will you help me water this grave? And this tree?'

The youngest looks at his two siblings for a reaction. They remain patient and as they lift the watering can together, he too places his hand on the can. I know they are eager to start the holiday I have long promised to partake in; eager to sample the magic of Mombasa that I have always talked about; to find the house their father was born in; the Old Town with its narrow streets and carved doors and its balconies propped up by bird-shaped supports; the old harbour where we, like Moti, first landed from Gujarat and where I wonder if dhows still land; the Blue Room ice cream, which they have already discovered; the coconut juice – they have even remembered my dubious theory that yellow, not green, coconuts bear the sweeter water. And they want that ride round Lighthouse.

'I am ready,' I say, and stuff the bundle of notes down the front of my dress, the way our mother-in-law used to. 'But before we leave, I want to show you how to make a frangipani button.'

ANOUSHKA BEAZLEY

The Interview

When it came down to it, it wasn't that difficult to walk away. Jags was a chameleon. He always made the best of a situation and did what he needed to do to fit in. He was so good at adapting and making it look convincing that no one in Southall would have imagined he had any dreams at all, but he did.

But that was a long time ago.

'You ready, Jagbir?' asked Michael Burns, a senior partner at Burns and Oleck – the third-largest law firm in London. As he proudly coached his latest prodigy, Jagbir could tell the man was a fan.

'When I interviewed you, I'll admit I was a son of a bitch. It's what I'm known for and it's what's needed,' he said, patting Jagbir on the shoulder. 'You proved yourself. You were different, and that's why you're still here.' They were nearing the conference room. 'Now, you've sat in on these before. This time you get to ask the questions.' He ushered him to the door where, through the square window panel, Jags could see the candidate. Still, in a state of undisturbed expectation. 'It's important you learn how to handle yourself in these situations. This person could very possibly be a member of our firm by the end of the week and, in the event of that happening, it's imperative that you establish control now, declare the hierarchy, know what I mean. You set the pace, the direction, maybe throw in a few surprises.' His eyes narrowed.

'And, remember, don't be afraid to make it uncomfortable.' Michael flashed a wolfish smile.

Outside, the sirens screamed past his window, screeching cars skidded round the corner. Jags lay on his bed, hands folded behind his head, watching a fly dance around the bulb. Stupid, dumb fly. Jags knew where the police were headed and wondered whether Sonny would be so stupid. Whether he would rob the corner shop like he was meant to, or whether he would stand there bigging it up, waving his toy gun around until the owner realized it wasn't real, called the police and Sonny pleaded six to ten for attempted robbery. If the pigs got there late and Sonny had cleaned up and out, Jags would be getting his cut in about three hours. That's how it worked. Jags set it up, decided what jobs the gang did, who did them and when. Jags always got the first cut; the rest was split between whoever was there, with a bit left over for the weed. They grew their own, smoked their own and sold their own.

The cigarette burned down to his fingers and he dusted the ash off his Adidas shell suit. There was half a spliff sat in the ashtray. He couldn't remember when from. He sat up, intending at least to find where he'd put the lighter when Daan opened the door.

'Don't you fucking knock?' Being surprised in his own bedroom made Jags see the room from the outside; suddenly it was opened up to the world. It could have done with a woman's touch.

'What are you doing here? I thought you were with Sonny tonight. You got a lighter?' He looked up at Daan: unshaven, dressed in a hooded sweatshirt and trainers, the darkness of the hallway swallowing him.

They were brothers, with less than two years between them, and over time everyone had assumed that Jags was the older one. 'What's the matter with you?' Jags asked his brother. He was tired. Just looking at Daan made Jags feel tired. Living in that house made him tired. He'd thought about moving out, but he couldn't. He'd feel guilty if he left them both, still stuck with their sadness, which had worn its way into the faded, embossed wallpaper. Daan held out a box of matches, but when Jags moved to take them Daan grabbed his hand, hard.

'What the?'

Daan's eyes peered out from his hoodie, rimless, black moons. He looked up at Jags. It didn't matter who was older any more. It should have done, like it did in most Asian families, but now she was gone they were all on their own.

'Saira's left me,' said Daan, his voice breaking. Jags could smell his breath, smell the Tennent's Extra. He was unmoved by the tears, which always flowed more freely after a can.

There was always some girl who fell for Daan and his pathetic stories. Jags would hear all the news from Sonny and Zeddy. They were reliable boys and he appreciated the heads-up. It was hard to keep track of which girl had broken his brother's heart this week; he hated them all. This latest one was no better, no different. Jags had to get out. Sonny and the boys hadn't arrived yet, but they weren't scheduled to meet for a couple of hours so there was no reason to think the boys weren't all right. He lifted up the edge of the net curtains. The night called him. A hazy, greyish blue: that part of the evening where the streetlights spilled into the sky and he couldn't tell what time it was; a sort of half-night.

On such nights he would just walk and walk. The house was better in the day, bearable, but in the night Daan prowled the corridors. Weed didn't agree with Daan, though you couldn't tell him that. It picked at his brain until it found his paranoia, chained up in a corner like a savage dog biting at its own collar, snarling at its own teeth, until it got fed. All the while their father sang, drank and wanked to a picture of a woman who had been taken from them the night Jagbir was born. Daan and their dad had been slowly drowning their feelings ever since. Their behaviour repulsed him. He couldn't breathe in there.

'I told you not to see her any more.' Jags scrambled for socks under the bed and found the lighter, hitting his head. He started to feel claustrophobic. Under the bed was a litter diary of the last seven days: a couple of empty, crumpled gold packets of Benson & Hedges, a packet of green Rizla with a few papers left inside, a Coke can and a chilli-sauce-stained kebab wrapper. His room was too small; the house itself seemed to grow smaller as darkness fell. Why did they all go so crazy at night? Anyone would think there really were monsters under the bed. He could hear his father, television blaring, watching a Bollywood movie with some drunken friends of his. The singing, dancing girl sounded like she'd breathed in a can of helium.

'Move.' He nudged Daan, whose long legs were between him and the door.

'I love her.'

Jags slapped him. 'Shut up.' He wanted to slap her out of him, but as he felt the slap reverberate on his palm he knew it was futile; the girl was just a body. Daan was in love with a memory. In some ways, they all were.

The meeting place was always the same: an abandoned petrol station on Junction Road, unless someone spread the word that the pigs were all over them and then everyone knew to go straight to Virginia Waters. The first time Jags had ever been to Virginia Waters was with Daan and his father. It had been the old man's idea. 'Take you boys out,' he'd said, 'see a real forest.' The fact that it was the tenth anniversary of their mother's death was incidental; what else were they going to do? The car broke down on the way and they had to flag down a passer-by for a jump start. A kindly old gent who rattled on about the reliability of German cars, which neither of them was driving, to the quiet trio of Asian males before setting them back on their way.

Jags had been surprised to see his father was right: it was a forest. Tall trees towered over them, casting shadows as their feet crunched the earthy floor. Unsure why they were there, together, they wandered, each alone with their thoughts. The silence of the forest promised to keep their secrets. Jags remembered that day as a kind of respite in the family hostilities and, when the gang needed a second place, another hideout the cops didn't know about, he suggested the forest of secrets.

He walked quickly down the high street, the smell of samosas from the many Indian restaurants hanging thick, waiting for the morning when people would waken and their hot breath and conversation would disturb the meaty air. He walked for miles up and down the same streets, bought more cigarettes and walked on. Asian boys, some friends, some not, drove around in their customized Ford Escorts: low suspension, two exhausts, big engines, treble bass with speakers fitted through the whole of the boot. And the cars never left Southall. Hell, they never left the block.

Heavy, patterned curtains twitched, as people surreptitiously tried to catch a glimpse of who was walking past their safe abodes so late at night. Before they could raise the lace, he was gone, moving on to the next house. A cat sat on a stone wall, agile and distrustful.

The car with blacked-out windows surprised him as it turned the corner, skidding abruptly to a stop at the top of the road, scanning. It was looking for him. It swung its nose around and paused for a moment; Jags locked eyes with the headlights and it sped towards him.

'Saaafe,' came the long drawl from the driver's seat as the darkened window came down. It was Asif. Sonny was in the back counting the money and Zeddy was slumped in the passenger seat, skinning up what was far from his first joint of the evening.

'Whass up, brudda?' Zeddy got out. It was a respect thing. Whatever the car, Jags always drove if he wanted to. If he made no moves to do so then the person in the passenger seat would offer their place and get in the back.

'Zeddy, watch my trainers, man,' complained Sonny, begrudgingly shifting his butt along the leather to make room.

'Whatcha get?'

'Two hundred from the tills and the guy's nephew gave us a grand from the safe if we promised not to kill his uncle.' Sonny was laughing so hard while recounting the story that it was impossible not to laugh with him. Asif had to finish.

'His uncle looked like *he* was gonna kill him.'

'Yeah, man. I think his uncle would have rather died than open that safe. We should go back and see if that kid's all right.' Jags relaxed and reclined the seat. It wasn't everything, but for now at least it wasn't home, so it would do.

'What happened to Daan, man?'

'Yeah, he wasn't at the pick-up.'

Jags was about to lie, but he hesitated a second too long.

'It's that bitch, isn't it?'

The weed was all he could smell now. He breathed it in and felt it caress him, soothe him, bringing him a peace he longed for. Zeddy had passed his joint around, but Jags wanted to build his own. It reassured him to know that there were two lit at the same time, and he enjoyed the process. Liked how his long fingers struggled to fit into the tiny plastic bag, enjoying the feel of the herb as he crumbled it, bit by bit, onto the tobacco, the Rizla cocooned effortlessly in the palm of his hand. He tore off a piece of cardboard from the Rizla packet for the roach, rolled it up and slid it into the perfectly round empty hole at the top of the spliff. If a spliff was built correctly you could slide a roach in no problem – it was an art. He opened his legs and inhaled deeply.

'Forget it.'

'She's asking him to leave the gang.' Sonny probably knew that if he was going to say anything at all he needed to get it out quick. 'She's from Heston. She's not a Southall girl. Didn't know who we were or who Daan was. He told her about tonight's job and she said if he did it she'd leave him *and* she'd go to the police.'

'She left him anyways,' said Jags.

'Who do these bitches think they are?'

Asif drove the Ford Capri round the corner smooth and fast and, from the inside, it felt as if they were on a straight road – or maybe the weed was just that good – the only thing that gave it away was the gold chain hanging off the rear-view mirror, swinging from side to side. It had belonged to Asif's father, who had passed away the previous year. Cirrhosis. Asif didn't talk about him. Come to think of it there was a lot they didn't talk about anymore.

Cause I get raw. Big Daddy Kane shook the speakers and the car bounced at the traffic lights.

What was the time? Nearly one. But it seemed later, like they had been driving around for hours. Maybe they had or, Jags wondered, maybe he was blending together the events of the past few years.

'My mum says I don't have to finish college if I don't want to. Says I can help her in the launderette, maybe run it one day,' Zeddy announced proudly.

'You gonna drop out a college and wash people's clothes?' said Sonny.

'Yeah, well . . . it's a job, ain't it?'

'You can wipe my arse, that's a job.' And everyone laughed.

'You ain't nuffin. You're only doing a BTEC in Business Finance.' Zeddy repositioned his hat, a nervous tic.

'I know I won't be weighing out fabric softener and rubbing the skid marks off another man's pants.'

'Mum doesn't handwash any more. It's too time-consuming, so now it's all done in the machine. Even mine. You should come down,' said Zeddy, happy again.

'Are you inferring your own pants have skid marks that can't be shifted without the aid of mechanics?' challenged Asif, who was studying A level law, but after his dad's death and the subsequent increase of his weed intake, no one expected him to sit his exams, let alone pass them.

'What about you, Jags?'

'Pull up. I'm hungry,' said Jags. The car had started to do his head in. Lately, they always seemed to ask him about his plans, ideas for the future. Now and then he contributed, but what he would actually do was irrelevant. He just needed to get out, do something anywhere but Southall, but he couldn't tell them that, it would crush them.

'Munchies,' screamed Zeddy. No queue at the kebab shop and, even better, Gnomi was working: free food.

'All right, boys.' Gnomi was wearing a red hat with a red shirt made out of a silky fabric that enabled grease and other food items to be wiped off easily. He had a wide-toothed grin, in which glinted a gold tooth, and unusually long fingernails, too long for clean food handling. Jags said that he reminded him of a garden gnome so, though his real name was Pradeep, everyone called him Gnomi.

A square sieve spluttered away in the corner of a metal deep-fat fryer. Three pieces of lonely-looking chicken sat on a shelf above it, and a precarious stack of empty boxes teetered to one side. Gnomi had dropped the large bag of frozen chips on the floor and was shovelling the lost potato sticks back into the white plastic sack when Zeddy threw his body onto the counter and stuck his head over the top.

'Don't gimme no three second rule, man. I don't want no chips from the floor, you skank.'

'No, yes, right, okay,' answered Gnomi.

'You on your own, Gnomi?' asked Jags, perusing the menu like it was à la carte, even though he always ordered the same thing. 'Okay, so I think I'll have the two breast pieces of chicken, large chips and two tomato sauce sachets, please, Gnomi.'

It unnerved Gnomi that, despite all the things he'd heard about Jags, he was always the most polite and best-behaved out of them all.

Sonny and Asif started play-fighting. Asif was taller and quicker but Sonny, stockier, had power behind him, and when his short reach eventually landed a punch Asif took a moment to steady his feet.

The kebab shop stayed open later at the weekends, but Mondays were slow. Now that the boys were here, Gnomi wished he had shut up shop ten minutes earlier.

Occasionally a car drove by. Because of the corner shop job, the boys were jumpy, but once Gnomi announced the food was ready, even the infrequent whirring of an engine didn't disturb them. There were no chairs in the kebab shop, but after much pressure Mr Ali had ordered two high, round tables, one in each corner of the shop over which the boys now leaned and ate. Such is the bond between boys and fried chicken that they did not look up immediately when Saira and her younger brother walked in. At the table in the corner, Zeddy nudged Sonny, who nodded to Asif, who whispered to Jags, who was surprised by what he saw. He hadn't expected a girlfriend of Daan's to be so sweet.

She ordered for them both. It was unusual to see a girl out so late in the area. She was dressed modestly, which was good: out here, the choice between a skirt and a pair of trousers after a certain time could make all the difference.

Gnomi saw Jags, chewed chicken meat in his teeth, skin and saliva hanging off his lips, a look in his eye, and he did his best to help.

'We're closing now; you can't eat in the shop, you must go. Now,' said Gnomi in his most authoritative tone.

The boy was happy to take his food and go and called his sister to come with him, but when he got to the door he turned around and saw something strange happening. His sister, rooted to the counter, and Jags were staring at one another and, even though no one had been talking when they'd entered, a deathly silence now filled the room.

'Take the boy home,' Jags ordered Zeddy, who was still eating his food.

The boy started to protest, but his sister calmed him, convincing him it was fine. She would be fine, younger brother, don't worry. Don't say anything to anyone; go home, she would see him later. It was obvious that she meant it.

'Lock up the front, Gnomi, and go home. We'll drop the keys to you later.'

Gnomi had turned the fryer off. There was a hum coming from a fridge against the wall and a more distant hum from a rusty extractor fan on the ceiling right above Gnomi's head. He moved from underneath it to address Jags directly, not that it had ever worked before.

'Jags, you can't do that.' Gnomi looked at the girl, whose eyes were suddenly hopeful, and he immediately realized that she might have got the wrong idea. He wasn't that brave. 'I have to take these keys to Mr Ali's house right now.' He knew how it sounded, but it was the truth. 'He's expecting me. They're doing inventory tonight and he's coming back about four. I'm serious, man. I wouldn't lie to you, Jags.'

Jags seemed to be studying Gnomi's face. His stance was almost meditative and, as such, Asif and Sonny knew better than to interrupt him.

His face detection finished, Jags moved towards the door and held it open while looking at the girl. 'All right, Gnomi, not a problem,' he said. 'We'll go for a drive instead.'

Sonny was right; she wasn't a Southall girl. And even though Heston was practically next door, she didn't have a clue who she was dealing with, to the point, he thought later – as they would all think about it later – that she didn't even look scared, but that was through ignorance rather than bravery.

When they got there, Jags pulled her from the car and not once did the boys involve themselves, in any capacity. She screamed right from the start, so Jags walked with her almost behind him, left arm underneath her chin and around her head, right arm over her mouth. She was wriggling and kicking her legs like a ladybird on its back and, as he dragged her into the woods, she lost the shoes she was wearing, her brown bare feet flicking up through the leaves.

The woods were not popular at that time of night. They heard an owl hoot near by, the echo of it remaining. When they stopped, it was without warning. It was so dark that the boys couldn't tell whether Jags had been to this place before or whether he just couldn't see any further. It was as if, for all of them, the point of their lives had simply been to get them to this dark, forgotten place deep in the woods.

Sonny and Asif didn't see her face, or look at each other's. They didn't see Jags smack her head into a tree or bend her over and flick her arms up around the trunk. They didn't hear the fabric of his pants crisp into folds as it slunk down around his ankles. It was only when she gasped an awful, hollow gasp that shocked them with the wounding of her, did they think about their sisters, did they know he was inside her.

A few weeks later, Jags left Southall and never looked back. That was seven years ago.

'You ready?' Michael Burns pushed the door open, allowing Jagbir to walk in first, and the candidate stood up.

'Jagbir Johar, good to meet you. You must be Eva, Eva Malus.'

Michael also shook hands and sat himself down on a side chair, leaving empty the larger, more central seat.

'Thank you for coming in to see us today,' Jagbir began, settling himself.

'Not at all, the pleasure is all mine,' she answered.

'Burns and Oleck is the third largest law firm in London. So, apart from the obvious, tell me, why us?'

'I'm not after easy. The challenge of working for a firm of your size and reputation excites me. I am forced in every situation to prove myself just to prove to you that by hiring me today you made the right decision. Those are conditions in which I excel.'

Jagbir noted an uneasy sense of déjà vu. He had given a similarly cocky response in his own interview and Michael, giving him a knowing nod, must have remembered it too.

'It says here' – he looked down at her particulars, though he could feel himself losing concentration, there was something about her – 'that your first work experience was for a conservation activist group. I'm hard-pressed to see the connection from them to us.'

'It isn't necessarily apparent, but an awful lot of bad things happen in the woods.' She politely turned to include Michael as she answered, but it was only when she spoke and looked directly at Jags that her words took meaning. 'Environmental law is a lot dirtier than people realize; there's a lot of money in it and as a result the legal ramifications need even more scrutiny and understanding. It was a great training ground.' Turning away from Michael, she focused her attention back on to Jags. 'Many people feel strongly that environmental abuse merits punishment. I'm a firm believer in making the law work for you if you know it well enough.'

'Sounds like something you would say, Jagbir. You two know each other?' asked Michael, but Jags, visibly shaken, wasn't listening any more.

'I don't think so,' she said confidently, but mulling over the question out of courtesy.

'Only joking,' Michael continued, looking down at her CV, 'you're not even from the same area.'

'No, that's true. Not any more,' she said. 'As you can see, I went to boarding school, but our old house was in Heston,' she said, smiling wide, pausing, for effect. 'Small place, near Southall, it was years ago, but you do look familiar.' They hadn't even taken her home; they had left her in the woods and driven back to Southall. It was a one in a million chance. 'Perhaps I do recognize you. Do I? I was known by my middle name then, Saira.'

Amina Zia

The Necklace of Golden Pound Coins

Najma sat on the wooden chair waiting for the blind muezzin to make his final call to the faithful from the mosque across the street. She sat still with her eyes closed in the darkness of her room. She was at peace. It was all in hand for tomorrow. The gentle whirring of the wooden fan in the ceiling lulled her into a meditative state. The four blades sliced the air rhythmically, circulating a warm draft of calm around the room. She sensed a frenetic movement around her. There was a feint, high-pitched humming sound. Something tickled the back of her bare neck. She jerked her right hand with a sudden controlled violence and slapped the life out of the culprit that dared to disturb her. It left a red speck of blood on her hand.

The slap was the cue for the muezzin. She heard the familiar clumsy bumping of the microphone and the mournful wail 'Allah Akbar! Allah Akbar!' The sound to remind the faithful of Lahore's affluent Gulberg district, that God is great. Najma rejoiced with him. She stood up to open the wooden cabinet, and grabbed herself the half-bottle of Murree Brewery's single malt whiskey. I could really have done with some ice tonight, she thought, pouring the golden brown liquid of Pakistan's elite into her glass.

The call to prayer had ended and it was now time to breathe again.

Standing at the porcelain bathroom sink, she splashed cold water on to her face and hands before running her long fingers through her cropped black hair.

The load of completed tax files was piling up at the government offices, and there wasn't a peon who could handle the pressure of the extra hour.

'Sir, Madam, if you wouldn't be minding so much . . .' they would begin, spouting phrases from their overly formal, illiterate grasp of the English language in the doorway to her office. She would dismiss their pathetic excuses with an outstretched hand.

But Najma's thoughts didn't end there. Her niece, Yasmeen, was in trouble. In desperation she had sent a note through one of the servants begging Najma for help. A month earlier, Yasmeen had been discovered kissing the gardener's son in the servant quarters. The son was immediately sent back to his village. After the incident with the blades, the bandages on her wrists, and the secret overnight stay in hospital, Yasmeen was being watched by the family twenty-four hours a day. It was the only way her father knew how to care for his lovesick daughter until his duties were fulfilled.

Najma felt her braces digging into her shoulders, so she unclipped them from her waist and took her shirt off, exposing a white vest. She struck a match and lit a candle that was carefully melted onto the white saucer it was standing on. The flame danced and flickered in the breeze from the fan. Protecting it with her hand, she carried it to the windowsill to light her cigarette before placing it into the black holder.

There was just one more part to her nightly ritual. She exhaled a few playful rings of smoke before turning to the black wooden box on the table. Unbuckling the lid, she saw the gramophone record with the crimson label in place on the turntable. She wound the handle on the side of the box as much as it could give and gently allowed the needle to fall onto the grooves of the spinning vinyl. Tapping her right foot to the scat emanating from the speaker, she closed her eyes, invoking her own prayer to the old man in the sky whom she did truly believe was great.

'Mr Sandman bring me a dream . . . *bung bung bung bung* . . . make him the cutest that I've ever seen . . . give him two lips like roses and clover . . .'

By the time Mr Sandman had tap-danced Najma to the lush green lawns of her youthful academic past in Cambridge and back to the stuffy heat of her civil servant reality in Lahore, she was lying on her bed contemplating the events of the following day – Yasmeen's marriage.

Najma's older brother, Mian Jamal Shah, was Yasmeen's father. He was a wealthy civil engineer who had overseen the construction of the country's dams. Mian Sahib had various agricultural business interests including the ownership of flour mills. His pride was his six beautiful daughters, who were the talk of the city's social circles. Their names all ended in 'een' – Shaheen, Mehreen, Naveen, Faheen, Nasreen. The most protected of them all was the youngest child, Yasmeen.

Najma remembered rivers bursting and homes being swept away in the monsoon floods. She was stranded on the roof top of her own father's house holding Yasmeen's heavily pregnant mother sprawled on a charpoi bed strung with brown rope. There were blood-curdling screams as Yasmeen was pushed out, three weeks premature. Overwhelmed by a need to guard her, Najma had wrapped the baby in a yellow towel. As the baby grew into a little girl, she followed her aunt everywhere. Najma had managed to convince her own mother that she wouldn't soil her brilliant white shuttle-cock burka when she went out to protest for Pakistan's independence on the streets. She had somehow managed to smuggle little Yasmeen out underneath the white tent she was wearing.

'We will not stop until this country belongs to us,' they shouted, marching together hand-in-hand.

Years later, Najma saw that liberalism and independence held no influence over her brother's intentions for his daughters. The first five had been sent to college to study home economics. The family was invited for the practical examination where each daughter had prepared a menu for breakfast, lunch and dinner. She was marked on her standard of presentation and the measure of her hospitality. After every graduation, Najma witnessed the defining moment when Mian Sahib turned to his daughter and remarked, 'The food was delicious. You will make a very good wife! I am very proud! Your reward, my child, is a good husband. He will be the best like you and I have found him!'

Every time Najma watched in fury, as her niece's face radiated excitement. You're being duped and bribed into thinking that the graduation gift is the greatest blessing – a chance to wear new clothes and golden jewellery, she thought. If only you could realize that it's nothing more than the chance to live within the confinements of performing wifely duties.

Each son-in-law was carefully handpicked: a police commissioner; a colonel in the army; a wing commander in the air-force; a politician and a judge. What more could Mian Sahib's daughters ask for? Or rather, what more could Mian Sahib have asked for?

But Najma's little protester protégé, Yasmeen, strived for her own path, set in different directions. She had pleaded with theatrical displays of resentment and misery. She had managed to evade the home economics course, convincing her father that she could study for a fine arts degree at the National College of Arts. Now that she had graduated, marriage was an unavoidable obligation. It was her grandmother's dying wish that Yasmeen should marry her cousin Yousaf.

Najma watched the scale and extravagance of the wedding preparations consume her brother's life. Invitations were sent out to the prime minister and various influential government officials. Yasmeen's wedding trousseau was lovingly assembled with a collection of Benares silk. There were twelve sets of golden jewellery individually encrusted with garnets, turquoise, sapphires and diamonds to match her selection of silk outfits. Najma's wedding gift to her niece was a solid gold necklace of pound coins, an insurance policy. In fact, she had gifted all her nieces with a necklace of golden pound coins on their wedding day, but this particular design was all the rage in the current wedding season.

In principle, the plan was quite simple. Having repeatedly played through in her mind the history of Yasmeen's troubled behaviour, Najma knew only too well that marriage was not a solution, especially now that her niece's heart belonged to someone else. Her staff at the office had been invaluable and exceptionally discreet in acquiring the necessary items. Najma didn't want to think about consequences, though. Instead she turned onto her side and drifted off to sleep.

The morning sun flared onto the windscreen as Najma strategically parked her green Moskvitch round the corner. It was out of sight and a turning away from the main Mall Road. She made one last check in the rear-view mirror. She tightened the knot in her brown silk tie and adjusted her sunglasses on the bridge of her nose. For the last time she felt the package hidden in the waistband at the back of her trousers, covered by her dapper double-breasted jacket.

Walking round the corner there was no mistaking the fact that there was a wedding in the neighbourhood. Huge steel cooking pots were lined up outside the house, which was adorned with multi-coloured lights. The huge brightly coloured and handstitched Shamiana wedding marquees could be seen behind the high walls of her brother's house. Najma walked through the white metal gate. Guests had already arrived. Sitting in their segregated part of the veranda was a row of men with black, pencil-thin moustaches dressed in Savile Row suits. She felt their gaze as she walked past into the house.

Thankfully there was no sign of her brother. He must have been sitting in one of the side rooms with the imam. She walked down the hallway towards the back of the house and the sound of girls giggling. Her palms were clammy with sweat and she tightened her fists as she entered the room.

'. . . you need to drink; you need to keep your strength up for the whole day!' Yasmeen's sister, Nasreen, was on her knees in her peacock-blue shalwar-kameez. She was holding the straw in a bottle of Coca Cola to Yasmeen's red-lipsticked mouth.

'You'll need to keep your strength up for the whole night as well!' piped up a voice from the group sitting on the bed. Another fit of girly giggles ensued.

Najma paused at the door and saw that all six of her nieces had their hair glamorously set in flamboyant bouffant styles and side curls. They were each wearing their necklace of golden pound coins. The younger girls of the family stared silently at her. They never knew what to make of Najma. She was the only aunt they knew who drove a car. Najma swallowed with unease knowing that their heads had been filled with all kinds of stories warning them to keep away.

'Asalaam Alaikum!' she nearly shouted as she walked over to the bride. Yasmeen greeted her with a look of discomfort. Burdened down with bridal gold, she was dressed in a vermillion bridal costume embroidered in gold thread. She wore a heavy and ornate golden necklace as well as her necklace of golden pound coins. Her hands, gold rings on each finger, were daubed in clumsy bridal patterns of red henna dye. Down the centre parting of her bouffant hair was a golden chain with a circular garnet encrusted bridal tikka. It took up the entire centre of Yasmeen's forehead. Najma bent down and embraced Yasmeen and whispered in her ear, 'Behind the toilet. Salik Street . . .' And, cupping Yasmeen's face in her hands, she announced, 'God bless you always! You are looking so beautiful today! Listen to your sister and drink; you will need lots of strength.'

Yasmeen sipped from the straw obediently.

Najma entered the adjoining bathroom and bolted the door shut. She turned the taps on. Unbuttoning her jacket, she pulled out the flat package from the back of her trousers and placed it behind the toilet seat. Turning to the window with the dusty metal grid, she forced the stiff latch upwards. It opened inwards and the hinges screeched, so she pushed it back slowly brushing the dust off her clothes with her hand. She yanked the long lavatory chain twice to flush and smoothed her hair in the mirror. She knew she was betraying her brother, but there was no time for guilt.

As she went past the bedroom, Najma took a last look at Yasmeen and winked. A barefooted young servant girl in turquoise was walking carefully down the corridor holding a tray laden with chilled Coca Cola bottles. Najma stopped to grab a bottle and immediately pressed it against her burning cheek. She walked through the empty dining room with the antique Russian samovar on the side board. She stepped through to the kitchen and the courtyard at the back of the house, and slipped out the servants' door leaving it open to a side road. There was the distant sound of a military brass band coming closer. It was the groom's wedding party approaching the house. After they had passed, she crept across the road, stooping swiftly back towards her Moskvitch on Salik Street.

Najma glanced at her watch. It was midday. The train was due to leave in half an hour and her heart was racing in the airless car. She stared into the rear mirror, wiped the stickiness from her forehead with the back of her hand and wound the window down. She opened the glove compartment yet again to check for the envelope with the money and the first-class train ticket to Bahawalpur. The nikah ceremony must have started by now. What if Yasmeen had been caught? She looked again into the mirror and saw a figure running towards the car. Her heart pounded in her chest as she turned the key of the ignition. The faceless little figure in the black burka, which had been so carefully pressed and folded into the packet, was sprinting halfway down the street. Najma leaned over and opened the passenger door and looked in the mirror again. Above the bare feet of the figure in the burka she saw a speck of turquoise. There was also a pair of black plimsolls in the packet, so why was Yasmeen running barefoot, and why was she wearing turquoise which wasn't the colour of the shalwar-kameez in the packet?

'Madam! Madam!' screamed the unfamiliar voice of a child from the burka. Najma leaned back and switched off the ignition. The black figure was at her window, panting and out of breath. All that was visible was a pair of brown eyes.

'Madam! Madam!' the voice squawked.

'Go to the other side and get in, child.' Najma didn't want to attract the attention of the whole neighbourhood.

'Madam! Madam!' the little voice continued.

'Come inside and sit down.' Najma patted the beige leather seat, and unveiled the young servant girl's face.

'Madam, Yasmeen Bibi told me to find you here and give you this.' The girl took a folded piece of paper out of her pocket and placed it in Najma's hand.

Najma swallowed as she unfolded the paper slowly.

The first word, 'Sorry', was written in English, and then, in Urdu, was a scrawl that read: 'This is my kismet.'

Najma closed her eyes for a second and, when she opened them, she saw that the servant girl's foot was bleeding. She took out the handkerchief from her breast pocket and pressed it against the girl's hardened sole.

'How old are you?' she asked, holding the little foot. The young servant girl's brown eyes sparkled.

'I think I'm eleven or twelve years old. My mother says I am. Isn't Yasmeen Bibi a beautiful bride?'

'Yes, she is. Now your foot is better, you must get back – and wash your feet before you go inside the house, otherwise you'll get into trouble.' Najma leaned over to open the passenger door.

'I like your car,' the girl said.

Najma closed her eyes, stroking her temples with the tips of her fingers. Then she bashed the steering wheel with a clenched fist. Yet again she heard the faint sound of high-pitched humming. Something tickled the side of her face. She wound the window back up on her side of the car. She jerked her right hand with a sudden controlled violence and slapped the life out of the culprit that dared to disturb her. It left a red speck of blood on her hand.

KAVITA BHANOT

Gust of Life

It was Nanji who found him. Or, as she would later tell the followers, he who found her. *Chose* her. Because it was no coincidence, she knew, their meeting outside the Guru Nanak Gurdwara at three thirty-five, that sunny afternoon in the October of '84.

She had done her matha tek in the gurdwara, had listened to the kirtan, eaten langar, drank tea and shared unhappiness-happiness with Kuldeep. Outside the gurdwara gates she paused to button up her coat and rearrange the shawl around her head and shoulders. She looked at her watch to check how long she had before the appointment with Doctor Gupta and was in the middle of distributing the weight of her carrier bags evenly between her arms when a young man walked past and smiled.

It was a remarkable smile. His eyes, already a light shade of brown and made luminous by the sun which seemed to increase in wattage just then, shone with it. His skin wrinkled into rainbows across his cheekbones. 'Sat Sri Akal,' he said with great enthusiasm. Nanji looked to her left and to her right, but there was nobody there. That smile, that greeting, had been just for her. It occurred to her that perhaps the boy was crazy, like Mr Gordon, or drunk like Chauhan from number seventeen. Both of them walked the streets all day talking and smiling and waving at no one in particular.

'You've just come from the gurdwara, mata,' he said. 'Why do you look so heavy? Your heart should be full of love and joy. It should be all over your face. You should be giving it to everyone you meet.'

Nanji sighed. She shook her head. 'You're saying the right thing, beta,' she said. 'I spend all my days going from mandir to mandir, from gurdwara to gurdwara, trying to forget this world and prepare for the next. But what can I do? The problems of this world just don't let me go.'

'What problems do you have, mata?'

Nanji looked at him, the young man standing on the pavement before her, his head tilted as if waiting for her reply. He was a smart boy. Although he was not very tall – she came almost to his chin, and he barely filled his jacket – he gave the impression of height and solidity. His face was familiar, not in the way an acquaintance was, but with an itching, can't-quite-put-your-finger-on-it resemblance to a face more known than your own. It was a manly face; the beginnings of a beard roughened its lower third, but did not disguise the clean lines of his jaw. His nose, large and flat, had made itself comfortable across his face, flaring a little at the nostrils. His hair, long and curly, was almost too pretty for the rest of him. It was surprising that such a boy had nothing better to do than listen to an old woman's problems.

'What can I tell you, my son. There is so much unhappiness in my life. There is nothing but pain. If I was to tell you . . .'

He stepped to the side, towards the gurdwara, so they wouldn't be in the way of people walking past. He took the carrier bags from her and put them on the floor. Sinking his hands deep into the pockets of his jacket he said, 'Tell me, mata.'

It was a temptation that Nanji couldn't resist; it wasn't every day that someone showed interest in her problems.

'I have a son,' she began. 'He's my life, my only son. He lives in Toronto. I want to go and live with him. I know he wants me to come too. I know how much he loves me, how he cries for his mother. But his wife – I don't know what kind of woman I have married him to – she won't let him send for me. We all used to live here together, but her family is in Canada and she took Raju and the boys there.

She said she would send the papers for me later, but each time I ask she gives some new excuse. Nearly five years I've been waiting for the papers,' she said, displaying the thumb and fingers of one hand. 'My two grandsons, Ajay and Johnny, they must be big by now. They must have forgotten their dadi. Johnny, the older one, he had just started the big school when they left; he used to look so smart in his blazer, now he must be finishing school.

'And I have a daughter, Kamu. She lives in Plumstead, in London. She is so unhappy. On the phone, she tells me she's fine, she doesn't want me to worry, but I hear it in her voice; I'm her mother after all. Her husband is so weak, he's not even a man; his mother tortures her and he doesn't say anything. They taunt her, that she doesn't have more children, that she only has a daughter, no son. I don't know what black magic the witch is doing to her, but my girl is always ill, she's wasting away. They won't let me see her, but when I saw her last, a year ago, she was like this.' Nanji put up a finger. 'My Kamu, who was so fat and healthy.'

As she talked the boy stood perfectly still. His eyes, now a darker brown, almost black, were fixed on her, watching her face as if it was a television screen, following, reflecting her every emotion. A few times, he leaned forward, turning his ear towards her mouth as if her words were so precious he didn't want to risk dropping even one. She would finish in a moment, Nanji told herself. She would be just a little late for her appointment; anyway they would just ask her to sit in the waiting room for a while before they called her name.

'And then I have this pain in my knees. Arthritis. I should rest but there's so much to do. It's better that I keep moving. Once I sit down, that will be it; maybe I won't be able to get up again. Then who will look after me? I have diabetes and high blood pressure too. Dr Gupta has told me I shouldn't carry any tension, it is stress that gives me this blood pressure and sugar. But how can you stop worrying about your children? I'm a mother. Of course I will worry about them. It's my fault, I married them to the wrong people. I spoiled their lives. But what could I do? I was all alone, there was no one to give me advice. He left me when they were still at school.' She started to cry now. 'He left me all alone. I didn't know how to do anything at that time. He loved me so much; he sat me on his eyelashes while he was alive. Now I'm all alone, I have to do everything by myself.'

He had opened a tap; the words were gushing out. Nanji hardly thought about what was coming out of her mouth; there was no neat packaging, no structure, no tidying up. Soon she was jumping from one complaint to another, going in circles, repeating herself. People she knew walked past, said 'Namaste', 'Sat Sri Akal', 'Radha Soami'. Nanji hardly noticed them. At one point, afterwards she wouldn't remember how and when, the boy put a weightless hand on her arm, lifted her bags, crossed the street and walked towards the park, where he sat down on a bench. She followed him, sat beside him without pausing, aware only of the words that continued to pour out of her, and his kind eyes, which didn't disconnect from her even for a second.

It must have been an hour by the time Nanji ran out of words. She took a deep breath, feeling good, clean and light. 'I don't know what you are,' she said. 'But you seem like a farishta to me. You've come straight from God. Nobody has ever listened to my problems like this before.'

Mostly she avoided talking about these things with anyone. She tried to keep her life private. People took advantage when they knew your secrets, that was what her husband had always told her. But sometimes, when she became too full of everything, when one hurt was so tightly packed on top of another that she was in physical pain, she would open up her heart to Kuldeep in the gurdwara or Geeta from number twenty-three or Mrs Moonga. But they were always so full of their own problems, she never felt that they were truly *listening* to her. She would start off telling Mrs Moonga about something that had happened that day, a scene that had been playing, rewinding and replaying in her head all day.

'I asked to speak to the boys today. She told me they were asleep. But she could wake them up na, to speak to their dadi calling all the way from the UK. I told her, and she said they have exams, their sleep is very important. As if I have no care for their exams. Exams *are* important, but talking for two minutes with their dadi doesn't mean they will fail. There is always something or the other whenever

I call; they're at school, they've gone to their nani's house, they're with their friends. She just doesn't want me to speak to them.'

'Haan, I know,' Mrs Moonga would say. 'In my house it's just the same. Sangeeta tells me not to give toffees to the children. "You're spoiling their teeth," she tells me. Look, a grandmother can't even give toffees to her grandchildren. But "just stay quiet", everyone tells me, "just keep hold of silence".'

'Who do I have in the world but my children and my children's children?' said Nanji. 'Without them I'm all alone.'

'It's a bad time,' Mrs Moonga would say, shaking her head. 'I suffered for fifteen years with Maaji, so much I suffered without a word of complaint. And, now when it's my turn, I end up with such a sharp daughter-in-law, and still I have to stay quiet. Always to stay quiet. How is that fair?'

In frustration, Nanji would stay quiet herself, letting Mrs Moonga cry about her own thing.

But this boy sitting beside her on the bench had listened to her problems as if there was nothing more important in the world. He had not interrupted to talk about himself – perhaps he was too young to have seen any problems of his own. He wasn't like other young people. She saw very clearly, when she talked to them, the signs that they were searching for a gap in the net she had caught them in, through which they could slip out, escape. They would shift from foot to foot, they'd disappear into their thoughts while bland eyes continued to look at her in a pretence of listening. They would be distracted; their eyes wandering towards the television, following an attractive girl, or, with relief, seizing upon some disturbance – an argument, an accident. They would drop hints, looking at their watch or, ever so slowly, gathering their things, moving towards the edge of their seat, uncurling and, once they were straight, taking small steps away from her. So Nanji became stubborn. She hardly breathed between sentences, she held them hostage with her words. No one had time to listen any more. When she was young she had happily spent hours listening to her grandparents or, as a daughter-in-law, to his grandmother and mother. And it had never seemed like something painful. As

Mrs Moonga said, when it had come to their turn they had been short changed in so many things.

Nanji remembered then, as if she had just come to consciousness, the appointment with Doctor Gupta, left abandoned somewhere in the midst of her outpouring. She had no regrets. She could see the doctor another time, any time. It was all she did, visit doctors. What else was left in an old person's life? Appointments with the GP, the hospital, the dentist, the optician, the physiotherapist, the Chinese doctor, the homeopath. That was her daily routine. But a boy like this didn't cross her path every day.

'I live near by,' she said to him on impulse. 'Just three streets away. Come to my house. I'll give you tea.'

She didn't expect him to say yes. She thought he would smile politely and say, 'Next time, mata.' But he shrugged his shoulders, curled his fingers round the handles of her carrier bags, and said, 'Chalo phir.'

He wouldn't let her carry even one bag. Light without them and with happiness, she seemed to float as she led him, chattering the whole time, past Hari's video shop, through the park, down Gilbert Street. 'Where do you live?' she asked him.

It occurred to her, as she asked the question, that she knew nothing about the boy. She wondered then if she was doing the right thing, taking him back to her home. He could be anyone. True, he was an Indian boy, not black or white. And he looked like a nice boy from a nice family; his clothes were clean and smart, his trousers carried a sharp crease, his black shoes were shiny. But no thief or murderer had their identity written on their forehead. She took a deep breath. She swallowed. On the television – *Crimewatch*, the news – they were always showing what happened when you let a stranger into your house. And her children were constantly telling her on the phone, 'Be careful, mata, don't open the door to anyone you don't know, leave the chain on the front door when you're at home.' Raju had even sent her money to make a porch, a second front door, for extra security.

They don't come themselves, thought Nanji bitterly, they just send their money and their advice. Maybe it will be good if something happens to me, then they will learn their lesson. But this thought quickly evaporated, and she just felt scared. The boy was telling her that he had come from India three weeks earlier. He was studying at the university. Surely he was a nice boy, thought Nanji. He was studying at the university and he had listened to her so nicely. Anyway, she couldn't take her invitation back now. She hardly heard what else the boy told her about himself. After some time, he stopped talking. They walked in silence. Mrs Moonga's face came into Nanji's mind, telling her the latest horror story about some crime that had been committed against a relative of hers, shaking her head as she said, 'It's a bad time, sister, a bad time.'

For the rest of the walk home, as Nanji unlatched her gate and opened it, as she kicked aside some of the leaves and crisp packets that were always blowing onto her path, as she searched the pockets of her handbag for her keys and opened the porch door, then the front door, Nanji chanted 'Radha Soami' over and over again in her head. Even through her fear, she was grabbing the socks and underwear she had put on the radiator in the hallway to dry, smoothing the plastic cover on the carpet with her foot. She had not been expecting a guest.

'Now, Maharaj Ji,' she said silently to the big photograph of Maharaj Charan Singh Ji that hung on the wall of the living room, 'my life is in your hands, it's up to you to protect me.'

'You're Radha Soami,' said the boy.

'Yes,' she said. 'This is my guru. I've taken naam. Maharaj Ji gave it to me himself when he did his UK tour in '75. My belief is very strong. I do all the rounds of mandirs and gurdwaras, but my heart is Radha Soami.'

'My parents are also Radha Soami,' said the boy. 'They are strong believers too. They both have naam and go to stay in Beas for some days every year. I believe too.'

Nanji wasn't scared any more. His parents were Radha Soami. He was Radha Soami. He wouldn't hurt her. Maharaj Ji, she thought, you've saved me again.

'Sit here,' she said, pointing to the settee. 'I'll be back in five minutes.' She returned with tea and digestive biscuits. 'Now, tell me about yourself,' she said, putting the tray on the coffee table and sitting down beside him. 'I don't even know your name.'

His legs wide, he placed a foot on his knee and leaned back into the sofa, filling it. His name was Veeru, he told her, taking the tea that she offered. Short for Veerendra. She asked again where he was from, what he was doing. She had not heard properly earlier, she told him, ashamed in the face of his generous listening.

He smiled. 'I know. You were worried. It's difficult in today's world to trust people.' She denied this but he smiled, as if he knew just what was in her heart.

He was from the Jatani village in Punjab, near Ludhiana. He had also lived, for some time, in Ludhiana, and in Delhi. He had come to England to study civil engineering at the university, had arrived just three weeks before. The university had told him that there was no accommodation for him, he had to look for his own. Some students had told him that Handsworth was an Indian area so he had come there to look for something. 'Do you know of any room?' he asked Nanji.

At first Nanji didn't think of it. She wanted to help the boy and in her head she skimmed through friends and neighbours who might have a spare room. It had to be a house where they didn't take meat or alcohol, said the boy. At these words Nanji felt such affinity for the boy; he was one of her own, no different to her own children. She couldn't remember the last time she had felt such a connection with someone who wasn't related to her by blood. And that was when the idea came to her, motivated also perhaps by her selfish reluctance to let such a fine pair of ears go.

'Why don't you stay here?' she said. The boy sat up. He looked round the sitting room as if chewing the idea over.

'It's a poor woman's house,' said Nanji. 'Very simple. But I'll look after you like your own mother. You can have the big bedroom upstairs. It used to be Raju's room. You can give me whatever money you can. It will be some help for me. And you'll be giving me company. The best thing is that this is not an eating drinking house, and you're not an eating drinking boy.' The boy was quiet. 'I can show you the house,' she said.

He shook his head. 'I have no problem with the house,' he said. 'It would be a very good arrangement for me; I can already see my mother in you. But you shouldn't decide so quickly. You might be feeling sorry for me, for my situation, but you should think about yourself first.' As he looked at her, his lips pressed together, he seemed so serious, so old for his age. 'Think for a day or two,' he said. 'Decisions should be made after thought. I'll take your number and call you.'

Her husband had been the same: everything he said and did was with a cool mind. 'Whatever you do,' he would say, 'do it after thinking and understanding.'

They talked for a while. Nanji remembered the surgery, it would be closing soon. She went to the hallway to call them. 'Can you tell me the time of my appointment tomorrow,' she said to Sheila, the receptionist. Sheila checked. 'It was today at 4 o'clock, Mrs Chauhan,' she said, annoyed. 'You've missed it again.' Nanji acted out surprise and confusion and asked Sheila to make her another appointment.

She returned to the living room with a glass of water and her ice-cream tub of medicines, various containers and bottles and packets. To make it easier for herself, at the beginning of each week she organized her week's worth of pills into little envelopes which she labelled in Hindi. One for the morning, afternoon and evening of each day of that week. But still she forgot to take them.

'This is what old age is,' she said to Veeru, placing in her hand the assortment of coloured pills that she was supposed to have taken that afternoon.

'Why do you have so many medicines?'

Having swallowed the pills, Nanji drank the water. 'They're keeping me alive,' she said, helping herself to a biscuit to take the taste away. Almost proudly, she showed him each bottle and container, told him what it was for; this one for her blood pressure, this one for her heart, the painkillers for her arthritis, the ones for keeping her sugar low.

'You have diabetes and you're eating a biscuit,' said the boy.

Nanji looked at it, a little guiltily. Just one biscuit wouldn't make much difference, she explained to him.

'There would be no need to take so many medicines,' he said, 'if you had discipline with living and eating.'

Nanji was reminded again of her husband. He too would tell her that she was weak, that she was led by the taste on her tongue. When he had been alive he had supervised everything. Their menu had been fixed for each day of the week; the whole family would eat their dinner together and afterwards he would cut up some fruit. Once a week, on Sunday afternoon, he would tell Kamu to make coffee for everyone. Just one cup. Sometimes Nanji would say, 'Let's have another one.' But he would refuse. 'You have to stay in limits,' he would say, 'nothing should become an addiction.' He had been a man of principle.

At that moment Nanji knew, as much as she had ever known anything, that she had to keep the boy in her house. He *had* to stay, she told him then, there was no question. She had made up her mind and wouldn't change it. He could move in that very day, could go now to get his luggage.

And that was how Nanji lost her sadness and acquired a new son. Now she was too busy and distracted to think about her pain. Now she had a reason to wake up every morning. She would lie in bed at night thinking of what she could make for the boy the next day for his breakfast, something different every day; aloo paratha with dahi, plain parantha with achar, beans bread, porridge. She asked her friends for new recipes, trying things she had never made before, dhokla, idli, fruit cake, gulab jamen. She packed something nice for him to take to university every day. After he was gone she went shopping, looking for the freshest ingredients on Soho Road. She sang as she cleaned the house; bhajans from the mandir, shabads from the gurdwara, film songs from Radio XL. She took things out of the cupboards, wiped each jar, each bottle, and then the inside of the cupboard, before putting the things back. She hoovered with more precision, getting into the corners of the rooms, moving settees and tables to swallow the dust under them. Her house was once again as clean (although a little more tatty and worn) as it had been when her husband had been alive.

The boy seemed happy too. He had called his mother, he told Nanji, to tell her that he had found a mother just like her in the UK.

After a few months Nanji saw that the boy was going to the university less and less. At first he missed the odd day saying that it was too cold outside or that he wasn't feeling well. Then he was going in just a few days a week. Soon he stopped going completely. Nanji didn't say anything; she was just happy to have him there in the house. Only once she asked him about it and he said he already knew everything they were teaching there; university was a waste of time for him.

Every day, from two o'clock in the afternoon until four, he stayed in his room, the door closed. Nanji assumed that he was studying. The rest of the time, the boy melted himself into Nanji's life. She didn't let him help her in the kitchen so he just stood there, keeping her company as she cooked. When Nanji fell down the stairs and was in bed for a week, it turned out that he knew very well how to make food, each day there was a new type of daal and sabzi. He could even make the rotis.

It was around that time that he took over responsibility of her ice-cream tub. It was a great relief for Nanji to hand it over to him. He would tell her when it was time to take her medicines, get out the right envelope, bring her water.

They would sit together in front of the television watching Nanji's favourite films. He was more interested in the ones with a nationalist or religious theme, like *Bhakt Prahlad, Jai Santoshi Maa, Shaheed* or *Shirdi Ke Sai Baba*. While watching the last film, Nanji noticed tears rolling down the boy's face, perhaps as he saw how the villagers who didn't believe in his power treated Sai Baba, or as he saw the pain of people's lives. He was lost in the film and didn't seem to notice as Nanji looked from the screen to his face in wonder, a little guilty that the film didn't create such a disturbance in her.

It was obvious that the boy had a keen interest in God and religion. He went with great enthusiasm to the gurdwara and mandir with her. He made friends with the pandits and gyanis and would sit with them for hours. Nanji would come home but Veeru would stay on, asking them questions, listening to them, arguing with them.

Then he saw some things that he didn't like. Not all the gyanis and pandits had an interest in spirituality, in bringing the ordinary people closer to God, in helping the unfortunate, he said. Some of them were trying to make money, running the places like businesses. That was not right. He heard them singing at the Anand Bhavan Mandir about how much money each person had donated. For the big donations he saw that they had put the names and amounts on a chart in the entrance. He heard a rumour that the pandit at the Narayan Mandir was keeping a large percentage of the donations for himself. Someone told him that a boy had not been served langar in the Guru Nanak Gurdwara because of his caste, because he was a Chamar, that Manjeet's girl couldn't hold her wedding in the gurdwara because she was marrying a Tarkhan boy not a Jatt.

Veeru stopped going to those places. Instead, he went shopping with Nanji, to Hari's video store, to her appointments. Soon Nanji couldn't remember a time when she had done all these things alone. The doctors didn't look at her; they told Veeru which pills she had to take, when and how many. 'You have to stop her from having sweet things,' Dr Gupta would tell Veeru and Veeru would look at Nanji and say, 'Don't worry doctor, I'll make sure.' Sometimes, Veeru and the doctor would get into conversations.

Wherever he went the boy made friends. Everyone remembered the handsome boy who asked lots of questions. Soon he was going around by himself, meeting all his new friends – he sat with Hari at the video store, with Dr Gupta at his surgery, with Munim Bhai at the grocery store, Jeetu at the garage; he visited other friends in their homes. He was spending less and less time at home, spending it instead with strangers.

One day he didn't come home for dinner. Silence echoed in the house as Nanji ate all alone. After her food he wasn't there with the ice-cream tub, making sure she took her medicines. For the next two hours Nanji muttered to herself as she walked round her living room, practising what she would say to him.

'It doesn't look nice,' she said, when he eventually returned, 'being outside the house so much, walking around the streets all day. This is your home, you should stay in the house. I've taken on this role of your mother, that's why I'm saying this to you. Otherwise there are so many lafanga boys around. Your parents have sent you to study, but you don't even go to the university any more.'

The boy listened quietly, seriously. And when she finished, he looked at her and said, 'You're right, mata. I'm grateful that you're telling me, that you care so much. I'll certainly keep it in mind.' Nanji hugged him.

He didn't go to the university after that. But neither did he go out much, except with Nanji. Instead, his new friends began to visit him at home. 'Is Veeru there?' Harminder from number seventeen would ask and Nanji would reluctantly let him in. He would stay all day drinking one cup of tea after another, demanding Veeru's time and attention. Soon they were all coming. From morning until night there would be visitors: Hari from the video store, Munim Bhai from the shop, Jeetu from the garage. 'Don't they have work to do?' Nanji asked Veeru.

One morning Kuldeep came to visit. Nanji left her in the living room with the boy and went to make tea. When she returned, fifteen minutes later, Kuldeep was telling the boy about her fourth girl, Jenny, who had been made pregnant by one of Handsworth's well-known gangsters. The girl was insisting, as if life was a Hindi film, that she would marry him and only him. At one time she had been a sensible girl with a beautiful voice – she would play the harmonium and sing in the gurdwara – but she had lost her senses over this boy. There was talk that someone must have fed her something. Kuldeep didn't normally talk about this with anyone, it was her shame, even if all of Handsworth was talking about it. As she poured her heart out to the boy, he listened. In the end he said, 'Let her marry him.'

'But her life will be spoiled. He and his brothers have such a bad reputation, they're the most well-known gangsters in Handsworth. And she's just a child, hardly eighteen years old. We wanted her to study. She always wanted to be a teacher.'

'You must let her follow her own destiny. I know you're thinking the best for her, but you can't control her fate. You've given your advice, now you must let her do what she wants to do. You can't force her. You can't lock her up. You can't control her with a remote control.'

Nanji could hardly believe the way Kuldeep was sitting quietly and listening; Kuldeep, who was so larakhi she never listened to anyone. 'Where have you been keeping this boy?' she said to Nanji. 'Bot beeba aa.'

Nanji sat quietly as they continued to talk. 'Don't you need to pick up Satinder's boy from the nursery?' she said at twelve o'clock, when Kuldeep didn't even look like leaving.

'Has it come to twelve?' said Kuldeep with surprise. 'I didn't even notice the time slip away.' She sighed. 'Man nain karda jaan da. Meenu's at home today, I'll call and ask her to pick up the boy.'

'The phone isn't working,' said Nanji. 'Anyway, Veeru needs to study.'

When before they would say they were too busy, now Nanji's friends had all the time to visit her.

'I don't know what it is in the boy,' said Mrs Moonga, 'that keeps pulling me back. He has such peace in him. It cools my heart to be near him. And when I tell him my problems it feels like they've got less just from telling him.'

'He's young in age,' said Geeta, 'but there's a very old spirit in him.'

There were always people in the living room now, drinking tea, telling jokes, sharing their problems. And amidst them, was the boy, sometimes giving advice, sometimes telling jokes of his own, but mostly just listening. He still disappeared into his room for two hours every day at two o'clock and nobody knew what he did there, but they waited for him.

Nanji began to enjoy the gust of life that had been blown her way. The days blurred into each other, disappeared into busyness: conversation, tea-making, eating, laughter and tears. Sometimes she missed that time when he had been hers alone, but how, she thought, could she have expected to keep a boy like that all to herself? And at least he was there, under her roof, cooling her eyes.

Sometimes she worried that she wasn't doing the right thing. Her children kept calling her, telling her off for trusting a boy she had picked up from the street, for opening up her house to all these people. 'What would Dad have said, mata?' Kamu asked her again and again.

He had been very strict about keeping a quiet, private life. 'The outside world should be left at the doorstep,' he would say. 'You shouldn't bring people into your home and if you do, you should know everything about their family, their background first.' For him, home had been sacred, the place to escape the world, not to let it in. And now all these people were invading the house and nothing was in her control anymore. It was his house, and she was walking all over his principles. When he started coming into her dreams at night, asking her what she was doing, Nanji resolved that she would speak to the boy. But then, what happened next, swept away her worries. It changed everything.

It started the morning that Veeru didn't come out from his room. At first Nanji thought nothing of it. It was unusual but perhaps he was tired, she thought. She didn't disturb him. After eleven o'clock friends started coming to see him. Hari came first, then Harminder. And then Mrs Moonga. 'He'll just be coming,' Nanji kept saying.

When he hadn't come down by twelve o'clock, Nanji left them in the sitting room and went to investigate. She knocked on Veeru's door a few times. He didn't answer. She tried the handle. He had locked it from the inside, something he didn't normally do. She rapped on the door again, called out his name and when there was no reply, she banged on the door.

That was when the fear entered her heart. He couldn't be sleeping so deeply. Perhaps he had fallen unconscious in there, or even died. She got down on her knees, trying to look through the one inch gap under the door. Mrs Moonga, who was coming up the stairs, joined her on the landing. Without a word she copied her. As they both peered under the door, they saw glimpses of Veeru tangled up; the soles of his feet, his knees, his thighs. As if he was sitting cross-legged. 'He hasn't opened the door all morning,' whispered Nanji. 'He's locked it from the inside. I've knocked and knocked, called his name, but he won't open it. I don't know if he's okay.'

Mrs Moonga called Hari and Harminder up. 'These boys can break open the door,' she said after explaining the situation to them. But Nanji didn't think that was a good idea. She was sure now that Veeru was okay, her door would be broken for no reason at all. She put up a hand, then went to find the box of tools she kept in the cupboard under the stairs.

'Can you take the screws out of this?' Nanji asked Hari, pointing to the handle of the door. 'Then we can see into the room.' They all stood to the side and watched as Hari got on his knees and used the screwdriver to take out the screws. He took out the last screw and removed the handle. The twin handle on the other side fell onto the carpet inside the room, creating a milk bottle sized hole in the door.

Hari peered through it. 'It looks like he's meditating,' he said. He stepped back to let the others have a look. Nanji put an eye to the door first. Still wearing the kurta pyjama that he wore to bed, the boy was sitting upright in the middle of the room, his legs crossed, his back straight, his eyes closed. Unflinching at all their activity and noise, he sat perfectly still. There was a serene, peaceful smile on his face.

'Can't he hear us?' said Harminder.

'We shouldn't disturb him,' said Hari.

'Who is he?' said Mrs Moonga.

'All I know,' said Nanji, 'is that he's not an ordinary boy.'

The rest of that day it was the same, and the next day, and the next day. For three days the boy didn't come out of the room, even for a glass of water. Nanji didn't know what to do. It wasn't a normal thing. But she decided to put her faith in God. Whatever He was doing, it was after thinking and understanding. More of their friends came, the word spread. As if it was a show, all kinds of people came to the house to peep through the hole, to see the meditating boy. They filled the house, sat around for hours, as if it was a blessing just to be near him. And Nanji, spending all her pension on food and tea, served the people tirelessly. She didn't turn a single person away. 'I knew,' she told Kuldeep, who had sent her daughters to help Nanji in the kitchen, 'that day I met him, that he was special. He has a direct link to God. God has sent him to help us.' And she would help him, she had decided, to help other people.

BIDISHA

Dust

Rosalind Ray had the indelible smile of a genie, a dry slab-like face and a metallic red crop. For the last ten years she had been the headmistress of Blackdean Boys' Grammar School. Blackdean: leafy, family friendly, laudably mixed, represented by a manicured philanderer of an MP who produced soundbites with the precision, speed and force of a circus knife-thrower.

It was nine o'clock on a Thursday morning in the first week of September and Mrs Ray was awaiting the new art teacher, Ryan Arrowsmith. This Arrowsmith soon came shambling up, solid and fifty-something in linen trousers, leather work boots, a canvas jacket and an old but carefully ironed shirt. On his walk he'd had an intriguing snapshot of local life: a cluster of tawny-bottomed mums outside the primary school, a few Croatian-looking chaps and several wenches and their gigolo boyfriends strutting towards the technical college. Blackdean, Ryan decided happily, had *flavour*.

Mrs Ray loomed up the steps.

'There you are,' she said, shaking Ryan's hand firmly, dryly, neutrally. 'I was beginning to worry.'

Mrs Ray had worked in education in the prison system before coming to Blackdean and still carried a whiff of incarceration and enforced punctuality about her. She had been awarded an OBE for her prison work, an honour which she concealed from her colleagues. Competitive jealousy was rife in the small world of English grammar school heads and she had no patience for it. Mrs Ray was also an expert hill walker, French speaker, hobbyist, breeder of dogs and leader of men – or rather, now, boys.

She proceeded along the walkway and Ryan followed, apologising. He'd been having some trouble with his van again, he explained.

The school campus was made up of the music, teaching, sports blocks and canteen on the right, the chapel on the left and the tennis courts and swimming pool around the corner. Behind the pool lay the playing fields, which were interrupted by clustered black trees growing so close together that they resembled conferring bureaucrats. The fields ran into a forest called Black North Wood.

'Have you got all your course plans and pens and pencils and whatnot?' said Mrs Ray.

'Yes. Yes, I have.' Ryan patted his cloth bag, which was printed with the curly logo of an Indian tea company.

'And where is it you've come from again? Remind me.'

'Ahm . . . my last post was at Crestwick. Very nice place. Friendly. Small.'

Mrs Ray had brought him to the chapel.

'Right,' she said, pushing the door open. 'I have to get back, but you're going to meet Ilora Sen –'

'Oh, *I* know that name. My son's got a book of her poems on the shelf.'

'Good, then you should make friends. Ilora's the head of pastoral studies here. She's back after a two year sabbatical. If you have any questions it's best to go to her before you come to me. In you go.'

Ryan found himself in a large, sparse office. Two gaunt wooden chairs stood against the wall like twin governesses. Sitting behind a presidential desk was Ilora Sen. She had dark hair, dark skin and a full mouth that ended in two distinct up-curving points.

'Hello,' she said warmly, shaking Ryan's hand. 'Please. Take a seat.'

Ryan smiled at Ilora and felt ancient, ugly, clumsy, fat, poor and pale. These days the scintillating gleam that had once enhanced his eye was the ghastly yellow of old ivory and his jokes came off as lewd inquiries. He'd turned into the kind of man at whom toddlers stared hostilely on the bus.

'So, this is where the school chaplain lives, is it?' he said.

Ilora grinned and shook her head.

'Not any more. It's now a common area for the students. This isn't a religious school. Come – I'll show you around. You sculpt, don't you? I'll take you to the art corridor.'

Ryan nodded.

'I do people's heads, in bronze. I was thinking I might put on a show, a local exhibition of my stuff.'

'You can use the art rooms whenever you like, provided no one else needs the space, and there's a studio at the end, but it's tiny . . . You're new to Blackdean, aren't you? Are you settling in?'

'We've got a nice flat on one of those Victorian blocks. The bricky ones,' he said enthusiastically. 'Me and my boy. He just came into the fifth year. He's sixteen. No, I lie, fifteen. Sixteen in December. I always give him one more than he's due. He walked up before me. Doesn't want to be seen with his senile old Pappy.'

'What's his name?'

'Cameron.'

'If you tell him to come by and see me for a chat . . .'

Ryan nodded, as he felt he ought. He didn't feel like a father figure, as such. He should be a sort of enigmatic, wizardly friend, hovering near and soundless, appearing through some innate paternal intuition whenever he was required. Ryan himself had been adopted at the age of two. His new parents had kept him, washed him and fed him, taught him to read, disciplined him, combed his hair and done everything they were supposed to do.

'Where do *you* live, Ilora?'

'Down the road. I've lived in the same house all my life.'

Ilora looked out of the window and had a quick, interfolded memory of doing the same thing one morning three years ago. Three years ago she'd just turned twenty-nine. Her old family car, a red Honda, had been parked where her Polo was now. Ilora preferred to drive at night; she enjoyed seeing the darkness melt like black wax before the headlights as she cruised to the linoleum mosque of the superstore under a marbled ink-in-water moon.

When Ilora was growing up, Blackdean still resembled the village it had been before the wars. There was the old toy shop, The Curiosity Box, which sold wooden animals, Halloween costumes and Ouija boards. There was Mr Kyriakos, the tubby tailor. There was the tea shop and its Formica tables of old couples. They were all gone now, so long vanished that Ilora wondered if they had really been as charming as she remembered. Perhaps they were all full of provincial racists. These days Blackdean was served by a Boots, a Ronald Brown optician's and a Pizza Express, squeezed into centuries-old buildings with leaded upper windows, powdered white cheeks and brows of frilled slate. The other day she saw written on the wall next to the cashpoint, CUNT.

Ilora had been born at Regents Oak hospital on the Blackdean–Hernlow border. Her parents were both Indian and had come to England more than forty years ago. Her mother, Radha, was an academic; her father, Dwarek Banerjee (Sen was Radha's surname), was an adorable naïf in public and something else at home. Dwarek died of cancer when Ilora was seventeen. At the expensive and pleasingly diverse Tapestry Guild Girls' School in Hertfordshire Ilora was cool, funny and popular, just like every other girl at the school. She went to Oxford and the London Political Institute. Then she brought out a collection of poems, which was politely received. But it made no difference. Observing the identical chaps she thought of as the Tobys and the Tims being parachuted ahead of her, swiftly, subtly, silently, automatically, she pawed the ground and made a few private observations on the state of play in the real world. She set her face, let her anger flare and harden, then filed it down to a cold, neat edge.

Around six years ago Radha met Mrs Ray at a conference. Mrs Ray floated the idea of a general tutor, who could act as a mentor to students. Radha suggested her daughter. It was an interesting job. It paid well. And it was very close to home.

Ilora reversed the Polo into a driveway bordered by powdery, khaki coloured fruit trees. A tall Somalian lady passed in front of her, elegant and rhythmic as a waving reed, her headscarf a folded white wing. Two policemen sauntered self-consciously down the middle of the road, gauche as debutantes – a white policeman on a black horse and a black policeman on a white horse. Did they notice everything or nothing? It was impossible to tell.

Ilora's house was called Red Stables. Ivy lay knotted over the red bricks and roof; she had been warned that the vines would wrestle the place to the ground within the next thirty years. Ilora went in, took off her rings and watch, changed into her home clothes, ate dinner, watched some films, set the burglar alarm, went upstairs and had a shower. In her bedroom she took a sleeping pill and lay down with the light on. Soon she was asleep, her face softened and chaste.

Ilora's parents had arrived from West Bengal and progressed to college lecturing jobs in London, in the years before the polytechnics and the universities merged. Both, when they arrived, observed the historic watchtower of native disdain. Ilora remembered the insults she'd witnessed directed at her parents when she was growing up: sugar-coated shrapnel delivered openly, calmly, with that legendary smiling rudeness. More than twenty years later she could still find herself turning the shards over in her mind. There was a book in that, she thought, if she was willing to dip a pen in her anger and write it.

Ilora's parents made themselves forget the sting of those scenes during their upward flight, which ended many years later in Radha becoming famous – within a certain circle – as her university's first Indian, feminist, political theory don. There was even a small annexe in the faculty library named after her. Radha had married Dwarek by arrangement but his stated intentions to complete his doctorate, conduct research projects and travel the world came to nothing. He found his place as a basic skills tutor in a semi-legit tutorial college in Hammersmith.

Two years and two months ago, Radha Sen delivered a guest lecture at Cambridge. Later, there was a candlelit dinner at which the discussion was as polished and sharp as the silverware. Driving away afterwards, Radha's red Honda was struck head-on by a student who was several times over the drink-drive limit and speeding the wrong way down the street. Both were killed instantly. A road safety camera recorded it all, its lens glinting like a watch face.

*

Ilora was about to make her modelling debut. Ryan Arrowsmith had come to see her, thanked her for helping him during the first week of term and asked if she'd pose for his local exhibition. She'd given a flattered Twenties cocktail laugh, a ribbon of miniature bells loose in the air. Ryan was an easy type – easy to understand, easy to disdain, easy to rebuff – the kind of older man who smelled of tobacco and body soap, who thought he could 'get around' women by flirting with them, who had an over-keen overweening manner, bright hungry eyes and a mouth full of winking words. That was what she'd thought of Ryan Arrowsmith when she first met him, and she hadn't thought anything of him since.

Ryan was in the studio at the end of the art corridor. The floor was protected by plastic sheets on which stood a bucket of water, a wooden stool, a block of clay covered in wetted rags and a revolving, flat-topped stand. On the stand was a rough oval of wire mesh. There was a large metal sink in the corner and a kettle, some chipped mugs and an assortment of biscuit tins on the worktop.

'*Here* she is! *Entrez, entrez, s'il vous plaît,*' Ryan sang when he saw her. 'Cuppa cha?'

'You seem very at home,' Ilora remarked, sitting down.

'It's cosy, isn't it? It's my little hidey-hole.'

Ilora peered out through the fire exit doors. The studio was high over the campus and the chapel sat in one corner of the view. A shadow passed over the fields and the school grew still and silent. Rain started to fall with a rustling sound, a multitude of guilty souls whispering their secrets in confession.

'Thanks for inviting me.'

'Oh, no need to thank me,' he said, laughing. 'I'm the one who gets to look at a pretty face all day. The show's going to focus on local characters of note. It'll be at the library in the spring. The Nelson Mandela library.'

'Yeah, they renamed it last year. Not sure why, they don't have a single non-white staff member.'

The librarian was a deeply menopausal Conservative Party fund-raiser type with a frosted hairdo, thought Ryan. She'd told him that the library usually invited people to exhibit, not the other way around, but Ryan eventually charmed her into showing him the exhibition facilities: a trestle table and a blue felt screen with three panels.

He gave Ilora his favourite mug – white and gold, with a picture commemorating the marriage of Charles and Diana – and shuffled the stand forward. He dunked his hands in the water and began to thumb fat nuggets of clay off the block, pressing them into the mesh.

'You can shut your eyes if you want. This is just to get the size and shape of the skull right. Tiny little heads like yours only need three or four sessions.'

He liked the way the clay responded to him. First it was dull and heavy, then he wet it and it spread in a thin opaque sheet, chilly and shiny around his hand. Steadily it warmed up, dried and tightened. The fine edge of it near his wrist began to flake off, cashmere dust.

'How're you enjoying Blackdean?' Ilora asked.

'Not bad. Not bad at all.'

He and Cameron had been living in Blackdean for over a month. This was their second move in four years and, as ever, they'd landed on their feet. Ryan had one afternoon and one middle-of-the-day off per week. In his spare hours he chatted with the girls in the secretaries' office or wandered along the High Street to buy cream horns from Martins Bakery.

'And how's your son settling in?'

'Oh, well, you know. He's a bit of a Norman No-mates, sorry to say.'

'Has he ever been bullied?'

'Not that I know of.'

'He's not cutting classes is he?'

'No,' said Ryan shortly.

Suddenly he was tired of the topic of Cameron and the interest it held for Ilora, who was clearly bringing all her professional acumen to bear on it. He picked up a curved metal ruler and callipers and lurked inches from her face, measuring her features. His shirt was hanging down and she balefully registered his chest with its mist of pale hair and draped breasts.

'You're such a nice colour,' Ryan murmured. 'Amber. Not pink like me. When I catch the sun I look as though I've been boiled in a pan.'

'Same here. I burn in a couple of minutes.'

'So, what are you?' he queried. 'English and – ?'

'Ah, no. Indian on both sides.'

'Really?' Ryan was fascinated. 'Are you sure? You've got quite a Hawaiian look. What are they, the Hawaiians? Is it Polynesian?'

He continued whimsically in this vein for some time and made anthropological enquiries pertaining to the language, belief system, occult fertility rites, arranged/forced marriages, tribal stoning, honour killings, folk customs and spiritual icons of her people. But, truth be told, her parents had not believed in anything. She did not believe in anything. And here she was, with proof that there was nothing – for had there been, given how much Radha loved her, there would have been some sign and some consolation. Radha's death had taught her nothing, except that what she thought she knew about life was no more than so much lumber waiting to be demolished. She was stunned by it as by a blow to the head, backing away with her arms out, seeing stars and wearing a silly smile of puzzled disbelief. She schooled her students in all the virtues but withheld the harshest lesson: that brute chance could flex and strike at any moment, breaking their soul, violating their world, destroying their beliefs. She sat in her office and felt her heart clench with fear whenever someone knocked on the door, in case it was an ashen-faced boy who'd just discovered the Law of Chance for himself.

Classes in the next studio came and went. Following some surface coyness, Ryan told her that after school in Devon he'd gone into the building trade, starting as a labourer and working his way up to foreman. He'd stopped when he had enough money to concentrate on sculpting full time. This coincided with his marriage to Cameron's mother, who happened to be pregnant and well-off. He went to a non-name art college and made most of his sculpting money through bullying acquaintances into having their children's heads and feet done. He was fifty-seven.

By half past twelve she could feel him tiring as he straightened up ever more laboriously after wetting his hands. The rain stopped, receding with the deliberate elegance of a queen drawing her skirts off the ground. Ryan cracked his knuckles.

'We're just about done, I think. You're a good sitter.'

'Thanks. I'd be interested to see how it turns out.' Ilora got up and stretched. 'I need a walk after that.'

'Going to wend your way to the enchanted forest?' said Ryan. From his studio he had watched her a few times, going around the side of the chapel to enter Black North Wood.

In the evenings Blackdean carried a scorched flavour which reminded Ilora of night-time Calcutta, a taste of dry smoke, dust and distance. That city often returned to her through the senses, early images as swift and vivid as a flash fire: gatherings, faces, family stories sprung clear from nowhere. She would recall the torn sky and flooded streets stirring restlessly after a monsoon shower, the speckled ridges of a gecko relaxing on the veranda wall or the marble floors of her maternal grandmother's house cooling her feet. She had spent every summer there until she was thirteen, reading American bonkbusters in the top floor room, protected from the sun by orange, painted shutters and green iron grilles. She remembered the chemical odour of the midge-repelling tapers, the pert yellow smell of peaking mangoes, the pale laps of the mosquito net and the light red liquor of expensive tea. She no longer knew anyone in India, her grandparents were all dead. The Calcutta house had been sold when it was clear that the children were not going to return. Her father's family home had been split into three large apartments for his remaining siblings after his death.

Radha had died in July during the summer holidays. Ilora inherited Red Stables, funded a yearly undergraduate essay prize at her old college and a scholarship at the London Political Institute, bought the Polo, made some repairs to the house and organized the cremation. Friends, ex-students, colleagues and disciples came from all over the world. The ashes went back to India with Radha's best school friend. Ilora had intended to spend July and August helping Radha edit a collection of articles, but all the contributors withdrew, not wanting to burden her. Three days after the cremation she received a letter from the Cambridge student's family extending their sympathies and reminding her of their own loss. She wrote back immediately on the reverse and told them in elegant terms that while their son's death may have been an accident, her mother's was murder. Their son had chosen to drink and assumed that the universe would make provision for him because he was a maverick, a boy genius destined for greatness. He paid for his mistake, he deserved to die and his family should suffer because it was surely they who'd brought him up to hold himself in such high esteem. She remembered writing the letter in her study, the window open, ingots of sunshine crowding the road outside. She had felt very alive at that moment, certain that she was writing the truth.

That September she returned to the school ready for the new year, but addressed the students in such an offhand, biting tone that they became afraid of her. She boiled with guilt over the letter, imagining the moment that it reached the grieving family. At the same time she salivated after revenge, but how or against what, she couldn't say. She could feel madness knocking on her door and loading her up. He wore a moulded plastic mask and carried a joker's rattle. She had violent, conscious fantasies about going for a run and murdering someone, then killing herself, in which she would savour the smallest details. She had never believed in God but now it felt as though she believed in the devil and that he believed in her. She began to watch the horizon with a kind of dark rapture, waiting, waiting.

Mrs Ray, who had been watching for some weeks, paid one of her visits and with humiliating gentleness told her to go home and rest. Ilora followed her advice for the next two years. Once inside Red Stables she watched time slow down, stop and then begin to run backwards. She began at last to dream about Radha and the dreams were terrible in their banality. When all her rage-dramas were exhausted she found that they'd been worthless after all, mere surface noise. The precise details of her life before Radha's death had crumbled into an amethyst dust. What remained was a loose and floating fragrance, a veil of brightness. It was stupid to say that her mother had been a clever woman, a strong woman, a good role model. Radha had been everything, and so much a part of Ilora herself that mere words dissolved before it.

Still, after two years she realized that even in loss there was such a thing as sheer boredom and that boredom itself was dangerous. At first she tried to demean its effects, as though death was an unwanted guest standing awkwardly in the corner of the room. Then she realized that she herself was this guest, the changed eerie person who had returned to live in the world, with different eyes and a different heart. Mrs Ray phoned a few times to invite her back to the school. Ilora returned, looked upon to guide, to reveal, but feeling feebler than the puniest of her students, suspicious of the world, hideously clear-eyed and yet certain of nothing.

It was a yellow and black city night and the school was hosting its annual preliminary parents' evening for the parents of all new boys, the first years and the upper-sixth students who were considering applying to university. Ilora doled out revision tips, handed over prospectuses, made overtures and confirmed or denied parental diagnoses of their sons' genius.

Ryan came up to her table during the break. He was purple in the face and either so drunk or so exhausted that his eyes were sliding from side to side like abacus beads.

'Ah, good evening, Ms Sen,' he oozed. 'Would you like to meet my *issue*? Cameron! Cam? . . . Cam! C'mere!'

Ilora looked past his shoulder. Walking towards them was a beautiful boy, the palest most beautiful-looking youth Ilora had ever seen. He was tall and long-boned with wavy dark blond longish hair and a widow's peak. He had a wide face with a pointed chin, a small mouth, the lips so dark they looked burnt, and deep-set eyes with straight sable brows and long, tangled, silver lashes.

'Nice to meet you, Cameron. I'm Ilora Sen. I'm the head of pastoral studies here. You can call me Ms Sen or you can call me Ilora, whichever you prefer.'

'But you can't call her *Miss* Sen, only Ms,' added Ryan, 'otherwise she'll smack you on the botty.'

'Take a seat,' said Ilora. 'Unless you have to be somewhere.'

'Tell her about Oxford,' Ryan told him. 'Ask her advice.'

'I will.'

'You never get the full information when you ask questions. You care too much about "bothering" people.'

'You have similar voices, you two,' Ilora noted, looking from one to the other.

'Cameron sings like a bird,' said Ryan.

'Yeah, maybe a bird like a duck, or a turkey,' Cameron quipped.

'See how we're all getting on?' said Ryan, laughing uproariously.

Ilora gazed into his sloppy face and he peered back closely, his bright eyes containing nothing except her reflection.

'Have you eaten any tea?' Ryan asked Cameron. 'He never eats lunch,' he said to Ilora.

'In my old school in Crestwick the staff canteen and the student canteen were in the same room, on opposite sides,' Cameron began, 'and –'

'I used to embarrass him in front of all his friends! Especially one *special* friend,' Ryan roared. 'Oh my God,' he added, yawning wetly, 'what a moon, what a night.'

He wandered away.

'I'm sorry to start with a telling-off but you really should have come and seen me by now. I'm supposed to have a chat with every new student,' said Ilora to Cameron. 'I'm in the old chapel. There's space to work there too . . . Your dad said you wanted to talk about Oxford. D'you want to apply? It's not until the year after next, so I think you might be jumping the gun a bit, but I can call my old tutor and ask if she'd talk to you. I'm sure she would. Tell me, the last school you were at, what was it like academically?'

'It was okay.'

'It must be hard, having to make a break in the middle of your GCSEs. Was it your preference or your dad's, to move?'

'Him. His.'

'And your first few weeks have gone okay?'

'Yes. Thank you.'

'And you like your classmates?'

'Yeah.'

'So it's all absolutely perfect, and you can handle just about everything in the world, all by yourself?'

'Y– no!' He laughed and she was amused to notice that she was pleased by it. Out of the corner of her eye she saw Mrs Ray watching them thoughtfully from the stage.

Ilora dismissed Cameron when she saw Ryan coming back to her table. Cameron and his father glanced at each other as their paths crossed, but didn't speak.

'So, that was the fruit of my loins,' said Ryan. 'The product of my bodily lust.'

'Where's he going now?'

'To splash around the pool. I told him to sign in with my staff ID.'

'Ryan! That is amazingly unsafe. And against the rules. What if he has an accident?'

'Nah, he swims like a fish. You can go in and haul him out if you like.'

'No fear.' She laughed.

It was nearly ten o'clock by the time all the parents had gone. Ilora decided to pick up a book she'd left in her office. She set off along the side of the humanities block, dangling her car keys in her hand. The chapel shone at the end of the walkway and she could hear the hum of the main road like a gramophone needle on dusty vinyl. Ilora wondered what it was about autumn that made the heart ache. It had an uncatchable, remembering scent and gave the strangest intimation, the long-gone beloved walking over her grave.

Seeing all the fathers in the hall had made Ilora think about her own father, something she usually never did. Dwarek Banerjee was a sadist. That was the sum of his personality, his manner, his object and his sole delight. She recalled his habit of faking a coughing fit or a stomach upset on the nights before she had a big test or outing so that her sleep was disturbed, the way he 'accidentally' blundered in whenever she'd invited friends over, coincided his days off with her own when he knew she wanted to work alone, waited for her on the landing whenever she came out of the bathroom, looked through her discarded rubbish, copied down her bank details and visited her friends' roads to see where they lived, called to her repeatedly in a vilely soft voice (replying 'Nothing' with a begging look when she finally responded), following her around the house so that he was never more than fifteen feet away from her, whispering her name slavishly, soft-eyed, with that horrible smile. He would come home from work every day and ask her eight or ten times in a row if she wanted him to make her a cup of tea, or if there was anything he could do for her – his face burnished with delight as she answered in greater agony every time. If she didn't answer he would stand at the door and lay his eyes entreatingly on her until she did, and then he would ask again. He would play the child's game of repeating everything she said, with a nod and that sick smile, as if he was merely fixing the information in his memory. He had excellent hearing, but pretended to be deaf so that she had to call him several times if the phone rang for him. Sometimes he would pretend to have lost something in his room and begin crashing around, pretending to cry and knocking things off the shelves in his search. He would run up and down the stairs pretending to look for it, hammering his weight on each step, then pretend to have found it and pant and pretend again to cry with relief. Each episode would take several hours and was conducted when Ilora had an essay to write or an exam to prepare for.

He had done far worse things to Radha in the early days of their marriage. He was a stalker and a wife beater. She couldn't leave because, if she had, he would have hunted her down and killed her. So she had to 'manage' him instead, and look over her shoulder, and smile in company. And all that time the ladies at his workplace thought he was adorable and charming and voted for him to be the office Father Christmas every December. Ilora remembered Dwarek's disgusting smile and his black, filmy, expressionless eyes. She remembered the nurses at the hospital, fluttering around him and being rude to Radha, whom they took to be a stupid, cold, uptight Asian wife.

When Dwarek died she realized that she'd been waiting for something, a last-minute reprieve whereby some crusading angel of karma would rev up to his bedside and crash judgement onto him. Nothing happened. The ease of his death was another of his victories – and she felt the injustice of it, that no matter what they did in the world, he and Radha had wound up in the same place. It was a regret of hers that Dwarek's cancer had not been more painful. Ilora gave her inheritance to a domestic violence charity. But still there was a coiling hatred that she carried with her and wanted to pour onto his face like acid.

As she came to the corner of the campus she saw Cameron Arrowsmith leaning against the wall of the chapel with his eyes closed. The moonless sky breathed an icy black and the white stone of the building gave off its own strong light in which he appeared in clear almost monochrome detail. His hair was wet and smoothed back behind his ears. His entire body, heavy and elastic from his swim, seemed to beat languidly in the dark.

Ilora stopped short at the edge of the gravel and cast her eyes spontaneously up and down his gleaming form. She looked at his tight white forearms and pictured briefly, with an athlete's eye, the lean muscles packed heavy as sand under his clothes, the long sculpted legs and narrow waist. How lovely it must be, she thought, to stand sinlessly, emptily at the beginning of one's life, bent only on enjoyment.

Cameron gave a start and opened his eyes. They stared at each other blankly for a few seconds.

'Hi, Cameron. Sorry to startle you. I was just collecting something.'

'No, sorry –' he said, mortified.

'Don't worry. I know you were swimming. Just be careful. Are you waiting for your dad?'

'Yeah. He said he'd pick me up. He – er – he might have gone over the road.'

'Over the road? Oh! To the Golden Lion. I see. I see. You don't go with him sometimes, I hope?'

'No.' Cameron scowled. 'I *hate* people who drink.'

They stood for some moments without saying anything. In the napped suede-like shadows, Cameron's face was moulded white with deep sockets, cheekbones that were high like hers, but wide – a Michelangelo face. Behind the chapel the playing fields were a silent, jet infinity. It occurred to Ilora belatedly that it wasn't necessary for her to keep Cameron company and that it was somehow wrong of them to be standing around in the forecourt at all. It was also for some reason worse for them to be silent than to be talking.

'Are you a strong swimmer?' she asked. 'I'm afraid of water, it makes me claustrophobic. When I was at school I was always the one who got stranded in the deep end and had to be fished out with a pole. But it's good. It's good to be active,' she ended blandly. 'Do you want to wait by the main reception? We can keep the light on for you.'

'No, it's okay.'

'Does Ryan have a mobile you could call?'

'No, I mean yes, but it's fine, he's always late . . . you don't have to chaperone me.'

'*Chaperone* you? I wasn't intending to. Unless there's any place in particular you'd like to go?'

Just then Ryan's white van tottered around the corner of the sports block. When he caught sight of them he began grinning and beckoning. He rolled down the driver's window.

'Come for a drink?'

'I can't, I've got to get my book,' said Ilora, leaning into the chapel doorway.

'You can meet me there, I'm just going to dump this one at home' – Ryan pointed at Cameron – 'then we're good for the night.'

'No, really. You go. I've got some stuff to finish up,' she said. It was the fourth or fifth time Ryan had pressed her to go for a drink with him.

As she drove out that night she overtook a police van, its tribal logo as fresh as war paint. It was passing the gates with creeping caution and the sound it made was an admonishing *Shhhhh* . . . Ilora hated the police with a feral, instinctive hatred, remembering the officer-boy who'd called when Radha had died: scripted solicitude tossed over a ditch of impatient disrespect.

At the superstore she drifted around, put some essentials into her basket and sampled a miniature sausage in the deli section. At the checkout she was served by a smiling woman with wide features and soft, cocoa skin. The woman was Gujarati and Ilora was Bengali – different looks, different generations, different colours, different languages, different regions, different classes – but here in England they could smile like comrades.

The following morning Ilora was waiting for her next modelling session in the art studio. Ryan walked in clutching a box of new pencils. He extricated himself groggily from his jacket. Whistling through his nose, he used a pencil to get some wax out of his ear. He disposed of the wax by wiping it on his leg. His face was bloated, his eyes floppy and bloodless as tinned lychees. He put the pencils into his bag with a shameless smile.

'Hello, dear. My head hurts,' he said at length.

'That's what happens when you drink too much tea.'

'Tea. Yes! A very dangerous infusion. A very – perilous *unguent*.' He laughed painfully.

Ryan took the cloths off the sculpture. He'd been working on it alone. His style was heavily textured, nail-scoops of clay laid upon one another like scales. It looked dreadful, thought Ilora, and nothing like her.

'Not long now at all,' said Ryan.

'And after this you put it in a kiln.'

'Yeah, but that's not the end of it. The final article's in bronze, not clay.'

'So . . .'

'This is the positive. I've got to make the negative. You put the clay head in the kiln, then you make a mould of it with this stuff' – he dug in his bag and came up with a scrap of a stiff blue rubbery substance – 'then you pour the bronze into the mould. *Then* you get the sculpture. Usually when you say you make heads in bronze people think you get a big chunk and then chip away with a hammer, but you can only do that with stone or marble. Or wood, I suppose.'

'How did you learn how to do that?' she asked, impressed. She speculated whether her disapproval of him was perhaps something more prosaic, like jealousy.

'Through being a builder, more than anything. I know more about materials than those bloody Royal College of Art charlatans.'

'That's hard work.'

'It's *heavy* work,' said Ryan. 'I'm thinking of renting this garage by the estates. That's where I'll make your mould.'

'How's the show coming together?'

'It's good, it's good. There's this girl who was in the *Young Musician* quarter-finals on telly. They did a thing on her in the papers. She lives by the way. But, you know, the library woman's being very difficult. Very unsympathetic. One of those women, nothing's ever enough for them.'

Things at the Nelson Mandela library had deteriorated after the optimistic start. His calls were going unreturned and his physical presence seemed to induce a sighing, an eye-rolling, a lumbering heaviness in the librarian. Still, Ryan was pleased that even the spotty young security guard from the technical college next door knew his face. His local fame was growing.

'Cameron liked meeting you. He said you were very nice to him about his university plans,' he told Ilora.

'I *was* nice.'

Ryan wet his hands and began sliding them over the sculpture.

'Well, he was very chuffed . . . You shouldn't take that Oxford-Cambridge thing of his too seriously, by the way. He only wants to go because *you* went there. You're one of his idols.'

'You *what*?'

'You're one of his idols. You fascinate him,' Ryan teased.

'Well, that is not possible because he would have been about . . . twelve when I wrote those stupid poems,' Ilora said hotly.

'Yeah, that's about right. Twelve, thirteen. They did you at school.'

Ryan gripped the clay and pressed it all over. He was sweating, with a hint of Beaujolais.

'And what's a teenage boy doing reading that kind of thing anyway?' asked Ilora, blushing.

'He's probably a queer.'

'Jesus, do people still *say* that?'

'They say it more than ever, Ilora, where've you been all these years? "Gay" is a well-known playground insult.'

'Cameron's very intense, isn't he?'

'You mean highly strung!' Ryan cleaned his teeth with his tongue, looking at her intently all the while. 'Listen. I'm not going to speak against my own son –'

'Of course not. I wasn't trying –'

'But I'll give you one little word of warning. Cameron's a tease. I don't like to say it, but there it is.'

'A *tease*?'

'Yup.'

'Why, what's he done?'

'Oh, you know. He fixates on his teachers. He follows the teachers. He wants a grown-up woman to pay him some attention.'

'Is that what happened at Crestwick?'

'Yes,' said Ryan softly.

'He harassed a teacher?'

'He certainly did, Ilora. He did. He's a harasser.'

He was smiling at her. The story of Cameron's Oedipal tendency seemed so minuscule – and she was so far from blaming anyone who wished to marry their mother and kill their father – that it made her view the boy with more rather than less pity.

'Well. You did the right thing by telling me, Ryan. I'll keep an eye on him.'

The sitting continued until twelve-forty. When Ilora had gone, Ryan sat down and rested his head on the table. There was obviously an industrial-sized franking machine several floors down that was sending shockwaves through the building. He and Cameron had got the van home last night after a few false starts and a tangle with a post box on the High Street. Cameron had been quiet, taking the fried onion omelette Ryan made for dinner into his room to eat alone – and wank in front of his computer, no doubt. Poor Cameron, thought Ryan. What a sissy.

They were halfway through the first half of term. Ilora had spent the morning writing university references, three hundred and fifty words of purring innuendo. She listened to the rain clacking over the roof, innumerable knitting needles purling out of sync.

She remembered Cameron Arrowsmith's interest in Oxford. She'd read his essays, which were fine, and decided to contact his old school in Crestwick. If she could bring in a favourable reference she might get in touch with her old tutor and pass it on. She phoned Crestwick and spoke to the head of the middle school. She couldn't help feeling that the woman had been expecting her call and that there was something assumed between them, which etiquette wouldn't permit them to say aloud. It was the way the woman said, 'Oh, yes. The son of Ryan Arrowsmith,' a flat clang, to which Ilora couldn't help but respond with her own leaden and recognizing, 'Yes.'

Just after the lunch bell went the phone rang. It was a well-spoken woman, speedy and nervous.

'Oh – hello, I'm sorry, I called the general number and they put me through to you, I'm trying to clarify some details about an exhibition by . . . Ryan Arrowsmith?' A folding of paper in the background.

'Ah, yes, he's one of the art teachers here.'

'Oh, he is!' said the woman with a rush of relief. 'Well, oh good, that answers one of my questions, so thank you for that –'

'Are you by any chance the mother of the young musician of the year?'

'Yes. Yes.' The woman was growing more reassured by the second. 'Only a finalist, not the overall winner, but still . . . Anyway, it's just that we got these letters on your school notepaper and we were very intrigued, but, you know, when a person you don't know sends your daughter a letter . . . but we were very flattered, and what can I say? We'd very much like to take part! I understand the sittings won't be taking place at the school. No, they're in Mr Arrowsmith's own studio, aren't they? Let me see . . . he's given a number for us to call. I think it's for a mobile. Is that . . .' She read out a phone number. 'I hope you don't mind me going over the details. I didn't want to be the overprotective mother, but you hear such awful stories.'

When they'd both hung up, Ilora put her work away and went to Black North Wood to think. The place was pervaded by a cool, almost metallic lime green light in which the stream clattered like a harpsichord. The clean air singed her lungs, a pleasant singe like a quality cigar. Soon she was fast inside the honeycomb of the forest. It was high autumn now and the trees shimmered like ruby chandeliers. She thought about Ryan's lively voice and his babyish, soapy smell, the Crestwick woman's voice, the mother of the young musician – the fear of the mother of the young musician. Ryan and Cameron were lucky; they were surrounded by a great discretion, innumerable protective layers of pillowy euphemism.

Plain stone benches were set every fifty yards along the banks of the river. When she came upon Cameron Arrowsmith sitting

reading on one she forgot to use her teacher voice and said carelessly, 'Oh, hello, what're you doing here? You're not bunking
are you?'

Cameron looked confused. He was swamped by his boxy school
duffel coat, his pale ribbons of hair splashing onto his shoulders.

'It's free period.'

'Oh, right,' Ilora faltered. 'Sorry. Didn't mean to accuse you.'

'I can go inside . . .'

'No need! Carry on.'

Out of politeness she made herself ask if he was reading anything
interesting. He held up the book: Marianne Brightman's *The Shoreline*.

'God, when I was a romantic teenager I memorised every single word
of this thing. Can I have a look?' She took it out of his hand lightly.
*'Marianne Brightman was born on the south coast of England in
1926. This, her debut collection, was produced in 1969, three years
before her death from MS. She is survived by her daughter, the film
director Natasha Brightman.'*

Marianne Brightman has been dead for more than forty years, she
thought, and still they read her. She was never going to make it. She
saw that now. She sat down at a respectable distance from Cameron.

'It's a shame. Marianne Brightman only had three years to enjoy
her success. She probably died not knowing *The Shoreline* was going
to become a classic. And she died very young,' said Ilora.

Cameron gazed at the book in her hands.

'Where are your rings from?'

'They were presents. My mum had them made for me. That's a
ruby and that's a pearl . . . I like Brightman's work. I like that poem,
"The Ballad of Rain Grey". I like romantic things.'

'So do I – but you're not allowed to say that, if you're a boy.'

'God forbid,' she replied, letting her own laughter spiral up.

'I was going to come and see you today,' he said. 'I was going to
make an appointment.'

'Oh?'

'I've got some essays with me. You said you wanted to see some
examples of my work?'

'Ah! Right. Hand 'em over.'

He reached forward and got them out of his bag. He was so beautiful, thought Ilora, that it hurt to look at him. She took the folder and looked at his handwriting, curvaceous blue, not the boys' usual unravelling thread. Three years ago, she thought, she would have been flattered by him. But three years ago he would have been twelve, and three years ago she had already been celibate for seven years.

'How's it going? How are your classes? Have you joined any clubs?'

'No, not yet.'

'You could do something for the drama club. Or swimming? They could use someone like you, I'm sure.' They grinned at each other. 'It'd help with your university application,' she added.

'Can I ask – is Oxford nice?'

'Yes of course.' *They'll love you. You're just their type.* 'But it's not very cosmopolitan. It could do with a bit more of that.'

It had been a shock, when she became an adult, to be reminded that she was not English after all. At Oxford the lecturers were unworldly, the town was small and the students were cold. They appeared to have been recruited from minor villages which contained no non-whites, Jewish people, homosexuals or women. Ilora couldn't find her way into 'Oxford society' at large.

'I can't join any clubs. We might not be here for long,' said Cameron.

'What makes you say that? Why would you be leaving? Even if you did, it's not going to be within the year, is it?' she replied, puzzled.

Cameron stared at the river, clenching his jaw. She could feel him thinking: tell the truth and make my family life seem sordid and pity-worthy; lie and maintain a sleek, outward cleanliness. That was a hard game, she had played it herself many times.

'Is he bugging you? My father.'

'No,' she said. 'Not at all.'

Her stomach rumbled and she put her hand over it. Their eyes met. Ilora immediately dropped her gaze. They watched the leaf-laden river, expanding forward, slinking back.

'D'you ever read *Valentine* back to yourself?' *Valentine* was her first and only collection.

'No, never. It feels like such a long time ago – a past life.'

'Was it about anyone in particular?'

'No, I wish,' she said without thinking.

It was very quiet in the forest.

'My dad says you're an old soul.'

'Oh, what else does your father say?' she shot back.

She turned to him and looked at his pale face, his dark precise eyes and lips. Her own eyes glowed like silver coins. Dazzled, he returned her look. There was a growing silence, thickness, clarity and heat. Ilora felt a surge of physical strength, a premonition of what could happen next and a terrible fear of what she was capable of. Then she thought of Ryan doing exactly the same thing and a long horror drew out slowly like a sword and shone, soundless.

'Cameron?'

'Yes,' he breathed.

'What happened at Crestwick? What has your father done? Has he – is he – is he – I just want to know –'

'Chop-chop, people, time to get back,' said a loud voice. It was Mrs Ray. She was standing solidly on the path, looking from Ilora to Cameron and back to Ilora. 'Off you go, Cameron. Have a grand day, Ms Sen.'

Mrs Ray watched until they were both, separately, out of her sight, then continued on her power walk, chin down, elbows out. She needed a ramble every day, otherwise her knees creaked. Mrs Ray was a country woman. She'd grown up in a village that seemed benignly floral at eleven in the morning, but was riven by drug problems, gang problems and worse. Her mother was a psychiatric nurse and her father taught languages at the local school. At the age of thirteen a school friend of hers was gang raped at a party and the local police did nothing except take her home, tell her off and tell her mother off for letting her out. She had seen young men, some of them her playmates or neighbours, going into prison for petty crimes of stupidity and boredom and coming out brutalized, bitter and angry. Encouraged by her parents, gifted at school, thick-skinned enough to take it, there was no doubt what she wanted to do, and do it she did.

Her last prison job was at Holloway. Mrs Ray left the prison service when she could feel herself growing sarcastic and unsurprised.

She hated cynicism, hated seeing it in herself and her generation of colleagues. It was time to retire gently into another full-time job with a high profile and lots of responsibility: Blackdean Grammar. The students at Blackdean were polite, well brought up, massively entitled and rightly optimistic about their future. Mrs Ray envied their ignorance of how the other four-fifths of society lived. It would serve them well as they pursued their ambitions; their certainty would not be troubled by reality. As she continued at the school, she, too, ceased to be troubled. She was a good headmistress because she was disinterested, pragmatic and wise, a good egg; and she brought this quality of distant care to Ilora, whom she liked with impersonal warmth because she was a bright young woman and the daughter of Radha, her friend.

It was one of the last modelling sessions.

'Ryan?'

'Oh, this sounds serious. Is it about the pencils?'

'What pencils? Oh, forget about that, everyone fiddles the stationery cupboard,' said Ilora. 'I was just wondering why you left Crestwick. You never talk about it.'

'They told me I was spending too much time on my own work,' he said easily. 'I wanted to do this exhibition –'

'Of?'

'Local life. Like this one. And I roped some of my students into sitting for me –'

'At your house?'

'No, the school let me use their studio. They had decent equipment as well. Beautiful kiln. And there was a financial aspect, as always. That's what you have to do when you're trying to get to the heart of something: follow the money. The school gave me a fair bit of leeway with materials and what-have-you, but I was so keen to get on I ran up quite a big bill,' he said.

'You stepped down in the face of a financial scandal?'

'I had to!' He worked her sculpture with light presses. 'The whole thing went a bit sour, and you know how people like to take sides, even your own students. You'd think they'd have better things to do, but no, they all want to put in their ten quid's worth. Not a tuppence, no. A full tenner. That was my rate for them to sit for me after school.'

'Ryan, I got a phone call from the mother of the young musician.'

'Oh?' Ryan had stopped working.

'A very nice lady.'

'Why did she call you?'

'Just to check the details. Make sure it's nothing dodgy. She mentioned that you'd invited her daughter along to your studio.'

Ryan said nothing.

'So she wanted to verify who you were before she sends her sixteen-year-old kid to a garage in the middle of nowhere,' Ilora went on.

'Well, I hope you told her I was nice. If I lose this one, my show's up shit creek!' Before she could say anything else he laughed and cleared his throat. 'Ilora, love, I wanted to ask, Cameron's not bothering you, is he?'

'No, why? He doesn't bother me at all.'

'I can have a word with him if you want.'

'No need.'

'He likes you.'

'Oh, I like him.'

'*I* like you.'

'Yes, I know, I like you, too,' said Ilora simply, subtly afraid.

Ryan frowned as he resumed work, remembering other models and other rooms. Crestwick was an old English hamlet ruled by a network of dried-up matrons who watched everyone with gimlet-eyed judgement. What happened there? Nothing. There had been an interesting girl with tumbledown hair, whose parents owned the local gallery-slash-teashop. Her name was Gemma. She was funny and loud, a saucy slattern, a bit of a tease. With her twin brother, she'd befriended Cameron. Ryan had invited her to sit for him and she did, because she was a daring girl. He'd put on the fan heater and they mixed up sachets of white hot chocolate that she'd brought from her parents' gourmet larder, sometimes with a little drop of something else for him. Many of her friends also sat for him. Occasionally the sittings turned into impromptu parties, when he would turn the radio up, lean back to watch them and feel a private river of delight coursing through him.

During the Christmas holidays a platinum coldness fell on Crestwick. Ryan and Cameron saw Gemma and her brother and their parents several times to talk about the exhibition. Cameron was happy for the first time in years, going to the girl's house as often as he could and letting her parents cook for him.

Ryan ran his hands over the clay. It was almost dry. He liked its warm, grabbing tightness. He watched Ilora for a few seconds. She was dozing as she sat. What had happened in Crestwick? The exhibition was scheduled for April and the sittings continued into the spring term. The girl was preparing for her exams and became busier, sometimes so busy that she missed their appointments altogether and he had to go around looking for her or slip a note in her locker. She and Cameron must have had an argument because she stopped coming to the flat and the phone didn't ring. Ryan was worried that Cameron might harm himself in a moment of silliness. He was very concerned about that.

One spring morning Ryan went to the school and found them all waiting for him: the head mistress, the deputy, a counsellor, the head of the middle school and someone from the police, a friendly man, not in uniform, thank Christ. That would have been mortifying. The girl had said that one afternoon during a sitting Ryan had taken off his shirt, and he had, but not like that. It got very stuffy in the studio. He remembered the click of the buttons when he threw the shirt on the table, and her sudden sharp turn. Gemma had left for a class soon after that anyway. She said he was phoning her in the evenings, and he was, with some minor but necessary queries. She had printed out his emails. She said he had offered her money to take off her clothes – and he had, for another sculpture, a classical torso. She said he'd drunk in front of her and offered her a drink, too – this he admitted with an embarrassed 'Oopsy, yes, I know that's bad.' Another time, when they were finishing up, the girl said that he'd cupped her face and kissed her on the mouth – and he had, in a fatherly way. He could remember her muffled scream of surprise – *Mmmmf?* – as his lips closed over hers; then he'd kissed her dryly, held her face for another few seconds and gazed into her eyes. She hadn't said no and she hadn't said yes.

Ilora's head jerked up and she wiped her mouth.

'Ugh! God, sorry,' she said. 'What time is it?'

'Three-fifteen, you're fine, go back to sleep,' he hushed.

Hearing the sweetness of his own voice, he remembered how many times he had used it with the girl, sugar in his throat. The policeman had said that the girl wasn't going to 'do' anything and he'd felt very, very relieved. He wasn't angry at all. He'd love to sit down with her and find out just how she was. But he never saw her again and neither did Cameron. During Easter half-term he looked into other jobs. His interview at Blackdean happened in May. He and Cameron kept a low profile until August, when they left.

That was the story of Ryan and Crestwick.

It was the night of the winter concert. The light in Mrs Ray's office was very unforgiving. In it, Ilora's face looked haunted and foxy. Mrs Ray eyed her over the top of a large photograph of her wedding to Mr Ray. The photograph was a shield against excessive intimacy or feelings of equality from guests. On the subject of Mr Ray it was generally assumed that he was a lesser variety of being compared to his wife: physically small where she was large, frail where she was strong, uncertain where she was zealous and bland where she was vivid. In fact, Mrs Ray's marital happiness was the big secret of her life. Mr Ray – Robert, never Rob or Robbie, even to his wife, who called him Dear Heart in private moments – was a scientist specialising in the effects of urban sprawl on bird migration. He was mild, intelligent, funny, well-read, fair and strong. They lived together in the Rectory in Hernlow, with Mrs Ray's yellow Porsche parked outside and Mr Ray's 1989 Volvo, a matt brown oblong, hidden behind. The two had known each other since they were three; they came from the same street of the same village and had always been together. Their conjugal might was not dented by Mr Ray's battle (and triumph) against throat cancer, which was treated by the saints at Gospel Oak oncology department, the same place Ilora's father had been treated. The Rays had two children: Rhiannon, who was away working with the UN, and Rory, who lectured in modern history at Durham. Mrs Ray had once been asked, by Radha Sen, the secret of a happy marriage. *Blind luck*, she had said.

'So, here we are, Ilora. The orchestra is playing as we speak. I wanted to meet with you before we break for half-term. How are you?'

'I'm good, Mrs Ray. Roz.'

'How's work?'

'It's good, it's good, it's great, thanks.'

'I remember we had a very fine atmosphere when you were here last.'

'I remember that, too.'

'You should have stayed in touch with your old friends. A lot of people asked about you.'

'And yet none of them says anything . . . Not that I want them to.'

Mrs Ray patted Ilora's hand and Ilora realized with shame that she had been too caught up in herself, these weeks, to see that Mrs Ray was an old friend, an ally.

'God, Roz, everything's so different now, it's all different.'

'I know.'

'I always thought that if my mum died, I'd die.'

'Well, that's the tragedy, isn't it? They go and you stay.'

'Then you're left with *this*.'

'You shouldn't think like that, Ilora, it doesn't help. Have you had any counselling about Radha?'

Ilora shuddered and put her hand to her throat.

'Don't say my mother's name, it hurts too much. I know she was your friend but I'm sorry, I can't hear it.'

'In two years, in more than two years, you haven't spoken to anyone at all?'

'I haven't had the chance. First I was too frantic to see straight. Then I felt too low. I've been having terrible nightmares – about my father, oddly enough. I used to have them once every four days or so, then they went away. Now they're back. It's always the same dream. I hit my father once. Did I ever tell you that?'

'No. No you didn't.'

'I punched him in the back,' said Ilora dreamily, remembering the oily, clinging quality of his skin against her knuckles. She was strong, but so was he – they had the same build.

'It doesn't help, does it?' said Mrs Ray.

'No, I felt worse. But I feel better now. Feels good being around people.'

'And how do you feel, being around Cameron Arrowsmith?'

Something shot Ilora in the chest, sending her hand flying to grip her heart.

'*What*?'

'Cameron Arrowsmith.'

'What d'you mean?' she said with a breathless laugh.

'You know exactly what I mean.'

'No! No! . . . God, no . . . I have absolutely zero interest in anything to do with that.' She raised her voice, 'I would *never . . .*' she trailed off, blushing and shaking her head.

'I saw you at parents' evening. And then I think about how you were behaving the other day, by the river. When I came upon you, all unawares.'

'And how did "we" behave?' asked Ilora sourly.

'*You were both enthralled*,' said Mrs Ray, and the hairs on Ilora's neck and arms rose, and all her spine turned to ice.

'You like him,' said Mrs Ray, 'and he likes you. But Cameron is a very disturbed young man. And you're vulnerable yourself, whether you like me saying that or not. You must stay away from him and that is that.'

'I know,' Ilora gulped, trembling, 'I won't, I won't, I wouldn't . . . I'm not going to see that boy again.'

'I think that's very wise.'

'I'm sorry, Roz,' said Ilora. She felt ashamed that this woman, herself a grieving friend, had witnessed her being so weak. She had demeaned herself.

'That's all right.'

They looked at each other, dry-eyed.

'There's something else, Roz. Mrs Ray. It's about Ryan Arrowsmith.'

'Ah!'

Ilora told Mrs Ray about her unease.

'Well, that explains a strange phone call I got from the library,' said Mrs Ray eventually.

'Yes, everyone's been busy on the telephone.' Ilora scowled. 'Now what are we going to do? And what's he been doing at the library?'

'Harassing the women employees. When I heard that, I did a bit of phoning around. Someone at Crestwick said they'd already spoken to you.'

'They have.'

'He's a groomer,' said Mrs Ray. 'And a statutory rapist. Or a coercer, if you want to be delicate. Or a sleazebag, if you want to be very forgiving indeed.'

'He's a dirty old goat,' said Ilora. 'He's a mucky little letch.'

'He's a filthy fiddler,' said Mrs Ray, cracking a smile.

'He's a dirty bugger,' Ilora joined in.

They giggled guiltily together.

'How old is the *Young Musician* girl?'

'Sixteen,' Ilora uttered. Mrs Ray looked thoughtful. 'You seem very unsurprised by all this, Roz.'

'I've seen much worse than Ryan Arrowsmith.'

'What are we going to do?'

'I've already told the police. They know who he is. They've been tracing his movements over a number of years. But it's hard to build up a case. He won't be returning after half-term.'

'What's going to happen to him?'

'Karma. Karma is going to happen.' Mrs Ray laughed blackly.

'What's going to happen to . . . to Cameron?'

'I can't answer that, Ilora, and you shouldn't think about it. Forget about him.'

Ilora was standing at the far corner of the fields, looking into the slavering blackness of the river. It was the last moment of the last night. In the assembly hall the concert was in its final throes.

'Cameron.' She didn't turn around. 'You followed me.'

'Do you want me to go away?'

'No. Just tell me what you want.'

'I don't know,' he said after a while.

'I didn't think so. And what are you doing here generally? At school?'

'I'm supposed to be taking care of the props for one of the drama skits.'

'And now you've left them all by themselves.'

She turned towards him grudgingly. 'Is there anyone you know coming to the concert? Friends, or family?'

'. . . No.'

'I suppose, at times like these, you miss your mother.'

'. . . No.' His voice got stronger. 'No, never. Never. My mother died when I was eleven. She drank too much. And they were both these, ugh' – he shuddered – 'they took drugs. But he's not an addict. He's not even really an alcoholic. He has too much ego to do real damage to himself. Two days after I found my mother I tried to kill myself by taking some pills. It was stupid, it didn't work and it tasted foul. Then we moved and my father got in debt, and after that we went to Crestwick. Now we're here. And that, Ms Sen,' he jeered, 'that is a little bit of what you've wanted to know all term, in all your curiosity.'

She stared at him, absorbing him, his unhappiness and his hate. For the first time she saw him in a dry, clear light, aside from his youth, aside from his beauty, aside from her own disgusting lust and failure and desperation. Now he was telling her his story, now it was too late. They would come for Ryan tonight.

'I'm so sorry, Cameron, I'm so, so, very sorry.'

'Yes, it all makes sense now, doesn't it?' said Cameron, his voice harsh.

They turned together and began to walk silently with slow cadence along the lip of the forest.

'It's four years since your mother died,' said Ilora eventually.

'It's two years since yours died.'

She sank back in dismay. 'How do you know about that?'

'I saw her obituary in the paper. I only noticed it because it said you were her daughter at the bottom. And she looks like you. I mean, you look like her.'

'I don't actually. You haven't seen my father, I look exactly like him . . . Only two years. A hundred weekends. They say it takes seven years to recover from a bereavement.'

'Then I should be feeling more than half recovered by now,' said Cameron.

'And do you?'

'How can I answer that?' he asked despairingly. 'My mum wasn't really "there" even when she was alive. I don't have good memories of her. She was very fragile.' He gulped. 'She cut herself. When she found out my father cheated on her. Don't tell anyone that.'

'I won't. I have good memories of my mother. Only good memories, in fact. But they don't make me feel better,' said Ilora.

'You're still lucky.'

'I realize that. I realized it when she was alive. At least she knew how much I loved her. I don't have *that* regret . . . You don't love your father, do you? You hate him. And he hates you. Let me guess, you look like your mother.'

A couple of paces on, Cameron nodded silently.

'Is he still involved with that world? Drugs, and –'

'No, he only drinks now.'

'My father had a lot in common with yours. He was this awful, creepy, sleazy guy, and he was such a good actor, everyone who met him thought he was so nice – they thought he was this sweet Asian dad guy . . . Don't you tell anyone that.'

'I never would.'

'Ryan told me you harassed a woman teacher at your old school. Is that true?'

'No. He groomed the students. He did it, not me. He did it. One of them was my best friend.'

She nodded, thinking it through.

'Of course. He can't do it to a stranger because he's too much of a coward, he needs a connection, or an excuse. It has to be a colleague or a friend of a friend. That's what grooming is.'

'She thought we were in on it together.'

'Yes, he uses you, he's jealous of your beauty. I'm sure he's jealous.'

'He always gets away with it, even when he gets caught. It never seems to stick. He's never *punished* for it.'

'Maybe he will be, one day.'

They followed a narrow footpath and stopped beside a slender silver birch. From here the chapel looked like a trinket wrapped in voile. Cameron was much taller than Ilora, but she felt radiantly strong. He raised his hands and smoothed back his hair, which shone like metal. Ilora lifted her head and watched him, not bothering to hide it.

'You're not shy,' she stated. 'Even though you're shaking.' Long moments passed. 'I liked you the moment I saw you . . . Tell me, Cameron, what are we doing here? What do you want? I want to know.'

They breathed in each other's scent, gazing at each other.

'We can't – we can't –' said Cameron.

'No, we must never do that,' whispered Ilora. *We mustn't behave like our filthy fathers.*

She made herself turn away. In a parallel dimension, she thought slyly, in another life . . .

'Ilora.'

'Ilora . . .' she repeated. 'Why is it so nice to hear one's name spoken aloud?'

'Depends on who's speaking.'

'Yeah, you can tell exactly what a person thinks of you from the way they say your name. I think we should stop talking now. In case we say anything we regret.'

'I won't regret it.'

Ilora threw back her head and laughed at the shattered onyx sky, exquisitely crunched and sharp. Here it all was.

'Why are you laughing?' he asked timidly.

'Nothing! I like you.'

They had come to a stop again. Around them the frost-spangled fields were soft and boundless.

'Aren't you cold? You're not wearing your coat,' said Ilora.

'No . . . I'm not cold.'

'I have to get back to the concert.'

'Your voice is so nice, Ilora.'

'So is yours . . . I have to get back.'

Unwillingly they backed away from each other. Ilora waved in dismissal, one fall of her palm as though casting a spell. She turned and began to walk towards the tennis courts and the sports block. Her body and soul ached. She kept her head down, didn't look back and walked straight into Ryan, who was dressed in a black anorak. He caught her and gave her a hearty squeeze that she stumbled away from. She gagged and gaped at him. He seemed to bear down on her in silence, putting out both hands as if he wanted to cup her face. She stared into his eyes and felt the warmth and smell of his hands approach. A rod of fear broke through her. He murmured something and, invaded by darkness, she lurched away.

'I saw you coming out – thought you were having a wee walkabout,' he said, 'and I said to myself, I'll go and keep her company. I was going to jump out at you but I'm too fat to do things like that.'

Ilora overtook him without a word, moving past the chapel, along the side of the humanities block, towards the assembly hall. She was going home now. She wouldn't return to the school. She had told Mrs Ray. Ryan followed her.

'Do I look debonair?'

'No, you look like a clown in a horror film.'

'We've had such a good time over the last few weeks. Even though they've cancelled the exhibition.'

'Ha! Oh, why, Ryan?' she said with sarcasm and hatred.

'Financial constraints. You know how it goes,' he replied, looking her straight in the eye. 'But you can keep your head. Your sculpture. I'll make a copy for you. You can keep your hats on it. Where are you going? Ilora!'

Driving out in the blackness, Ilora passed the students who'd been performing at the concert as they came back to the music block to drop off their scores. They looked like child ghosts in her headlights. If only there was a way of keeping them young for ever. They would all trade their innocence, not for knowledge, not for happiness, not for freedom but for their opposites, something ambiguous and purgatorial, a fleet departing light that they'd spend their lives glimpsing and reaching for.

ROHAN KAR

Sepulchre

What would you say to a person who asks you to scatter their ashes on the Tomb of the Christ when they die? 'You're mad,' you would say? If a Catholic, 'You're blasphemous, raving.' But Ma had asked me to do this very thing. I'd missed her death, and was left with remorse – a second, lingering death. The only things I have of her are a small silver vial of her ashes and her pocket book copy of Frost, which I take with me everywhere.

Yesterday, in the massing crowd of the Old City, my wallet was lifted. The back of my jeans sliced clean with a blade; where there had once been a pocket there is now only a seam with loose, dangling thread. Without a shekel, I feel vulnerable. My other pocket, thank God, still contains the book.

It's getting dark. Amid reports of muggings by Palestinian child gangs and an old, black Ethiopian porter's lament about a break-down of ordinary life, I leave the King David YMCA with a single purpose, as if pushed by an invisible hand. There is a gilded mirror in the YMCA foyer, but I can't stand to look at myself any more. My beard and hair have grown. I must look feral.

This morning a Palestinian burned the Israeli flag in a mosque. The resulting curfew means the Old City can now only be accessed in the afternoon, the first free slot in three days.

It is difficult to know what is true. Before coming to Jerusalem, I had Ma's idealized sense of this place as an old time machine: traders in ancient souks selling relics to pilgrims; a labyrinth of conflicting faiths; Christian bells; the wail of the muezzin; stones from a jumble of ages – Roman, Byzantine, Turk. Now, the Old City is full of soldiers. The acrid smell of tear gas is in the air. In some areas, its vaporous fingers reach deep into the lungs making you retch.

I stand on the stone wall running along the city perimeter near the Jaffa Gate, one of eight gates into the Old City. Israeli soldiers, their heads shorn, gather below me, moving shiny steel-capped batons from hand to hand, looking edgy. Both Arabs and Jews pass by them: the Jews in Hasidic black tunics, bespectacled, dishevelled, carrying books and shopping; the Arabs in baggy pants, some wearing dark leather slippers, some barefoot even in the winter cold. The older Arabs look nervous, but the younger ones seem defiant in the face of the soldiers' suspicious gaze. Three of the squaddies are adolescents with bad skin and pouting mouths. Experience produces silence, but these Israeli soldiers are noisy, garrulous babies. In the settlements they have had to turn on their own people. Images now come to me of children; empty homes, scattered toys.

We moved home often when I was a kid, which left me with a sense of displacement. But each time we moved and I moaned, Ma would point her skinny pianist's forefinger at a book of verse by Frost: 'Home is the place where . . .' and then – a single parent, her feline eyebrows arched – she'd look at me, expecting me to fill in the blanks with a higher wisdom I'd yet to understand. The memory of this makes me smile. I should have told her I loved her – for saying this, for giving me the book.

To my left, the modern city: rolling hills dotted with cypress and pine trees. To the right, the Old City: staggered rooftops laden with crosses, turrets, and mosques. Dominating the skyline is the Dome of the Rock, the mosque with its roof like a giant golden light bulb. To approach the Tomb of the Christ, I will have to go back down into this labyrinth, despite my fear.

My ankles are weak, causing them to bend inwards in the cold. I move awkwardly, slowly towards the spiral descent to the Jaffa Gate.

The vial in my pocket is heavy and clumsy, but I am so filled with her it makes me shine, like the Dome, brightly inside.

At the crematorium, I had pulled the white cloth over her shrunken face and closed the casket. I promised her then I would scatter her ashes at the Holy Sepulchre. Sacrilegious? Yes, but when the thick metal oven door slammed shut and the sudden roar of the burners reverberated through my bones I felt her absence like the sky over the earth.

When she died I was not there. I had no chance to say goodbye. She would have liked the view up here on this wall, in her favourite season.

She'd had a window of opportunity. Six months and I could have brought her here; her cancer *healed*.

'Please take me there, Mikey,' she'd said in that persuasive, almost childlike voice I'd come to love as she got older. If I'd had the sense I would've stayed quiet, but I didn't.

It had started with her fall on the stairs. In my mind she wanted a cure only for her hip.

'Where, Ma?'

'The Holy Fire.'

'*Jerusalem?*'

She nodded, smiling like a little girl.

'Ma, stop chasing after miracles. You can't travel.'

'I'm not.' The smile gone, she crossed her arms. 'Even invalids can travel by plane, you know,' she said, trying to sit up defiantly in her wheelchair. The wrinkled white skin of the back of her hands was peppered with moles.

I looked at her, wishing I were not alone, that I had a father and she a husband. How did she think she would manage with her chair in the Old City – or was she expecting me to carry her up all those cobbled streets on my back? Her frame seemed tiny inside her green cardigan, emaciated apart from her stomach, which stuck out as if a small football had been shoved up her top. Once, I found tablets hidden under her pillow. The white label with black print suggested a repeat prescription, but I couldn't be sure. I never found them again. But I found other things: a small blue trunk in the attic.

I refused to budge. 'You shouldn't have come down those stairs in your old slippers,' I said. The fall on the stairs had taken away the use of her legs. 'I told you to throw them away, you stubborn old fool.'

I regretted this as soon as it was out. Her eyes looked sad, a dark gaze. 'Don't talk like that, Mikey.' She turned her head away. 'Can't you hear them? Can't you hear what they're saying?'

'Hear what?'

'You'll scatter them. You promise me?' Then she looked at me as old people do. Her legs started shaking. 'I don't know what's happening to me.' She was about to say something else, but suddenly stopped.

I kept silent and just stared at her, at her skeletal form in the wheelchair. There was so much about her that remained unsaid, as if saying it would frighten me. She must have known for a long time then about the demon growing inside her.

I wanted to comfort her, but couldn't. It was only a few months ago, but I was much younger then, too focused on myself. How many times do we make mistakes? Sometimes they fall into the white noise of life and disappear; often they don't.

Slowly, I make my way down steep stone steps so worn they dip in the middle. It is cold, the biting crisp cold she liked when younger, especially when she took me out sledging on a nearby farmer's field. I hate the cold, probably a result of my father's blood – just about the only thing I know of him. Every morning, she'd walk along that muddy track beside the raggedy cornfield to get away from the matchbox-shaped houses on the estate we were living in then. She loved the open spaces, tracing the memory of her ancestors' land. She had the hard graft of those Inverness men built into her bones, but in fact she seemed more like a kid getting her wellies caked in mud: always curious, always welcoming.

The Tower of David rises up in front of me like a giant stone finger. It seems complex, disjointed. Nauseous, I continue on weak legs across the opening of the Jaffa Gate and towards the interior. Armed soldiers in thick fatigues stand guard by the gate's base. I keep my head down. I can't help the way I walk. It's bound to attract attention. If they body-search me and find the vial, I will have a hard time explaining. I'm not the first martyr to pack a chemical weapon. They are sure to take her from me, look inside.

As I pass the gate, I hear raised voices. A tanned, blond Israeli soldier is shouting at a young Arab man. Gesticulating arms, pointing fingers; the soldier is stony-faced. In one corner, just behind them, a man frying falafels on an open stand watches the scene unfold. The air fills with the sweet scent of cooked ceci.

And then the soldier looks at me. Fear grips my stomach. I have done nothing wrong and yet I feel the vial in my pocket radiating knowledge of the sin to come. For an instant our eyes lock and in his blue gaze I see a question arise. But, distracted by the young Arab, who starts to walk away, he turns and begins shouting after him.

I tell myself I am doing this for her. I have to press on. Through the gate, steady streams of people pass in both directions. I seize my chance and scurry across the square.

An alley to my left; dark stone walls and intricate iron grilles. The wall feels icy against my back; my breath is unsteady, gasping like a fish out on sand, reminding me of my madness in agreeing to this. I'm shivering from fear. People pass the alley, but I am in the shadows away from the nervous shifting gazes and questioning looks. A small miracle to escape – or is it? I hear her now: 'Mikey, a young man who suffers with your legs must think of himself as a secretly chosen being.' No. Not me. A miracle would be an irony, as life has always carried too much reality. Belief in a God, yes, but no miracles. Faith has its limits.

Sinking to the freezing Jerusalem stone, everything coming at once, I wish she was here now, and wonder if she is: a miraculous white ghost sitting beside me, seeing and knowing my pain.

Her vulnerability when it came, sudden and harsh, made me desperate for the goodwill and duty of strangers: young doctors, nurses who had no knowledge of her as a human being – of her kindness, the support she gave to those close to her. Like most people who don't believe in miracles, I was ready to receive one. Six months after the fall, just when her hip had healed and the doctor whispered of finally discarding the wheelchair, I came home from work and found her in bed lying rigid, her mouth locked in a mocking toothy grin. She was paralysed from the neck down. But the stroke wasn't the worst of it – in fact, it concealed the real evil from me: her ovaries were the size of balloons; a ticking bomb.

But hadn't her tummy always been big? Just a year ago, I'd playfully approached her like Basil Brush, shouting 'Boom boom' and touching it gently with my head. For how many years had I been blind? I told myself we had too much trouble, sometimes moving two or three times a year: a landlord kicking us out for the piano noise; shit through the letterbox; the local skinheads throwing stones at our windows or bullying me for my rolled-in ankles and funny walk. Once, a gang of six skins followed us as we walked home through our estate in Hackney. One of them came up behind me and mimicked my walk, exaggerating it like a drunken penguin. And then he switched, following her, puffing his cheeks like a gecko and making like he had a huge belly. I looked across at Ma, terrified, gripping her hand, but she just looked straight ahead, completely confident, smiling and reciting in her chirpy sing-song way:

'Home is the place where, when you have to go there,
They have to take you in.'

The line is now in my head and 'The Death of the Hired Man' in my pocket next to my leg, the last thing she gave me at the hospice before she died.

The attention of a group of dark-skinned youths dressed in raggedy clothes and ill-fitting shoes makes me uncomfortable. Young people here scare me. They are used to more violence than I've seen in a lifetime; Arab and Jew, spilling each other's blood and yet having to share not only their holiest shrines, but the folklore that goes with them. I know little of their troubles. I am here by accident. Or is it fate?

Once, I read that the stone on which God called upon Abraham to sacrifice his son Isaac is the very stone on which the Dome now stands; the same stone Muslims believe carries the imprint of Mohammed's foot as he ascended to heaven. I have often wished for a father to tell me these tales, to hear his voice teach me the truth. Arab, Jew, both of semen and ovum; it doesn't make sense. Nothing does.

The youths watch me with amusement or maybe curiosity because of my ankles. It is easy to imagine curved Moorish knives hidden in their clothes. The hungry black gaze of one of the older boys, a gangly lad with arms too long for his coat, fixes upon me like an animal. I bury my hands in my pockets, fingering the pages of Frost for comfort, hurrying on to get out of sight. I turn a corner, straight into a group of five Israeli soldiers.

The soldiers approach me. They wear gas masks. I can only just see the eyes of the man in front through his Perspex visor. Silhouettes of nearby buildings reflect in shiny, tinted plastic. Two old men seated on mats in a corner further along the street look vaguely at us, then quickly look away, chattering on in a harsh form of Arabic.

The soldier points his baton at my stomach, prods me. I wonder whether to gently remove it, but my legs begin to buckle, so I step aside. Time passes slowly. The soldier's breathing sounds alien through his mask and his gaze flashes from my jacket to my trousers, which bulge with the vial.

And then, they are gone, trotting off in their khakis, fat shaven heads with black straps bobbing up and down. My body goes numb.

I continue slowly towards the old men, strength returning to my legs.

'Hello, hello,' someone shouts from behind.

Turning, I see the dark youth from earlier. He approaches with a confident swagger that makes me watchful.

'Where you go?' the youth says, rolling his 'r's with a deep Arabic sound I've come to recognize. The boy's tone is even, enquiring. I stay silent. It is just one thing after another here; a place of madness, without end.

'Where you from?' the boy persists, his intense black eyes unwavering. 'You *dark* like me.'

I stare at him. And for a moment, I want to open my mouth and howl, scream, laugh, anything to relieve the pressure within. I should have expected this, but don't know how to respond. Perhaps the boy is just as confused. Yes, I'm dark like a Palestinian, brown, but not one; this is surely the reason why the soldiers stopped me.

What can I say to this boy about something I've never discussed, not even with Ma? I don't hate my father, but I have many questions for him.

'Where you go?' the youth repeats.

I am unsure about mentioning a Christian church, given the boy looks like an Arab, possibly a Palestinian Arab. If he only knew of the sin I would soon commit.

'The Holy Sepulchre.'

'The church? Come, I take you. You go wrong way. You go this way,' he says, striding off. But I remain where I stand. He stops and looks back.

'Come, I take you.' This time his inflexion suggests a command, as if it is an insult not to follow.

I look at him, trying to measure his sincerity. I don't have any money to give this boy.

'Come, English, we go this way. Come, I take you. Do not worry, this place is my *home*, I know it.' He is confident, engaging even. He comes up to me and takes hold of my arm, pulling me in the opposite direction to the way I've been going.

There are many shadows in the light. I can smell spices, fried oil, the narghiles of the Arabs sitting around smoking and playing what looks like backgammon. Thick, red meat cuts hang from iron hooks.

Now would be the time to say I have no shekels, but I don't want to be abandoned with no idea how to get back. I don't know how long we will be in this quarter, a few minutes, perhaps ten or fifteen. My steps quicken.

We pass through a narrow archway into another alley. It looks safer here. Small children work as tailors, pumping on old Singer sewing machines, skilled with their hands and bare feet; tourist trinkets – shiny bead necklaces, clay lamps, belts and brassware – dangle from string in doorways. And then in the midst of all this cheap trade, I hear the sound of a piano.

It's strange to hear *this* music now, as if it is a sign. I take comfort from it. A child sitting on a wooden stool is weaving a basket. Ma kept her favourite music in a wooden stool. To her, music was like a dream, different to waking hours. She was a reluctant performer, but I'd often make her get out Beethoven: the *Moonlight Sonata*, its sombre melody a long poem creating a sense that somehow, something is about to change.

The youth is still in front of me. His shoulders begin to slouch as if he feels more comfortable here, away from the soldiers. We are coming to the end of a long alley and I can see it will soon open onto a wider square. The sonata has faded. My fingers are moving to its memory. She made me play classical and later I became a teacher like her. I stumble, almost falling into the boy. Stupid! With my clumsy gait, I have to keep my eyes on my feet on these uneven cobblestones. The youth has started to sing, something low and quiet in Arabic, but in tune; he has a good voice.

There is something about this voice, its loneliness or timbre that reminds me of her. She would sing to herself like this, often to clear her head. She heard voices. *His* absence did that. She got worse as she got older. She would complain that the neighbours had cameras and were watching her and that they could see into her head. Maybe she sensed what I'd done.

I found the small blue trunk hidden in the attic, covered with dust. It was one of those old-fashioned ones with brass levers and a small Champion padlock, which was easy to pick with a pair of cosmetic scissors. Inside, the musty smell of old paper, yellowing copies of *The Lady* that he must have given her, a few simple letters in faded blue ink and broken English telling her when to meet, where, how excited and happy he was to be with her. His handwriting had the sharp angles and loops of Arabic, except in Roman lettering. There was also a black-and-white photograph, partly torn, but you could still make out the face of a pretty young white girl, timid in a puffed chiffon blouse and a hat, and a man with long brown artistic hands, dressed in a pin-striped suit. His head was torn away. And then there was a crumpled letter from a GP: short, handwritten, difficult to read, telling her that she was to be admitted to a home to have a little 'rest'. It was dated the year of my birth. Her madness. And now, there but for the grace of God go I.

I look up from my feet.

The youth has disappeared. *Where?* I look crazily around the small square like a man who's lost his child. There are some trading stalls to one side. A group of children as young as three or four approach me, hovering around my legs. One of them touches the pocket with the vial. I push him away, harder than I intended. He falls back onto the ground, bumping his head on the stone. He's going to cry. I freeze.

I don't want to look up: the traders will beat me here and now. But the boy just pulls a monkey grin, revealing sharp black-stained teeth. He bounces up like a jumping bean, now pulling at my other trouser leg. He has a muddy-coloured birthmark across one side of his face. I look around for the youth, but can only see Arab traders staring back.

'English, why you walk that way?'

I spin around. '*Where did you go?*'

'You find church for miracle?'

'What?'

He points at my legs. I follow his gaze down to my feet, not knowing what to say. 'Transitional,' the midwives had said, but this boy wouldn't understand. The source of weak muscle tone that has plagued me from birth, the reason she wanted me close, a force I'd always resisted – 'Mikey, you might look poor and weak, but, because of this, your inner world will be richer and stronger than most.' He stares at my legs as if they are a pair of circus stilts.

'Why you go to church?' he repeats calmly.

The kids gather around him. They are now all staring at my legs. The youth has one or two of his front teeth missing and the question whistles through his remaining bad ones. Being tall and gangly there is unpredictability in his movement. Now I'm closer I can see his face has more maturity than I first thought. There are little scars around his mouth and crow's feet around the eyes. I don't want to get too familiar with him and so pretend not to hear, but he looks at me with such a penetrating gaze that there's little point.

'I'm going to the Sepulchre.' I imagine myself already there, fumbling with the vial and Ma's ashes. The idea makes my mouth dry. What will happen if they catch me? Here, the Muslims cut off hands for theft. What will the priests do for blaspheming the Tomb of the Christ – of God? And yet, to me, it is not an act of blasphemy, but love.

'You are Christian?'

'Yes,' I say quietly. The youth falls silent. I watch him very carefully, wondering whether to tell him that I too have a father who is Muslim and whom I've never seen. Suddenly, the youth waves the others away, winking at the younger child with the birthmark, who appears to be holding something. The child nods and vanishes up one of the alleyways like a genie.

We continue to walk. I keep nervously glancing at the youth's back and around at the alleyways. I look at my watch. We have to hurry if we are going to make the church in time. The sun has gone down. The evening curfew is set to start in one hour.

We pass through many streets and I settle into a routine of lifting my feet to avoid uneven stones, steep steps or small piles of rotting fruit. We've been walking for some time and my ankles hurt. I sense we are nearing the Sepulchre.

In her last months, I hired a private ambulance to take Ma to a Christian healer. It was expensive, but I was desperate. I'd gone to the hospice nearly every day, stealing time from work just to be with her, helping to turn her body and clean her mouth with pineapple juice and a tiny pink sponge on the end of a white tube, like a lollipop. With it sticking out of her mouth she looked like a child. She would stare out of the window, blinking at the grey, wintry sky and the skeletons of swaying trees, their arms reaching in every direction, and I would wonder what was in her mind. Sometimes, I would clean her quickly and leave with a sense of shame.

She lost the power of speech. Gradually her skin became sallow and hung from her body like folds of old paper. She ate less and less, and eventually refused even fluids. The morphine couldn't dull the pain. In solitude, with no family, I saw it all – a unique feature of hell, to see down to the last detail.

I became paranoid, constantly switching between wonderment at the hospice staff for their daily compassion and suspicion they were injecting her quietly in the night, killing to free the bed.

My solitude grew, becoming fat like a pig. You think I was mad? But then one day, when I found her left in her own excrement, I reached the end.

The paramedic helped me wheel her out to the ambulance. It took three hours to get her to the healer. I listened to Ma groan, strapped to a stretcher. She could never stand me being distant and I wanted to touch her, comfort her, but couldn't. I sat listening to her breathe, the rain pat-patting on the roof, when suddenly both back doors flew open and the healer stood before us, like Jesus in white.

We enter the Christian Quarter, which is very different to its Muslim counterpart. I feel the anticipation in my body rise as I look upon more familiar sights: short thoroughfares decked out with neat arches and plasters, built, paradoxically, by the Ottomans.

We pass through an archway leading to a large cobbled forecourt.

'Wait,' I say, stopping by the archway. The youth comes up to me and stands very close, almost unaware of my own space. I smell his fuggy odour: fried oil and musk. The Christ was once here: the Via Dolorosa, the route marked out by the fourteen Stations of the Cross – his last walk. I look past the boy to what seems to be a church, but I cannot be sure.

'Her spirit has already left her body,' the healer told me. 'You must let her go.'

I feel the broken skin on my lower lip. In the failing light, it has begun to get very cold.

'Leave us,' I said. I couldn't let go, there was too much unresolved, too many kinks. Back at the hospice, I tried but was unable to hold her; her body almost bone. In frustration I stepped out of the room, just for a few minutes.

'Is this . . . the Sepulchre?' I stammer, barely able to contain the tension.

Even now, I cannot understand why I left her there alone. In the time I was out, barely ten minutes, she died. In that green room, as I stood staring at her just an hour after death, her face carried a gentle dignity, still holding a sense of the spirit once within her, her hands clasping a small Gideon bible. I couldn't believe the energy that gave her eyes life – their soulfulness – and her skin its luminescence could vanish without residue after only sixty-three years. I wondered then where her spirit had gone.

A wave of emotion lifts me in an endless shifting sea with no sight of solid land. I look up at the ancient stones that make up the walls of the church, a giant mosaic, an anchor, and the old wooden doors, bleached by the sun and rain. Finally, I can place Ma's ashes on the Tomb of the Christ, with the miracle of the Holy Fire, a blue indefinable light, burning from the stone on which the body of Jesus is said to have been laid. She never got to touch the light, never had a chance to be healed.

I wipe my eyes so quickly the boy doesn't see.

'This is Anne's church,' the youth says flatly, spitting.

'*What?*' I shout at him. 'But I want the Sepulchre. You promised me the Sepulchre.'

The youth laughs.

'Sepulchre?' he says, his tone mocking, indicating he's known all along. He rubs the thick glob of mucus into the cobbles with his heel, reminding me I am a stranger in his land. 'That is too *far*. Look at time,' he continues, gesturing at my watch. 'You think the Israelis will let you pass *now*?' He spits again. 'Believe me, English, Inshallah, if God wishes, they are all the same. What does it matter what church, English?' he says, pointing at the wooden doors.

I stare at him for a long time, enough to see him look away. I crouch down. Stupid bloody boy. Bloody idiot. But then, he doesn't understand; how can the Arab understand? I feel tired enough to lie down on the cobblestones and fall asleep.

'I am going into this church,' I say weakly. 'Thank you, but I'm going.'

I take the vial out of my pocket and clutch it.

The youth steps forward, blocking my way.

'I help you, English,' he says menacingly, glancing at the vial. He holds out a dirt-smeared hand. 'You give me five shekels for showing.' His gaze fixes on the silver tube now luminescent in the light.

From their dress, head to toe in black, a group of Armenian nuns pass. We stare at them in their silence. The boy's head turns as he watches them disappear through the archway, the tendons of his neck taut. It suddenly occurs to me while looking upon the dark profile of this Palestinian – just a boy like countless others – that in some strange way perhaps he is right, that it really doesn't matter. Seeking comfort, I reach into my pocket for the book, but it has gone.

Confused, I search frantically through all my other pockets. My mind works quickly and then I realize. I look past the boy's head to the church, its stone walls dark.

My gaze flickers to the vial in my hands and then to the tall, wooden doors. For the first time since coming to this city of ghosts I feel a sense of peace. No matter what happens now, here with this boy, I know she will understand.

Home is the place where, when you have to go there,
They have to take you in.

ABOUT THE AUTHORS

Rajeev Balasubramanyan was born in Lancashire in 1971. His first novel, *In Beautiful Disguises*, won a Betty Trask Prize and was listed for the *Guardian* Fiction Award. He won the Clarissa Luard Award for the best British writer under 35. He has published short stories in various anthologies, including *New Writing 12*. His second novel, *The Dreamer,* came out in India this year, and will be published in the UK in 2012. It is based on a short story that won an Ian St James Prize in 2001.

Anoushka Beazley studied film at the University of Kent. She lives in Cricklewood, London, with her husband and two children, and has just finished her first novel.

Kavita Bhanot grew up in London and lived in Birmingham before moving to Delhi to direct an Indian-British literary festival and then to work as an editor for India's first literary agency. She spent two years running a guest house in the Kangra Valley of Himachal Pradesh and is now a PhD student at Manchester University. She has had several stories published in anthologies and magazines.

Bidisha is a writer, critic and broadcaster who began her career at fourteen, as a journalist for arts and style publications internationally. She signed her first book deal when she was sixteen. She presents and contributes to arts shows and documentaries for BBC radio and TV, writes on the arts and on social politics for the *New Statesman, Financial Times* and *Observer* and she has a weekly column in the *Guardian*. She judged the Orange Prize for Fiction in 2009 and the John Llewellyn Rhys Prize in 2010. Her latest book is *Venetian Masters*.

Rajorshi Chakraborti was born in Calcutta in 1977 and grew up there and in Mumbai. He is the author of four novels – *Or the Day Seizes You, Shadow Play, Balloonists* and *Mumbai Rollercoaster* – as well as essays and short stories. He lived, studied and worked in the UK for fourteen years – in Hull, London and Edinburgh – and was, between 2007 and 2010, a lecturer in English Literature and Creative Writing at the University of Edinburgh. At present, he lives in Wellington, New Zealand.

Divya Ghelani read English Literature at the University of Hull and attained an MA in Creative Writing from the University of East Anglia. Born in India, she now lives in Hong Kong, where she is completing an M. Phil in literary studies and writing her first novel.

Niven Govinden is the author of novels *We Are the New Romantics* and *Graffiti My Soul*. His short stories have appeared in *Five Dials, Pen Pusher, First City, Time Out, 3:AM, Shortfire Press, BUTT* and on BBC Radio 3. He was shortlisted for the 2011 Bristol Short Story Prize.

Kavita Jindal is a critically acclaimed and widely anthologized poet and short-story writer. She also writes song lyrics. Her poetry collection, *Raincheck Renewed*, was published by Chameleon Press. She was born in New Delhi and lived and worked in Hong Kong for several years before settling in London.

Rohan Kar was born in London, but spent his early years in Sri Lanka. Several of his short stories have been published in anthologies and, in 2005, he was a winner of the Scottish Open International Poetry award with his poem, 'Seeing True'. He studied at the Universities of Kent and Harvard, and graduated from Birkbeck College's Creative Writing MA with distinction. His first novel explores, through the 2004 Boxing Day tsunami, how the accidents of childhood shape man.

Ishani Kar-Purkayastha completed a medical degree at Oxford University, where she was co-editor of the literary journal, the *Pestle*, and won a commendation for her writing in the STA and the *Guardian* Young Travel Writer Award. She now works as a doctor in the field of public health and, in 2010, won the *Lancet*'s Wakeley Prize for her essay, 'An Epidemic of Loneliness'. Her first novel, *The Dancing Boy*, is published by HarperCollins India in 2011.

Dimmi Khan studied at Manchester Grammar School and the London School of Economics, and holds a MA in Islamic Studies from Birkbeck College, London. His writing reflects his experience as a British Asian man raised by a single parent in a working-class area of Manchester, but who attained a scholarship to a private school. His debut novel is to be published in 2012.

NSR Khan is of Scottish and Pakistani parentage. She was a criminal defence barrister by trade until acute mental illness abruptly curtailed this career. She lives in Edinburgh and London with her family who span three generations and have roots in four continents. She is currently working on a sitcom and a first novel that draws on her experiences of the mental health system.

Azmeena Ladha is a native of Kenya and now lives in Devon. She graduated as a graphic designer and worked in publishing and for a trade union in London for many years before retraining to work with refugees and asylum seekers in south London. Her short stories have appeared in *New Writing*, *The Reader*, been translated for *Vrij Nederland*, and broadcast on BBC Radio 4. She is working on a collection of stories which explore frailties and resilience among settler communities.

Gautam Malkani is the author of the novel *Londonstani* and has been a journalist at the *Financial Times* since 1998. His writing has also appeared in *The New York Times* and *Prospect* magazine. He was born and raised in Hounslow, attended his local comprehensive school and studied Social and Political Sciences at Christ's College, Cambridge.

Bobby Nayyar was born in Handsworth, Birmingham in 1979. He studied French and Italian at Trinity College, Cambridge, and then Comparative Literature at the University of Chicago. He has worked at Faber and Faber and Little, Brown, and now runs his own publishing house, Glasshouse Books. In May 2011, he published his debut novel, *West of No East*.

Madhvi Ramani was born in London and lives in Berlin. Her short stories have appeared or are forthcoming in publications such as *Stand*, the *F Word* and in PARSEC Ink's *Triangulation: Last Contact* anthology. She also writes children's literature, screenplays and non-fiction articles.

Reshma Ruia was born in India and grew up in Rome, Italy. After a postgraduate degree in Economic History from the London School of Economics, she moved back to Rome where she worked as a development economist with the United Nations and subsequently with the OECD in Paris. She is the author of *Something Black in the Lentil Soup* (2003). She is now based in Manchester, where she is submitting her PhD thesis at Manchester University and finishing her second novel.

Suhayl Saadi is based in Glasgow. His varied literary output includes novels, short stories, song lyrics and plays for stage and radio. He has authored the books, *The Burning Mirror* (2001), *Psychoraag* (2004), *The White Cliffs* (2004) and *Joseph's Box* (2009), and, under the pseudonym Melanie Desmoulins, the erotic novel *The Snake* (1997).

Nikesh Shukla is a London-based author and resident poet of the BBC Asian Network. His first novel, *Coconut Unlimited*, published by Quartet Books, was shortlisted for the Costa First Novel Award 2010. Nikesh's work has been featured on BBC radio, and his writing has been widely published. He has written a sitcom for Channel 4's Comedy Lab, called *Kabaddasses*.

Harpreet Singh Soorae was born in London and grew up in Birmingham. He is working on a series of novels that bounce around the lives of Punjabis in England from the 1960s to the present.

Amina Zia was born to Pakistani parents in Cambridge, and has a degree in Russian from London University's School of Slavonic and East European Studies. After enjoying a varied career working in radio and television at the BBC, she is now about to complete her MA, training as a professional actor at ALRA. Amina began writing poetry, short fiction, plays and autobiographical stories while studying for a graduate certificate in creative writing at Birkbeck. 'The Necklace of Golden Pound Coins' is her first published short story.